ALLWORLDS AWAKENING

Joel E. Roosa

Cover Design by Erin Roosa

Dedicated to my wife and kids, with gratitude for putting up with me while I wrote this.

Part One: Prologue

Chapter One
Awakening

A dark, vertical hole showering rainbow sparks appeared in the air of a dirty alley. A seven-foot-tall man in a stovepipe hat poked his head out of the hole. His massive, blond handlebar mustache shook slightly as he looked about, assuring himself that the portal had not been noticed. A disheveled man asleep next to a wine bottle was the alley's only occupant, and was thus ignored. Looking down from the hole's second-story height, the man sighed, then jumped.

He brushed his suit down after landing, and then reached up to grasp the hand of a woman gently falling from the portal, trailing more of the colorful sparks. She held up a decorative pastel blue parasol, which seemed to be slowing her fall. As they clasped hands, her feet pointed down, then gently impacted the ground as her fall came to a graceful end.

"Apologies, my dear," said the man.

Winds swirled around her, ruffling her voluminous skirt fiercely as she examined the alley.

"Indi, I'm sure you'll get better at positioning portals, but you know a fall is of no consequence to me. This alley, however, is another matter. I find the filth offensive."

She raised her hand to gesture, but Indi gently tugged it down.

"Rae, having just committed ourselves to the Wyrd, would you violate its restrictions already? We are not allowed to interfere in another world without consequence."

"Please?"

She batted her long eyelashes at him and gave the sad eyes.

Keeping a stern face, Indi said, "It's not up to me, so there's no point in wasting your charms trying. I do appreciate them, though."

He cracked a small smile.

"As I see it," she said, "the Wyrd only restricts willful interference. I'm curious as to what might happen were I to stop suppressing its winds."

With a relaxed expression from Rae, the winds buffeting her expanded out, engulfing the entire alley. Indi put a hand to his hat. Trash swirled about in several mini-tornadoes before merging as one.

"Now, Indi, since you haven't yet closed the portal, you might set it for departure and we'll see what the pressure change does."

Indi raised an eyebrow, but gestured at the portal. The remaining rainbow sparks were sucked in, as was the tornado of trash.

"If you would close it now, please?"

Indi tipped his hat in the direction of the portal, which vanished. He cocked an eye at Rae.

"What?" she asked. She rose up a foot above the ground. "I still have my powers."

"I suppose. Apparently, you got away with violating our terms and conditions."

Rae smiled.

"I violated nothing. The winds did as they would, picking up the debris. You just changed the portal from 'in' to 'out.' Where's the harm in that?"

"Not for me to judge, but we haven't lost our powers or been struck by lightning so I suppose we're fine. It's just amazing how random winds scrubbed this paved alley so thoroughly that there isn't a speck of dirt to be seen. Even our sleeping friend seems presentable, though I'm surprised you didn't shave him."

"Let us get on with it. I'm here for a vacation."

She pointed out of the alley, then strode ahead, finger showing the way.

Indi followed her as she stopped at the train station across from the alley.

"There it is," said Rae, "the worlds-famous Orient Express, and we're going to ride it."

"Why? We could travel under our own power much faster."

"Of course, but where is the fun in that?"

"Fun? We're immortal beings now, with all the responsibility that entails," said Indi.

"What responsibilities? We have nothing to do at the moment, which is why I want to enjoy myself as much as possible. A good start would be a five-night luxury train ride from Paris to Constantinople."

"That's Istanbul, not Constantinople," said a male voice behind them.

Rae and Indi whirled about to see the man from the alley, his blue coat lustrous, with snug white pants tucked into scuffed, black boots. Middle-aged, he sported at least a week's worth of beard growth.

"Istanbul? When did that change?" asked Rae.

"Few centuries ago, I guess. Yes, you act like immortals all right, doing what you want, when you want, and damn the consequences."

Indi had walked behind the man, then back to Rae.

"Even his backside is clean. Yes, I'm sure your winds lifted, scoured, and placed him randomly back in the same position."

"About that," said the man, "I, Aristide Achart Archambeau, thank you, but I also find offense that you took a perfectly good, half-full bottle of the finest wine and disposed of it. I would challenge you to a duel, Madame, if such a thing were not an even bigger affront to my honor."

"Bigger than being drunk in an alley?" asked Indi.

"I am French, sir, and can hold my wine. I was merely resting after a long day. I saw you enter the alley and thought perhaps my wine had been laced with opium."

"And now?" asked Rae.

"And now I seem to have fallen into the realm of higher powers once again. Or rather, they have fallen across me."

"A regular sort of occurrence for you?" asked Indi.

"Not regular, no, but it has happened a distressing number of times."

"See, Indi, he is habitually the beneficiary or victim of random events. Not my fault at all if the winds decided to clean him thoroughly."

Indi cocked a smile at Rae.

"Once the extranatural has made an impact, one is more than likely to experience it again. It's like driving a wagon on a dirt road. The wheels tend to fall back into the same ruts," said Indi.

"Be that as it may," said Rae, "this gentleman has introduced himself, and we would be gauche to not do the same. Mr. Archambeau, we are the ValDurians. I am Raelani and this is my husband, Indra."

Aristide took her gloved hand and kissed it.

"Enchanted, Madame. Call me Aristide, if you please. As for the matter of my wine, I have changed my mind. Let us say the cleansing of my attire more than makes up for it. I'll be on my way before I become embroiled in your affairs any further."

"Nonsense," said Raelani, "this should cover the cost of a fine wine."

She pulled out Aristide's hand and dropped several gold coins into his palm.

"Well, yes. More than cover it actually. In all honesty, it wasn't that high a quality to begin with."

Aristide moved to return some of the coins to Raelani. She held up her palm and shook her head.

"Keep them. Money is of little use to us."

"It will buy train rides though," said Indra. "Speaking of which, it's time we did that. Pleasure meeting you, Mr. Archambeau."

Indra tipped his hat, then turned to Raelani and offered her his arm, which she took. They started through the crowd, toward the station.

"Wait, my dear," said Indra, "you're missing that little hat thing you had clipped to the side of your head. Did your winds take it?"

"It's called a fascinator, which I haven't been wearing since before we got here. I didn't want to lose it between worlds."

She reached into a skirt pocket, pulled out a yellow hat thing and clipped it in her silver-blond hair just before her right ear.

"Most becoming, my dear," said Indra. "Shall we be off?"

The sky darkened briefly until flashes of purple lightning

brightened it.

"Oh, bloody hell," said Indra. "What now?"

Worry lined Raelani's face.

"Dimensional rifts are forming in the sky. Paris is being invaded by demons," she said.

"Blast. And I really was looking forward to the train trip as much as you. I suppose we have no choice but to leave this world," said Indra.

Aristide had rushed to their sides while they spoke.

"You're going to just run away?"

"We have no choice," said Indra. "Not that you need to know this, but Raelani and I have become part of the ValDurian Wyrd, our fate, our guiding destiny. It grants us great power and eternal youth, but with strict conditions. Among other things, we may not interfere with other worlds. While we could defend ourselves from the demons, that might end up interfering with this world. Better we just leave."

Aristide's face clouded with anger.

"And leave Paris to be raped by demons?" he yelled. "You probably brought them here. Are you not responsible?"

"Just our bad luck they picked now to invade," shouted Raelani. "We did not bring them here."

"Did you not?" asked Aristide as he pointed to Indra. "He talked about falling into the same wagon ruts and mere minutes ago you made a portal into this world. I see convergence rather than coincidence."

"I am sorry," said Indra. "Even if we attempted to help our powers would soon fade, dooming us as well. You may come with us if you like. That isn't interfering to any great degree overall if most Parisians will die anyway."

"Never. I will fight for France and die if need be," shouted Aristide. "Give me a horse and a sword and I will fight to my last breath and beyond."

Indra and Raelani looked each other in the eyes.

"You know this will probably kill us," said Indra.

"Maybe, but I got away with the alley stunt. If we can't help people any longer what is the point of being immortal?"

Aristide bowed from the waist.

"Most immortals would sooner walk over you than acknowledge your existence by changing their path. I salute your potential sacrifice, but there is something you have not considered: those demons are the invaders. Wouldn't defending us count as stopping their interference? You would be the keepers of balance, not purveyors of disorder. How could that be bad?"

"We are new to this," said Indra. "It seems your experience in such matters is beyond ours, despite our long lives before. You shall have your horse and sword, though I pray you won't need them."

Indra waved his hands about, manifesting blazing mist which solidified into both ghostly horse and glimmering blue saber. Aristide pulled himself up into the phantom saddle, then Indra handed him the sword.

The sky grew brighter as the purple lightning intensified. Now the diving hordes of winged demons were plainly visible to the crowds below. Panic ensued as the populace scrambled for cover.

"Rae, you take the rifts while I deal with the horde," said Indra.

Blazing shafts of light resembling wings burst from Raelani's shoulders as she headed for the sky.

Aristide gaped in awe.

"An angel," he whispered while crossing himself.

"Aristide," said Indra. "Guard the streets from loose demons while I assault the horde's bulk."

Indra's form changed to that of a man-sized star as he roared into the air. Aristide crossed himself again.

While Aristide watched, multiple volleys of white lightning sprayed from Indra, incinerating clouds of swarming demons as they approached Paris. Raelani flew higher, singing a tune without words, dodging demons as she sang rifts closed, one by one.

One rift was closing on a demon, catching him halfway into France. Its legs remained trapped in demonland as it struggled to free itself. With a look of alarm on her face, Raelani grabbed both the creature's arms and pulled it free. The demon shook its head, then grinned and came after Raelani. She flew out of its reach as a bolt of white incinerated it.

"Two more rifts yet, Indi. How are you doing?"

"Fine, though I'm becoming dizzy. Expending a lot of power, but we've got this handled."

"How can you become dizzy when you don't have a head at the moment?"

"Never mind. Our new friend is doing well, don't you think?"

Raelani glanced down to see Aristide galloping through the streets, routing demons with his glittering blade while shouting, "Long Live France!"

"Yes," she said, "I think he's doing admirably. Now, let us do so as well."

She started her song once again while electrocuted demon corpses fell from the sky.

In less than an hour it was all over. Every visible rift had been sealed and all demons were crumbling debris. Indra flew off to see if there were openings elsewhere on Earth while Raelani started to magically heal injured Parisians. Aristide's sword and steed melted back into mist while he, clothes stained with black blood and demon gore, approached Raelani.

"Excellent job, sir," said Raelani, not raising her eyes from a patient.

"Thank you, Madame," said Aristide. "There is a matter most troubling, however."

"Continue, good sir."

"I happened to see you free that demon from the closing rift. Yes, Sir Indra quickly eradicated it, but why would you do that?"

Raelani bit her lip but stayed focused on her patient.

"Really, Madame, I must insist on an answer," said Aristide, glowering.

"Insist if you wish, but an answer I cannot give you at this time. I ask only that you wait until Indra returns."

"Very well. Until then."

Aristide checked his pocket watch several times over the next hour until Indra did indeed return. First as a star, then he assumed human form in an eyeblink.

"Sir Indra," said Aristide, "I—"

"I know," said Indra, "and the lady may not explain, but I shall. As part of her Wyrd, she may not cause harm to any living being. Even though the demon being bisected was not intentional it would still have been a result of her power. She could not take the chance it would violate her Wyrd."

"Then why did she not merely say so?"

Raelani stood, and Indra kissed her.

"She may not," said Indra. "As another condition of her Wyrd she may not explain such matters to non-family members or attendants to such. My conditions are different, so I may say whatever I wish to whomever I choose."

Aristide shrugged.

"Very well. As I have no further matters of import, there is a café calling me. I hope it has not been destroyed."

As Aristide turned to walk away, Raelani put her hand on his shoulder.

"I have an important matter, Ari, if I may call you that. Since we ValDurians may not seek out invasions and incursions throughout the AllWorlds ourselves, apparently, I ask you to work for us and with us."

"Pardon? Ari? I rarely get so informal with people I have just met. As for the job, why not? I have few demands on my time at the moment. As for the AllWorlds, what are they?"

"The AllWorlds are what we call the multiverse, if you understand that. Literally all worlds that occupy the same time and place but with different vibratory rates. Invisible and immaterial to one another most of the time, save when situations make them collide, like today."

"We'll start an order of champions," said Indra, "people that work for us and go where we cannot, actively looking to prevent trouble between different worlds."

"Yes," exclaimed Raelani. "We'll call you the Knights of the AllWorlds, at least until I think of a better name. That we protect those who cannot protect themselves, is the least we can do for a multiverse sometimes beset by events such as we just witnessed. I can think of no better calling for the ValDurian family."

"I'll get you some permanent equipment," said Indra. "What I provided you earlier was merely illusion given solid form for the duration."

"With pay, of course," said Raelani. "Kneel before me, good sir."

Aristide dropped to one knee and Raelani manifested a blade of light in her hands. She tapped him on the shoulders with it.

"Rise, Sir Aristide Achart Archambeau, first Knight of the AllWorlds."

Part Two
Keeping it Low Key

Chapter Two
Weekdays at the Office

On the cusp of midnight, at the top floor of a weather-beaten six-story walkup, in a dingy, cluttered office, a man slumped back in a wooden swivel chair. With feet up on the desk, gray vest unbuttoned, and fedora pulled down over his eyes, he snored. City lights through the hall window silhouetted the form of a woman in a wide-brimmed hat standing outside the office door's frosted glass. She disappeared for an instant, and entered without opening the door. She stepped forward and a floorboard creaked.

A halberd appeared in the man's hands, the point motionless near her throat as he stood.

Sudden dead silence echoed.

"Thought I was done with your kind," he snarled through clenched teeth, "give me a good reason for you being here."

"Allow me a moment, Aurus."

She slowly removed her black, red-banded hat. She had long, raven-black hair that tumbled down a slick, black trench coat, revealing gray eyes, and a stoic face.

"I tried not to disturb your slumber. Don't know who you think I am, but I'm Nea and you're expecting me. I'm here and on time."

"That tells me nothing. I had just dealt with a group of dead-god worshipping wizards, and they dressed similarly to you. After I made sure their god was extra-dead, we came to a truce. Figured one of them thought better of it and wanted revenge. How did you know my name and why are you here?"

"I'm your new partner. Someone should have told you I'd be arriving today."

The halberd vanished, then he pushed the hat back on his blond hair. "I'm sure someone did, but the whole subject of 'today' is a tricky one. What day is it?"

"Tuesday."

Aurus rubbed his eyes, then pulled a bottle and two glasses from a desk drawer.

"That's a start at least. Drink?"

"I don't drink alcohol."

"Neither do I. This is pure water from the Primal Source. As pure as anything taken from it can be, anyway." He poured two and she took one.

She flipped back a lock of hair and took a sip.

"That's . . . really something. I can't begin to describe the taste."

"Why are you here? I don't need an assistant."

"Partner. Not a question of your needs. I'm a DemiKnight, so the full-stars assigned me to a senior Knight."

She held up her right hand, palm out, and in it appeared an eight-pointed golden star badge with a circular, smooth-cut black onyx in the middle. The cardinal points of the star were twice the length of the lesser points.

"Great, I get stuck training a rookie, but I will grant that you're cool under pressure. Do you know what the Knights of Valeron do?"

"Only from general, public knowledge. The full-stars didn't tell me much when I was recruited. Just that something big is coming up and they need more Knights."

"They're like that. They tell you almost enough sometimes, but it's like they expect you to think for yourself or something. Come back in the a.m. and we'll start. You got a place to stay?"

"It's all been arranged. I have a penthouse apartment."

"Somebody rates high with the full-stars. All I have is this office with an attached apartment. Welcome to Downtown. In any event, see you tomorrow morning. Then you can explain how you walked through my closed door."

#

Nea returned bright and early the next morning. Against that brightness she had added a pair of large, dark glasses to the previous night's slouch hat and trench coat.

"Well," said Aurus. "Don't you stand out?"

Nea pushed the sunglasses back on her hair, like a headband, and put the hat and coat over the back of a chair. She wore a short red dress, but his attention was drawn to her belt holding a rapier and dagger.

"Okay. That stands out even more. Let me clue you in. People don't usually wear swords or daggers in New York City on this world, and it could get you thrown in the slammer."

"I know that, hence the coat. These are my traditional weapons."

"And I'm fond of halberds, but do you see one around? No. I keep it low-key. I'll help you get wise to the ways of this world, but that's for later. Just as an example though . . ."

He twirled about, showing off his white, button-down shirt, gray vest, tan fedora, fingerless gloves, gray pants, black shoes, no socks.

"I'm just another hipster. Nothing to see here, folks. Apart from that, I like the vibe of old detective movies, hence my office. Now, drop the cutlery and we'll get to work.

"First of all," said Aurus, "what's your flavor, um, what abilities do you have? How did you walk through a closed door?"

"Oh, nothing remarkable for our line of work. I can do magic, but primarily information-gathering spells. I'm partial to shadows and stronger in the shade. I didn't walk through your door, I traveled in shadow. There are some interesting things I can demonstrate, if you like."

Aurus smacked his forehead.

"This is somebody's idea of a joke."

"What do you mean?"

His body glowed faintly, then brighter and brighter until Nea had to look away. He dimmed his glow and grabbed some crumpled paper from the wastebasket.

"Put your sunglasses back on and watch."

She did, as a ray of light lanced from his eyes, incinerating the paper he held, leaving a curl of smoke.

"That's what I mean. Light and heat are my things, my flavor. We're going to get on like fire and ice."

"I can't leave until the full-stars say so."

"True. I'll make the best of it, but can't go easy on you. This will seriously cramp my style though."

Aurus blew the paper ash from his hands into the wastebasket. He opened the door in the wall to the left of the office door, letting them into his apartment.

"I'll show you how I get assignments."

Aurus opened the bathroom door and bowed before the mirror over the sink. He ran the water and his eyes heated it to vapor in his hands. The mirror clouded, and then blazed with fiery sparks. When the sparks cleared, mystic letters remained in the foggy surface. Aurus read them before wiping the mirror clean with a towel.

"The mirror writes out anything they want me to know. If I don't check it often enough, it gives off this fingernails-on-a-blackboard noise until I do. It said Thursday we're on Loki duty. Today we train."

#

Thursday morning arrived along with Nea. Actually, morning arrived first, but Aurus wasn't awake yet. What woke him was Nea knocking at his office door, which had the shade pulled down. After a few knocks, Aurus stumbled from his apartment to the door. His blue eyes were bloodshot.

Nea had on relaxed-fit blue jeans, white sneakers, white button-down shirt, white sun hat, and the same old sunglasses.

"You said we were on low-key duty. I'm trying to blend in."

Aurus smiled with brilliant, white teeth.

"Good attempt, but I'd almost rather you'd worn the same dress. I didn't say 'low-key' duty, I said 'Loki' duty."

Nea gave a blank stare.

"What?" she asked.

"Loki. Norse pantheon? The troublemaker?"

"Oh. Father of Fenrir? What kind of duty is that?"

"Have a seat and I'll explain."

He poured her a glass of pure water.

"Among the many duties Knights of Valeron perform, we ensure that wayward deities don't cause trouble on worlds where they don't belong. We scope them out, make sure they're clean, and take them out if they aren't. Maybe call for backup if they're over our pay-grades. Simple stuff."

"I never dealt with a god before, not professionally anyway. What's our mission, and what does my fashion sense have to do with it?"

"I'll explain when we get going. For now, come here."

She followed him into his apartment, where he opened a drawer and pulled out an electronic tablet device.

"This is the Fabricon, a magic wardrobe. It can create almost any outfit we might want. I'll set the selection for Loki-appropriate clothing and wait for you in my office. Come out when you're ready, and we'll get going."

He tossed her a half-dollar-sized gold disk inset with black glass on one side.

"That's your energy shield. The gold will stick to skin, so see if you can hide that somewhere. I got neutralizer handcuffs for you, but there's no place on you those could hide, so I'll hang on to them."

"While you're in an explaining mood, may I ask a question?"

Aurus nodded.

"I was told your name was Aurus, so why does your office door say something different?"

"Around here everybody knows me as 'A. Harry Keaty,' like the door says, so I saw no reason to change that. Harry is my middle name. Used to run a private investigator business, like in the old film noir. Sort of still do, but that was Harry's business while Aurus is more focused on being a Knight of Valeron."

"About that, I know we had been the Knights of the AllWorlds. When did that change?"

"Years and years ago. We're named for the full-stars' place of power, a mini-dimension called Valeron. It didn't exist when the

Knights were started. Now, can you pick out a dress?"

He walked into his office and waited. And waited. And waited. He pulled a copy of Shaw's Man and Superman from his desk drawer and began reading. After fifty eternal minutes, Aurus, now in a black tuxedo, yelled, "Hey, you okay in there?"

"Fine," came her muffled voice. "Just seeing which one looks best on me."

"Pick one. We don't have all day."

Twenty-four interminable minutes later she stepped into his office, resplendent in a white, sparkling, ankle-length gown.

He put the book away.

"We need to get going. Come up to the roof with me."

His office was on the top floor, and they made a quick trip up the stairs to the roof, their speed hampered a touch by the tightness of Nea's dress.

On the roof he handed her an emerald pendant.

"Thank you. This dress cried out for an accessory. Do we meet Loki here?"

"Hah. No. We're going to a party. The pendant is an Eye of Overview."

"Considering the selection of gowns, I assume you want me to seduce him?"

"What? No, for cryin' out loud. It's just to get Loki's attention, and to make sure he gets a good, long look at the Eye. We've got traveling to do, and I'll give you the rundown on the way. Now for the invisibility field."

He pressed a button on his large wristwatch.

"We're invisible to outside eyes, despite being able to see each other. Let me apologize in advance. Now we do the Lois and Clark thing."

"The what?"

Aurus scooped up Nea in both arms.

"Put your arms around my neck."

With that, he carried her into the sky, the wind whipping her long hair.

"I've never flown before," yelled Nea against the wind.

She tried to keep her face expressionless, but finally turned her head as though she was looking at something on the ground. When Aurus couldn't see her face she broke out in a smile.

The Big Apple shrank below them as Aurus flew to dizzying heights.

"Glad you like it. We had to get away from the city so we can travel to another Earth."

"How do you travel?"

"With a fragment of Bifrost, the Rainbow Bridge, from the same mythos as Loki. This is how we activate it. We sing 'Here we go, into the rainbow yonder,' in the original Norwegian."

He sang, "Her skal vi gå, inn i regnbuen over horisonten."

A rainbow appeared beneath and before them, and they left the world.

Chapter Three
Ain't No Party Like a Mansion Party

Aurus and Nea appeared out of a rainbow into an early evening sky. They flew invisibly a few miles to the swampy alder woods near an enormous mansion. Using tiny binoculars, they scoped out the situation, and saw hundreds of fancy-dressed people arriving by limousines and other high-end cars. Those folk presented gilt-edged invitations to a couple of dark-suited, burly men at the stair-top mansion entrance.

Aurus picked waxy, white mistletoe berries hanging from the white-barked alders while he watched.

Nea slapped them out of his hands as he brought them to his mouth.

"Those are poisonous."

"Yes, to humans, damn it, but not to me, and I love 'em."

He grabbed a few more berries.

"How much of an idiot do you think I am?" he said.

"I have no idea how much of an idiot you are. I've barely just met you."

Aurus nodded.

"Anyway," he said, "Do you see the couple that resembles us? He in a silver-gray suit, she in a sparkly gown? That's our ticket in."

"We're going to waylay them and take their places?"

"Hell, no. That'd kick up too big a stink. Just wait here and watch me work." Aurus shivered slightly, shimmered, and shrank to the form of a brown hawk. He flew into a row of red rose bushes to the left of the entrance. Concealed from view, he became humanoid once again, and pressed the button on his wristwatch, fading into invisibility. He watched as the silver-gray suited man with sparkly-gowned female companion handed an invite to the guard on the right, looking up the stairs, who tossed it into a wooden box behind him. Aurus reached over the bushes, and grabbed that invitation out of the box, as the man tossed another toward it.

The invitation hit Aurus on the head and bounced to the ground.

Aurus hastily pulled himself behind the bush as the guard cursed under his breath and picked up the fallen invite. Transforming again into a hawk, Aurus worked his way out of the bushes and flew back to Nea, carrying the card in his beak.

Returning to human form, he smoothed the beak-creases out of the card and showed it to Nea.

Logan Farber Celebrates the Fiftieth Anniversary
of His First Movie, Springtime Heartbreak
July the 26th
Festivities begin 7:00 p.m.
'Armando Cullen and Guest'

"I'll impersonate this Armando, while you're 'and guest.' "

Aurus's features melted and re-formed, taking on a somewhat more effeminate cast.

"This is pretty much what he looked like. Should be enough to get us past Tweedledum and Tweedledumber."

"Is his left eye supposed to droop like that?"

"Like what? Do you have a mirror?"

"Oh, yes. I've certainly got a mirror hidden in this dress. No, of course not."

"I should have had you carry a clutch purse. Can you push the eye to where it looks good?"

Nea pushed his eye around, and it stayed where she put it.

"That looks good," she said. "Since this fellow is already inside, won't his fraternal twin showing up cause some commotion?"

"Not if I have this figured right." They walked from the woods, to blend in with the crowd of new arrivals.

Along the way, Nea asked, "Why did you turn into a bird? Couldn't you have just flown down invisibly and grabbed an invite?"

"Invisibility is for the rubes, not anybody important. The big mooks work for Logan-Loki. I figure a better than even chance they could see invisible. Anyone who is anyone has defenses just for that kind of sneak thief nonsense.

"Now, when we get to the stairs, stay on my right. We're going to the guard on the left, since he didn't check in Armando and guest when they arrived. I'll change to my own face right after we pass the gate keepers."

#

They quickly mingled with a crowd of Hollywood names and wannabees in the great, arch-ceilinged redwood ballroom. Emerald drapes over the windows kept the fading evening sun at bay, while dozens of golden chandeliers alight with actual candles cast a soft glow over the gala. A twenty-piece big band played hits of the fifties as the crowd mingled. Aurus, back in his own face, faded into a sea of tall, handsome men, while Nea literally stood head and shoulders above another sea of attractive women.

She chatted and laughed, finding out what she could about Logan Farber without drawing attention to her ignorance. Before long, she attracted the glances of an old, but energetic man who asked her for a dance.

Nea batted her long lashes at the short, handsome, gray-haired gent in a dark, pinstripe cashmere suit with red tie.

"Really, Mr. Farber, the world is dying to see you in another movie. I know I am." She pressed herself closer, and at five-eleven, plus heels, the emerald pendant sparkled before his eyes.

"Call me Logan. I think the world will survive just fine without a new movie from me, but if I can do anything for you, just ask."

"Well, if it isn't too much, could you show me around your mansion? I've never seen any place so lovely."

Logan's green eyes twinkled. "Of course, my dear. I'll give you the personal tour. My guests won't miss me for an hour or so."

While Nea worked on Logan/Loki, Aurus explored the house. After he was done with that, he went outside to the rear garden. He went discreetly invisible to avoid the eyes of the crowd.

Nea's tour ended in Logan's mahogany-paneled den, complete with lit fireplace, mounted jungle cat heads on the walls, and an upright, stuffed grizzly. A large many-paned window overlooked the mansion grounds. She breathed in the earthy scent of sandalwood.

Logan sat next to Nea on the big leather couch.

"Could I draw you?" she asked. "You're the most famous celebrity I've ever met. Have you pen and paper I could use?"

"I do, and certainly."

He handed her a pad of paper and pen.

"It won't be long, Logan. Just sit there and look handsome. That shouldn't be hard for you."

Logan beamed as Nea sketched rapidly for a few minutes.

"There. Done," she said, as she held it out for Logan to see.

"Remarkable," he said, "but you shaved a few decades off me, I think."

"That's how I see you. Would you mind autographing it for me?" she said as she handed it to him.

"Certainly. You know, I could talk to people about getting you art jobs, assuming I still have the pull I used to. I'm a little out of favor these days, what with my Old Hollywood lifestyle. Speaking of which, I must apologize for the hunting trophies. It seems they're considered tacky by the Hollywood elite these days."

"Ooh, no. They're very manly. Did you bag them yourself?"

"I did, but as a young man, not this brittle, old scarecrow."

He poured two Cognacs from an ornate coffee table decanter and offered her one.

She swirled her brandy.

"Old? You still look like a man in his prime. You can't be that old."

"I confess I've forgotten just how old I truly am, and right now you make me feel young again."

"How kind of you . . . Logan."

She smiled sweetly.

He drained his drink and stood. "Now, perhaps you'll tell me what's going on here?"

"What do you mean?"

She set her full glass on the table.

"You're heavier than you look, stronger too. That pendant has some sort of divination magic, and I'm quite sure you've never seen one of my movies. I only ask the courtesy of knowing your purpose."

"Fair enough. I was sent to determine whether you are a threat to this world's well-being. The pendant is supposed to read that."

The casement window smashed open as an animated stone gargoyle knocked Aurus through it from the outside. They fell to grappling on the shag carpet as the couch turned into a cage around Nea.

"Don't you mean 'we were sent?'" asked Logan. "I notice everything, and you arrived with that man now ruining my carpet, I believe."

Aurus's body blazed with a light so bright Logan had to shield his eyes. When he could see again the gargoyle lay in pieces on the smoldering carpet.

"Young fellow, invisibility is rather rude, you know," said Logan. "The gargoyle wouldn't have attacked had you not been in stealth mode."

"It wasn't meant to hide me from you. Just to avoid attention from your guests. We need to know your intentions, and I was monitoring you from outside."

"I'll let you explain that in a moment. Shall we introduce ourselves properly? As you no doubt know, I'm Loki Farbautison, among other names." While he spoke, his skin smoothed and his hair became a bright, but natural, red.

"Aurus. Aurus Harry Keaty."

Loki asked, "And your name, miss?" He turned to the cage, but Nea was not there. She appeared from the shadow of the stuffed grizzly.

"I really am Nea, short for Daernea, no last name, but I am called 'The Undark.'"

"So, can we avoid a fight, Mr. Keaty?" asked Loki.

Aurus grimaced. "I hope so, but I prefer 'Aurus,' if you don't mind."

"Not at all. It seems as though I'm not the only fallen pantheon represented here, Mr. Horus Harakhte. Would you mind appearing in your true form?"

Aurus shrugged. "Why not?" He shimmered as though seen through a blazing hot day in the desert. He blurred, and regained clarity as a bronze-skinned man with a gold-feathered, human-sized, hawk-head, wearing only a wrap-around cloth about his waist.

Loki turned to Nea. "You aren't Nyx, are you?"

"Nyx? Who? No, why?"

"Greek goddess of night. Just wondering. Now, could you explain yourselves, please?"

Aurus's voice crackled with power, like a distorted loudspeaker. *"We are Knights of Valeron."*

He returned to human form, wearing his fedora and casual clothes.

"Sorry, I know my voice is really grating in that form."

He held up his right hand, and in it appeared an eight-pointed golden star with a quarter-sized hole in the middle. Nea summoned her badge the same way, though hers had a black onyx in the hole.

"Ah, I see. The plainer of the two badges shows you to be closer to true ValDurian, then?"

"No, it just makes me her senior in rank," said Aurus. "And you'd probably be better off not saying that name. It has a habit of drawing attention. We just call them full-stars."

"All right then," said Loki, after drinking Nea's Cognac. "You were going to explain yourselves, were you not?"

"Yes," said Aurus. "Nea's pendant showed me your life since you came to this Earth. She had to get close to you long enough for me to read you through this companion piece." He held up an emerald ring on his right hand. "I was looking at the holographic display outside while invisibility covered it and me. My apologies for the intrusion. You don't seem to be a threat to this world."

"Oh, I'm so glad to have passed your test."

"No need to be sarcastic. I've seen too many worlds savaged by displaced deities trying to regain their former glory, or taking out their frustrations. You, however, seem to be mostly harmless."

"Oh, I'm far from harmless." In the air above him formed the images of a massive snake, a snarling wolf, and shimmering eight-legged horse. "Right now though, I only want to enjoy my very long life. So, is that it then? I was rather looking forward to getting to know this young lady better."

The images faded.

"Another time, perhaps," said Nea.

"We have other matters requiring our attention right now," said Aurus.

"Pity then. Logan Farber will die soon. It's time I took on another identity, as this one has begun to bore me."

"You'd give up all this?" asked Nea.

"In a heartbeat. It's just stuff, and I've set up a number of accounts for my new identity. Logan is old, and I need to be young again."

"We'll leave you to it then," said Aurus. "Sorry to have bothered you."

He and Nea moved to the smashed window.

"No bother at all. This was the most fun I've had in years. That makes it all the more clear I need to move on. One more thing though. Aurus, the cover name is a bit of overkill. I mean; Horus and Harakhte in the same name? Nea, dear, would you mind drawing me a portrait of yourself, just in case we never meet again? I hope we do though."

"Of course," she said, and did.

Logan smiled and waved goodbye.

With a run and jump, Aurus carried Nea out the window invisibly, and into the night sky. He did a U-turn in midair and dove to the garden.

"Almost forgot," he said, and without touching the ground, snatched up a satchel tucked behind a stone bench. Then he launched into the sky again, all in one move.

"So, he's safe to leave alone?" asked Nea.

"I read his life, or what I could digest. These past fifty years he's been a peach, and a hero, in my opinion. That's all assuming he didn't alter my readings somehow. I'll have the full-stars check out my findings. I read a little further back, from before this world, and he saved his own Midgard from Ragnarok by changing the Bifrost connection to a dead world."

"Oh. Then I'd say yes. I still think you could have told me though."

"Told you what?"

"That you're a god."

"Could have, but didn't, because I'm not."

"So why did you tell Loki you were a god?"

"I didn't, just gave him the nod. Besides, if the original Ghostbusters movie taught me anything, it's that when they ask if you're a god, you say 'yes.' "

Nea nodded hesitantly.

"If you say so. Would you have fought him then, if you had to, seeing as you aren't a god?"

"I wouldn't have been sent if the full-stars didn't think I could handle him. Same for you. I'd die serving them if need be."

"What inspires such loyalty?"

"It's my duty. The full-stars saved my life, and gave me the body you see, just because. You know how they are. My birth name is 'Ch'Kar', and I'm officially 'Ch'Kar-Harakhte', but I hate 'Chuck'. I call myself Aurus Harry Keaty, because the pronunciation is nearly the same as the god's name. My own little joke."

Nea nodded.

"Having finished with Loki, what's next?"

"Finished? We aren't finished."

Aurus laughed.

"There's more than one Loki in the AllWorlds, and it's still Thursday."

Chapter Four
Number Two is Trouble

Back in Aurus's office, he and Nea changed into gray, skin-tight outfits with pouch belts, hers supporting a rapier and dagger. She also donned a hooded gray cloak that she called her Cloak of Mystery. Aurus struggled into a backpack that had been leaning against his desk when they arrived.

"Are we going camping?" Nea asked.

"This is ordnance for the next Loki mission, courtesy of 'Q'."

"Who is that?"

"The full-star in charge of special equipment. I'm surprised you haven't met him. Anyway, this holds a bunch of condensed planar-phase pylons, and some upgrades for a superhero we're going to meet."

"Superhero?"

"How do I explain superheroes? Um, beings with powers and abilities far beyond your average chump on the street."

"That describes about half the people I know."

"Okay, but these tend to wear colorful costumes while fighting crime and/or evil."

"Oh, like the legendary Ulandar Lionheart?"

"Yeah, but often with logos emblazoned on their chests, and names like Lightning Man, or Thunder Woman."

"Is this another scouting-to-see-if-he's-dangerous mission?"

"No, this Loki's a major prick. It's a stomp-him-until-he-stops-moving mission. He's created some sort of ectoplasmic creatures he calls the Einherjar, after the eternal warriors from Valhalla. The superhero group ICON has been dealing with him for a while now."

"Icon?"

"Superhero teams usually have some fancy name, like The Legion of Justice Avengers or The Fantastic Doom Squadron. ICON is an acronym, but I don't know what it stands for.

"Anyway, let's get moving."

With a quick trip to the roof, they rode the rainbow.

#

Half an hour later that same Thursday, on yet another Earth, Aurus flew down next to Nea and a silver tech-armored figure. Behind them in the dry field lay hundreds of stacked-up steel cylinders looking much like scuba diver oxygen tanks.

"I've finished placing the pylons," Aurus said.

"THIS IS MAJOR TOM TO GROUND CONTROL. DO YOU READ?"

Aurus and Nea yanked out their earbuds. Aurus swore.

"Dammit, Major. Are you trying to blow our heads off?" They turned to the silver-armored man.

The Major opened his faceplate, revealing a brown-eyed Caucasian male. "Sorry, I had the volume set too high, but they work, yes?"

"Yes," said Nea, "but what's that about ground control?"

"Oh, you know, like the song?"

Aurus frowned.

"We're not originally from an Earth, Major. Don't expect us to get any cultural references. It's lucky we speak the same language at all."

"I'll download some Bowie for you later. I've adjusted the output. Let's try them again."

He closed his faceplate.

"Radio on. Can you hear me now?"

"We could hear you before," Aurus said, "but now we'll be able to keep hearing afterwards."

"Are we ready to start the operation?" asked Nea.

"I'm ready," said Aurus. "Major?"

"Good to go, but what are your code names going to be?"

"Code names?" asked Nea.

"Sure," he said. "Not only are code names standard for an operation, the supers and I use them as a matter of course. I'm Major Tom Hollen, but my code name is Major Mechon. Because I wear power armor."

Nea raised her right eyebrow.

"So you pick something that suits your flavor, your style?"

"Exactly."

"Then this is what Aurus was talking about. You can call him Hawkman, and I'll be Shadow Lass."

"I wouldn't," the Major said. "I'm pretty sure those names are owned by a comics company. We're very careful about treading on trademarks."

"I'll be Aurus and she'll be Nea then," Aurus said. "Are we clear on the plan?"

"Of course," said Nea.

The Major said, "Like you laid it out. I assault the main complex with my war-drones; take out his facilities and the Einherjar, while the two of you go after Loki himself in the other building."

"That's it," said Nea. "Simple is best."

Major Tom said, "Leaving me only two questions: Are you sure I can take out his monsters now, and should I call in any other ICON members for reinforcements?"

"The modifications to your weaponry make it one hundred percent effective against ectoplasm, compared to the thirty percent you experienced before we got here," said Nea.

"I placed planar phase-pylons around the entire neighborhood, so he can't teleport away," said Aurus. "We've got this. The rest of your organization has the loose Einherjar to deal with. If they can't handle them the full-stars will have to send in their strike forces, but only if they can't."

"As you say. Mission is a go." The Major pointed to the great stacks of tanks, which immediately soared overhead and then hovered in a great circle.

"War-drones; apply Search-and-Destroy mode on programmed

targets. Initiate." The drones and he flew off toward the setting sun and the rundown warehouse district.

Aurus and Nea zipped up the cowls of their one-piece gray bodysuits, then Aurus pressed his wristwatch, making them fade from sight. With Nea on his back, Aurus flew low, winding through city streets until they reached a dilapidated warehouse. Upon regaining visibility, he set Nea down and materialized a large, golden halberd in his right hand. He wound up for a two-handed swing at the steel door, but Nea stopped him.

"Let me get this," she said. She merged with the deepening shadows by the door, disappearing. In a few heartbeats the door swung open.

"How'd you do that?"

She frowned at him.

"Have you not been paying attention? My style is shadow. I merged with the shadow under the door, and stepped from the connected one on the other side. I've shown you this."

"I watched you move from one end of a room to the other in a shadow. I thought you went through the glass in my office door. Didn't know you could squeeze those puppies under things. I've been concentrating on not wiping out your advantage with my light powers. That's why we attacked at sunset."

"There was no point, and we're wasting time."

They moved through the building at a terrific clip, Aurus flying and Nea flitting through shadows. As Aurus traveled, he looked at a crystal disk held in his left hand.

"Do you have a fix on him yet?" asked Nea. "Maybe we should have had Major Mechon send some drones to help search?"

"No, they couldn't find him. The Major is only a distraction to keep Loki's attention off us. He'd be no help here."

The Major's voice came over their earbuds. "I can hear every word you say. These are two-way radios. Which I made."

"Sorry, Major," Aurus said. "I'd have been less condescending if I knew you were listening. I only meant that you literally can't help against Loki. He's magical and you aren't. We have protections against his brand of bullshit."

"Magic? You serious? I know he's tricky, but . . ."

"Magic," said Nea. "It's a thing, and he has it. So do we."

"Like this," said Aurus, gesturing pointlessly with the crystal disk. "We have a magic scanner, the All-Seeing Eye."

The Major asked, "I've been wondering. Why is he bothering to hide if he's a god? Why not just attack you?"

"Fallen god," Aurus said. "His power isn't what it once was. Plus, Loki's a cautious type. He doesn't know how tough we are, so he won't start a fight he might lose. Good on him, 'cause he wouldn't be the first displaced deity I've taken down. That's what we Knights of Valeron do."

"Okay, then just take him out. If he manages to replace world leaders with his Einherjar ecto-clones we're all in deep trouble. Mechon out."

Aurus turned his attention back to the crystal disk. "Loki's here. Above us, I think. The Eye has only a top-down view, so it can't give the relative height between us and him. Damn thing is only slightly more useful than a paperweight."

Aurus carried Nea up and set her on the ceiling's exposed metal framework. "He should be more-or-less right above. He keeps moving, so the signal isn't distinct. Of course, Mechon's drones couldn't see him at all."

"Why?" Major Mechon's voice interjected again.

"Spells," said Aurus. "He's shielded so as to be undetectable to anything but normal, living senses, like sight and sound. Your drones use video feed, so they couldn't see him."

"And your magic will?"

"No, not at all. The Eye detects everything else in the area, so anything that can't be detected shows up as an anomaly. He may as well be wearing a beacon on his head."

"Cool. Let me know how it goes. Mechon out."

Aurus focused light rays from his eyes on a finger-width spot above him, quickly burning a tiny hole through the ceiling. Nea vanished into the shadow above.

"Clear," sounded her voice over the radio. "It's a small room, and he's not here."

Aurus burned a larger hole, transformed into a golden hawk, and flew through the hole, carrying the earbud in his beak. Once in the room, he changed back to human form and rematerialized his halberd.

"The Eye shows he's likely just outside the door," Aurus said, as he hit the wooden door with a flying kick and smashed into the next room.

The room was piled high with crates and boxes, and a metal stairway led to a higher level. Aurus checked the Eye, and found the anomaly behind him. He turned to see Nea skewering a green-and-gold bedecked man with her rapier.

Nea straddled the prone figure and manacled its hands behind it with a pair of crystalline handcuffs.

"He went down awfully easy," said Aurus. "Something's not right." As he spoke, the figure changed into a nude woman with two long fox tails.

"Fox spirit," said Nea. "I caught a whiff of her perfume before she could strike. She's still breathing; maybe we can get some info?"

Aurus checked the Eye. "The neutralizer cuffs cut her non-detection spells. All right now . . . Son of a bitch. He switched his protections onto her."

He waved his hand over the Eye. "There. He's got to be on the roof from the way he's moving." Aurus grabbed Nea and they flew up the stairs, smashing through the door to the roof. Near the north end, a man in a cream-colored business suit adjusted a cloak of brown feathers over his shoulders and jumped off.

Aurus dropped Nea to the roof as a falcon replaced the man who had jumped. "No, you don't," Aurus yelled, and willed his own transformation. A golden hawk took his place and sped into the night sky after the falcon.

Closing the distance in seconds with magically-enhanced speed, Hawk-Aurus dove at the falcon. Again and again he swooped and struck, the falcon now trailing blood and feathers. With one final strike, Aurus transformed to human form, and bore the falcon to the ground in a hundred-foot drop. He slowed his fall at the last second with his flight power, still driving the falcon into the dirt.

Kneeling, Aurus grabbed a wing in each hand and pulled. The wings came off as the feathered remains of a tattered cloak, transforming Loki into a man. Aurus gave a victory grin. Loki punched Aurus in that grin, knocking him back ten feet.

While Aurus spit teeth, then picked himself up, dazed, Loki

gestured and formed a mostly transparent dome about himself. He stood and held up the remains of the cloak. "I've had Freyja's Falcon-Cloak forever, you bastard. I'd stop and kill you, but I think I'm still at a disadvantage. Since I can't fly now, I'll just walk past this interference you've set up and teleport to another base."

"Not happening." Aurus summoned his halberd, and swung at the barrier. To no effect.

Streetlights flickered to life along the nearby sidewalk, pushing back the night.

Loki laughed, and brushed dirt from his torn and bloody suit.

"I'll send you a bill for the suit. Armani, you know. Oh, and I must thank you for using radio communication. I heard everything you said from the moment you entered the warehouse. It certainly helped make informed decisions."

Aurus grabbed at a section of concrete sidewalk and tore out his fingernails clawing it up. Straining, muscles bulging, he hurled the bloodied slab at the dome. To no effect save for a shower of broken concrete.

With a deep chuckle, Loki started walking. "This barrier is really quite delightful. I doubt there's anything you can do to penetrate it, at least not before I get past the interference zone." He waved his hand, firing a bolt of lightning at Aurus, who dodged it.

Aurus lit up like the very sun itself, and his eyes sent a blazing beam of power at the barrier, which turned dead black on the side facing Aurus.

"Won't work, you know. I've read too much science fiction. I'm well aware that transparent force-fields can be penetrated by the proper light attacks. Hence it's photochromic. Ironically enough, your Major Metalhead has a sonic attack that could work, but he'll be kept busy by the last of my Einherjar for too long."

Aurus replied by sticking his halberd in the ground before the slowly-clearing dome, but found himself unable to slow its progress. Loki fired another bolt at Aurus, missing, while he maneuvered the dome around the halberd.

Nea's voice from behind the dome gave Aurus pause. "I can stop him, Aurus."

"Of course. It's nighttime. Your powers should be at their strongest."

"Afraid not," she said. "My power lies in shadow, not darkness alone. I've been trying to tell you that night does nothing for me."

"Then die," said Loki, striking her square in the chest with a bolt of crimson energy.

"Not tonight," said Nea, while a nimbus of orange surrounded her.

Aurus said, "We have protections too, asshole."

"I can stop him." She stepped between Aurus and Loki, facing the dome, spreading her cloak open behind her. "Backlight me."

Aurus glowed, darkening the dome again, except for a large patch facing Aurus. Nea was nowhere in sight.

The ensuing sounds of struggle, and a male voice in pain, were music to Aurus's ears. The dome faded, leaving Nea with her knee in the back of a facedown Loki. His hands had been manacled behind him with crystalline cuffs, which she held high, twisting his arms up.

"Nea, way to go," Aurus yelled. "Wait, you took your cuffs off the fox girl? Is she dead?"

Loki gritted his teeth. "Oh, I hope not. She was a lovely girl . . . or whatever I wanted." He gasped for breath.

"No, Aurus, she's still alive. These are your cuffs. I figured I'd need them. He wasn't very tough without magic."

Aurus felt in his back pouch. "Did you take them with your shadow powers?"

Nea laughed. "In my youth I was a sleight-of-hand artist."

"A pickpocket?" Aurus asked. "You were a criminal?"

"I've been many things. Right now I'm Daernea, the Undark, DemiKnight of Valeron."

Loki grinned, and then grimaced. "My dear, I really think you should be working for me. We'd make a wonderful team, yes, we would." He winced and stopped talking as Nea twisted his arms up higher.

"Thank you, but no. I'm quite happy with my current situation, even if Aurus here could pay closer attention to what I say, instead of the things I wear."

"Okay, okay, sorry."

Aurus picked up his scattered teeth and Loki, while Nea called Major Mechon.

After she finished, Aurus asked, "How did you penetrate his dome, and how did you get down here so quickly?"

"I told you, my power is shadow. Shadow requires light. I traveled via the shadows created by the street lamps to get here. Then you gave me a shadow right into his dome and I went through it. Our powers can work together, if you listen to what I tell you."

"Huh, and here I thought the teaching was my job."

"No reason we can't both learn, is there?"

Chapter Five
And Loki Makes Three

Invisible, Aurus and Nea rode the rainbow over their New York City.

"So, what will they do with the prisoners?" asked Nea as Aurus picked her up and they flew. The rainbow vanished.

"Don't know much. I just drop 'em off. From what little I do know, Loki'll be thrown in the slammer and given the chance at rehabilitation. Same for the fox dame, but in a different clink."

"How do you rehabilitate a god who's outlived his worshippers? Especially a known trickster."

"No idea. Grapevine says the full-stars can do almost anything except interfere personally in other worlds, unless their Wyrd lets them. Maybe they reincarnate him as a pigeon or dung beetle."

They flew to the roof of Aurus's building, where they became visible.

"Do we get Friday off?" asked Nea. "Two of Loki in one Thursday is too many."

"Sure, but it's still Thursday."

"Can't be. It looks about noon, and we already had evening on that last world."

"Nonetheless, it's still Thursday here."

He pointed to his wristwatch.

"It keeps time with this world, and here it's Thursday. It has to do with how Bifrost works. We could have been gone a week as long as the connection was maintained and it wouldn't matter. Except sometimes. I get confused on the issue myself."

They entered Aurus's office, and he went to the sink in his bathroom. There he scrubbed the blood from his torn but already healing fingers. He also washed the dirt off his loose teeth and reinserted them into his gums. Upon returning to his office he flashed Nea a full-grin smile.

"They'll hold solid in a few minutes. It'd take a long time to regrow them from scratch."

"Handy. Are you sure they're in the right spots? They look a little off to me."

"That's just 'cause they're still wiggly. Fortunately, I have each tooth numbered on the back for just such an emergency."

"Really?"

"No. Now then, we have one more target on another Earth today. First though, I'll make us some lunch, and you can get some sleep if you want."

"Sounds good. Meanwhile, I'm going to draw that Loki and the fox spirit, just for my collection."

"You can draw me, if you like," said Aurus.

"Why would I do that? These are pictures of defeated foes and the briefly encountered. Chances are I'll be seeing you every day."

#

One pasta meal later, Nea declared herself fit for duty.

"I'm impressed with the meal," she said. "It was really good."

Aurus smiled and his eyes literally lit up.

"Um, thanks. Don't usually cook for others, so I'm glad to see my tastes aren't too weird."

"No, that was great. I'm just a bit surprised a man can even cook, especially considering the line of work you're in."

"With how much I have to eat, it only made sense to learn some culinary skills. I've got some game, but I'd not be likely to win Chopped or Top Chef."

"I don't know what those are. What do you mean by 'have to eat?'" said Nea.

"Those are TV shows that feature cooking competitions. As for the eating, this body burns a lot of calories, about three times that of the average superhuman. Figured I might as well learn cooking for myself. Do you need a nap before we start out again?"

"I don't sleep much anyway, Aurus."

"Neither do I."

He leaned back in his desk chair, knocking a pile of DVDs off the desk.

"Maybe that's something the full-stars look for in a Knight."

"So they can work us twice as long?"

"You might think, but we do get time off to relax or whatever. Speaking of which, for relaxation I have these."

He picked up the spilled DVDs and stacked them haphazardly on the desk.

"Old detective movies?" asked Nea.

"I do like those, but I like these too. I'm a sucker for romance movies."

He tossed one DVD to Nea.

"Springtime Heartbreak?" she said. "That's Logan Farber's first movie. So that's what was in that satchel you went back for."

"Chatted with the guests while we were vetting him. His movies sounded good, so I went through his collection while you were distracting him. He had so many I doubt he'll miss these. That's the real reason I went outside, to hide the satchel. I had already gone through his life story from the Eye of Overview while I was inside, but the gargoyle caught me when I was coming back in. I have a DVD player, so maybe when we have a break, you might want to check them out with me?"

"That's for the future. For the present, is the second Loki what I was recruited for, the 'big thing' that was coming up?"

Aurus laughed.

"Him? He's just Thursday. Nothing much out of the norm for a team of Knights. I have no idea what the Oracles or the Omnimind may have seen on the horizon, but it's gotta be something bigger than a lousy fallen god."

"I know of the Oracles, in a hearsay sort of way," said Nea. "Traditional, mysterious predictors of the future that the full-stars use to get ahead of trouble, I guess? What is the Omnimind?"

"There is little traditional about the Oracles, but you're basically right. Using all sorts of mystical means, they predict trouble so we have time to deal with it. The Omnimind is what you might call artificial intelligence. It gathers info and compiles that into files to give us heads-ups on possible troubles. More extrapolative than predictive, I think."

"So, which has been giving us these missions?"

"Can't say. Maybe both. Didn't ask. Doesn't matter."

"Why the hurry to deal with three Lokis in one day?"

"Can't say for sure. I don't think the full-stars see time the same as we do. They determine something has to be done, and we do it. The whys and wherefores are above my pay grade speaking of which, we're back on the clock."

Aurus opened up a cluttered desk drawer and pulled out a gold-rimmed black disk the size of a half-dollar. He flipped it to Nea.

"My spare energy-shield. Loki put yours into the orange with one blast. Another hit and he'd have been through. Use that while yours regenerates. Now, pick out an outfit from the Fabricon and we'll be on our way to a new world. You'll be taking the lead on this one. Just remember what we decided about Number Three during lunch."

#

Nea and Aurus strode the dark streets side by side. Nea wore a white shift dress, short red jacket, and silver high heels. Aurus wore a simple, well-tailored black suit, black fedora and black Italian loafers without socks.

"I'm still a little surprised you're in such bright clothes, considering your style," said Aurus.

"From the guy with light-powers dressed all in black. My sobriquet is 'The Undark', not 'The Dark'. I dress to suit the occasion, and this one is as a buyer of questionable commodities. Do I have carte blanche to buy anything needed to come off as authentic?"

"The full-stars will cover anything you need."

She adjusted the emerald Eye of Overview so that it hung just below her throat.

"I'll do my job as we discussed: Flash this, and keep Loki, slash,

Carl Helsir, talking so it can read him. I play the boss, you're the stoic muscle."

"Yeah, that's about it. It helps if he looks at the pendant, which I think he will, considering the placement."

Nea said, "If things go badly, follow me into shadow. I created one end of a shadowgate at that abandoned convenience store we stopped at, and I'll make another end if we need a quick escape route."

"Shadowgate?"

"Something I'm experimenting with. I should be able to step through one gate to another without any connecting shadow in the physical plane. The connection comes through the Plane of Shadow, which theoretically connects every shadow everywhere. The drawback comes from having to create both ends of the gate in this world."

"So that's what you were doing there. Cool. Thought maybe you were powdering your nose, if you'll pardon the euphemism."

He looked up at a darkened office building.

"We're here. Stay on script, and since we're undercover, remember to call me 'Harry,'" he said.

#

After a long elevator ride, they were patted down and scanned with electronic wands by a male-female pair in dark suits and dark glasses. The man touched his earpiece and nodded.

"Mr. Helsir will see you now."

The man opened an ebony door and the woman waved them in. The door closed behind them with the echoing sound of a prison cell door slamming.

They walked down a long, bright, white hallway with only one other door at the far end, and no windows.

Aurus rumbled in his throat.

"Huh, what the hell kind of setup is this? I thought we were meeting Helsir, not getting our exercise for the day."

"Yes, it is odd. Be on your guard; something doesn't smell right."

A panel opened in the ceiling and two women dressed as ninjas dropped down. Before they even landed, Aurus punched one out of the air, smashing her into the wall. Nea dropped the other silently with a roundhouse kick to the head.

Nea tugged her hem back down into place.

"She's lucky I didn't kick her with the heel. I hope there won't be much more of this. My dress isn't made for fighting."

"And here I thought it was a combat skirt. You expect more?"

"No other reason for the long hallway."

They walked on. Halfway down the hall a panel opened on each side, both disgorging a man wearing plate armor and wielding a two-handed sword.

Nea said, "You take them. I don't want to break a nail."

Aurus grunted, and ducked the swing of the nearest 'knight,' losing his hat. He picked up the man and threw him into the other. Both went down, and Aurus made sure they stayed down, by ripping off their helmets and knocking their heads together.

Aurus checked the alcoves they had been hidden in, but found nothing. He picked up his hat.

"You expect there's more of 'em?"

"Of course. We aren't there yet. Onward."

Just as they neared the door, four people in high-tech flak armor popped up from the floor on a rising platform. Two men and two women, each armed with automatic weaponry.

Aurus glanced at Nea, who shook her head. He folded his arms behind his back in an "at-ease" pose.

"We only want to see Mr. Helsir," said Nea. "There are items I need, and it's been said he can get them. Unless, of course, he doesn't want our business."

One of the four put his hand to a headset, and then nodded. The door slid up, and the four moved aside, a matched pair to each side, allowing passage.

The penthouse office, dimly lit and tastefully spartan, sprawled over an area that could have held four buses, should someone find a way to bring them up. Cedar-paneled walls bore a few paintings, all mountain scenery. The marble-tiled floor had a gold-accented path that led to a mahogany desk with only two chairs in front of it, and a high-back chair behind. That chair faced away from them, toward the sole window. A low, quiet voice came from the chair.

"I'm told there are certain items you wish to acquire?"

"I'd rather see your face," said Nea.

Aurus looked at her in surprise.

The voice spoke again. "Anything can be had for the right . . . What?" It ended on a high note.

"I'd like to see you, Mr. Helsir. I came here to do business face-to-face, not face-to-chair."

"Dart?"

The chair spun about, revealing a slender, blond man in a herringbone suit.

"Hello, Eddie. I'm called 'Daernea' now, 'Nea' for short. I thought that was your 'business' voice. Long time no see. Do you always treat clients like intruders?"

"Oh, girl, give us a squeeze."

Eddie jumped over the desk and picked Nea up. She hugged him back and smiled.

"Oh, how long has it been, sweetheart?" asked Eddie.

Down on her feet again, she adjusted her dress and jacket.

"I'd hate to say. I don't want to number the years for either of us."

"It's okay, girl, I'm not vain," he said, as he patted himself up under his chin. "The corridor lets me know what I'm dealing with. The quicker they wimp out, the more I charge. Plus, if they can beat the last four, I'm out of here."

"Your clients are okay with being assaulted?" she asked.

"No, but I apologize for the security system error and give them a 'discount' for the inconvenience. It helps me gauge their levels of desperation and how much to gouge them. The cameras only show the fights from above, so I didn't recognize you. It was fun, right? Now, what can I do for you?"

"I need things, Eddie, and I know you can get them."

"Oh, fer sure, but call me Carl. For the time being I'm Carl Helsir. What are you doing in this world?"

"I could ask the same of you, Ed, uh, Carl. I needed a pipeline to some esoteric and potentially illegal materials, and Mr. Helsir's name floated to the top of the list on this world, in this city."

"For your employer?"

"Customer. I work for myself now, Carl, but I have clients with extraordinary tastes and the wherewithal to satisfy them."

"Give me a list and I'll see what I can do. In the meanwhile, you might introduce me to your pretty muscle here."

"Carl, this is Harry, and yes, he is pretty. Harry, this used to be Eddie Singer. He taught me my first magic."

"Charmed," said Aurus.

"Ooh, he talks too. Do you have to pay extra for that?" Carl brushed his eyebrows into place with his fingers.

"I don't pay him; we're partners. I do the planning, he does the heavy lifting."

"Um-hmm. I'll bet he does. Well, anyway, let's see what you need."

Nea wrote her list on the pad of paper Carl handed her. She tossed it and the pen back.

"You have some very interesting clients. Even for me, some of this is hard to come by. Basilisk gallstones? In this day and age?"

"Then go somewhere that isn't this day and age, Carl. I'll make it worth your while."

"Of course, of course. It'll take some time, so you can drop off your contact information. Or you can leave Harry with me, and I'll send him back to you when I'm done."

"Sorry, Carl," said Nea, "but I need Harry with me."

"I'll just bet you do. Your loss, Harry, but I'll get right on this."

#

Aurus flew Nea through the night sky. Holographic scenes from his ring played in front of them.

"You threw me, going off script like that," he said.

"You recovered quite well. I couldn't act like he and I were strangers. He's right though; you're pretty, at least when you're perplexed."

"Aw, shucks, ma'am."

He used his shapeshifting power to make himself blush deep red.

"Did you get what we needed?" asked Nea.

He shut down the holo images.

"I got enough. He isn't a very good guy, but mostly harmless, I'd say."

"I could have told you that. We used to run cons together in an interdimensional scumhole, back in our youth. Well, my youth anyway; he's obviously older than he looks."

"Sounds like you had an interesting childhood."

"Some sort of hint to open up about my sordid past for you? I suppose that's only fair.

"Eddie saved me. Literally picked me from the trash and gave me purpose. That was mainly as a pickpocket, but it was a purpose. I had to leave him eventually though, as my body was a wreck and became worse with time. Couldn't do the jobs and didn't want his pity. That's when the full-stars found me.

"They repaired my body and filled it with a piece of the Plane of Shadows. That's where my power and strength comes from. That's why I work for them now and will continue to do so for the foreseeable future. Any more than that I'm not yet ready to tell you."

"Don't worry about it. Not like I'm in a position to judge from on high if that's what worries you."

"All things considered, can we leave Eddie be?"

"I think so. Didn't you tell me you'd never dealt with gods before?"

"I hadn't thought so. How was I to know? Eddie must not want anyone to find out if he wouldn't tell me. Knowing him, he'll get skittish if he finds out we learned his real name, so let's just play along."

"Fine. I'll report it that way."

"Aurus, do you suppose they knew?"

"Who knew what now?"

"The full-stars. That Eddie and I used to be a team."

"Best guess from years of experience? Yes."

"Then why didn't they tell us?"

"Easy answer: they, particularly the Oracles, like to mess with people. I think it's probably more complicated than that, but close enough.

"Probably just one of their whims. They'll never set you up in a bad way on purpose, but I like to think they look for a few giggles here and there."

"Oh, good, then they'll get a kick out of being stuck with a shipment of hundred-year-old zombie testicles every month."

"You know, I think they just might."

Chapter Six
Aftermath

Raelani wafted down a green hallway, white gown billowing. The door at the end vanished ahead of her, allowing access into a huge, glowing white room. It was decorated with tiers of frosted circular crystals, set in all the walls, as high and wide as the eye could see. She passed through another vanishing door into a much smaller room with a coffin-like crystal cylinder hovering in the air horizontally, at waist level. In the cylinder lay an unmoving man.

"Indra, are you about?" said Raelani.

The air rippled with light as Indra manifested in human form.

"I am. Just stepped out for some cellular refinishing agents. What can I do for you, my dear?" he said.

"Aurus and the new DemiKnight, Daernea, performed admirably. I'd say he was in top form. Told you it would work."

"What would work?"

"Pairing him with Daernea. He'd been in a slump for so long I knew he needed something to wake him up and bring out his full potential."

"I suppose so," said Indra.

"Hmm, and she's smart too. If she can get him acting smart again, instead of falling back to just smashing foes to a pulp, we're all better off."

"As you say, my dear. And the Lokis?"

"That's three Lokis assessed with only one needing

incarceration."

"Very good. How many does that give us now?" asked Indra.

"An even dozen, with three well on their way to reintroduction amongst the AllWorlds."

"Excellent," said Indra as he turned to the cylinder man.

"Aren't you done with that yet? You have other responsibilities," said Raelani, pointing to the man.

"Almost, and I know. I've already sent Julian to assemble a team for the upcoming campaign and it will have to include Aurus and Nea."

"They've had little time to rest, you know."

"I am aware, but it's not like we have unlimited Knights," said Indra. "Even with the time-stop ability of the Bifrost shards we don't have enough of them."

"And fewer all the time, it feels like. This set of missions would have been perfect for Ari," she said with a sigh.

"Agreed, but Aristide Achart Archambeau is no more and has been gone for over fifty years."

"That doesn't mean I don't miss him. He was our first Knight, you know."

"Yes, I know. I was there. You need to find another Knight to dote on. Meanwhile, the campaign is in play, and I really need to work on this."

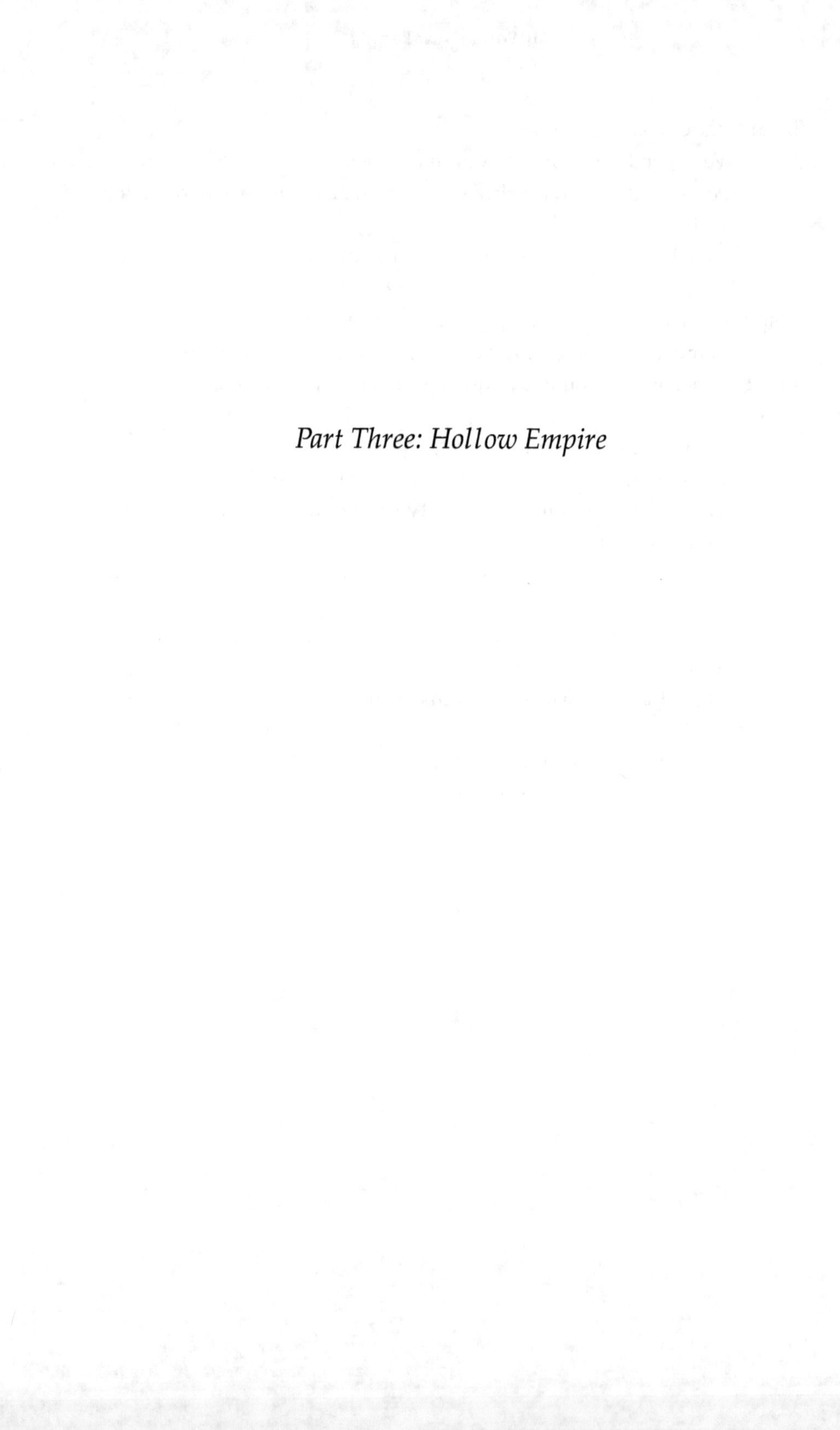

Part Three: Hollow Empire

Chapter Seven
Prelude to Horror

Aurus raised an invisible fist and knocked on the penthouse door. He waited for a few moments but got no response. He glanced about the posh, blue-carpeted hallway and saw no one. He checked himself in an ornamental hall mirror to ensure he was still invisible then knocked again, harder this time.

Nea's voice came from a small, gray screen to the left of the door. "I can only assume this is Aurus since I can't see anybody. Use the com-pad."

Aurus shrugged and looked for buttons on the tiny screen.

"Oh, you've probably never seen one of these. Just touch the screen and talk."

He gingerly touched the screen.

"Yeah, this is Aurus. Let me in. We have a new mission so I came over straight away."

"I won't even ask why you're here instead of calling so I could have had time to ready myself, or why you're invisible."

"Lost your phone number, and this way I bypassed building security."

"Whatever. I'll meet you on the street soon as I can."

Thirty minutes later Nea, in dark glasses, hair scarf, and tan trench coat, left the building to find Aurus nearby.

"Sorry to have kept you waiting. Got ready as fast as possible."

"That's okay. Now let's get going. I hope Master Julian isn't upset with us."

#

A quick rainbow ride later, Nea and Aurus were seated at a round table in a circular room with two other people. One was a brown-skinned, brown-eyed man with a green head scarf and leather jacket. The other appeared distressingly average, save for having short, dark hair. Aurus started introductions.

"Gents, this is Daernea the Undark. She goes by Nea usually."

"Nea Nystoros. I picked a last name after meeting the first Loki."

The two guys nodded.

"Been on god duty then," said the first one. "That's a little above our pay grade. We only get called in for the more down-to-Earths jobs."

"These two are Marvin Dees," said Aurus, waving his hand at the first guy, "and Zen. No last name. They may be DemiKnights but you can count on them in a dust-up."

"Just so long as it ain't *too* dusty," said Zen.

"Did you forget that *I'm* a DemiKnight? How dusty is it?" asked Nea.

"Dusty enough," said a voice coming from a gray doorway that had suddenly appeared on a wall.

A man stepped through the doorway. He had wavy white hair with a matching goatee.

Nea gave a slight bow.

"Master Julian."

"Nea. How pleasant to see you again. Greetings to you all: Zen, Marvin, Aurus."

As they all nodded back, Aurus turned to Nea.

"Nea, when did you meet Master Julian?" asked Aurus.

"He recruited me, or rather inducted me after Lord Caerelon recruited me."

"Just so," said Julian. "Now that we're all introduced we can get down to business. There's been an upturn in interdimensional trafficking, the human kind."

"You mean slave trade?" asked Nea.

"I do, but more than that, and by 'human' I mean numerous sapient beings. Zen has personal experience in the matter on his home world, but we're going to try and shut down every such operation across the AllWorlds."

#

Nea pivoted in the front passenger's seat and examined the rear interior of the van, windowless on the sides and back doors. The walls were lined with electronic equipment, replete with a plethora of tiny lights.

"Let me be blunt," said Nea. "I have no idea what most of this stuff is. I don't normally deal much with technology, so I don't know why Master Julian assigned me to this."

Zen shrugged.

"Don't need a tech nerd. What I need is someone to monitor me and do deep infiltration when called for. I hear you're the best at that last."

"Depends on what I have to infiltrate."

"That would be the interdimensional spaceship we're approaching. The specs I gave you should help. Just memorize and then destroy them."

"Why destroy them?"

"If you're discovered, it's one less thing you'd have to explain to any authorities."

"Will do then. I'll also be setting up one of my experimental shadowgates until it's time to meet with you."

#

Zen embraced the young woman, passion spent, sweat glistening. He caressed pale, hot skin until his tanned fingers found the small of her back. He jerked away from the chill.

Her ice-blue eyes opened wide, staring at him. She brushed back her long, auburn locks, then caressed his short, dark hair.

"You know what I am. Are you displeased?"

Zen gulped.

"No, no. Just startled at the difference in body temperatures."

"The real me uses heat more efficiently than a human. We've had physical sex. Do you wish to continue with emotional sex?"

"Yes, of course. Could you do me a favor first?"

She waited, unblinking.

"Might I see the real you? Not the Receptacle?"

She blinked.

"A most unusual request. Are you sure?"

"Yes, please, if it won't trouble you."

She stretched out on the bed facedown, her lower back a furrowed, dinner plate-sized area of mottled green. As Zen watched, said area rippled and humped up, peeling away from the skin around the edges. After several spasms, her body finally lay tranquil.

Before the green mass separated from her completely, Zen stuck fingers in his mouth. He pulled loose a hard plastic capsule that had been glued to the backside of his front teeth and then tucked it between his cheek and lower gums.

The moss-colored pillow of a creature pulled free from the human body, save where still attached to her lower spine.

There, it said, in a high-pitched, electronic voice. *This is me, free of my human host. Do I repulse you?*

"Not at all. You have a beauty beyond the human."

The creature's underside was all tendrils and thick mucus. The human cavity was blood-red but not bleeding, coated with the mucus secretion. Her upper spine ended just below the rib cage, where it had been connected to the creature's backbone.

"Is it permitted to speak with the Receptacle?"

Certainly. In fact, I encourage it. Ask your questions.

He cleared his throat.

"I'm Zen. You probably don't remember, but —"

"Oh, yes."

She giggled.

"We just had sex. Was it as glorious for you as it was for me?"

His eyes widened.

"It was great, all right. I didn't know the human remained conscious as a Receptacle."

"Always. The V'Laubi share everything with us. Every day is a joyous day, especially when I can share myself with other humans."

"The V'Laubi don't resent us?"

"Not even a little bit. They didn't know our polluted air would be so poisonous to them, so how could we have known?"

Zen nodded, then changed his expression and voice timbre to that of a wide-eyed fanboy.

"When this fantastical, flowerlike spaceship landed and they disembarked, it seemed like the herald of a new age. Hundreds of beautiful, emerald-green people; alien faeries, I thought."

"Oh, yes. Me too," she said. "I wanted so much to meet them, but then the horror happened."

He shuddered extra-hard for effect.

"So awful, their skins bubbling, then melting, due to man's thoughtlessness."

She turned her head to the side, looked up, and beamed him a radiant smile.

"Not all, thank the Maker, else I would not be bonded with my new soul. They only ever wanted to help, even now. Thankfully, humans are not as vulnerable to foul air."

Zen smiled back before he spoke.

"Praise be, they had unbonded young ones aboard the sealed ships, but it's unfortunate none of their original Receptacles survived. Out of caution, they had me shower and have my clothes dry cleaned before I boarded the ship."

A tear rolled down her cheek, onto the sheet.

"I feel so glad they needed human Receptacles, but guilty the old ones had to die so that I could experience this."

"How long will you stay with them?"

"Forever, I hope. I'm so happy now." Her eyes were glazed, her smile a little too wide. "Please, may I reconnect?"

Zen looked closely at her upper spine, barely able to see the thin filament remaining connected to the V'Laubi. He rubbed his cheek, pushing the hidden capsule between his teeth. Inhaling, he paused, then bit down and exhaled at the underside of the V'Laubi.

The creature writhed to an electronic scream.

Zen grabbed the filament, suffering a shock that dazed him

briefly. A hard yank snapped the connection, then the host screamed. He grabbed her head.

"Can you hear me?" he asked as they locked gazes.

"So much pain, too much, too much. Yes, I can hear you," she half-screamed.

"I'm sorry I had to use your body, but it was the only way to avert suspicion. I apologize for the pain, but we had to be sure."

She grabbed his hand.

"Not pain from you, from them. Every day hooked to it is torture. Please, kill me."

"Can't you quit, have your back replaced?"

"No. They don't surgically remove it, they eat their way in. Then they feed on our pain. Nobody ever leaves; we can't, even if they'd let us. We'd die soon without them being attached. Please kill me, before it recovers."

"I don't think it will. We'd found some alien remains that hadn't quite dissolved, so we were able to experiment on them. I blasted this one with a dose of ragweed pollen. That's what really killed their first hosts, pollen, not our 'polluted air.' They took an unexpected setback and played on our sympathy, hoping well-meaning environmentalists would be on their side."

She bit her lip.

"They seemed so helpless, and they're still playing, but also on our greed now. We volunteers came here because the government people said they'd help our families, then we'd be rich when our service was up."

"The government was happy to help the V'Laubi, because they promised us their tech," said Zen. "The feds didn't care about you at all, even if they had their suspicions."

"The V'Laubi goal has always been domination," she said. "The 'emotional sex' is supposed to give humans healthier minds, but it's really brainwashing. It convinced me to give up my body for them."

She gave a bitter laugh.

"Are there any unbonded girls in here?" he asked.

"None. The process takes less than a day. If you had thoughts of rescue, forget them and me. I need to die; otherwise another of those things might use me."

She gazed at him and pleaded with her eyes. He stared back, his face emotionless, as though carved from stone. He knocked her out by striking the carotid artery, and then snapped her neck. Zen dressed, then peeled off two patches of fake skin on the backs of his upper arms. He stuck one patch on her body and the other on the V'Laubi. Then he snorted out a plastic bulb of liquid from his sinuses. He squirted both patches with the liquid, then tossed the bulb. The patches began dissolving.

He left the room and nodded with fake, dazed happiness to other Receptacle girls as he walked to the airlock. It opened just as Zen heard internal fire alarms, and he knew the bodies were engulfed. Partly outside, standing barely inside the airlock so it wouldn't close, he dropped the happy act and spoke to Nea, who had remained in the van.

"It's worse than we feared. All the girls are beyond recovery, living every day in hell. No need to hold back any longer."

"I heard and saw the same thing you did, and memorized the targets," she said. "Time to bring hell to the body snatchers."

Nea stood, dropping a clipboard with a drawing of the flower ship she'd just finished onto the seat. She left the van and merged with the shadows.

Zen strode away nonchalantly as Nea slipped aboard, just before the hatch spiraled shut. She made her way down the hallway which was mad with blinking emergency lights. Power shut down as fire suppression measures began. The convenient shadows and fire extinguishing mists gave her an easy path throughout the ship while she stopped in several locations to attach black hockey puck-sized and shaped devices in unobtrusive locations.

Receptacles ran about, making electronic screaming noises.

Nea killed all of them she could, when she could, with quick, mortal strikes of her rapier, sparing those girls from what was to come. Finally, having placed all her devices save one, she entered the engine room and stuck that one behind transparent pipes of noisy, bubbling, scintillating liquid.

Finding a bare patch of golden wall, she traced a rectangular outline on it with black chalk, chanting to herself as she did so. At a sudden sound, nearly unnoticed over the bubbling liquid, she snapped her body to the left. A flare of pain tore through her right shoulder as a bolt of emerald light grazed it while striking square on the standing rectangle. Her right arm numb, with her left she flung a dagger into the throat of a Receptacle girl as it pointed a golden tube at her again. An emerald bolt struck the pipes of liquid, bursting them and making Nea scramble.

No further bolts were forthcoming as the girl had fallen. Nea retrieved her dagger and the golden tube, then stabbed the V'Laubi that was attempting to disengage itself from its host-corpse. She began chanting in front of her rectangle again.

The rectangle became solid black and Nea put her arm through up to the elbow. With a satisfied expression she stepped through. . . and found herself in the back of Zen's van. The shadowgate on that side vanished as she exited it.

"The charges are in place," said Nea. "Bring the hell."

Zen stabbed a console button. Almost immediately a rumble sounded in the distance. Grabbing binoculars, Nea looked through the front window and saw the V'Laubi floral ship bursting into flames.

"Your bombs are highly successful," said Nea.

"I've transmitted all relevant information to Marvin and Aurus, so they should be starting their mission about now."

#

A thousand miles away, Aurus and Marvin began their mission.

"Got the info," said Marvin, standing at the edge of a forest. "We now know how to distinguish between possessed humans and normals. If you could give me a lift, please?"

Aurus nodded, and picked up Marvin, then triggered his watch's invisibility field. Marvin and Aurus both wore heavy backpacks while Marvin also carried a scoped rifle. Unseen to prying eyes, but not each other, Aurus flew Marvin into the night sky.

"We're probably far enough away that we won't set off any of their sensors," said Marvin while pointing at a second grounded flower ship, "but they still might be using radar, and invisibility won't help against that."

Aurus nodded.

"Like I told the new girl, anybody who is anybody has defenses against invisibility. How close do you have to be to use that thing?"

Marvin shook his rifle.

"This 'thing' is an M1 Garand, said to be the greatest rifle ever made. Certainly the greatest ever produced for the US military. Absolutely the greatest American rifle ever designed by a Canadian."

"No disrespect to the rifle intended, but you didn't answer my question. How close?"

"A great shooter would probably have to be within 500 yards. I can hit my target at 1,000. We should be well outside the range of their scanners."

"You're better than a great shooter?"

"I am the greatest known marksman in the AllWorlds, with the exception of Florinald ValDurian. Florinald, however, cannot use self-propelled missiles, like bullets from guns, being geased to use things powered at least partly by his muscles, like bows and throwing knives."

"Interesting that you should know that. I didn't think the full-stars were in the habit of revealing their geases to those who were not full Knights."

"Oh, yeah, shouldn't have said anything. Please don't spread that around and I shouldn't have either. Florinald and I bonded, being fellow marksmen, I guess."

Aurus shrugged.

"Makes no nevermind. You tell me where to take you and I will. It's your show at this point and I'm the taxi service."

After a minute Marvin had Aurus take him to a treetop where he could see the V'Laubi flower ship clearly. It was in the middle of a clearing two thousand feet in diameter. Within moments, his night scope was sighted in, and he let fly four rounds at apparently random sections of the blossom-like hull. Aurus then took Marvin to a tree on the ship's other side where he launched four more rounds. When he finished, there came a metallic 'ping,' as the Garand's empty clip ejected. Marvin caught it with practiced ease and put it in a belt pouch. He replaced the top-loading clip with a fresh one of eight rounds, flush with the top of the rifle when closed.

"Now what?" asked Aurus, hovering near Marvin, both of them

still invisible.

"We snoop on the enemy," said Marvin, as he shucked his backpack and slung the rifle onto his right shoulder with one movement.

He drew out a tablet-style monitor from the backpack and flicked it on.

"Those bullets should let me monitor the interior and interfere with their sensors, based on what Zen found.

"Zen had contact lenses that were recording devices powered by his own body's electricity so that the V'Laubi wouldn't detect them. He not only got footage of the girl explaining that all Receptacles were completely controlled by the V'Laubi, but body scans enabling us to tell exactly who were fully human and what were not. Zen and Nea got lucky in that none of the girls were still human, so they could destroy the ship indiscriminately."

"Not so lucky for the girls, of course," said Aurus.

"No. I didn't mean to make it sound that way. It just made their job easier. We aren't so lucky, which is lucky for some of the girls. There are a dozen full humans awaiting their turns to enter hell, but we can't let that happen. Now it's your show, Aurus, and I'm just the tech support. I'll connect to the ear piece you got from the superhero world and direct as you go. That's amazing tech, by the way. I should look into getting more of them."

Aurus put in his ear piece and flew off toward the flower ship. While he remained invisible, Marvin did not, after the invisibility watch moved away. Under Marvin's guidance he chose a section of the hull and began cutting a four-foot diameter hole with his eye-beams, but not cutting all the way through. When that was done he called Marvin.

"Ready now. Are the girls still in the same place?"

"Yes, but I received new information from Zen. The V'Laubi have energy weapons that the body shields won't stop. Not deadly, he thinks, but Nea's arm is still numb from a graze. If it's a paralo-ray then it might shut your heart down when fully effective. They are hand-held gold tubes that fire green lights."

"Thanks. I'll be on the lookout. Going in now."

Aurus flew to the hull at high speed, kicking the cut area as he hit. The section flew inward with a great noise from impact and more from hitting the floor. There was almost no distinguishing the two sounds as they became one impressively loud noise.

Alarms sounded as strobing laser lights filled the hallway and revealed Aurus's position by outlining him. He turned off the useless invisibility and flew down the hallway, pausing to open an elevator and enter it. A push of a button sent it silently sliding down to the ship's lowest level.

"That was surprising. I expected they'd have shut it down."

The doors slid open at the lowest level, where Aurus entered a short hallway that ended in sliding double doors.

"Is this it, Marvin?" asked Aurus.

"My sensor bullets say so," said Marvin, through Aurus's earpiece.

"Then I'm going in."

Aurus manifested his golden halberd from nowhere and slashed at the doors where they divided in the middle. Letting the weapon vanish, he put his fingers in the new slit between the doors and strained mightily. Veins popped out on his neck and forehead while nothing else happened for a moment.

With the sound of screaming metal the doors slid open with a whoosh. Aurus ran into the room, shouting.

"Girls, it's time to leave. The V'Laubi are trying to kidnap your bodies. It's not the paradise they pretend and I have proof."

There were six doors, three on each side of the golden room. As one the doors each slid open a crack and twelve pairs of eyes peered at him, but none entered the room. Aurus set a tapered silver cylinder point-up on the floor.

"Watch this please. Your lives are at stake."

A holographic recording of Zen with the Receptacle played, followed by weeping and crying from the girls.

"It can't be true," said one, "this has to be some sort of trick."

"I know her," said another, "that's Sandy. She's the reason I came here. Didn't you listen to her voice? I know pain, and that's pain. Why would anyone try to trick us? Take us out of here, mister, please."

"That's what I'm here for," said Aurus. "All of you follow me." He grabbed the projector, and shoved it into his backpack as he waved the girls out of the room. They all ran down the hallway behind him as the elevator doors slid open, disgorging two Receptacles carrying golden tubes. Before they could fire, Aurus lit his chest like a blinding sun.

Receptacles and human girls cried out, and before the V'Laubi could react, Aurus pulled out his halberd and beheaded them both with one wide stroke. Then he stabbed the possessors themselves. He called out.

"Sorry about that, ladies. No time to warn you. Link arms to follow me if you can't see."

He led them a short way to the elevator, and they waited while he pried the doors open with the halberd. All twelve girls squeezed in and Aurus entered last.

"I was concerned about this. They cut power to the elevator. I can get us out though."

He pulled the doors shut and flew to the ceiling. The elevator was dark, so he radiated a gentle light. With his back to the ceiling he slowly lifted the elevator while those girls that could see started murmuring.

"Oi, my God. He's lifting the elevator."

"Can't be. This is some sort of trick."

"No. Look at the lights. There aren't any. He's really lifting it. I can feel it move."

"Are we in a movie?"

"It's real, ladies," said Aurus, "and dangerous. I'm taking us to the very top because they're bound to be waiting at the main entrance, since it's the only entrance. Or exit, for that matter."

The room stopped moving.

"We're here," said Aurus. "I can get you all out. Do you trust me?"

"Trust you?" asked one. "We just met you. Not like we have a choice."

He jammed the halberd through the wall, holding the elevator in place. He dropped lower, and burned a two-inch hole between the doors with his eye-beams.

"It's going to get weird now, ladies. Stay with me."

"Get weird?" said one. "You've got laser eyes, glow, and can fly.

How much weirder can it get?"

Aurus transformed into a golden hawk and went through the hole.

"Sorry I asked," said the girl as she dropped to her knees.

He quickly examined the hallway and it was empty. He changed back to human form and pulled the doors open.

"Last stop before freedom. Everybody out."

The girls stumbled into the hallway, then Aurus reached into the elevator and touched his halberd. It disappeared and the elevator dropped almost faster than Aurus could pull his arm back.

"All of you watch both ends of this hallway while I work on getting us out."

He began cutting a large hole in the wall with his eye-beams. In a minute or two he'd burned through, then gave the loose section a kick. The burned bulkhead sailed into the night.

Aurus pulled rope ladders from his backpack, then wrapped one around his waist and the other around his legs.

"Here's how we're doing this: I'll carry one girl in my arms and one on my back. Two can hang from the ladder-ends around my waist and two from my legs. We can make this in two trips that way."

The girls, numb by now, nodded dumbly. Aurus flew out the first terrified load to a short distance from the flower ship and dropped them off.

"Run now, fast as you can toward that copse of trees. I'll bring the others straight away."

He flew back and found the girls fighting with three unarmed Receptacles. He crushed the enemy in short order.

"Everybody okay?"

A round of affirmatives later, Aurus had everybody up and out. He caught up with the running girls and set the others down.

"Keep running, all of you. This isn't done yet. Marvin, we're all clear, so it's your show again."

"Roger that. Fire in the hole."

From the copse of trees the girls were running to came missile fire aimed at the ship. They struck through Aurus's first hole, exploding on contact. Aurus met up with Marvin in the treetops as the last missile was fired from a launcher made of tubes. Aurus hovered nearby and looked back toward the ship.

Flame exploded from its every hole as sharp reverberations rocked the air.

"Any minute now until the engine blows," said Marvin.

Indeed, scarce seconds, later the entire ship exploded, showering the countryside with debris.

"Wow. That was impressive," said Aurus. "If we hadn't needed to rescue the girls you could have done this yourself. From now on I'll call you Marvin the Mighty."

Chapter Eight
It Begins in Earnest

Indra, deep in thought, bent over that body in the hovering tube from earlier. The tube was now open, the top half having split open and peeled back.

"Indra," called out Raelani, "Valeron is in flames and we must flee for our lives."

He didn't react. With a quiet sigh, she flew over him, and then sank lower, upside down, her long, silver-blond hair dangling. She waved a paper file folder before Indra's eyes. He looked up at her.

"You could have just said something," said Indra.

"Tried that. You're too absorbed in your work."

"Sorry. What do you need?

"Not about what I need. The Omnimind sent new info on our current problem."

She handed him the folder.

#

Nea, Aurus, Zen, and Marvin sat in a half-circle at the round table, listening to Master Julian.

"Nice work on that last, but it's only the tip of a larger operation. We need to focus on one still working in hopes of cracking the entirety of it."

"What the hell is that supposed to mean?" asked Zen.

"Sorry," said Julian. "Hoping that getting into one will get us into their entire setup. I have a literal plan of attack for V'Laubi incursions across the AllWorlds, but before we get to that I need Zen's report on the cleanup at his end."

Zen cleared his throat and stood.

"My Earth has marked the destruction of the V'Laubi ships as an effect of our polluted air finally eating into them. No mention of the real circumstances to the general public, which I think is for the best. Even though I sent footage of my encounter to the US government I feel there's no point in adding to the tragedy by letting parents and loved ones know the Receptacles were essentially zombies in continuous pain. As-is, this will give more fuel to environmental agencies in a push to clean up the environment. Even though it's not nearly as bad in the first place as some would like us to believe, cleaner air and water is never a bad thing.

"As for government collusion with helping the V'Laubi in return for alien tech, that came to nothing with the destruction of the flower ships. No government gained anything apart from promises, and the destruction was so thorough that nothing salvageable was left, except for this."

He held up the golden tube-weapon.

"I feel no need to turn this over to the American government, but it doesn't work anyway. I'm guessing it used broadcast power from the ship, so it's dead now."

"I fiddled with it when we got back," said Nea. "If you hold it like a gun there's a very slight bump that depresses like a trigger, but I couldn't make it work either."

"I'll take that," said Master Julian. "Maybe Morninglight can figure out how it works. Since it would be obvious to anybody watching your recorded footage that you caused the disaster, are you concerned that transmissions from V'Laubi cameras to your superiors in the US government will lead to your capture by those you work for in your day job?"

"Not at all. It's unlikely they would ever know it's me."

"Master of disguise, are you?" asked Nea.

"Again, not at all. I am hard to describe, and extremely average. They call me . . . nobody. I have no flashy codename."

Turning away from Nea, he asked her, "What color are my

eyes?"

She hesitated.

"Green," she finally said, as he turned toward her. "Oh. Well, brown, I guess, with green highlights."

"And this is why I'm not worried about being identified. Even if you've met me before, you'd only have the nagging feeling that you'd seen me somewhere."

"You have black hair and tanned skin," said Nea.

"Do I?" said Zen as he held up an arm of average Caucasian color, then rubbed it through his brownish hair.

"You did, I thought. But you aren't a master of disguise?"

"I am a Master of No-guise. It may be a psychic ability, but I can blend into a crowd of one. I have to use makeup to stand out, like the tan makeup from before. My possible picture on V'Laubi camera means nothing to anybody. Even facial recognition software won't peg me. I must admit that you noticed more than most people though."

Nea nodded, pleased with herself.

"The funny part of all that," said Zen, is that I ended up doing what I do as a means of gaining recognition. Thought I might be hailed as a hero, maybe get a medal and a statue someday. Instead, I'm less recognized than ever before."

"Well, I recognize your worth," said Nea. "We all do, even if maybe we wouldn't be able to pick you out of a crowd."

Everybody nodded, while Zen gave a curt shake of his head.

"I'm concerned about that weapon," Nea said. "It penetrated my energy shield, but was apparently only a paralytic, not physically damaging. Why it destroyed the engine tubes is a mystery if it only harms the nervous system."

Julian held up the tube and waggled it about.

"Morninglight will soon have the answer for us, I have no doubt. As for the main problem though, I'm assembling strike teams and infiltration units. Since you four did such a good job I'll keep you together for the time being. You'll act as both strike and infiltration."

"Are you coming with us?" asked Aurus.

"You don't need my help. I only hang with the weaker teams. By which I don't necessarily mean they aren't powerful in their own rights, only that they lack key elements for being independent teams.

Altogether, you four have mobility, strength, stealth, long-range attacks, the ability to plan, and adaptability should a plan fail."

"Aw, stop. You'll make us blush," said Marvin.

"Grab your ordnance suggested by the Omnimind and be on your way to the next world," said Julian. "Meeting adjourned."

#

Nea walked the dirty, neon-glazed streets. She dressed in business attire, but the kind of business that dealt with feather boas, spike heels, short skirts and fishnet stockings. Her ear bud beeped and Aurus spoke.

"Having any luck?"

"Depends on how you define 'luck' I suppose. Had an encounter with a sex worker who said I'd better show up at the Verdigris Bar if I want to keep working these streets. Had seven clients so far who must have spread my reputation. I'd given them a quick 'Forget' spell and a minor memory rewrite so they think they had the time of their lives. So good that I figured it was only fair to relieve them of an appropriate cash amount. Can you believe one actually asked if I took credit cards?"

"In this place? Yeah, I'm a believer. Been asking around, but haven't found out anything specific yet. The Verdigris has come up in conversation though."

"How long do you want me out here?"

Her earpiece beeped.

"You can both get back to base for now," Zen said. "Marvin and I found out a few things."

#

Aurus, next to a robed Nea, sat on a couch and listened.

"There are three procurers of note in this area," said Marvin. "One of them operates out of the Verdigris, so that sounds like our target, and Nea already has an invitation."

"That jibes with what I heard," said Aurus, "but she's not going in by herself. I'm going with her."

"You sure?" asked Zen. "They might try to eject you."

"They might try, but they'd regret it. I don't see any reason to hold back if they do."

"Well, we are trying to keep it a secret operation. Don't want to scare away any V'Laubi, since they'd just relocate," said Zen.

"Okay, fine, I get that," said Aurus. "I'll be good, but why are we looking in this particular area anyway?"

"Because the Oracles of Valeron told us to do so," said Marvin.

"They couldn't have narrowed the search down for us?" asked Nea.

"That's not how they work," said Aurus. "Like most oracles of myth and legend they provide vague hints and suggestions and it's up to us to work with them to the best of our abilities."

"Could be worse," said Marvin, "at least they don't give riddles. We don't have to look for 'the man with one understanding' or that sort of nonsense. My understanding is that they don't have much, if any, control over what they foresee."

"Control or not," said Zen, "their visions have helped the full-stars stay ahead of multidimensional crises for many average lifetimes. Now, of course, there is also the Omnimind. Regardless of who gave what information, let us be thankful we know where to start."

Nea and Aurus nodded.

"Now then," said Marvin, "Zen managed to find online banking information for a 'Catherine Zygmeir.' She operates a charity that finds homes for runaway girls, but has no disclosed source of income apart from charitable donations. All donations are in cash, so we're stonewalled there, but she makes a surprising amount of money. And that's only the funds we can access. I'm sure there are large sums of cash changing hands on a regular basis."

"We're also sure she's using casinos to launder money from prostitution," said Zen. "That's a whole different kettle of stinky fish."

"This V'Laubi operation, stinky as it is," said Aurus, "is a much more efficient one than that last. They're worming themselves into the criminal underworld and establishing an economic powerbase. It'll be harder to just shake them out with physical force."

Nea nodded.

"If they have the smarts you suspect, there will be humans in key positions who have no idea this is the spearhead of an extradimensional invasion. We need to bypass this lot and find out who and where the higher-ups are, but in a way that doesn't disrupt this operation. Don't need them on high alert."

Aurus smiled approvingly.

"Much as I want to pound heads, the lady has a point. Once we infiltrate their command structure the targets will be clear, then we can kick the snot out of the hollowbacks. One swift strike could free this world of their influence entirely, without alerting the entire V'Laubi race."

Marvin and Zen nodded in sync.

"All right then," said Marvin, "Nea takes a meeting and Aurus goes with her, but keeping himself hidden. Decide on what sort of equipment you might need, but I insist on you wearing the contact-lens cameras, Nea."

#

Two burly women in black, midriff corset tops flanked the canopied entrance to the Verdigris.

"Whaddaya want, sister?" one said to Nea.

"I was told to see your boss about permission to work the streets."

The two bouncers glanced at each other, then smiled.

"Sure," said one. "No harm in asking, right?"

"You look like the right type," said the other.

"We'll see," the first one said. "Follow me."

She turned on massive high heels and Nea followed her into the bar.

Aurus hovered in the night shadows with his flight power.

"Definitely not V'Laubi," said Zen's voice in Aurus's ears. "Not that you couldn't tell already, what with being able to see their lower backs. Still, for the record, the scan revealed pure strain humans. I'm getting video and audio feed from Nea's contacts, but she can't hear me."

They'd determined an ear bud had too great a chance of being discovered if Nea were searched, but it would be unlikely they'd find the contacts. Even if they did, contact lenses were common.

"We'll let you know if she's in any immediate danger," said Zen.

The bouncer led Nea to a room in the back and ushered her in. The room was well-appointed, with emerald curtains on three out of four walls, the one where she entered being oak paneled. No windows. Two muscular women in neck to toe black leather, combat boots, and a plethora of decorative silver spikes, rocked black buzz cuts. They flanked a mahogany desk behind which sat a smaller but still imposing woman wearing a dark business suit. She brushed back long, auburn hair and gave Nea a withering glare.

"Definite hollowback," said Zen to Aurus. "The boss I mean."

"How is it you think interrupting my business meeting is a good idea, Cindy?" said the boss in an icy voice, as she closed a laptop computer.

Cindy gulped.

"The girl said she was told to come here, Madame Zygmeir. She's a new street worker."

"I should see a common streetwalker?" the boss asked. "I have underlings for that."

"Said she was told to see the boss," said Cindy. "T-thought she looked like the right type. Figured I'd better bring her straight to you."

"Huh, and so you did. Cindy, you can go back to your post."

Cindy bowed and left with haste.

"Now you," said the boss, pointing to Nea, "you got potential. You're big enough, not some skinny tramp. I've already heard about you if I'm being honest, and I like to be that way every now and again. Your rep precedes you with a trail of glowing reviews, so we'll be talking at length."

"You two get out, and don't come back for a few minutes," said the boss. "I've got private business with the lady."

The two women left the room.

"What sort of private business?" asked Nea.

"The paying kind of business. I can use someone like you, and not just as a hooker. There are all kinds of opportunity in my organization, so we'll see how things shake down. Interested?"

"Might be. Always interested in betterin' myself. Can I leave if I don't like it?"

"Right now you can walk if you want. Once you get in deep it might be a different story, so walk now if you're worried," said Madame Zygmeir while leaning back in her chair, arms folded behind her head.

"I'm in."

#

The two bodyguards each took a smoke in the alley behind the Verdigris.

"The boss said to give her a few minutes and it's barely been one," said the first.

"Time enough to grab a drink at the bar, I'd say," said the second.

"Stole the words right outta my mouth. Careful where you put those fingers, yeah?"

They laughed, and at that instant, Aurus, now a black hawk, silently swooped over their heads, then through the open rear entrance before they moved back toward it.

"Jeez, was that a bat?" said the first one, stopping in her tracks.

"What if it was, you pussy? Not gonna get tangled in our hair," said the other.

She brushed a casual hand across her buzz cut and then the other's. They laughed while going through the door, which they then pulled shut until it locked.

"Not gonna blame us if vermin wanders in."

Aurus kept to the shadows in the corners of the room. There was plenty of decorative bric-a-brac to hide behind, so he did just that while working his way toward Nea.

#

"So, what's your name, girl," asked Madame Zygmeir.

"Dart," said Nea, appearing nervous as she glanced around the elevator.

"Just 'Dart?' asked the Madame.

"It's all I've ever needed. Do you need more?"

"Short and sweet suits me fine. Just wondered."

The elevator came to a smooth stop and the doors slid open.

"Here we are, Dart. This is where my real operation is handled."

She waved Nea out of the elevator into a typical-appearing office hallway. Touching Nea's shoulder, Madame Zygmeir guided her three doors down to what appeared as a spa.

"The girls here can work wonders. They'll scour that half-assed paint job off you, then apply some quality makeup. You've got good bone structure, so making you pretty is a cinch. The trick is to not make you look like a whore or drag queen."

"I've been doing okay on my own so far. I mean, nobody complained."

"And they wouldn't. Even ugly whores can turn a cheap trick, but we want high-end clientele. I'm going to make you a head turner even without the tacky clothes and overdone eye shadow."

"Never realized I was such a scuzzbag," said Nea as she threw down the feather boa.

"Don't get pissy. Just calling it like I see it."

#

Aurus silently slid through the shadows of various hallways as a hawk. He didn't have to use his wings to fly, so he pulled them in and stuck to traveling along seams between walls and floors, carrying his ear bud in his beak. He found the 'board room' where Nea had met Madame Zygmeir, and he became human-shaped to open it. Once inside, he checked for cameras and found none. He did find the elevator behind a wall drapery, but was unable to open it without causing obvious damage.

He put his ear bud in.

"I'm back online, guys."

"About time," said Zen. "Why were you offline in the first place?"

"Had to remove my ear bud or it would have given my hawk form a splitting headache."

"Why doesn't it transform with you?" asked Marvin.

"I can only change my own body. My clothes are part of me, even my hat, so they change. The ear bud is not me, so it doesn't."

"Your watch changes with you," said Zen.

"Made from me, so it tastes like me. Don't know just how the full stars pulled that off. Maybe I'll get Morninglight to make an ear bud from me, but don't know if I'll need it that much anyway. Now, can we get back to the mission at hand?"

"Already on it," said Marvin. "I peppered the place with sensor bullets in sensitive spots, so combined with Nea's transmitter contacts we've got a good picture of the place. The elevator has a fingerprint scanner to open it. Can you change your prints to match Zygmeir's?"

"Suppose I could if I knew exactly what they looked like and had a few free hours to concentrate. It isn't like magic, guys, there's a lot of effort involved."

"Huh, okay then. Never mind that," said Zen. "I infiltrated their electronics through Marvin's bullets, and might be able to do a little fiddling with their security."

Zen hummed while he fiddled.

"Shit. Elevator's on its way up. Maybe you can get in when the doors open," said Zen.

"Easy, but let me prep."

He moved the draperies back in place, then turned into a hawk once again, holding the ear bud in his beak. He hovered tight against the wall above the elevator door as it slid open below him. Madame Zygmeir strode out, and Aurus shot into the elevator. She stopped for a moment, looked around, shook her head, and moved out into the office.

Aurus waited a few minutes, or at least he thought it had been a few minutes. Hard for him to tell since his watch was part of his feathers at the moment. Returning to human form, he replaced the ear bud.

"I'm in the elevator. Can anybody use it from the inside, not just the boss?"

"Probably," said Zen, "but it might set off alarms. Better to fly up through the elevator hatch to the very top of the shaft. Since this is a human-style elevator there'll be a big access panel for repairmen to work on the elevator mechanism. Go through that and you should have freedom of movement."

Aurus flew up and out of the elevator, closing its hatch. As Zen had said, there was an access panel at the top of the shaft that he exited through. He examined the area briefly, finding it to be a dirty, concrete blockhouse of a room with one door, no windows, and two air vents.

"I'm here. Now what?"

"Hate to say it," said Zen, "but you can use the ventilation system to get around the entire complex."

Aurus groaned.

"Just like in the movies? How lame. I didn't think it was actually possible for a person to move around in them."

"It usually isn't," said Zen, "and wouldn't be in these, but it's a breeze for something hawk-sized. You will have to tear through the occasional air filter, but that's easy enough. I won't be able to direct you while you're in bird form, so let's get your directions straight first."

#

Twenty-three minutes later Aurus was flying through the air ducts and nearing Nea's location. He peered out the last vent and saw Nea naked, facedown on a table, getting a hot stone treatment. Perplexed, he wondered if he should keep watching to make sure there was no funny business or wait until she was done and dressed. His better nature won out and he turned his hawk eyes away from the vent. He still had to peek every so often to make sure she was done, of course. Finally, Nea was clad in an emerald robe and sitting in a chair, while a woman worked on her face from a tableful of makeup.

Aurus stared while Nea admired her new face in a mirror. Finally, the spa woman left.

He pushed at the vent covering, popping it out with his mighty beak. He caught the piece before it could hit the floor.

Nea glanced up in total lack of surprise and nodded.

"About time you showed up, but then, I'm glad you waited until she was finished. What do you think?" said Nea as she stood up and pirouetted.

The robe fell down slightly, exposing her shoulders.

"I'm not going to lie. You look absolutely stunning. Here I was afraid you were undergoing torture of some sort."

"I was, in a way. Don't get used to the look because it probably won't last. You'd better get out of here right now before Madame Zygmeir gets back to see her new toy, me."

"You don't want to get out?"

"I do, but I'm in a unique spot to learn more now. She likes women on the tall and strong side, so I made it right into her elite squadron of seductresses. I think she plans on using me to snare high rollers and big spenders. I can only assume her ultimate goal is world domination, but I don't know how she'll get there."

"What –"

"Never mind. I hear high heels in the hall, so get out."

Aurus gave the vent cover to Nea, then flew back up to the air vent as a hawk and entered it. Nea reached up and snapped the cover into place.

Madame Zygmeir stormed into the room, flinging the door wide.

"They did a nice job, sweetie. Drop the robe and turn around a few times."

Nea let the robe fall, then turned in place, slowly.

"Very nice, but ease up on your exercise routine, Dart. Trim is good, but hardbody doesn't sell for the clients I have in mind."

"Yes, Madame. Now what happens?"

Madame Zygmeir continued to watch Nea, approvingly.

"Now we get a couple of good meals in you and start your training tomorrow."

"Training, Madame?"

"We're going to teach you how to seduce men. You might think you know, but you don't."

#

A troop of mauve lizard-women in yellow metal armor opened

fire on an earthen barricade. Their bullets sank harmlessly into the dirt while pale-skinned humans took cover behind it. The humans clashed their rifles upon green kite shields and hooted.

"Hoo-ora, hoo-ora," they shouted, over and over, daring the lizards to attack in person.

Behind the lizard lines, one of the mauve soldiers spoke into a black mirror.

"O Grand Elder, the humans are held, but we cannot advance through their projectile fire. We also know from experience that our forces are no match for theirs in close quarters."

A green elfin face appeared in the mirror and answered.

"V'Laubi forces outnumber theirs, so just engulf them and fight to the death. Anything, so long as we win this, Javis. Achieving dominance here is imperative."

"Begging your pardon, Magnificence, but we no longer outnumber them as their counteroffensive wiped out over half our forces."

"Just do it. I don't care how. My position as Grand Elder depends on it."

"Of course, Magnificence, but if you lose many more troops here your standing will suffer regardless."

"Maintain your position and I will be there shortly. In the name of the Divine."

"In the name of the Divine," said Javis.

"Hold fast," she shouted to her troops. "The Grand Elder herself is coming."

Indeed, within a few minutes a small, golden flower-ship descended, landing behind the lizard lines. A golden-armored woman leapt from the ship and stormed the barricade. Gunfire pinged off her armor as she tore earthen piles and humans apart, flinging heads and limbs with maniacal glee. She ground her heel into the eyes of the last living defender, crushing his skull.

"The useless males are dead, V'Laubi," she screamed. "Surely you can handle it now."

"Of course, Grand Elder," yelled Javis. "You have given us victory."

"As I do. Now deal with the mess."

Chapter Nine
Learning Curve

For the next several days Nea learned her lessons. In the meanwhile, Aurus had the run of the complex in hawk form, breaking into all their secret places. Zen and Marvin processed as much information as possible, but lacked further video feed since Nea's transmitter-contacts had died.

In Nea's room, Aurus finished her huge lunch.

"Thanks," she said, "they always give me way too much."

"You're welcome. Anyway, have you found out anything significant that's mission-related?"

"Maybe. I've learned seduction isn't always about being overtly sexual, but instead becoming the woman a man or woman wants them to be."

"That's mission-related?" asked Aurus.

"In a way. I know that many of the girls Madame Zygmeir took off the streets were trained that way. Some have been sent around the world as part of a very high-end courtesan slash spy service. I suspect others were sent to different realities. If any have been possessed by V'Laubi I don't know. Didn't see any others besides the Madame while my contact lenses were still working."

"Zen and Marvin have all the info we're likely to get from their records. Now it's a matter of deciding how to proceed. Do we shut this place down or leave it and travel to another V'Laubi base?"

'I say leave it," said Nea. "It's relatively harmless, apart maybe from providing bodies for the hollowbacks to puppet. Beyond that, the Madame has taken broken girls from the streets and given them a new sense of purpose. Yes, they're sex workers, but is there really anything wrong with that? They have a lot more control over their life-courses now, and any children they have are raised and educated. Criminal organization or not, they've done some good. Not sure what happens offworld. Besides, a hard takedown here could send ripples throughout their network before we're ready to take them all out."

"Agreed. I don't have the rosy look on this operation that you do, but we'll leave it alone for now. When we've found where to go next, and you can leave without arousing suspicion, we'll move on, saving this place for last."

He reached up and pulled off the vent cover, handed it to Nea, then became a hawk. Ear bud in beak he flew into the opening and then Nea snapped the cover back in place. She had scarcely turned around when Madame Zygmeir entered the room.

"Well, Dart, here's where things get interesting. Turns out we have an intruder."

Nea's face went blank. Then the Madame smiled.

"Not to worry, it's only a rat, we think. During regular maintenance they found all the air filters had small holes in their bottom edges. We're going to seal the system then gas the sucker."

She pushed a button on the vent cover until it clicked.

"There," she said into her phone, "last vent is closed. Let the gas rip."

Nea stood under the vent and yelled, "Hear that, mister rat? You're gonna get gassed now."

Affecting an unsteady hand, Nea stood back from the vent.

"I thought I heard skittering noises from the vent last night. Wasn't sure if I should say anything. I hate rats."

They heard a rushing of air behind the vent, then the cover practically exploded from the vent, followed by a black hawk and dark blue gas. Nea dove to her right of the vent while Madame Zygmeir dodged to the left.

Trailing gas, the hawk fell to the floor, writhing. The Madame yelled into her phone.

"Cut the gas, reverse it. We have a breech in 3B and it's a bird."

With one great spasm, the hawk became Aurus, gagging on the floor. Nea screamed and grabbed a ceramic vase from a table. She hit him in the back with the vase, shattering it while seeming to have hit his head. At the same time, the Madame zapped him with a green ray from a gold tube. He stopped moving.

"I got him," yelled Nea. "What the hell is going on here?"

"Nice job, Dart, but it was this that did most of the work," she said, holding up the tube. "As for what's going on here, don't know what yet, but it's more than rats, much more. Oh, and the cost of that vase will come out of your pay."

#

After the Madame left and her bulked-up women had carried off a barely breathing Aurus behind her, Nea examined the spot where he had fallen.

"Not here. Has to be near."

She put her hand up to the open vent and conjured with shadow. To an onlooker, her hand would have appeared to separate from her wrist as it explored the inside of the vent. After a few moments of exploring the vent, she smiled, and pulled Aurus's ear bud from it. Using a damp towel from the bathroom, she wiped any residue of the gas from the ear bud. She placed the bud in her ear.

"Marvin, Zen, this is Nea. Aurus is down."

"Zen here. How did you get his ear bud?"

"Long story. The Madame took him down with one of those gold tubes, plus poison gas."

"He was the strongest of us," said Marvin. "If they could take him down—"

"You're Marvin the Mighty. You could make this place a hole in the ground," said Nea.

"Yeah, but it won't help rescue him. Um, he is alive?"

"I think so, and I can rescue him if you help."

"How?" said Zen and Marvin as one.

"You know the layout of this place by now. Tell me where they're holding him."

While waiting for an answer, Nea went through the outfits

Madame Zygmeir had provided recently. She dressed in a red body stocking and tied a black scarf around her face.

"Anything yet, gentlemen?" she asked.

"I think so," said Zen. "He's probably being held on the next lower level in a secure room. Don't know what else they'd be used for. Also don't know which one it is."

"I know," said Marvin, "it's 4C."

"How can you be sure?" asked Nea.

"I get these hunches sometimes. I'm right, trust me."

"I'm off then. I'll keep the ear bud in so you know when I get there."

"But how can you get there?" asked Marvin.

"I have my ways. Trust me."

Nea tore a blanket from her bed, then draped it over herself and the ventilation hole. Conjuring with shadow, she disappeared into the air duct, then in a near-instant found herself at another vent in another room, still in the duct. She knocked the cover out with her fist, then squeezed her body through, if only just.

And she wanted me to put on weight.

As the cover hit the floor, the Madame's two buff women, who had been standing by a metal table, pulled golden tubes from their belts and fired in Nea's general direction. They missed by proverbial miles, giving Nea time to tuck and roll between them.

She hit one behind the knees and the woman dropped. Then Nea grabbed her by the wrist and took the gold tube. Nea used the downed woman for cover, keeping her controlled with a wrestling hold. The other hesitated, as she couldn't get a clear shot. Nea could, and the armed one went down with a small hole in her chest. Nea disengaged, keeping the tube trained on the remaining foe.

The woman crawled to her downed companion, tears in her eyes, cradling the still figure in her arms, ignoring Nea completely.

"B-Beth, no. Please, no. You can't be dead. This was supposed to be a fun gig. What am I going to do without you?"

Her tears fell on Beth's face.

"I'm sorry," said Nea, "I thought these weapons only paralyzed."

The door opened and she darted behind the metal table where Aurus lay, held down in gold shackles.

"That's usually true," said Madame Zygmeir, peeking in from the hallway, holding out her own gold tube, "if the target is a woman . . . you must have squeezed the trigger too hard."

"Look," said Nea, "I'm just here for my friend. Let us go and I won't give you any more trouble."

"We'll talk in a minute. Bonnie, get Beth to the infirmary. I think she has a chance. You okay with that, Dart?"

"Fine with me. Got nothing against any of you personally."

The gold tube and the Madame's eye still held the doorway as Bonnie carried out her companion.

"I think this needs to end just like the first mission, minus the explosions," whispered Nea.

"Okay then," said the Madame, "it's just the two of us, Dart. How does this end?"

"Don't you mean 'the three of us?'" said Nea. "I know what you are. I don't think this can end amicably."

"Huh. Some kind of interdimensional cop then? Knew you were special."

"Okay then," said Nea, "how about you let us and all the girls go, shut down your operation, and get the hell off this world?"

Madame Zygmeir laughed loudly.

"After all this work? We could salvage some of it, especially the money, but then we'd have to start over somewhere else. I'd probably be eliminated for gross incompetence, so it's not in my best interest. Why don't I just seal this room and pump in the Zyklon B?"

"I'd get out the same way I got in. You want to control the situation and come out on top, right?"

"Of course, and I will. My reinforcements will be here in moments, so you can't win. We might as well chat until then, so maybe start with who you are?"

"So you've been stalling? Smart. They call me Daernea the Undark, and I actually was called Dart at one time."

"You got in through the ventilation? You a shapeshifter too?"

"No, I've got other powers."

"Powers? We specifically chose this world because it didn't have superheroes, or wizards, or super-wizards."

"Well, as you guessed, I'm not from around here, and just for the record, I've been stalling too. Fire time, guys."

The fire alarm kicked on and the power went out. The emergency lights blinked, and Nea dove across the room in shadow. She grappled with the Madame and drove her chin to the floor, but got thrown off before she could get a good hold. The Madame pointed her tube at Nea and squeezed it, but nothing happened. Nea punched her in the throat and drove her to the floor.

"So sorry, but we knew your power shuts down for safety reasons when the fire alarm goes off. No power, no zapping."

Nea twisted the Madame's arms and legs behind her and tied them with her scarf.

"I've still got people coming," croaked Madame Zygmeir. "You won't be able to get your friend free without the key, and Bonnie has that."

Nea turned back toward Aurus and held up a small gold cylinder, sparkling under the blinking lights.

"Took this from Bonnie's belt while I grappled her. I can free him just fine."

She inserted the gold key and popped the manacles one-by-one, hands and feet.

"I'll be taking him and you, my dear Madame Zygmeir."

Nea turned to see the Madame's V'Laubi scuttling up the wall to the vent, then slithering through.

"Damn, got too cocky. Guys, do you know where she's going?"

"Only in general," said Zen. "Can you sweep her into your shadow?"

"Not how it works. I can get ahead of her, but I'd have to guess her destination. Any hunches, Marvin?"

"I can tell you where she's going," rasped Madame Zygmeir.

"You want revenge," said Nea.

"No, but I want her because I'll die without her. Put her back in and we'll talk."

"Tell me where."

"The portal room, lowest level."

"That's what I was going to say," said Marvin. "I'll direct you."

"Better get after her," said the Madame. "She'll try to leave."

"I can't leave my partner."

"Go," said Aurus, barely audible. "I'll be fine in a few minutes now that those shockers are off me. Without those tubes there isn't much they can do to me."

"You're okay, thank all the gods," she said.

"I will be anyway. Go get it."

He struggled to a sitting position as Nea merged with the shadow and entered the vent.

#

Some time later, Nea dumped the squirming creature out of a blanket to the floor next to the Madame. The fire alarm had stopped and the power was back on.

"You'd better call off the alert or a lot of your people will die if they come through this door," said Nea.

She put a phone to the Madame's mouth.

"This is Madame Zygmeir. The alert is canceled, situation normal. Return to your stations, code Albino."

"Why'd you say that?" asked Aurus, stretching and bending to get his circulation going.

"If I hadn't said it, we'd still have had armed visitors. We're good now."

"She's telling the truth," said Zen. "We can see people turning back from your level."

"The voice in my head says you aren't lying," said Nea. "Now we get out of here and talk."

"My back first. I won't be doing much moving without it."

"But then we can't trust you," said Aurus.

"There's a little filament, like a fiber optic coming from its part of my spine. That's the part that gives it full control over me. If you could burn that off I'm still me."

"That tracks," said Zen to Nea, and she relayed the message to Aurus.

He grabbed the filament, ignoring the minor electric shock, and melted it to a glob with his eye beams.

The creature, almost with a sigh, crawled into the Madame's back. With a shudder, the V'Laubi sealed itself in. Nea untied her, and

Madame Zygmeir stood, hale, hearty, and full of life.

"We can go to my personal quarters," said the Madame. "Dart won't draw any attention, but the man will. There are no other men here."

"Not a problem," said Aurus, transforming into a hawk.

They walked into the hallway, Nea keeping the gold tubes and Aurus wrapped up in her scarf.

Madame Zygmeir's quarters proved quite comfortable, with overstuffed sofas and recliners, plus a vast selection of alcoholic beverages which both Aurus and Nea declined. The Madame helped herself to a long drink of Scotch.

"One of you two might as well start this conversation. How about Dart, or Daernea, first?"

"Where to start?" said Nea. "It's our job to stop the hollowbacks from eating their way into any more humans. Anything you can do to help us with that would be appreciated."

"Hollowbacks, heh. Gotta say I like that one. Why would I help you, and how much appreciated?"

"That depends on the info," said Aurus.

"The women are talking, boy. Don't interrupt," said the Madame.

Aurus's eyes glowed red.

"I don't know who the hell you think you are, but I outrank Nea," said Aurus. "I'll jump in if I feel like it."

"I'm *so* sorry. With the V'Laubi only women are of any import."

"That may be," said Nea, "but I will defer to him. This is a three-way convo."

"Fine then. What do you want to know?"

"Let's start with why you're so comfortable having your body hijacked by an alien parasite."

"It was hard at first, but I got used to it," said the Madame before she finished her Scotch. "We are very similar in nature: I want to grow my business and put women in positions of power. She wants to harvest woman hosts for the benefit of her race. Our interests overlap rather nicely."

"Your parasite is female?" asked Nea.

The Madame patted herself on the lower back gently.

"Of course. All the V'Laubi are. They can only inhabit female hosts, so males are irrelevant."

Aurus put his hat on the sofa and leaned forward toward the Madame in her recliner.

"No males means no offspring, as a rule. How do they reproduce?" asked Aurus.

"Budding. No idea how, as she hasn't done it yet," said the Madame, hooking a thumb over her shoulder to point at her back.

"Fascinating," said Nea. "We mainly need to know their goals and operations. Can the various races of the AllWorlds coexist with the V'Laubi?"

"AllWorlds?"

"What our people call the multiverse."

"And who are your people?"

"No reason you shouldn't know," said Aurus. "We are Knights of Valeron and work for the ValDurian family."

Madame Zygmeir shrugged.

"Never heard of you or them," she said, as she poured herself another Scotch.

"It's a big multiverse," said Nea. "Our main goal is to keep peace between the dimensions. No invading other realities allowed."

"Then you have a problem. The V'Laubi need women, preferably humanoid."

"That's the problem with not having men," said Aurus, "it's hard to replace your hosts if they can't give birth."

The Madame made a show of swirling her Scotch in the glass, then downing it with one swallow.

"Oh, their hosts can give birth through artificially induced parthenogenesis."

After blank stares from Aurus and Nea, she continued.

"I don't understand it myself, but it essentially makes a woman give birth to a clone of herself. The problem, as my passenger puts it, is they don't always end up as exact clones. More and more suffer from diploid variation as infinitesimal bits of genetic material are lost. The current state of affairs is that less than twenty percent of the VLaubi have viable hosts from their world."

"So they decided to get hosts from elsewhere," said Nea.

Madame Zygmeir poured herself another Scotch.

"Yes, and while they were at it, decided to conquer nearby dimensions to ensure a plentiful supply of two-legged vehicles."

"The kidnapping and conquering are what we have problems with," said Aurus. "Even previously-willing hosts end up in constant pain in a life of living hell, as we understand it."

"Well, I don't know about that. We've been fairly compatible from jump. I didn't mind at all, since it expanded my business and let me attend to the local lost girls."

"And now you'll help us expand our business in taking the V'Laubi down?" asked Nea.

"Why should I do that?"

"It's either that or this place becomes a smoldering crater," said Aurus. "Not only that, since we can't allow the invader to run unchecked, it'll have to be removed from your back."

"Didn't say I wouldn't help, but my rider probably won't cooperate."

"About that," said Nea, "what's to stop her from scuttling off while you're asleep?"

"Now that I can control," said the Madame.

She got out of her chair and rummaged around in a filing cabinet, finally pulling out a rectangle of black cloth.

"Dart, if you could cinch me into this, it takes care of one problem at least."

She unfurled the cloth, revealing it as a corset. Then she removed her jacket and blouse. Nea went behind her, put the corset in place, and pulled the laces tight, hiding the V'Laubi.

"There," said the Madame, "that keeps her out of trouble for the time being."

"Can't she eat her way through your abdomen?" asked Nea. "I know they eat their way into the back."

"That last is true, but they can only do it once. The young are all globby and such. They don't come back-shaped at birth, that's just how they end up."

"So you're in no danger from within?"

"Not so far as I know. Now I'll see if I can help. Luckily for all concerned, the Arbiter was here just last week."

"The Arbiter?" asked Nea.

"An observer for the V'Laubi that checks on their outworld operations and reports directly to their Grand Elder. She shows up once a month, so we'll have time to make sure this setup stays looking legit. So long as I keep sending money and supplies we should be fine."

#

"Greetings, O Grand Elder," said a dark-suited woman with close-cropped red hair and black gloves.

"And to you, Arbiter," said a green-skinned, hooded woman in golden robes. "Show me the standings."

"That is why I'm here, Grand Elder."

The Arbiter grabbed a folded tripod and easel pad that had been leaning against the wall, fumbling with them until they were standing properly.

"This would be so much easier if technology or magic worked here," said the Arbiter.

She then pulled an extendable pointer from her jacket, snapping it out to its full length and hitting the pad.

"On the left, in blue, that bar represents the Morvalan faction, the purple is the Jagonnal, and the gold is you Voaminids."

"Yes," said the Grand Elder. "My faction's bar is twice the height of the Morvalan, but the Jagonnal are closer to us than last evaluation, nearly three-fourths our height."

"Two-thirds, Grand Elder, but—"

"Even you don't get to correct me, Arbiter," said the Grand Elder, venom in her voice.

"My apologies. They've gained because of the recent disaster where you lost two dimensional ships and their contingents."

"I lost nothing. It was the fault of incompetent underlings that I myself would have killed were they not already dead. What of the other two factions?"

The Arbiter struck the red bar.

"The A'Rittan gained at the expense of the Morvalan," she said, then smacked the green, shortest, and final bar. "The L'Orenn have done little, so they gained nothing and lost little. I see nothing to challenge your supremacy, Grand Elder."

"As it should be. Our domination of all is assured. Praise the Divine."

"Praise the Divine."

Chapter Ten
Down to Business

"This is the last of it," said Aurus, as he set down two wooden crates he'd had on his shoulders. "How soon before we're operational?"

Zen glanced up from an electronic console.

"I have to connect everything. That's the slow part because none of you can help there. I appreciate you and Nea getting our bunker dug out though. That saved a ton of time. Marvin's nearly done setting up his firepower, so maybe five hours?"

"Good enough. I'll start setting up the smokeless stove so nobody dies of hunger waiting for the mission to get underway."

"Eat some ration bars if you're hungry," said Zen.

"I burn a ton of calories, so I'm always hungry, but I want actual food if I can get it."

Aurus opened the crates and set up a gas camp stove, then connected it to a vent pipe that went through the ceiling of their little cave.

Nea finished stringing up fine wire all about the cave, making it glisten like the lair of metallic spiders.

"The disrupter wire is hung," said Nea. "We should be able to use electronics without fear of discovery now. Once we have any electronics to worry about, that is."

"Funny," said Zen. "We will, soon enough."

"Gun emplacements are ready," said Marvin. "Cannons are camouflaged and waterproof. Missile tubes are covered and ready."

"What do we know?" asked Nea.

Marvin unfolded a wooden camp chair.

"Since Zen is busy, I'll take this: With Madame Zygmeir's help, we were able to access most of their computer files. Something we couldn't do with the flower ships."

"Why not?" asked Aurus.

"Time, mainly. The V'Laubi were making Zen's world extremely nervous and his people wanted them gone fast. We've had plenty of time to dig in to Madame Zygmeir's complex and figure out where to go next. That would be to here."

"Then from here to their homeworld?" asked Aurus.

"Or the next strongest base, yes. Master Julian made the decision given what we now know."

"I know that, but why?"

"I can answer that, because I was paying attention at the meeting," said Nea. "We don't know how strong their homeworld is. Hitting this base will let us test ourselves against their full tech in an entrenched base, while simultaneously cutting off a source of supply to the homeworld."

"Not only that, what we learn here gets passed on to other teams," said Marvin. "Those can strike multiple outposts simultaneously while we hit the home base. Julian thinks we have a good chance of taking out their high command, government, or whatever."

"Seems kind of a stretch. None of the teams have more than eight people, and I don't think that's enough to take on a world, even a bubble world like this one. Wouldn't it make more sense to send in the Huntsmen of Valeron en masse?" asked Aurus.

"The Huntsmen are only for mass attacks," said Marvin. "What we and the other Knights are doing would be surgical strikes and rescue missions. Once those are done then the Huntsmen can obliterate whatever is left, if need be."

"Sounds like your job, Marvin," said Aurus.

"Hey, I'm as surgical as the next guy, while the Huntsmen are loaded with nothing but devastating power. I can pick and choose my level of devastation."

"Aren't they called 'Untari' now?" asked Nea.

Marvin and Aurus shrugged.

"A distinction with no difference," said Aurus. "We Knights of Valeron used to be Knights of the AllWorlds. Still the same people with the same goals."

"Yes," said Nea, "and my goal is to get some rest before the dawn. Come first light the mission is on."

#

Aurus greeted the emerald dawn with a smile as the verdant sun peeked over the horizon. The pale vegetation took on a green cast that would have been at home on most any world. Unfortunately, everything else also took on a green cast.

"This world's a kick," said Aurus, "but the unrelenting green could become tiresome after a bit. Gods forbid I wear anything red. Preliminary surveillance showed us what the natives look like, so do you think I nailed it, Nea?"

He wore rough, homespun trousers, a peasant shirt, sandals, and a broad-brimmed straw hat wide as his shoulders. The centerpiece of his look was a second set of eyes where his eyebrows would normally be. He stared at Nea with all four eyes and blinked them in unison.

"The clothes are good, but the extra eyes are amazing," said Nea. "Were they difficult to do?"

"Tricky, but not overly so. I used a mirror so I could get them just right. The only issues are that they won't blink or move autonomously. I also can't actually see with them, but that's an advantage in that the extra sight would confuse me otherwise. I am worried the natives see in a different range of the spectrum though, so let's hope I don't miss simple painted signs outside of my visual range.

"By the way, I made the hat with the Fabricon, not from myself or native straw."

"Have a nice trip. Wish I could go with you."

"Not until I find a way to hide that you only have two eyes."

#

Walking through the forest, Aurus spied a clearing ahead and saw several humanoid forms milling about in the shadowed area.

"Time for first contact," he said to himself. "Let's hope there are no language issues."

Striding into the clearing, those people already there scattered into the surrounding trees.

"Well, that was rude of them. Or was I the rude one? Hey, everybody, I just want to talk."

"You don't want to hurt us or spit on us?" said a voice from the trees.

"Of course not. I am new to your part of our glorious world and wondered if you might direct me toward anyone that might be willing to hire cheap labor?"

"I am not the sort to direct anyone's life. I might only suggest that over that rise up ahead in your current path lies a collection of homes and businesses."

"Thank you, but I am not used to speaking with someone hidden from me. Might we speak face-to-face?"

A short, four-eyed man wearing a backpack dropped lightly from the overhead branches.

Aurus blinked all four eyes. Then again.

"Just wanted to ask a few questions," said Aurus.

"You may, but I cannot guarantee correct answers."

"Fair enough. As I'm new to these parts, is there anything important I should know about the city? I mean, things I should do or not do?"

"I'd say 'don't enter' but I don't suppose that'll help. Don't really know much about the city save that the people don't like us forest-dwellers. Beware the Riders, as they patrol the land and shoot people who threaten the city. That's all I know."

"That's something at least. Thank you."

"By your direct words, you are not from around here, you could repay me by saying where it is you are from."

"Fair enough. I am from the mountains."

Aurus waved his hand to where he had come from. The passerby's eyes all went wide.

"The Teeth of Clermann, Edge of the World," said the man. "Is it true that there is nothing beyond Clermann save the endless stars? Could one drop off the edge and sail amongst them?"

"I don't know. We do not live in the mountains or beyond them, so the mystery is the same for me as yourself, just usually closer at hand."

The man nodded and bowed.

Aurus tipped his hat and left.

"No hint of V'Laubi," said Zen over the earbud.

"Why would there be? According to Madame Zygmeir, only females can become hosts."

"I was checking the entire area through your contacts. There were other people about, hidden in the foliage. Remember?"

"Oh, yeah. Either way, are the contacts working okay?"

"Transmission's clear as crystal. We'll talk later. Zen out."

Aurus shrank himself down about a foot after having discovering he towered over the forest man. He continued on.

Though he caught glimpses of small animals in the trees and underbrush, none were ever seen clearly. No birds at all were spotted. He resisted the impulse to pick the plentiful fruit from nearby trees, not knowing if any might be toxic to him. In short order, he topped the rise of a hill and saw a village spread out before and below him.

The village was quaint and colorful by his standards, primarily filled with conical one-or-two story buildings, save the odd dome or two, and a central building that was a three-story tower with a glass dome. He headed toward the tower.

He saw a few people enter the village, trudging as though they'd rather be elsewhere. He changed his confident stride to a humble shuffle and he hunched forward a bit.

Upon entering the village proper, he was stopped by a man in dark pants and a white jacket trimmed with brown fur.

"Here now, supplicant of the sacred city," said the man. "Prostrate thyself and give thanks to the day before continuing on."

Aurus knelt and the man motioned for him to go lower. Noting the curved gold tube on the man's belt, beneath the jacket, Aurus thought perhaps it would be best to comply. He lay flat, facedown on the cobbled street. Stretching his arms out ahead of himself, he spoke.

"Oh, great light above, I give thanks for this glorious day on fruitful Clermann."

"What? Clermann? You forest-dwelling frog humper, the proper name of the world is Voldflass. Get that right and I'll not run you out of town straightaway. Get up."

"Yes, benevolent sir," said Aurus as he climbed to his feet. "Voldflass. Got it."

"Be on your way then, tree-licker. See that you don't run naked or shit in the streets."

"Yes, sir, of course, sir," said Aurus as he shuffled away.

"What was that about?" asked Zen.

"Religious differences, I suppose. To the forest-dwellers this worldlet is Clermann, but to these folk it's Voldflass. Already getting complicated, but I'll walk around with hopes of not causing a major incident between the two peoples. I hope it's only the two."

The village was not densely populated that he could see, unless perhaps most people were in their homes. The cobblestone streets were empty, while the flagstone sidewalks were lightly dotted with pedestrian traffic.

Aurus reasoned that, as an apparently obvious outsider, asking stupid questions of the locals would not be seen as unusual. With that in mind, he approached a man who wore jacket and trousers of purple.

"Pardon me, benevolent sir. I'm new to the village and—"

"Yes, you're clearly not from here, so it's pointless to mention it. Your premise is also irreparably flawed in that I am not benevolent and this is a city."

Aurus wasn't sure if either laughter or anger would be appropriate, so he went with a neutral expression.

"I merely wished to ask of you a few questions, if that is allowed."

"I suppose. You may proceed with your questions," he said, brushing down his jacket.

"Thank you. Are there many people in the city? I see very few on the streets."

"You see none on the streets, as we keep to the sidewalks. As to your actual question, we number in the thousands, but most have precious little time to go joywalking about the city during work hours.

I am an exception, being enormously wealthy, so may do as I please."

"I see. That brings me to my next question: Why are the actual streets empty? I've seen no vehicles of any sort."

The man gave him a four-eyed stare.

"You have but to wait a moment and the answer will be plain," he said, pointing into the street behind and to the left of Aurus.

He whirled to see a mounted animal charging down the street, bearing a woman on its back. The creature resembled an ungainly cross between camel and cougar, having the general body-shape of a camel, but heavily furred, with a catlike head and wide, padded cat feet.

The woman stood upright on the hump, appearing at ease with the beast's gait. She bore short, pale fur and wore a black dress that hung to mid-thigh. From her polished, brown leather belt hung a curved gold tube on the left side.

"Stop," she yelled.

The beast came to an instant halt, gripping the cobbles with massive, clawed feet. She remained upright and steady, then jumped down gracefully. Towering over Aurus's current height, she glared down at him.

"Remove your hat, outsider, that I may see the face of he who shuffles along Turrinbingle's sidewalks."

Aurus held the hat over his chest and looked up at the woman. Her brilliant green eyes stood out over anything else.

"Give me your name, hat-boy."

"Harry, if it may please your greatness."

"It doesn't, particularly, but I suppose there's no helping that. I am Lyndia of the Talons."

At the mention of her name, Aurus dropped his gaze to her feet, as she did have massive, downward-curving toe talons, with a large heel talon on each foot. None on her fingers though.

"My eyes are up here, Harry," she said, pointing to her four-eyed face. "Why is a forest dweller wandering about in the greatest city on Meifiera?"

Not another name for the world, thought Aurus. *Best not to say anything, I suppose.*

"I'm not wandering, your greatness. I'm specifically heading toward your central tower."

As he spoke, another camelcat ran from the direction of said tower, passing Lyndia on the way out of the city.

"Meet you in the arena tonight," shouted the other rider, galumphing off.

"I'll be there," said Lyndia.

Her camelcat sniffed at Aurus, wide nostrils snorting afterwards. A greenish mass on the back of the creature's neck reached down with a tentacle and touched Lyndia's face. After a moment of contact the tentacle retracted.

"Now, Harry, you may follow me to the tower. Ask for me by name at the door."

She vaulted back to the top of her camelcat and this time Aurus could see her talons digging into the beast's hump. The beast galloped off.

"And that, Harry of the Forest, is why we keep our travels to the sidewalks," said the man in purple. "Those creatures don't always stop if somebody is in their way, no matter how rich and important they may be. Still, they guard the world from invaders, so we should be grateful."

Aurus moved on, alone save for the voice in his ear.

"Who is Harry?" asked Zen.

"Harry is my middle name, because Danger was taken. I tend to use it undercover because 'Aurus' is far more recognizable. Never know if my reputation has preceded me."

"According to Madame Zygmeir, they've heard of neither the Knights nor the full-stars, so probably not."

"What's in a name anyway?"

"Doesn't matter. The important thing is that the lump on the camelcat is a V'Laubi," said Zen.

"What? I thought they were all hollowbacks. Now they're beastriders?"

"I don't know, but Zygmeir said they don't start out back-shaped. Maybe that was a young one or a different variety. Too big to fit in a normal human woman's back though."

"I'll figure it out eventually. Meanwhile I'm here."

The central tower was an affair of rose-colored bricks three stories high, with a crystal top dome. The cobbled street ran straight to a large white door tall enough for Lyndia to have ridden through while still standing, and wide enough for four riders abreast. He thought it looked rather like a typical garage door, save for the size. The sidewalk ended at a much smaller side door with a man beside it. He was dressed in dark pants and a white jacket trimmed with brown fur, like the first man Aurus had encountered in the city. He carried a gold tube in his right hand.

"Now it gets harder," said Zen. "They're all armed and you'll be enclosed, so you can't fly away at will."

"I'm not big on retreating anyway. I've doped out a defense against their nerve blasters, I think, and without those they aren't much of a threat."

"What defense? You don't know just how dangerous the toe talon girl or the camelcat are in close combat either."

"We are going with the name 'camelcat' then? Fine. If a fight breaks out we'll see if my defense works, and just how tough they are."

Aurus stepped up to the guard.

"Her benevolent presence, Lyndia of the Talons, has requested that I appear in the tower."

The man tightened the grip on his tube and stared eye-to-eye with Aurus.

"I wasn't told," he said with a sour glare.

"Sorry, but I'm sure if you check –"

The guard opened the door for him while Aurus stared.

"In this world there are those who know, those who need to know, and those who don't matter. I'm the last. She never tells me anything, so go on in."

He stepped back to clear the doorway, and Aurus nodded to him, then entered.

"I'll tell the magnificent one you're doing a great job," said Aurus as he walked past him.

The man sighed.

"May the grace of Voldflass, or Clermann, or whatever, be with you. Don't bring me up, please. I'd rather be unknown and unknowable than have her actual attention focused on me."

He closed the door behind Aurus.

#

A mauve lizard-woman brought in a completely assembled suit of golden armor on a two-wheeled dolly.

"The one and only divine Battle Presence, solely dedicated to and controlled by the Grand Elder, thoroughly examined and found to be in perfect condition," she said.

The green-skinned Grand Elder did not look up from the gilded book she held.

"Ah, Elder?"

"GRAND Elder, unless you find my full title is too cumbersome."

"My apologies, Grand Elder. I meant no offense."

"What IS it Attendant Javis? I have matters requiring my full attention."

"Um, where do you want your Battle Presence?"

"You can't figure it out for yourself? Along any wall, facing out."

Javis wheeled the armor to the nearest wall and slid it off the dolly, facing out.

"I shall take my leave, Grand Elder, unless you require something further."

"Not at present," said the Grand Elder. "What took you so long? Leave me."

"Gladly," mumbled Javis under her breath as she exited the room.

Once Javis was gone, The Grand Elder dropped her book to the table and moved to the armor. She polished it here and there with the sleeve of her robe, looking at her reflection in the sealed helm's eye lenses.

"You and I," she said to the armor, "we will make our V'Laubi the multiverse's supreme race. By ourselves if need be."

Chapter Eleven
Those Left Behind

Not long after Aurus had trekked off into the forest, Nea and Marvin explored the area near their cave while Zen monitored things. Nea was armed with gold rapier and silver dagger while Marvin carried his trusty rifle.

"I don't like the idea of Aurus going off on his own," said Nea.

"You needn't worry, as he isn't on his own. He's got Zen watching through the transmitter contacts and talking through an ear bud."

"I need to focus on something else meanwhile. I've tried doing a portrait of Zen, but I'm not having much luck."

"Oh, do you have it with you? I'd like to see."

Nea pulled a small pad of paper from a belt pouch, opened it, then handed it to Marvin.

"I see," he said, as he flipped through the pages. "These are all just preparatory rough sketches?"

"They weren't supposed to be, but I can't do his face, like I've got a mental block."

"He did say he thought it might be a psychic ability," Marvin said as he handed the pad back.

"I guess. Did you okay though."

She opened the pad to later pages and handed it back to Marvin.

"Oh, I say, this is splendid. You certainly don't lack talent."

Nea took the pad back.

"Bored now," said Nea. "Have you any stories to regale me with? I know you've been a DemiKnight a lot longer than I have."

Marvin smiled, and polished the rifle stock on his sleeve.

"I haven't lived that exciting a life. Mostly just shoot things we're having trouble dealing with. I mean, what else would I do? It's the only way I can prove my skill since Florinald ValDurian and I don't use the same weapons. He uses bows while I use rifles and pistols. He is the greatest archer in the AllWorlds while I'm the greatest rifle sniper. Don't know which of us is the absolute best marksman."

"Sort of apples and oranges then?"

"Yes." He smiled. "Speaking of which, there are lots of colorful fruits hanging about. We could gather some and test for poison back at base, but we've got plenty of rations to tide us over, so it probably isn't worthwhile."

"The way Aurus eats? Who can tell how long we'll be here? I know he can eat things that would kill humans, so if a bird could survive it, so would he."

"Better than holing up in a literal hole. Let's do it."

They busied themselves in gathering multiple varieties of tree fruit which Nea carried in a sack she made with her cloak.

"I've been working on a variation of my shadowgate spell that could let me create storage pockets of shadow on my person," said Nea. "Would certainly be more convenient for carrying fruit, if nothing else. Now there was something I've been wondering —"

"Yes, uh, raincheck on that discussion. Come with me this way," said Marvin, gesturing to their right.

Nea followed him to a large tree, which they climbed. It had broad, five-pointed leaves which gave them deep shade.

"What's going on?" she whispered.

"One of my hunches. Just stay quiet and watch below."

She did, and before long a furred woman standing atop a camelcat stalked below them. Its nostrils flared, and then it snorted. From the creature's fur she pulled a long gold tube, like a rifle to the gold pistol-tube on her belt.

Nea chanted briefly and quietly, making a patch of shadow on the tree trunk. She put an arm into it and pulled Marvin through behind her.

They appeared in their cave-base, coming through the wall behind Zen, who spun about at the sound.

"What the hell? When did you two get back?"

"Just now," said Nea. "I'd made a shadowgate on the wall for emergencies, of which this was, I think."

"Explain."

Nea gave him the situation.

"I see. Aurus came across the riders in the city a short while ago. One of the citizens said the camelcat riders patrol this worldlet against invaders."

"Which we would be, technically," said Nea. "I'm glad we left there then. I'm sure they track by scent. That's why I got us out. They can probably backtrack our path to here."

"I have some sprays to confuse bloodhounds," said Marvin. "They've got to be in a crate somewhere, so let me check. Didn't think we'd have visitors so soon. Didn't even have a chance to spruce the place up."

"The entrance is camouflaged well," said Zen, "but if your scent leads them right to it. . ."

"Yeah, they'd find it easy enough. Along with Marvin's dog spray, why don't I mash up some of this fruit to help mask the odor?"

"Why do you have — you know what, never mind. Let's do it."

Zen and Nea smashed up fruit in a cookpot, then they mixed in water, making a fine slurry. The resulting mess was quite fragrant, and Nea dashed about the immediate area, slopping it around. She did her best to not leave obvious traces of mashed fruit.

"Done," she said. "My fruit sack, otherwise known as my Cloak of Mystery, could shroud the area in fog, but scent is the one thing it's useless against."

"That sounds like a handy gizmo," said Marvin, "but for some other time. I could just shoot whatever pokes its nose in here."

"I know you could," said Zen, "but I don't want them to get the idea that anybody at all is here. Don't have any other ideas right now though."

"Got one," said Nea. "I can rig up a shadowgate on the door covering so that it looks like maybe the start of a dark cave. If they step through they'll end up far away. Might confuse them at least."

"Excellent. Do it, please. I have to keep monitoring for Aurus coming back online."

"What does that mean? Aren't you in contact with him now?"

"Not since he went into their city's central tower. Beforehand he said not to worry, because he had figured out a defense against their nerve blasters."

"What do you mean 'he has a defense against their nerve blasters?' Maybe he should have discussed it with his partner, me, and the rest of you first? He's going to be cocky now. Cockier than usual, I mean."

"I don't know what he meant. He didn't elaborate."

Nea sighed and rubbed her brows with both hands.

"Based on clues Madame Zygmeir gave us, we're pretty sure the paralo-ray only does physical damage versus living material, and matter in contact with that. Even then, only if they turn up the power. We had wondered how the rays blew up their engines, but as it happens, the engines use a living fluid that generates energy. The rays made it explode."

"That does explain much," said Zen, "but not his supposed defense. He's not even wearing armor."

"I don't know. How about you keep checking on Aurus while Marvin and I deal with the tracker. I'll make a new portal on our door that connects with the one I left on the tree, then I'll be back."

"I'll shoot anyone that breaks in while you're gone. Not a brilliant plan, but it'll do."

As good as her word, Nea made their entrance a new shadowgate back to the tree where she and Marvin had been. She deactivated that portal. Checking for the beast rider and not seeing her, she climbed down and made another portal a few hundred feet away under the shadowed boughs of an even bigger tree. She dove back through to their base.

Emerging at the outside of their entrance, she deactivated that portal long enough to step inside.

"I'm back, boys. Any news of Aurus?"

"He just checked in," said Zen. "He's on his way back and can fill you in himself."

"Good, I—"

A rattling noise came from their vent pipe, followed by a stone falling from it onto their camp stove. Nea picked up the rock, which had a piece of paper wrapped around it.

She unwrapped the paper, which turned out to have illegible writing on it.

"Everyone be on alert," said Zen. "Somebody found us and knew to avoid Nea's trap at the entrance. This could have been a bomb."

"Not sure what it is," said Nea, "but it's not much of a note. I can't read it."

"Let me see that," said Marvin, "penmanship may not be the issue here."

He took the note and looked it over for a time, humming and ah hah-ing.

"It's in a common tongue, but the characters are odd. Somebody is saying they know we're here, obviously, and would like to talk to us outside. Oh, and they led off the beastrider."

"We're clearly compromised, so let's talk," said Zen. "Can you two handle it while I stay at my station for Aurus?"

"Certainly," said Nea.

She deactivated the shadowgate, then she and Marvin went outside.

"All right then," she announced to the air, "we're here, so let's talk."

"As was my intent," said a short, brown-robed man who appeared from the bushes. "We've known you were here from the moment you arrived, but thought it would be safer to find more about you first. To that end we listened in, first through the rock itself, then from your vent pipe. It seems your goals may actually coincide with our own."

"And what goals are those?" asked Nea.

"Why, the freedom of our people and the entire worldlet of Clermann. Those you call the V'Laubi have controlled our affairs for far too long."

"Ah, you called it a worldlet," said Marvin." May I presume you understand what the bubble worlds are then?"

"Of course. Incomplete shards of a once-larger world. We did not come from here originally."

"How may we work together?" asked Nea. "I'm not so sure our goals are the same."

"You want to defeat or destroy the V'Laubi. We want that also. Whatever we each also want is irrelevant to the larger picture. We can't defeat their ray-weapons, but we can help you get to their bases without being detected, just as we did with your companion, Harry."

"Harry?" said Nea. "How would you know his middle name?"

"We led the beastriders away from him as he walked to the city, though he did not know this. He introduced himself to the beastriders of the city as Harry."

"Ah, his undercover name. Makes sense," said Nea.

The forest man scratched his head.

"Undercover? Like this?" he asked, pulling at his robe.

"It means he's in disguise, pretending to be somebody else, so he uses a different name."

"Oh, I see. My name is Khersmel. I speak for the tree dwellers as they are too shy to speak for themselves."

"I am Nea, this is Marvin, and Zen is still inside. Aurus is on his way back."

"Yes, I know. All of that. Aurus will be here . . . now."

Aurus appeared from the bushes on cue.

"I feel like I'm missing something," he said, as they all stared at him.

#

After everybody caught Aurus up to the present, Zen joined the discussion, and Nea asked Aurus what he'd been doing.

"That might take a while. We can go inside and get comfortable."

"I'd rather stay outside," said Khersmel. "I'd feel trapped in there."

"Very well," said Zen. "I'll bring out chairs. When Aurus is ready he can start."

#

They undulated in their movement, though moving and undulating was not what they did, nor did they think of themselves as "they."

The presence that was not a presence puzzled to itself in terms with no meaning to any but it themselves, but might be interpreted something like this:

The threads of the AllWorlds exist, all in glorious disharmony, each with their own glory, each with their own song, all woven through each other, separate yet together, untouching, disparate, yet a whole. Now though, the strands tighten, becoming more perfectly aligned, more harmonious, more perfectly woven, yet the songs clash in brilliant cacophony. The strands grow taut with harmony. How much more perfection can the AllWorlds take before the strands snap, the threads unravel, the music shatters?

If the AllWorlds go, will we go with them?

Chapter Twelve
A Tale of Daring

Having followed the beastrider to the central tower, its side door closed behind Aurus, leaving him in a dim hallway. Following the light at the end, he came to a well-lit, large, open floor space with a high ceiling. On his left was the large door to the outside that Lyndia had entered through, and on a ten-foot high stone throne before him was Lyndia herself. The camelcat slept curled up, off to his right. The V'Laubi was not on the back of its neck.

"Well, Harry, here you are and here I am."

"Quite so, but why did you say that, it being obvious and all?"

"Just that I didn't really expect you to enter. I know you tree-dweller types don't like to be closed in."

"I suppose that would be true if I were of the forest folk, but why would you assume I am?" asked Aurus, frowning.

"You could be nothing else, as you appeared at the city gates unheralded. Had you come from another city, you'd have been followed along the entire way. No, only those of the forest could appear without having been seen well in advance. So your origins are not in question, only your reasons for entering what is very dangerous territory for you."

Aurus shrugged. "I can see why this is strange for you, as it's also strange for me. I wasn't trying to hide, so it is odd you didn't spot me. I'm not known to be stealthy on accident. I only wanted to talk with the city leaders."

"Then talk. I can offer you that much."

Aurus cleared his throat, then took off his wide, pointed hat and held it on his chest.

"The technology you use to oppress people is not yours by right. I would like it returned, please."

"What? Are you insane? The V'Laubi have used it for hundreds of years."

"Indeed, and it's time they stopped."

Lyndia snarled in response and fired her ray tube. Aurus responded by firing his eye-rays. Her ray deflected harmlessly off his hat while his rays destroyed her tube. She screeched and flung the tube away, then blew on her fingers.

"What are you?" she shouted.

He moved his hat up over his face for an instant. When he took it down his skin had become blue, and his head elongated, with numerous needle-like teeth. Lyndia had meanwhile leapt to her camelcat and dug a long gold tube from its fur. She fired at him again.

He calmly deflected her blasts, then destroyed her weapon with his eye-rays.

"Careless of me," he said. "I didn't know you had another. No matter though. I am Harry of the Olgun, whom you call the Ancient Builders. Nothing from our technology may harm me. Now will you talk to your people? You are no longer allowed to use our machines."

"This is crazy," Lyndia said, "but I am not one of your machines."

She snarled and pounced, followed by her steed. Aurus fell with her on top, as the beast bit at his legs. She attempted to pin Aurus's arms at his sides while going for his throat with her teeth.

"Such ferocity," said Aurus, struggling to appear calm. "It's a wonder you need weapons at all. Still futile though."

He kicked at the beast's head with one leg to free the other, then flew up, still horizontal, Lyndia on top, and he pushed her against the ceiling.

"Assuming you don't wish to be dropped, can we discuss things in a civil manner?" asked Aurus.

Her knees bent backwards, and she dug her toe talons into the wooden ceiling beams, pulling herself from his grip. Then she jumped down to the beast, digging into its hump with her talons.

"My, how impressive," said Aurus. "I never saw that —"

The beast jumped at him.

Aurus tried to dodge, but the beast was too big. It virtually engulfed him, knocking him to the floor while biting his face.

"— coming," he said, through the camelcat's fur.

"Bite his head off," shouted Lyndia. "I don't care what he is, but he dies here."

The beast sucked in Aurus's head and tried to bite it off. After gnawing and chewing for a moment, it spasmed, then lay still.

Aurus pried its jaws open, then pulled his bleeding head out. The beast's teeth had left a dotted line of oozing punctures around his neck.

"What? No. What have you done?"

She grabbed the beast's neck and shook it, but it didn't move.

"Sorry, but I had to kill it," said Aurus. "It couldn't really harm me, but I saw no easy way out. Never try to eat someone with blaster eyes."

Aurus wiped his head on the beast's fur while Lyndia hyperventilated, then he picked up his hat.

"You still have to give up our tech," said Aurus. "I feel bad for your beast, but the fault is yours."

"Eeeeh, aaaah, my mistress will have me flayed for this. Do you have any idea how hard it is to raise those properly? How can I be a beastrider with no beast?"

"I'm more interested in the V'Laubi that was attached to it. Talking with you has brought about only death, no resolutions."

A loudspeaker crackled.

"*There will only be your death now. We do not accept your ownership of our technology.*"

The overhead door slid up, revealing three beastriders armed with rifle tubes. They moved in and Aurus dodged behind the stone throne while holding his hat in front of himself. The riders fired at him, not even hitting the throne, let alone him.

Lyndia's eyes widened, and with a grin, pounced, grabbing the hat from Aurus and shredding it mid-flight. Unfortunately, a stray ray blast caught her and she fell to the floor, paralyzed, but still grinning.

"Damn. That makes things harder. Time to leave, I think."

He activated his watch and disappeared. At almost the same time the overhead door slammed shut. He flew up and was instantly highlighted by red lasers. Cursing, he did a barrel roll toward the side door while shots flashed all about him. He hit the side door hard as he could, feet first, smashing it to splinters. Lasers in the side hallway lit him up again as he flew for the exit.

For a slim moment the hallway was clear of ray fire, then the three riders, beastless, tried to enter the hallway, hampered mainly by them trying to all enter at once. The brief congestion gave Aurus time to reach the door, which he smashed through with a shoulder. He flew out, once again bracketed with rayfire. One beam grazed his foot and he felt himself stiffen slightly. Marshalling all his willpower, he flew into the sky, still invisible, but no longer highlighted by lasers.

#

"And here I am," said Aurus. "Feeling fine now, without even a tingle from their ray blast."

Nea applauded while Zen and Marvin shook their heads.

"But how did you protect yourself from their rays?" she asked.

"The hat. As I'd guessed, the ray only works on biologics, and must be nearly touching skin. A normal, thick coat isn't enough, but my hat had inner cross-straps, so I just held on to those. It kept the rays more than three inches from my skin."

Khersmel was wide-eyed, but with a confused look.

"I didn't understand much of that. You are an Olgun? An Ancient Builder manifest?"

"No, that's only what I told them."

"So, you lied?"

"Yes, sort of. It's called improvisational acting, and it came to me on the spur of the moment. I have no idea where the V'Laubi tech came from, but an Olgun origin isn't that much of a stretch."

Khersmel stood and began to pace, appearing agitated.

"Wait, you said you became an Olgun?"

"In appearance anyway. Like this."

Aurus turned away and changed his look to the Olgun-face again. When he turned back around Khersmel was gone.

"Where'd he go?"

"Don't know," said Nea. "I think you freaked him out. Never saw anyone vanish so fast without magic. Then again, maybe it is magic."

"Khersmel, it's still me," said Aurus, "just a disguise, acting, like making up stories for your kids and doing a scary face."

"Oh," said Khersmel, now behind Aurus. "You folks bring a lot of new and scary stuff with you, so pardon my skittishness. Actually we all tend to be that way, and for good reason. The beastriders used to kill our men and capture our women a lot, so calm, sluggish people don't last long around here. Even if all that weren't true, your Olgun-face is terrifying."

"He's got a point," said Marvin. "That isn't a face I'd like to come across in a dark alley. How do you know what an Olgun looks like anyway?"

Aurus shrugged and grinned.

"Don't really. Just made it up because it was an easy face to do. Didn't think they'd know either, and apparently they didn't."

"Okay then," said Zen. "The big question is why you did it. It was supposed to just be a reconnaissance mission. Are you going to go rogue like this all the time?"

"First of all, I was playing it by ear. I couldn't resist the invitation to the tower. Second of all, I don't like your attitude."

"What?" said Zen.

"You act like you're in charge of this mission, while I've been keeping the AllWorlds safe since before your dad's sperm assaulted your mother's womb. If you don't like how this team runs then take it up with Master Julian at the next meeting. Meanwhile, I'm the only full Knight on the team, so we do things my way. Do you have a problem with that?"

Nea had a gleam in her eyes while she covered a smile with her hands. Marvin kept his expression neutral. Zen's mouth dropped open and he had trouble speaking for a moment.

"No, no, I'm fine with how things are going for the most part. It's just been a lot to take in the past few hours, with both you and the forest people."

"Consider that this was all spur of the moment. I had a moment where I realized we could make them think the Olgun were trying to reclaim their technology, not that Knights of Valeron were looking to rescue countless kidnap victims."

"Not sure that makes any difference," said Marvin. "They'll still be on high alert for intruders. Does it matter what intruders?"

"I think so. They'd be protecting their bases against something designed to take out their tech, not someone trying to free slaves. That means slaves would be relatively unguarded," said Aurus.

"Plus, the Olgun are ancient and mysterious," said Zen. "If the V'Laubi really are using Olgun tech then this could rattle them. If not, Olgun are still scary, and one of the oldest known legendary races."

"Of course, Aurus did run from them," said Nea. "That might put a little crimp in the legend."

"Yeah, but they didn't actually see me flee. For all they know, I was just sauntering off. They may be able to Detect Invisible, but they didn't know I was desperate. The only problem is breaking back into their bases now. I don't know if they can detect me outside of their buildings, but that's only part of the problem."

"Then you don't have a problem," said Khersmel. "We can get you into their bases on Clermann."

#

All mine, thought the Grand Elder. *Every world, every bubble, every place that can support life, all mine.*

She addressed Attendant Javis, who stood next to her.

"I must go over plans and strategies with myself, and it's better if I speak them aloud. They are not for you to hear, so go now and leave me alone for an hour."

Javis bowed and escorted herself from the chamber.

"Yes, indeed, Attendant Javis. It wouldn't do for you to hear my secrets, and they are so much more delicious when said aloud. All the worlds will be mine, the thoughts of all women under my control. Our race will die without new hosts, but our woeful situation gives me a golden opportunity to bring all the resources of the V'Laubi toward that one goal. All for my benefit.

"But of course all is for my benefit, as the high-born chosen of the Divine."

She laughed.

"Not poorly done for one who was not actually high-born, but I cannot brag about that in public. A pity. It would drive the fact of my supremacy home even more strongly.

"If only they knew, what would they think?" asked the Grand Elder.

Chapter Thirteen
Let's Get On With It, Already

"And that's how we do it," said Khersmel. "We could have broken into their bases before, but had no defense against their ray tubes. Not to mention their beasts would have smelled us in close quarters."

"This why you prefer the forest?" asked Zen.

"No. We prefer the forest because that's where we like to live. Now though, it's become a necessity. I wouldn't mind visiting the city once in a while, but we can't anymore."

"After this you should be able to," said Nea. "Well, this, then the other four cities you mentioned."

"Are you sure my people don't have to fight?" asked Khersmel. "We would if we have to."

"Just getting us there is fine," said Aurus. "We'll handle the fighting."

He flexed his fingers and a golden halberd appeared in his hands. He whirled it about his head and then struck a battle pose.

"Very impressive," said Zen, "but why don't you just vaporize them with your laser-eyes?"

"Not really meant to be used that way. They project precision beams suitable for fine work and pinpoint attacks. I can't use them if my head is moving too much, because it requires focus. I could blast the inside of the camelcat head because I had that chance to concentrate. And for the record, it's a thermal ray, not a laser, even though it can cut without much residual heat if I really focus."

"What's the difference?" asked Nea.

Aurus made his halberd vanish.

"Lasers are light, concentrated and focused on a specific point. They are intended to only cause damage at that point. For instance, if you had an inflated balloon inside another one that was clear, you could pop the inner balloon without harming the outer."

"Cool. Your ray doesn't do that?"

"No. If I miss it'll leave a burned scar until it's stopped by something. It'd be awesome if I could spin in place and just spray heat rays, but I can't. Been working on it though, but no luck so far."

Zen interrupted.

"I think you have the precision we need for this job, so let's go with the plan I helped lay out, okay?"

"No problem," said Aurus with a smile. "It's okay to disagree with me, you know. I'm not going to jump all over you just because I established some ground rules."

Zen nodded.

"Just don't want friction to ruin the teamwork. Now, everybody grab the new ray shields I made."

Zen handed out what looked like folding personal paper fans.

"Khersmel, are you ready to take us?"

"Indeed. We all are."

Khersmel and a dozen other forest-dwellers, all loaded down with wooden boxes, surrounded the Knights.

"Everybody link hands and close your eyes," said Khersmel.

"Do we have to think happy thoughts?" asked Aurus.

"No. Why would we do that? Just keep them closed until I say otherwise. You may experience nausea."

The Knights felt a flickering sensation and they all felt nauseated.

"Open them up. First stop," said Khersmel.

They found themselves on a grassy knoll, under the noonday green sun, with the city of Turrinbingle about half a mile off.

"Khersmel, if some of your people can help me with the boxes the rest can be on their way," said Marvin.

"I thought we were using natural powers to travel through tree roots," said Zen. "Where's the tree?"

Khersmel pointed to a small, green shoot poking up from the grass at the top of the knoll.

"All the roots are interconnected or overlap. We kept the tree small so as not to draw attention. Now, what's this about 'natural powers?' "

"You know, tapping the power of nature to travel through it?" said Zen.

"It's magic, pure and simple," said Khersmel. "I wouldn't call it 'natural' exactly. We use the biologic energy inherent in the trees to power our transport spells, and the roots are convenient conduits."

"Basically, you can fast-travel to anything with a connecting root," said Aurus.

"Yes, the power given us by Clermann herself, and connecting the entire worldlet. It's why we named it Clermann in the first place."

"Why the other names then?" asked Zen.

"Voldflass was the original name for this bubble world. The city dwellers didn't like when we changed it, and it helped drive a wedge between our peoples. Meifiera is what the V'Laubi call it, for reasons that escape me. And there you have it."

"Peachy," said Marvin. "Now can we set up here while the rest of you get going?"

"Of course," said Aurus. "Everybody partner up."

Each Knight save Marvin held hands with a forest dweller while Khersmel stood in the middle of their small circle, his hands on the backs of Aurus and Nea.

"Close your eyes again," said Khersmel, "and we're off."

"Second verse, same as the first," said Aurus. "Blerrgh."

"We're here. Open your eyes."

They had appeared in an overgrown garden on the outskirts of Turrinbingle.

"Why couldn't we appear inside the city," asked Zen.

"Because there are no gardens inside the city," said Khersmel. "They suspect our ability to hide and evade has something to do with trees and plants, but no idea of what it actually is. They've done just enough to stymie us though."

"Then we'll have to break into their tower on our own," said Zen. "You said you'd get us in."

"And so I shall. We've been growing a really long tree root under the city for years now, and it's finally close enough to break into their basement. We haven't dared to yet because they'd wipe us out in any kind of battle, but with you here the odds are suddenly in our favor."

"How kind of you to say so," said Nea, "but it's still going to be tricky. Can you make the root grow through the cellar wall now?"

"Working on it. It's really just the shoots sprouting through and I hope that does the job, because I can't make the root grow any faster than normal. We were worried the V'Laubi would notice if a root broke through, and . . . yes, it's through," he yelled.

"Copy that," said Zen. "I just told Marvin. The attack starts now."

Even as Zen said it, multiple streaks of different-colored smoke came from Marvin's knoll toward the tower. Aurus flew up, invisible, and gave the play-by-play.

"The missiles are hitting the front of the tower and exploding with minimal damage. Most hit the foreground of it, but they'll be shaken up inside. The smoke leaves a clear trail back to the knoll, so the V'Laubi would have to be stupid not to find it. When the beastriders come out, that's when we go in."

"And?" asked Nea, trying to appear calm, and mostly succeeding.

"They're out," said Aurus. "Time for us to go."

He landed and became visible.

"I could make four of us invisible when we get there, but it's a tight radius of effect, so I don't see the point. Especially since they'll probably have sensors going."

"Speaking of going, here we go," said Khersmel. "Close the eyes."

#

With a great cracking sound, the Knights and forest dwellers appeared in a dark room. Aurus brushed dirt and debris from his head, then lit himself with a dim glow to see the others also brushing themselves off. They stood amidst a pile of rocks and dirt in a rough-hewn room.

"Sorry about that," said Khersmel. "The shoots didn't break through as much as I'd hoped, so we ended up doing most of the breaking ourselves. Is everybody well?"

General grunts of assent said that all was well.

"Where to next, Zen?" asked Aurus.

"I don't have the layout to this place, so I'll need to hack their electronics first. I also can't contact Marvin through the ear buds for an update; same problem as when you were here, plus I switched on a radio jammer before we entered, to be on the safe side."

"He'll be fine on his own," said Aurus. "I pity the beastriders that find him."

Khersmel's people gathered together, separate from the Knights, then vanished.

"They are of no use in a fight, and would only get in the way," he said. "Now their panic of being closed in won't be an issue and we needn't be concerned over them."

"What about you though?" asked Zen.

"Oh, I'm of no use in a fight either, but you might need a way out later, so I'm staying. I'm also not as prone to panic over closed spaces," he said. "And I have an idea where the prisoners are being held, so I can guide you."

Zen hefted a backpack the other forest dwellers had left. He also wore one on his back and carried a pistol on his right hip. He unholstered his gun and gestured with it.

"You know," he said, "Marvin would have loaned you pistols if you wanted. This is one of his. We didn't have to do this medieval style, with swords and halberds."

"Never fired a gun," said Aurus. "Need to go with weapons I trust."

He gestured and a halberd appeared in his right hand.

"Same here," said Nea, "though I have fired guns before. My rapier and main gauche will do just fine, especially if you shut down the power."

Zen nodded and they left the room, heading down the hallway. Khersmel had them turn at the next right, then at the next left.

"We're almost in their secure areas," whispered Zen while looking at a handheld device. "I'm picking up electromagnetic activity ahead."

They rounded a corner and the walls were now sheathed in golden metal. The lights were dim, but bright enough for Aurus to shut down his glow.

"Straight ahead," said Zen.

He ran his device along the wall as they moved, until he suddenly stopped.

"Right here, Aurus. If you can cut a three-inch wide hole just deep enough to expose the wiring please? One-half inch deep; don't cut the wire."

Aurus stared at the wall briefly, then red rays lanced from his eyes, quickly cutting out the desired hole. Zen stuck another device into the hole, tapping into the wires. He pushed a few buttons, then stood back.

"Any second now, if they have the same system as Zygmeir and the flower ships."

The fire alarm sounded and the lights dimmed.

"Good," said Zen. "They damp the power during a fire because the living fluid in their generators is too unstable around heat."

"Follow me," said Khersmel.

He led them down the hallway, through a couple of turns, then stopped before a closed door.

"In there. I memorized the layout based on sounds we heard through the stone."

Aurus jammed his halberd into the door's edge and levered it open to reveal an empty room.

"Clermann's Blood, we're too late," said Khersmel. "I should have struck when they were first taken."

"And done what?" asked Nea. "You didn't know how to shut down their power and would likely have been helpless against their weapons."

"I guess. Doesn't help to know that though."

They searched the remainder of the level and found no women, but did find the generator room. Zen opened the backpack he'd been carrying.

"I'll rig explosives on the pipes and trigger it when the power comes back on. The rest of you look for the portal and computer rooms and I'll be along when I can."

Leaving Zen, the rest found the elevator.

"I can carry us up the shaft," said Aurus, "this is like on the spaceship, but you'd think they would have emergency power in case of, well, emergencies."

"Maybe they don't need it," said Nea.

Removing a glove, she felt along a wall next to the elevator and pushed a nearly invisible panel, causing a door to swing open.

"Emergency ladder," she said, then bowing and waving at the spiral staircase within.

"All right then, I'll fly back to tell Zen where we're going, then fly up the staircase," said Aurus.

He flew to Zen, and was back in moments.

"Had a thought while you were gone," said Nea. "The emergency lights create enough shadow for me to work with, so I should go up first."

So saying, she vanished into shadow. Moments later she gave the all-clear, and Aurus flew Khersmel up the staircase.

The upper floor was much the same as that they left below, and Nea recognized the layout as similar to the one from Madame Zygmeir's complex.

"Portal room should be down this way," said Nea, pointing to their left. "This place is the same as Zygmeir's, except it has a lower dungeon level. Computer room should be one floor up."

She flowed down the hallway as shadow, confirming the last room on the left was the portal room. After they had all entered, Nea began snatching what fancy parts from the portal she could. After helping her disassemble part of the portal frame, Aurus stopped.

"Why are we doing this?"

"I can answer that," said Zen, who had just entered. "Prevents them from using it, and gives us a head start on building our own."

"Why would we need to build our own?" asked Aurus. "We already have the Bifrost shards for interdimensional travel."

"Not sure, but that's the reason I was given. Probably a directive from the Omnimind. Should have hit the computer room first though. We need more information than we could get from Zygmeir."

"Then let's do that," said Aurus. "We can come back to this later."

He stepped into the hallway and immediately jumped back to the room and slid the door shut.

"They have guns. Regular guns."

#

Marvin scanned the horizon toward the city with a pair of binoculars. He saw a dozen beastriders following the smoke trail. He smiled.

"You lot get on out of here," he said to the forest-dwellers, "and take my excess equipment with you. There's no need for you to be a part of the firefight coming up."

Leaving him with smiles, they vanished, along with most of the boxes. What they'd left were three machine gun emplacements equidistant around the perimeter, plus boxes of ammo, steel shields encircling the knoll's crest, and a rocket launcher with thirty missiles.

"I'd like to see your rays work now, you assholes, especially after the gang shuts down your power. Wait, what's that?"

He focused the binoculars on the beastriders, then frowned.

"This lot has conventional gunpowder weapons. I don't even see the ray tubes. . . Zen, do you copy? Oh, right, radio blackout. No matter; the plan remains the same. I just might die more than expected."

As the beastriders neared the knoll, the camelcats put on a burst of speed as the riders leveled personal machine guns on the hill. Marvin smiled and seated himself behind his own machine gun.

"I bet none of you have ever fired full auto from animal back."

They loosed an intense round of gunfire that struck the hill or otherwise missed completely. Marvin didn't.

In mere seconds, five out of twelve riders were down from explosive rounds, followed by their beasts and the V'Laubi attached to them. The other seven beasts with riders dashed left and right, into the foliage, out of sight.

"Oh, now you've got me. I couldn't possibly defend against a multi-pronged attack."

He leapt to the left-hand gun emplacement as all seven beastriders dashed from cover, surrounding him. He took down four on the left with withering gunfire, and yanked on a cord behind him, triggering the right-hand gun. It didn't hit any beastriders, but they broke left and right, charging up the hill.

"Had a hunch you'd do that," he said as hidden claymore mines on the side of the knoll went off ahead of the beastriders, decimating two of the camelcats.

One beastrider continued on, leaping over Marvin's shield wall. He grabbed his rifle, but the beast landed on him before he could fire. Grimacing, he pumped eight rounds into the camelcat's chest, and was showered with blood and flesh as the rounds exploded.

Marvin struggled from beneath the camelcat and wiped the blood from his eyes.

"Had a hunch one of you would get through," he said, then shot the rider in its head with a pistol.

A wave of blackness overwhelmed Marvin's senses and he went down again, but in searing pain now as taloned toes sank into his abdomen and legs from behind. He dropped the pistol, and as he tried to twist free, the rider behind him snarled.

"You didn't get us all, demon from below. I will hunt you Olgun until you're extinct again."

While she ranted, Marvin pulled a knife from his belt and reached over his shoulder, stabbing her in the leg. Screaming, she hopped back, freeing him. He grabbed the fallen pistol and emptied the clip into her head.

"Should've saved a few rounds, I guess, but I think she was it. Better check. Don't know what she did to me, but I can see fine now."

He peered over the edge of the shield wall with binoculars, then moved left around the inside, still looking out. He saw no living enemies. What he did see was a trail of blood on the ground behind him and all around the inner wall.

He reached around to his back and his hands came back dripping blood.

"Oh, that's not good."

He sat on the camelcat carcass.

"Zen, having serious blood loss, and I can't reach the wound,

but I got them all. . . Zen? Damn."
    He fell, eyes closed, unmoving.

Chapter Fourteen
Are Things Going As Planned?

"Don't panic," said Aurus. "There's only four of us, so I can get us out invisibly and still hit the computer room. Since the power is out the sensors won't reveal us."

The lights came on.

"Son of a bitch. I've got to stop saying things."

"What now?" asked Zen.

"No shadows, no stealth," said Nea, "and I'm not bulletproof. Options?"

"Only force," said Aurus. "I'm more bullet-resistant than you three, so let me handle it. When I step out, close your eyes and close the door."

Nea put her hand on his arm.

"Are you sure? My cloak can generate fog to hide us."

"Keep that in reserve. It wouldn't stop them from firing blindly, which is going to be the only way they can fire in a few seconds."

He stepped out, intense light bursting from his very pores, so strong even hands couldn't completely block it. Screams and sounds of gunfire filled the hallway for uncounted seconds until a knock came at the door.

She opened the door to see Aurus bleeding profusely. He limped in.

"Oh, dear gods," she said. "I thought you were bullet-resistant."

"I said 'more bullet-resistant than you three' and I am. Still hurts a lot though, and I suppose death was always an option. You might not want to look because this will be a little gross."

Nobody turned away when he put his hand into his chest, fumbled about for a bit, then pulled it back with a gushing of blood. Khersmel went white and Zen shut his eyes briefly.

"Told you it would be gross. This is what I was doing."

He held out his hand, and in the palm lay an expended bullet.

"You do surgery on yourself?" asked Zen.

"Not exactly. I expanded the bullet hole enough to get my hand inside and pull this out. I've closed the skin to stop bleeding all over the floor, but I'm not healed yet. I do regenerate pretty fast, but faster if I can pull the bullets out. Give me a couple of minutes here."

Nea pulled two daggers from her belt.

"I have a light touch with daggers. Can I help? I could pincer them out, and you wouldn't have to open up bigger holes."

"Yes, please."

"While you two are doing that, I'll hit the computer room, okay?" said Zen.

Aurus nodded, and Zen stepped into a hallway full of decapitated, bisected bodies of toe-taloned riders, but no V'Laubi or camelcats. He picked up one of their automatic weapons and a spare clip while he walked.

At the door to the computer room he put a handheld device on the lock plate and sprung the door. Inside, a mottled green, blobby V'Laubi quivered in the chair at the console, its tentacles plugged into it.

"I'm impressed you could shut the fire alarm system down," he said, "but I'm pretty sure you've been locked out of anything else. Why don't you ooze out of that chair so I don't have to shoot you? Not that I would mind overly much. You things disgust me."

Zen knocked the creature out of the chair and sat there. He checked the system and nodded.

"Thought so. I overrode access to everything else. Now that I'm here I can shut down the generator, communications, and your jamming field."

How can you do this? Humans are too primitive to understand our technology, it said in a high-pitched, electronic voice.

"Some are. I'm not. Got a chance to hack your systems before, and they're not the great shakes you body snatchers think. About time you scum got what's coming to —"

Zen fell to the floor, shaking, as a V'Laubi tentacle pierced his neck.

We are not defenseless, as you now see. I cannot control you but I can electrocute you.

It struck with another tentacle and Zen spasmed.

Die, useless male.

With great effort, Zen raised his arms and grabbed each tentacle, then clenched firmly.

You cannot resist.

"So sue me," Zen yelled, as he tore the tentacles loose from his neck, and dove for his machine gun.

The tentacles came at him again as he fired on full auto.

An electronic scream filled the air as the bullets tore the creature into stray globs of green. Zen collapsed, breathing heavily.

"Got here after we heard the gunfire," said Aurus, standing in the doorway, still bleeding. "You okay? What happened?"

Zen held up a finger while he caught his breath.

"I mistakenly thought the V'Laubi were harmless without their hosts. Won't make that mistake again. Turns out their tentacles act like tasers."

"How did you beat it then?" asked Aurus.

"Enough adrenaline can give you the strength to endure a taser, and fear for your life can generate a lot of adrenaline."

Nea walked through the doorway.

"I heard all that. Got lucky when I bagged Zygmeir's V'Laubi then. Why don't we all stay here while Zen works on the computer? I'll finish picking bullets out of Aurus in the meanwhile. Zen, do you need medical attention?"

"I'm just jangled. I'll be fine, eventually."

"Good, because I'm not sure what I could do with knives and bandages."

#

Nearly an hour later, they had finished collecting everything they could from the portal and computer. Zen finally managed to turn off the comm-jamming field and then called Marvin. After a tense minute he turned to the others.

"Marvin isn't responding. Let's get back to the hill we left him on, ASAP."

"I'll have to call the others," said Khersmel. "I can only take one of you."

"No time," said Nea. "I think I can make a shadowgate that connects with the one in our base. I'll bet your people are nearby."

"Why didn't you do that back in the portal room?" asked Zen.

Nea smacked herself in the forehead.

"Didn't think of it. Was like a cloud over my thoughts and I couldn't think of anything. Sorry, Aurus. It's still new to me, but I could've saved you from a near-death experience."

Aurus shrugged.

"Apology accepted. At least, this way we cleaned them out of their base."

With her cloak blocking the light, she created a patch of shadow on the wall. The four of them stepped through, and ended up back in the Knight's under-hill hideout.

"It's me, Khersmel," he yelled. "I need the team here."

They all went outside, and saw six of the forest-dwellers waiting. A woman spoke.

"Praise Clermann. We didn't dare return to the tower, so some of us waited here and some are at the knoll. Marvin was badly wounded. He's back at our sacred clearing, but isn't doing well."

"Take us there," yelled Aurus.

And they did. The entire group appeared in a clearing surrounded by giant trees. In the middle, lying down on a sarcophagus-sized stone block, was Marvin, made comfortable on a thick bed of moss.

"Where was he wounded?" asked Nea. "I don't see anything."

"In the back," croaked Marvin. "Those damned toe talons really smart."

"Thank goodness you're alive," she said, "but why haven't they healed you?"

"Our magic is only for travel," said Khersmel. "The best they could do is wrap him in medicinal leaves."

"Yes," said one of the women. "We know he has internal injuries, but we can't help with those. We did give him some herbs to chew for pain relief, but I'm pretty sure the wounds are infected."

"There's a hospital back on my Earth that deals with injured government agents all the time. They won't ask questions if I take him there," said Zen.

"Then do so," said Aurus, "before the sun goes down and we can't use the Bifrost shards."

Marvin coughed up blood.

"Make sure they collect up my equipment and stash it in our hideout. Just be careful on the knoll, because I have claymore mines all over it. You can leave those until I get back. If I do."

"You will," said Nea, "you just get better. We were just about to have a long conversation before the V'Laubi happened."

Marvin smiled while Zen frowned.

"You two should get back to the tower and secure it against returning V'Laubi," said Zen. "When I get back we can proceed with the remaining plan, but I might have another idea. Aurus, can you give us a lift skyward? It'll be easier than me carrying Marvin up from the ground."

"Are you going also?" asked Khersmel. "You're pretty ripped up as well."

"I should be fine in a few hours, enough you wouldn't be able to tell I was ever wounded," said Aurus.

He lifted Marvin carefully while Zen wrapped his arms around Aurus and hung on. Gently, he flew toward the sun, while Zen sang forth the rainbow.

#

Aurus threw more golden rifle-tubes on the pile, next to captured machine guns and ammo.

"I think that's the last of the weapons in Turrinbingle. I think our next step is to find who ran them guns."

"That's mostly a Zen thing," said Nea. "Sounds right up his

alley. Meanwhile, the forest-dwellers took out all the dead bodies and disposed of them."

"There were supposedly thirty beastriders originally," said Aurus, "and we've only killed thirteen camelcats. Why haven't the others showed up? Went to the other cities?"

"In my talks with Madame Zygmeir, she'd gathered the impression that V'Laubi are splintered into factions, so maybe the cities here don't play well with each other."

"That would explain why there have been no reprisals yet, but that can't last forever. There has to be some interaction, so questions and investigations are inevitable," he said.

They heard running in the hall, the tappity-tap of hard-soled shoes coming in their direction, until Zen burst through the open doorway.

"Damn," he huffed out, "I could hear you both down the hall and I missed my cue." He breathed heavily for a moment.

"What cue?" asked Nea.

He finished panting.

"I have answers to your questions. Before I came back, I stopped to chat with Madame Zygmeir. Her hollowback was full of information when I told it what we'd done. It may actually be scared now, as it tried to make a deal with me. In return for keeping the Madame as a host, it filled me in with greater detail as to how the V'Laubi work."

"And Madame Zygmeir was okay with that?" asked Nea.

"Completely, since she'll die without the body snatcher. Anyway, the situation is thus: there are five V'Laubi factions, all at odds with one another. They mostly stay out of each other's way, but will actively move to undermine another's situation when possible. On their homeworld, the highest-ranking clan is the ruler. They have some sort of complicated point system to determine who ranks highest.

"They don't help another clan under any circumstances, even if it means their own deaths. Regardless of whether they know what happened here, there will be no attacks forthcoming from the other cities. They can't even try to expel us for their own good, as it could be perceived as overtly helping themselves at their rival's expense."

"That seems incredibly stupid of them. You'd think they'd try to get rid of us and rack up points for themselves," said Nea.

"I've seen a lot of weird worlds and worldlets," said Aurus, "and that isn't the screwiest thing I've come across."

"It only helps us," said Zen. "We don't have to worry about a concerted counterattack. The beastriders probably don't even know what happened here yet. Better yet, we can commandeer this tower for use as our new base. We can use its generator and construct the portal jammer right here."

"That's some good news at least," said Nea, "but how's Marvin doing?"

"Pretty well for guy who was basically stabbed with six daggers in the back. The docs say he'll be down for a couple of weeks at least, but that he should make a full recovery."

"That's great," said Aurus, "but without his firepower we're going to have to delay the plan."

Zen sat down, and waved his hands over all the captured weapons.

"We've got plenty of firepower right here. I can use the weapons and train others in their use, but not with the finesse Marvin would have brought."

"We aren't supposed to raise a local army here, if that's what you were saying," said Nea.

"Yeah, I sort of was, but we don't need to do that, as Marvin suggested a replacement shooter."

"Really?" asked Aurus. "I'd like to see the guy that could take Marvin's place."

"I'll bring him, if I can find him. I'll also fill Master Julian in while I'm out and about, as I know where and when to find him."

"You do that," said Aurus. "We'll keep watch here in case the beastriders come back. I'm going to see how the local populace is taking this."

#

Aurus stepped out the side door he had originally entered through. The same man from before stood by the entrance. On his right hip rode a gold tube.

"How are you doing, sir?" asked Aurus. "I'm surprised you're still here after that bombardment earlier."

"Oh, I ducked inside during all that. It just shook the ground and made some holes. When it was done I came back out."

The grounds were a mess with the holes from Marvin's missile fire. Their colored exhaust had left multicolored patches about, lending it an air of surprising beauty.

"So, is Her Benevolent Presence, Lyndia of the Talons, done with you?" the man asked. "You've been in there a long time."

"She's done and gone, I'm afraid. I've been in and out a few times since then."

"Didn't see you leave."

"You wouldn't have. I'm sorry to say I had to kill her and many of the other beastriders."

The guard reached for his tube, but stayed his hand.

"Didn't kill all of them?"

"No. They may return, but I control the tower now. I appreciate your restraint in not drawing that weapon, but it wouldn't matter since we turned off the broadcast power from the generator."

"Don't care, really. Not here because I want to be. They've mostly left us alone since they arrived, except when we bring in food, or when they take the women. Other than that, we're ignored."

"I'll see what I can do about letting you all live your own lives again, but the beastriders may still be dangerous for a time. I'd appreciate it if you continue to guard the door until then, and let us know if any riders return."

"Sure. And I appreciate that you're doing something for us, though I get the feeling our lives are only incidental to you."

"Hey, I'll do what I can for you. Right now I've got some scouting to do."

He launched himself into the sky, leaving the guard with a slack jaw and wide-eyed stare.

Chapter Fifteen
New Kid on the Block

Near the end of a very long day, Aurus, Nea, and Zen welcomed the newest member of their little clique. The newcomer wore black pants, green jacket, and had red hair. Zen introduced him.

"This is Dorian Fell, a marksman highly recommended by Marvin. We need to explain what's happened and what we're trying to accomplish here. Just bring him up to speed."

"Before that," said Aurus, "how about he shows us what he can do, so we can plan accordingly?"

"Fine with me," said Dorian. "For starters, throw something expendable into the air."

Out of a wooden box he'd been snacking from, Aurus grabbed a yellowish, hockey puck sized disk, and tossed it up. It fell, instantly transfixed by a dagger.

"Nice," said Aurus. "Do more, since these aren't much good for eating anyway. They're either mashed popcorn, or Styrofoam."

Aurus threw another half-dozen disks, each struck dead center by a dagger.

"Where are you getting all those daggers from?" asked Nea.

"What daggers?" asked Dorian.

When everybody glanced at the fallen disks not a dagger was to be seen. Dorian held one in each hand.

"Magic daggers?" asked Zen.

"Yes, but only in that they can strike creatures immune to

normal weapons and will return to my hands instantly if I will it. Oh, and I never need to sharpen them.

"Throw one up again, and I'll do a trick slow enough for you to see it."

Aurus tossed another disk and Dorian struck it with a dagger, which vanished, then another hit as it fell. When Aurus picked it up, dagger still in place, he saw only one hole. Dorian reached, and the dagger appeared in his hand.

"Is this for real?" asked Aurus, "the second was in the exact same hole. You sure that isn't magic?"

"Maybe it is, but it's my magic, not the dagger's."

"That's great and all," said Zen, "but how are you with rifles?"

"Never touch the stuff," said Dorian. "I'm more of a bowman."

Nea raised an eyebrow.

"That's going to be something of a problem," said Zen. "In all likelihood we're going to need the firepower, more than bow-and-arrows can provide."

"I'm sure I'll make do. Just tell me what needs to be done, and I'll do it."

"I don't know about that," said Aurus. "Marvin gave you the green light, but —"

"I'm here," shouted Master Julian, who had just walked through the doorway. "Fill me in on everything and introduce me to the new team member. Wait."

He stared at Dorian for a moment.

"Florinald, sir, I didn't recognize you with red hair at first. Pardon me for interrupting."

Dorian/Florinald slapped himself in the forehead.

"Great. Thanks for blowing my cover, Julian. I've been here like a minute."

Julian blinked and stared for a moment.

"I don't understand," he said. "You're undercover?"

"Using a fake name, anyway," said Florinald.

"Oh, I apologize. Why?"

"So I could be just one of the gang, with no special privileges or high expectations."

"You *are* Florinald ValDurian then," said Nea. "I had suspected, from something Marvin said, but why hide your true identity?"

"You're Nea, right? Like I just said to Julie here, to be nobody special, just your average substitute Knight off the street."

"Thought we'd treat you differently?" asked Aurus.

"Of course you would, and will. I technically outrank everybody here, so I could screw up an entire mission by giving orders when I don't know what I'm doing. Which would be all the time."

Looking to make a comment, Zen raised a finger, then changed his mind.

Florinald continued.

"I'm not the powerhouse the rest of my family are. In fact, it wouldn't be a stretch to say I'm the least of my family. The only thing I have going for me is my skill with missile weapons, but that's exactly why I can be here right now."

He hesitated, but nobody else said anything.

"My multilayered and mysterious family is prevented from doing a lot of things by our Wyrd. It protects and empowers us, but also restricts us. As you probably all know we can't interfere all that much with other dimensions usually. In this case though, the dimensions in question are interfering with other dimensions, so that gives me something of a loophole. Even more, since my power level is so negligible I can't upset the overall scheme of things very much. In fact, you're all probably more powerful than I am."

"Then, with all due respect, Sir Florinald," said Zen, "why are you here?"

"No 'sir', just 'Florinald.' As to why I'm here; because I can help, despite my shortcomings. Tell me what needs to be done and I'll do it if I can."

"Can you use Marvin's ordnance?" asked Aurus.

Florinald made his dagger disappear.

"Depends on what it is. I'm not allowed to use self-powered projectile or energy weapons, but I have a possible, clumsy workaround for that. I can also set landmines or booby-traps with the best of them."

"I'm sure you'll be great," said Nea. "Now then, Master Julian, aren't you here for a meeting?"

"Of course. Does this place have a conference room?"

\#

The five sat at a large, wooden table. Julian handed out electronic tablets all around.

"That's what the other teams have learned. You've all done a spectacular job in containing the V'Laubi menace thus far. To this point we've managed to avoid calling in the Untari for an extinction event, and I hope that continues. The V'Laubi have several strong bases remaining though, and I may have to combine you with other teams for the toughest ones."

"Who would be in charge of a combined team?" asked Zen.

"That depends on the resulting team. I'll make sure it's all figured out before any missions commence. Don't want to ruffle anybody's feathers. Before that, I'll make sure everybody is properly equipped."

He pulled a tablet device from a box he'd placed on the floor.

"Could you hand me your scanner, please, Florinald?"

Florinald took a red lens from his jacket and tossed it to Julian, who placed it on the tablet. Julian poked a few buttons on the tablet, and then tossed the lens back to Florinald.

"I just added some modifications. It'll reveal the presence of V'Laubi to you now, just like Zen's contact lenses."

"Cool," said Florinald.

He put the lens over his left eye and it stayed in place, then he looked about the room.

"Welp, none of you are controlled by the blobbies, so I guess we're good. Wait, what if *I'm* controlled?"

"They only possess females," said Nea, "though whether that's merely preference or a biological limitation we don't know."

"I have the contacts in," said Zen. "but I don't see what's scanned for myself."

He held up a laptop, the screen of which showed whatever he was looking at.

"The contacts transmit to my equipment. He's clean."

"As if there were any doubt," said Julian. "To continue, I have a battle plan, or the precursor to one. Aurus and Nea will return to their home base, briefly, with the rest of you."

"That's a plan?" asked Florinald. "What will that accomplish?"

"As they used their Bifrost shards to travel here, little time has passed on that Earth, relative to us. You'll all go there and start the next mission from about a day ago, relative to Clermann. We can hit them while this was going down here, before they could possibly hear about it."

"You see why I get confused about what day it is?" said Aurus to Nea. "This is why the Knights can be so many places at once, despite our low numbers."

"I've got Clermann sealed off," said Zen. "With the portal parts we took, my counter-portal will prevent them from traveling in or out. I've also armed the forest-dwellers with automatic weapons to hold the tower for us while we're gone."

"I thought you weren't going to do that," said Nea.

"Wasn't, but I knew we'd be gone, and I don't want the hollowbacks to take over again."

"What if they just send interdimensional messages instead of using their portals?" she said.

"That isn't a thing," said Zen. "Communicating across dimensions requires the creation of a portal in the first place to open a channel. Even the full-stars can't do it easily. I have no idea how they contact us with magic mirrors and the like."

"Nor do I," said Julian, "but it matters not right now. I'll be bringing in some of the weaker teams to gradually take care of the other towns while you are gone, and I'll be helping them out. Read the info I gave you, then get to Nea's Earth. From there, head out to the next target, given us by the Omnimind. Any questions?"

Nobody said a word.

"Very well. You're dismissed, and good luck."

#

"Pardon my office," said Aurus, "I wasn't expecting company."
"Would it have mattered if you were?" said Nea.
"Not really, no."

135

"Are we ready to move out?" she said.

"By my thinking, yes," said Zen. "Our next target is five armies of V'Laubi possessing very powerful women. They're nomads with no permanent bases. They kidnap and leave, so they'd be hard to track normally, but we know where they're going to be in a few hours, so we can get the drop on them."

"Sounds like fun," said Florinald. "Reminds me of my younger days as an adventurer, and I think we make quite a team. Archer, tech wizard, warrior, and thief, if I may be so bold, Nea."

"I've been called worse, sir."

"Oh, no, not you too. It's 'Florinald,' please."

"Of course. Shall we go to the roof and see what Master Julian has left for us?"

"I have what I need," said Florinald, "but yes."

He held an ornate, golden longbow, and wore a large, arrow-filled quiver upon his back.

They took the stairs to the roof to find stacks of boxes awaiting them.

"Oh, my," said Nea. "A lot of it is Marvin's stuff, and it's heavy. Are we supposed to make several trips?"

"That wouldn't work," said Zen. "What Marvin and I did in the first place was to put all the boxes on little casters, then rope them together and pull the lot like a small train, up over the rainbow. There's more now though."

"I can pull it all, easily," said Aurus.

They went through the boxes to find rope, casters, and steel screw-eyes. With one continuous length of rope, which they knotted at each screw-eye (on the top front of each box), they were lashed together in a line. At the bottom corners of each box, they inserted the casters.

When the boxes were all properly tethered, Zen summoned Bifrost. It started on the rooftop and vanished on the horizon.

"That should give the locals something to point their cameras at," said Zen.

"All aboard," shouted Aurus. "Departing now from Dullsville for Somewhere Over the Rainbow."

"You had to say it, didn't you?" said Zen.

"Yes. Yes, I did."

#

Attendant Javis nodded toward the Grand Elder.

"You may speak," said the Grand Elder.

"The worldlet of Meifiera has fallen."

"Meaning what?" asked the Elder.

"That it is no longer under V'Laubi control."

"Impossible. Those pathetic scum? Refresh me on them."

"Basic, average humanoids, but possessing four eyes in the fronts of their heads."

"Yes, pathetic, little, four-eyed losers. It is impossible they could have rebelled."

"They had outside help, which has commandeered the portals. You, of course, do not need them, as you have access to other dimensional travelers."

"Of course. A small matter which will be dealt with at our convenience. You may go."

Chapter Sixteen
MegaBrawl

They had finished unpacking Marvin's equipment on a low mesa overlooking cracked and dry plains. Amidst the litter of boxes and many deep fissures was a triangular, teepee-like structure, set aside from big gun parts. The sun hung high, and was what they considered normal in color, being a bright yellow.

"Kind of a relief from the green on Clermann," said Zen, who was scanning the horizon with computerized binoculars. "Why wouldn't the hollowbacks pick this mesa, as it's the tallest feature in the area?"

"The question is not why, but how we know they'll be here," said Florinald.

"You aren't used to travel by Bifrost shard, are you?" said Zen, continuing to scan.

"Correct. I have other means. Could you explain, please?"

"Of course he can," said Aurus, while fitting a barrel into the mini-howitzer. "He loves explaining things."

"I do. The shards are keyed to the time frame of a world when we leave it. When we returned to Nea's world we were a day or so in the past of the Clermann we left. The full-stars knew where and when the V'Laubi had entered this worldlet, so we just arrived before they're going to."

"So we can destroy them before they get started?" said Florinald.

"No. We don't want to change any events, and I'm not sure we can anyway. What we will do is destroy their entry point while they're away, then they're stuck here, incommunicado. At that point we'll deal with them."

Florinald rubbed his eyes and shook his head.

"So, you're all on Clermann at this point? Could you or I travel there and warn them of what they'll go through?"

"Hasn't been tried for a long time," said Aurus. "A group of Knights attempted it once and were never seen again. Presumably exterminated by conflicting time lines."

"So, let's not do that," said Zen. "We'll go with the plan Master Julian laid out for us. The hollowbacks are here, or just about. Look where I point."

He handed the binoculars around and they all saw a bus-sized rip in the air, at ground level, half a mile away. It churned with a mix of stars and roiling purple.

"That's it," said Zen. "We wait until they're done and gone from there. Meanwhile, make sure that gun is operational."

While they assembled, so did the V'Laubi. Ponderous parts pulled through the portal were built into a dull metal arch until the portal was sealed, leaving normal air in place of it. The portal was activated, manifesting as a black patch within the arch. As Zen watched, dozens of vehicles and hundreds of beings poured through, arranging themselves into ranks, leaving an open pathway from the portal.

"Is the gun ready?" asked Zen.

"All but the loading," said Aurus, as he stepped away from it.

He grabbed a shell from a nearby pile, then loaded it into the breech.

"Now it's ready."

"Okay. Florinald, you said you had a workaround for using the big gun," said Zen.

"I can't use it myself, but I see no reason why I can't sight it in. I'll get it ready, but someone else has to fire it."

Zen handed him the binoculars, but Florinald waved them away.

"My scanner's all I need," he said, pointing to the red lens over his left eye. "This baby's got everything, including telescopic vision."

Nearly an hour later, the portal was closed, and the assembled forces departed in five different directions.

"What's that they're riding in?" asked Nea while looking through the binoculars.

"GEVs," said Zen, "Ground Effect Vehicles."

"What? I don't know what that means."

"Hovercrafts. A cushion of air keeps them off the ground. An ideal transportation for terrain that broken. May I have the 'nocs, please?"

Nea handed them back.

"I really should have brought more binoculars," said Zen. "I'll tell you when they're far enough away to fire."

Aurus tapped continuously on the howitzer barrel until he annoyed everybody. At about that point, Zen spoke.

"They're over the horizon, and the GEVs make too much noise for them to hear what we're about to do. Fire when ready."

Florinald waved at the howitzer with a flourish.

"Be my guest, madam."

Everyone put on noise-muffling headphones, then Nea fired the gun. Florinald made an adjustment while Aurus loaded another shell.

"Again," said Florinald.

Nea let loose another blast, and that went on for six more rounds while Zen observed the target.

"Nothing remains standing," said Zen. "Stop firing and move out."

They broke apart the triangular structure, which turned out to have been three hang gliders stacked tip-to-tip, points up. They linked them front to back by cables. The first in line had a cable with a triangular handle that Aurus grabbed.

"Ready," he said. "Take your positions and start walking. When I start flying, you start running."

With everyone belted into their own glider, Aurus started walking. They followed suit, and when he thought they were ready, launched himself into the air. They scrambled to keep up, and by then were at the edge of the mesa, feet dangling in the air.

Nea screeched with delight while Zen held his control bar with white knuckles, and Florinald hummed. They made their way swiftly to the portal site while they got a better view of the area. It wasn't worth the look, being a dry, bland, cracked desert.

"We're landing in a moment," yelled Aurus, "so detach your cables and land how I showed you. Don't worry if there's a problem, because I'll help if need be."

They all detached the snap clips on their cables and were flying on their own, though Florinald began wobbling off course. Aurus reined him in and everyone landed safely.

The area was mostly a cratered hole, but there were remains of portal tech and two damaged hovercrafts. The few bodies were of a mauve-skinned lizard race with fangs and finlike ears. Aurus pulled off the yellow plate armor on one, and found a dead V'Laubi in its back.

"Well, that answers the question nobody asked out loud," he said.

Aurus waved his Bifrost crystal around the portal site until the shard pulsed, then he put it away.

"I've connected my crystal to the dimension they came from, so once this mission is put to bed we can assault their presumed homeworld."

"Check it out," said Florinald. "These GEVs don't look so bad off. Maybe we could use them, instead of Aurus towing us everywhere?"

Zen gave them a once-over and determined they could cannibalize parts from the more damaged vehicle to repair the better one.

"One hovercraft coming up," he said.

"We're going to call it a landspeeder," said Aurus.

"What? Why —" said Zen. "I don't care. Landspeeder it is."

#

Half an hour later they were on their way. The landspeeder sat six in a pinch, so they were quite comfortable, even with the weapons Aurus had brought down from their mesa camp.

"I'll fly on ahead," said Aurus, from the front passenger's seat. "That'll also give us a chance to test the speed on this thing, as there's no speedometer. Kick it to the max, Zen."

Aurus launched himself skyward and left the landspeeder behind. Zen grinned and gunned it with a squeeze of the hand throttle. There were no foot pedals.

Zen caught up to Aurus in moments, keeping pace right below him.

"That was easy," yelled Zen. "I don't think this is even at half power."

Aurus shifted into a hawk and shot ahead. Zen gave the throttle a death grip and caught up again, but not as quickly as the first time. After they stayed neck-and-neck briefly, Aurus took his seat in the landspeeder and resumed human form.

"Might want to ease off on the throttle a bit, Zen, just for safety's sake," said Aurus as Zen did just that. "My normal speed as a hawk is between 40-45 miles per hour, but with my magical flight ability I can push it to at least double that, so this thing is pretty fast. I'll go on and act as advance guard."

Aurus shot on ahead as a hawk.

Zen squeezed the throttle, keeping Aurus in sight, but hanging well back. After about an hour, Aurus returned to the speeder, and landed on Nea's outstretched arm, around which she had wrapped her cloak. He hopped into the front seat and returned to human form.

"They have a base camp up ahead. We need to park this soon, so we don't kick up a dust cloud."

They parked the speeder behind a grassy dune, and Aurus gave Nea his watch.

"You three go invisibly and I'll go as a bird. If we try to move as an invisible four-person band there's too big a chance somebody will step out of the perimeter and be seen. I doubt they've identified the birds of this world yet, if there are any, so I shouldn't arouse any interest."

Nea activated the invisibility field and they all glowed bright orange.

"Son of a bitch," snapped Aurus, "this wordlet has built-in defenses against invisibility. That happens often enough, as the rules of magic and science can change from bubble to bubble."

Nea handed him his watch back.

"So, we're stuck with normal stealth then," she said, "since me summoning a fog would probably be suspicious this late in the day. I'm okay with that, since there's a lot of broken ground for cover."

Aurus scouted as a hawk while the others moved as stealthily as they could, each carrying a small mortar with backpack of shells, He returned after a while and told them to set up on a low, sparsely wooded hill. The terrain had changed, now growing meager grass, and was lightly dotted with trees.

"When you're ready, I'll start the attack. Look for my signal."

He transformed again, then flew off. Florinald kept his eye on him.

"Small or not, I can see his heat easily with my scanner, via the infra-red spectrum. I'll let you know when he does anything."

After a tense few minutes, Florinald shouted.

"There it is. Let's go."

A thin red ray lanced from the sky at a V'Laubi hovercraft, then its fuel tank exploded. Aurus hovered above the site in human form, picking more targets with his eye-beams. The rest of the team fired their mortars into the chaos, over and over until their ammo was gone. Nea and Zen ran toward the chaos, using the smoke for cover, while Florinald stayed behind and carefully picked off single targets with his bow.

A gigantic woman warrior in high-tech plate armor fired a large blaster at Aurus, sending his energy shield into the orange, and forcing him to gain altitude. Several women in lesser armor with backpacks dropped to all fours and scattered, running from the target area. Three such ran straight into Zen and Nea.

Moving as though she expected them, Nea ran her gold rapier down the throat of the first, but lost her grip on it as the creature tore away in its death throes. Another one came at her, but she ducked into the shadow of a tree and vanished. The creature paused and looked about, until Nea dropped from another nearby tree and drove her dagger into its right eye. It screamed and died, giving Nea a chance to free her rapier from the first creature.

Zen emptied a clip from his machine gun into another creature until it died. He whirled to see four more charging him and quickly loaded another clip.

"Getting tight here," he said, "and close combat is not my forte.

Little help?"

Even as he spoke, two arrows each took out a creature.

"Much obliged, Florinald."

"My pleasure," said Florinald over his earpiece. "I'm calling them quadramorphs, by the way. Huh, gotta go. Under attack."

His arrows took out three creatures before they closed with him, then he dropped the bow and pulled his daggers. The four-legged mob surrounded him, hesitating, taking their measure of him for a moment.

They rushed him as one, savagely biting at his limbs, dragging him down by sheer weight. He disappeared under the mass of creatures, which continued to tear at him.

The pile lay still until a shredded arm wielding a dagger shot up through it. Quadramorphs were flung left and right until Florinald stood again.

Those creatures still living began to slink away, and he stood in a pile of those unmoving.

"No, you don't, dammit. You don't get to chew on me and just walk away."

He pushed aside the bodies until he uncovered his bow. Then he fired half a dozen arrows in a blur of continuous motion as the creatures broke into a run. Six died, but the others scattered, coming at him from six different directions.

A creature clamped to each of his limbs, apart from two quadramorphs that yanked his bow away and ran. Once again, the others tried to pile on him, but their numbers were far fewer this time, and they only dragged him to his knees.

His daggers were pointed toward his wrists, knife-fighter style, so he slashed the snouts of the two holding his wrists. As they let go, he rolled, dragging the ones on his ankles with him, until a blade in each of their brains ended that threat. The two that had been on his wrists thought better of the fight and bolted for the cover of the forest. A dagger to each back leg hobbled the one on the left, letting Florinald limp after it.

Florinald recalled his daggers, then jumped on the creature, ending its life as the other one turned on him.

In a short, furious, bloody struggle, the only remaining

quadramorph near Florinald was dead. Breathing heavily, he checked himself.

"Blast, I should have worn old clothes. I just bought this shirt. At least it'll make decent bandages."

He tore off his shirt, revealing lacerated skin leaking purple blood. He removed both bracers, then bandaged his arms with strips cut from his shirt.

"My boots were tough enough to protect my feet, so I don't think I'll bleed to death, after the first aid."

He kicked one of the dead quadramorphs.

"You'll need bigger teeth than that to bite clean through my hide. Even a low-powered ValDurian has at least semi-armored skin. And one of you two has my left-hand dagger."

He flexed the fingers of his left hand and a dagger appeared in it.

"Wish I could do that with my arrows, because I'm almost out. 'Course, if I can't find my bow, it won't matter. Can't just chase after them, because I'm sure they'll outrun me."

Florinald stared into the forest, focusing on V'Laubi, and saw two signatures nearby. After adjusting his visual ranges in the scanner, then testing the wind with a wet finger, he gave each dagger a mighty fling.

There was no sound, no reaction, but the V'Laubi faded from his scanner.

Florinald strolled up to his targets in the bushes, finding two quadramorphs transfixed between the eyes with his daggers. The V'Laubi were struggling to leave their dead hosts, but he recalled his daggers and finished them. His bow lay on the ground before them.

"Hey, Zen, Florinald here. I need to collect up my arrows or I won't be of much use around here. You okay with that?"

He got Zen's assent on his ear bud, so he went on an arrow hunt.

Meanwhile, Zen had finished off another quadramorph, while Nea had killed two.

"I think we got lucky," said Zen. "Most of what Florinald is calling 'quadramorphs' have gone after Florinald and Aurus, or just died in the shelling."

"I'm not worried about Aurus," said Nea, "but I hope Florinald is okay. Maybe we should go after him?"

"No, anyone from that family should be fine, despite his assertions to the contrary. Let's move on to the main area we shelled before and hunt for survivors, then trail Aurus."

They jogged ahead to the main spot they had targeted, finding destroyed GEVs and the remains of corrugated metal, pre-fabricated huts. There were several dead quadramorphs, all still in two-legged form and carrying weapons.

"We're out of long-range weapons. Do they have anything we can use?" asked Nea, while poking through a burned-out GEV.

"Maybe. I'll try to figure them out quick-like, then we go after flyboy."

Zen pulled out two heavy rifle-like devices and aimed one at a tree. It fired a cantaloupe -sized projectile at a tree, which became wrapped in tendrils upon impact.

"Huh, a netcaster. I've seen more primitive versions of them. I was really expecting something explosive, to be honest."

"A netcaster makes sense if we assume they're looking for host bodies," said Nea. "That's their whole mission right now, or so we believe. Wouldn't want to blow up somebody useful."

They each grabbed a netcaster and loaded their empty backpacks with projectiles, then took off after Aurus's last known location.

#

Aurus hid in a grove of trees bearing greenish-gray fruit. The armored warrior-woman stomped about, smashing down trees with her armored fists. She looked about warily, pointing her weapon randomly, but not firing.

"Didn't want you, just the women," she thundered, "but you attacked us, so now you die. Could have just left us alone, but no. Now you're mine."

"Should have never come here," said Aurus. "It's my job to see you don't leave under your own power."

He threw a broken tree at her, which she dodged, if just barely, by ducking into standing trees. He flew up again.

"Not bad for a pathetic male, but try this."

She grabbed another broken tree and heaved it at Aurus. He dodged the trunk, but the wide branches caught, pulling him down into a pile of other broken trees.

The woman laughed, then searched for him in the fallen branches. She was joined in the search by two howling quadramorphs armed with netcasters. Meanwhile, Aurus had become a hawk and flitted through the branches to evade discovery. Once free of the branches he became human and killed one quadramorph with his eye-beams, then flew up a large, intact tree.

The warrior stopped searching in the branches and blasted at the tree, making it rather less intact than earlier. Hidden by a flurry of leaves, Aurus hawked-out again and flew to another tree behind the women. As the leaves kept falling from the first tree, the quadramorph kept yowling at it, while the woman looked around.

Still in hawk form, Aurus dove at the warrior from behind in a blur of speed, transforming to human at the last millisecond, knocking her down while the quadramorph kept barking up the empty tree.

He materialized his halberd in preparation for head removal, while the warrior struggled to rise.

He went down as a net hit him in the back, wrapping him with tendrils. He spasmed as an electric charge surged through his body, and dropped the halberd. The quadramorph, still barking, dropped the netcaster and went on all fours. The warrior rose slowly, shaking.

"Unbelievable. That one puny male could knock down Kelvaana. Inconceivable. Time to put the universe to rights by ending you. None of this ever happened."

She grabbed her blaster from where it had fallen beneath her, but as she picked it up it fell apart. She screeched while frantically trying to reassemble the flattened, misshapen mass of useless tech.

"No, no . . . No matter. I'll kill you with your own weapon. How fitting."

Kelvaana picked up the halberd.

Aurus snapped his bonds as two nets stuck Kelvaana in the back. While she untangled herself, he flew up, shredding what was left of his net while electronic shrieking filled the air.

"How come the nets don't hold her?" asked Nea, standing over the now-dead remaining quadramorph.

"My sisters would never harm me," yelled Kelvaana, "but the same cannot be said about you."

She flung a net at Nea, missing, then the other at Aurus, who dodged.

"There's one for the records," said Zen, "The nets *are* V'Laubi. I thought that death scream sounded familiar."

"Regardless, if we can't restrain her she must be killed," said Aurus.

"Nobody restrains Kelvaana. You speak as though you control the options, but even at three to one you are no match for Kelvaana."

She spun the halberd about and sized them up.

"Wait," said Aurus, "There's no need for all of us to fight. Tell you what, Kel, I'll fight you myself, and if you beat me, you get to leave this worldlet under your own power, if you can."

She stared at Aurus intently.

"Why would you give me the advantage? I'm bigger, stronger, armored, and I have your weapon."

"While I'm lighter, faster, and can fly. We both have something to prove here and it won't work unless we go mano a mano. Or is that mano a womano?"

" 'Mano a mano' literally means 'hand to hand,' " said Zen.

"I don't care," thundered Kelvaana as she swung the halberd at Aurus, who dodged easily.

"Figured you'd strike while we were talking," he said. "Typical, not that I blame you, since you know you're going to lose."

He flew up out of range.

"Nea, you and Zen stay out of this, please. I need to vent on her."

"Coward," yelled Kelvaana. "You want to fight, but fly out of harm's way? Face me . . . man."

Aurus dove and kicked her in the gut, knocking her down, but she turned it into a roll and came back to her feet. She swung the blade but he ducked under and rained a flurry of punches to her chin. Staggered, she did an overhand chop that he dodged by closing with her. He grappled with her briefly, then touched the shaft of the halberd, making it vanish.

She froze in astonishment as he broke free of her grip, then jumped back.

"And now you don't have my weapon."

She leapt and grabbed him around the middle, pinning his arms to his side and squeezing.

He tried to position himself for a body throw, but she dropped and rolled over, taking him with her and smashing his head on a tree stump. She came to her knees and drove his skull into the stump again, but his head won, breaking the stump into kindling. Kelvaana got a better grip on Aurus, then glared into his eyes and slammed him against the stump over and over until it was splinters.

Aurus had worked his arms free while she was stumping him, then he punched her unarmored throat with both fists while she still held him. She let him go and fell back, choking, while he attempted to stand and failed.

Head ringing, he only pulled himself erect via his flight power as Kelvaana stood once more. She was at least as unsteady as him and breathing raggedly.

"I can take anything you've got, man. Walk away and live."

Aurus flashed a toothy grin.

"That's a desperate bluff. Here's your motivation: we've destroyed the portal and killed all the rest of your people. If I walk away you're going nowhere. What now?"

Kelvaana screamed and fell to her knees, pounding the ground with her fists.

"Sorry about that, but you were here to kidnap—"

She ripped loose a massive clod of soil and threw it in Aurus's face. His head snapped back and he fell. Kelvaana leapt on him, knees in his gut. His breath exploded out and she grabbed his throat with both hands, then squeezed.

Zen aimed his machine gun at Kelvaana, but Nea pulled it down.

"He asked us to stay out of it. I believe he's got this," said Nea. "Besides, are you a good enough shot to hit her cleanly without hitting Aurus?

Zen shrugged, but lowered his gun.

Aurus punched Kelvaana in her jaw, breaking it. He forced his way free while she was stunned, then kicked her in the head for good measure. She lay unmoving while he pulled her hands behind her back and cuffed her with crystalline manacles that expanded to match her size.

"Not even sure she's alive," he said, "but why take chances?"

Nea ran to him.

"Are you all right? You took quite a beating."

"She took a worse one, and I'm fine, but thanks."

Nea walked around Aurus, brushing dirt from him.

"Besides," he said, "I'll survive anything I can walk away from."

Zen examined the fallen warrior.

"She's alive. Why didn't you blast her in the face with your eye-beams?" asked Zen. "Wouldn't that have been easier than punching her?"

"But not as satisfying. Also, it's hard to concentrate with my airflow cut."

"What happens to her now?" asked Nea.

"Well, I'm not going to just snuff an unconscious foe. And it's not like she chose to be a hollowback. Probably. But that's for another time. We'll keep her restrained, and move on."

They all heard the whining roar of an approaching hovercraft.

Nea and Zen made themselves scarce amongst what remained of the trees, while Aurus awaited the vehicle as he stood with a foot on Kelvaana. As the GEV neared, Aurus saw Florinald driving it.

"Everybody out," said Aurus. "Incoming friendly."

Zen and Nea stepped from hiding as the landspeeder roared to a stop and Florinald leapt out, dressed the same as before the battle, clothes pristine.

"I recovered all sixty-four arrows, so I'm good to go. Now what?"

"We load in the big girl and take her back to their base camp remains," said Aurus. "We'll rig up a holding cell from their scraps, then go after another group."

Just as they were about to leave, there was a moaning, wailing, and crying from the shattered woods. Upon inspection, they found three wretched, bedraggled, pale-skinned people roaming about, whimpering.

"Can we help?" asked Nea.

The three natives looked about, as if unsure where the voice had come from, then went back to crying, moaning and mumbling.

Florinald held up his finger for quiet, listened carefully, then nodded.

"I can understand them. They're bemoaning the destruction of the trees, specifically the loss of fruit, if you can call those gross things fruit. They call them 'dreamfruit.'"

"Meaning they induce dreaming?" asked Zen.

"That's what I'm getting. It's their entire lives, their only source of entertainment and joy."

"What you're saying," said Zen, "is these people are basically lotus eaters."

Facing a sea of blank stares, Zen continued.

"It's from stories related to the Greek pantheon. The lotus was a highly narcotic plant that essentially enslaved the inhabitants of an island. They lived only to eat the lotus and experience the constant euphoria. This sounds like the same thing."

"The problem is," said Florinald, "dreamfruit trees have been destroyed and most of the fruits with them. What hasn't been destroyed is virtually inaccessible to them, being covered by broken trees."

"We bear some responsibility for that," said Aurus. "I can probably collect enough undamaged fruit for them, and maybe even the smushed fruit is good enough."

"The question is though, should we?" asked Nea. "We'd be contributing to the dissolution of a race."

"A race already dissolute," said Zen. "We'd only be repairing some of the damage we caused. Well, mostly caused by the V'Laubi, of course."

Florinald shrugged.

"I don't really know how this should go. I'll take a dreamfruit back for cousin Morninglight to analyze, so that should put us on the right track. Can we get this lot some fruit, then take Giganta to a holding cell?"

"Sounds good," said Aurus. "Once we finish this mission, we'll get instructions on how to handle the lexus eaters."

"Lotus eaters," said Zen.

Chapter Seventeen
This Is the Song that Never Ends

"Is this going to be the master formula for all our battles on this worldlet?" asked Aurus.

Florinald was gathering up his arrows after having helped decimate a horde of tailed, clawed women. Zen and Nea were in close combat with the stragglers, while Aurus was facing a large woman with four bladed tentacles instead of arms.

"Seems pretty normal to me," said Nea with a blank expression, "but would you rather I face the tentacle monster instead?"

"No, that's okay. Nice of you to offer though."

"Think nothing of it," she said, while skewering a tailed woman. "Only offered because these lesser evils are boring."

"Even this one is dull. She's certainly no Kelvaana," said Aurus.

The woman-thing screeched, and lashed at Aurus with renewed intensity.

"You dare compare me with that weakling?"

Two tentacles grabbed and halted his halberd while the other two slashed him with greater fervor.

"I dare compare. She had the flair, while you're naught but air, so there."

The halberd vanished from his right hand and reappeared in his left. He pierced her abdomen from the front, one-handed, skewering through to the V'Laubi in her back. The halberd vanished again, and, as she fell, it reappeared for a two-handed stroke that removed her head.

"Why bother killing her?" asked Zen. "She'd have been helpless with her puppet master dead."

"I didn't want the host to suffer. I could give her that much."

His halberd vanished again, and his lacerations and clothing were visibly healing.

"Nice trick with the halberd hand-switch," said Nea. "Never saw that before."

"First time. I've been wanting to try that for a while, and this creature seemed weak enough to risk it. Wouldn't have tried that with Kelvaana."

"You seem taken with Kelvaana. Are you sweet on her?" asked Nea.

#

The Knight crew was ensconced on a cliffside, the landspeeder far below at ground level.

"I can see their next encampment," said Zen. "This one is in full swing, with holding cells and prisoners. This one we can't just blow to hell without killing innocents."

"Just as well," said Florinald, "we're starting to run low on Marvin's ordnance. Looks like we're talking 'stealth mission' this time."

"My specialty," said Nea. "I'll go in for a close look."

"I hate stealth missions," said Aurus. "But then again, one slip-up and it's a brawl, so we'll probably end up in a fight anyway."

"Well, let's try to avoid that for now, if you could. I've got the audio-video contacts in, so if you could give a gal a lift?"

He picked Nea up in his arms, then jumped skyward.

"Where to?" he asked.

"That clump of thick woods on the left," she said, pointing.

He dropped forward slightly, and she put an arm around his neck to hold on tighter.

"Don't worry, Nea. Just a little fluctuation in air resistance. I'd never drop you."

"I know, but you missed our target back there."

She pointed behind them.

"Damn. Sorry. Distracted."

He doubled back, then they landed in the forest.

After getting her bearings, Nea created a shadowgate on a large tree.

"That's in case I need a quick getaway. Could you please wait here, in case I need help? I'll be able to contact Zen through the lenses, and he can contact you through the earbud."

"Or I could just follow you as a bird?"

"Perhaps, but we haven't seen any other birds, so you might attract attention."

"Okay, fair point. I'll keep an eye out from here."

"You won't see me, but stay alert."

She melted into the underbrush.

"Zen," he said, "you there?

Aurus heard Zen over his earbud.

"I'm here. How are things on your end?"

"Fine. I'm a little worried about Nea though, walking alone into the lioness's den."

"She'll be fine. This is what she does."

"I suppose. Doesn't mean I can't worry."

#

Nea flitted through shadows, made easy by the setting sunlight on crude holding cells casting shadows. Full holding cells. All women, of course.

She sent the encampment's layout to Zen while scoping out the enemy. They had ten GEVs, ten cells, and twenty metal personnel huts, along with what looked like electric street lamps, currently off. The grunt forces were four-eyed women.

"I wonder where *they're* from?" asked Nea, who had ensconced herself in a nearby stand of trees. "And yes, I was being sarcastic, if you're listening. Haven't seen many four-eyed people besides the ones from Clermann, not counting those who wear glasses.

"Once Florinald has himself together, can you send him to the point opposite Aurus in case I need aid? I don't plan on starting a pitched brawl, and I'm hoping to free the women so that we can shell this place. Failing that, I'll skulk about and kill them one by one.

"For the record, there's about seventy grunts, and their leader is a beastrider, minus the camelcat. Just a big, four-eyed, toe-taloned, furry lady now, but armed. Not with paralo-ray tubes, because they probably don't have a generator going yet. Energy blaster, like the one Kelvaana had.

"Basic machine guns for a few of the grunts, plus clubs and swords, with netcasters all around. The mission proceeds at my discretion, so I'm going in."

Nea faded into the shadows and examined the holding cells. They were simple buildings of corrugated metal, with padlocked doors. The simplicity made her laugh silently.

Freeing the women is easy, but they won't get far unless I take out the guards. Hmmm; big girl or little girls first?

She examined the guards' buildings and found them to be little better than those of the captives. No padlocks, but simple inner deadbolt locks for their own security.

I should be able to do this without mass slaughter, and I just thought of how to get the women out.

She went to the nearest holding cell and slipped under the door in shadow. The pale women gasped as she materialized, but Nea put a finger to her lips in the apparently multiversal sign for 'zip it,' and they did.

"I'm here to get you ladies out, so bear with me for a moment."

She went to the rear wall, which had the best shadow available, and created a shadowgate.

"Four of you hug me as tight as you can, and move when I do."

They nodded, then Nea walked them through the gate, and back to the tree by Aurus.

"Aurus, start leading them off, single file, but make sure the last girl is within sight of the tree. I'll keep adding more to the line as we go. Girls, he'll watch over you until I get everybody out. Going back for more."

She stepped through the tree.

#

She cleared out the cell in fairly short order, then decided to try something to ensure the entire pack of guards couldn't follow. Going to each guard hut, if they were occupied she locked the deadbolts from outside with her lock picking tools. She then phased pebbles into the locks through the keyholes with her shadow powers to make them unable to be opened by any traditional method.

Nea went back to rescuing the women, and succeeded in freeing those from six cells, but after she had delivered the latest batch to the end of Aurus's line, they heard the clamor of alarm bells from the encampment.

"Damn," said Nea.

She sped through the forest to the head of the line to talk with Aurus.

"Somebody was actually doing their job and checked in on the prisoners. Either that, or some hollowbacks tried to get out of their huts and couldn't. Regardless, Aurus, could you escort these girls away at their top walking speed?"

"Can do. Ladies, if you would pick up the pace, please? Stay in single file, if you would. Keep it orderly and the invaders will have trouble following us."

While the girls marched off, Nea spoke to Zen, or so she assumed.

"I know you heard all that. I'll try to free the remaining girls, but we'll probably need Florinald to take out some guards for a distraction at the very least. I know you can't respond to me directly, so I hope you have a way to contact Florinald."

Nea slipped back through the shadowgate, to the cell she'd just emptied.

"Four more cells to go. I can do this if Florinald keeps the guards occupied."

She looked out of the cell to see dozens of guards milling about. They scattered in all directions when fireballs exploded amongst them. They were driven from the area of the remaining four cells, so Nea slipped out through the shadows.

In haste, Nea slipped into the next cell and began transporting the prisoners. When they arrived at the shadowgate tree, Nea spoke.

"Your friends and fellow captives are up ahead, but you'll get lost going after them in the dark. Hide here, and watch the fires at the base. If you see any guards coming this way then run. If not, stay put, and I'll get you away when I can."

Nea returned to the base and transported the remaining women from the seventh cell.

"Only three cells to go. I can do this. If that's Florinald firing at them, tell him to keep it up as long as he can."

The next cell had a dozen guards hiding behind it, outside, because they'd apparently figured out where the fireballs were coming from. A lone guard approached from the left and gestured wildly to the ones already there, then pointed to the distance and off to the right. The dozen guards ran in the direction the new one had pointed.

"That was convenient," said Nea, as she stepped from the cell's shadows and killed the new guard.

"Zen, this dead one directed a batch of them that way," she said, pointing.

"If they've found Florinald's position, tell him to move. I'm going into this cell."

Nea filtered into the cell through the slotted windows. This one had only eleven women.

"Hi, ladies. The pandemonium is a prison break. I'm going to get you out. Already freed most of your friends."

There were nods and no chatter as Nea made another portal. In a couple of minutes she had freed the eleven.

"Two cells to go. I've got this."

She slid outside under the door just as the electric street lights snapped on. The local shadows were gone, and Nea cried out as she fell to the ground. Several guards turned at the sound. Weakened, Nea whipped her cloak around herself, then fog billowed from it. She crawled to the side of the cell as guards stumbled around the fog blindly where they had last seen her.

Panting lightly, Nea got back to her feet. Moving swiftly and silently, she left the fog and found the shadows at the edges of the street lights.

As Nea was about to melt into the shadows an impact knocked her to the ground.

Tentacles wrapped her tightly, and shocked her to numbness.

Let my warmth enfold you and comfort you. In the end we will stride the land as a queen. None will stand against us. All will bow before you.

Nea reeled against the mental assault as she struggled to focus. She lay half in the shadow and willed herself to use its power, but could not.

Resistance is not only futile but pointless. Why would you deny the power I can give you? That hurts us both but mostly you.

The V'Laubi kept its grip, but Nea's cloak, wrapped around her body, spared her the worst of the electric shock. She tried to wriggle down, out of the cloak.

The electric lamps exploded, one after the other, but in almost the same instant. The V'Laubi, startled, relaxed its grip slightly, letting Nea shed the cloak and V'Laubi with it. Her gold rapier flickered in the firelight as she slashed the hollow back to pieces.

She re-donned her cloak.

"Zen, I'm free, but weakened. I couldn't get the rest of the girls out yet, but I haven't given up. If Flor can keep up the barrage I might make it."

A blazing star lightened the night sky briefly, then the light condensed to Aurus as he bore down on the camp like a meteor. When he hit the camp's center, light exploded, dazing most of the grunts, but Nea had shaded herself with her cloak. The beastrider, having been the focus of Aurus's impact, lay in a crater of his making. So little of the beastrider's body remained it was scarcely identifiable.

The remaining grunts scattered into the surrounding forest.

Nea rushed to the nearest full cell and opened it. The bewildered girls rushed out and Nea pointed them to the woods. She opened the final cell.

"Follow your sisters, that way."

She pointed into the woods as Aurus landed in front of her.

"Good work," she said, "but those girls in the woods are going to need your help, especially with all the escaped grunts."

"Don't sweat it. I ran into an army of their people in the woods, and they weren't about to take this invasion lying down."

"Thank the ValDurians."

Nea's knees buckled, but Aurus caught her.

"Easy, I've got you. Not that you really needed my help. You freed most of them already on your own."

"May I sleep now?"

#

The Knight crew gathered at a table in one of the hollowback huts, with a pale man and woman from the local populace.

". . . and that's the story," said Zen. "They want your women and we want to stop them."

"And thank you we do," said the pale man, "we want our women to remain."

"Of course you do," said the pale woman, "without us you'd have to do all the work yourselves."

"All? Men already do all the hunting, heavy lifting, and hut building. Women pick fruit and cook."

"Don't even get me started," she said. "Men would be lost without us."

"AHEM," yelled Zen. "We aren't here to help you through a cultural revolution, we're here to stop aliens from kidnapping women. You can work out the division of labor on your own time.

"Thessera, how goes the training?"

"With excellence, Lord Zen," said the woman. "The girls are learning to shoot those captured guns while the men are trying to drive the flying cars and build defenses."

"Please don't call me 'Lord.' How is the driving going, Racknuh?"

"We've only broken two of the floating vehicles, but we're getting the hang of it. Wouldn't it make more sense for the women to drive and the men to shoot?"

"No. Women tend to be better shots than men. The panel is still out on driving. All we want you to be able to do is defend yourselves if any of the hollowbacks return. We aren't trying to give your people advanced weaponry, and will likely take all of what you have with us when this is all over.

"If there are no further matters that need tending to, you may leave."

He nodded to the locals, who left the building.

"Are there Knight matters that need tending to?" asked Zen.

"A few questions, anyway," said Nea. "Florinald, I assume it was you that shot out the street lights?

"It was. Easy shots."

"Thank you for that. Zen, how did you contact Florinald so that he'd know to attack the enemy base?

"Simplicity. I lit some tiny torches, snuffed them out, and held them up in a rack when needed. The number of them was a code, and he could see the remaining heat easily in the infra-red with his lens."

"Okay, but where did all that firepower come from, Flor?"

Florinald gave a sheepish grin.

"I've always had it, but try to conserve it. With my bow and arrows at full power I'm nearly the equal of the other family members, but such arrows are expended in one shot, irrecoverable. You can see why I try to stretch it out."

"Not really," said Aurus. "I'm sure you could get more, but we'll talk about that later."

"I have only one more item," said Nea. "When we were getting the training set up, I talked with the women, and they were eager to give me an earful. Their men are not the most enlightened, so we had long gab sessions, but that's not the important part right now. It turns out that dreamfruit we came across has been something of an issue amongst these people for quite a while now. Many towns have been devastated by it, completely falling apart when the inhabitants are on the fruits constantly. This group hasn't had it so bad, but the women are trying to take action against the fruit suppliers, and I'm afraid the modern weapons would give them that opportunity."

Aurus frowned and scratched his head.

"I understand your concern, but we have to focus on the V'Laubi right now. If the women take the law into their own hands it's their law and their hands. We didn't supply the weapons. They're booty from an alien invasion."

"We did train them though," said Zen.

"I know, but we can only deal with so much at once. If these women end up doing something good I'll be happy, even if we can't condone it officially," said Aurus.

"I have one more item of some concern," said Zen. "I wondered if it should be mentioned. When the outside lights came on and weakened Nea they shouldn't have. I checked their system and they were timed to come on at least twenty minutes later."

"That is concerning," said Nea. "Did someone take the initiative to light the camp for their benefit?"

"Seems unlikely," said Zen, "but I don't suppose we'll ever know. Just thought I'd mention it."

"Anyway, we still have active hollowbacks to hunt," he said.

Chapter Eighteen
Bad Vibe Hunting

Aurus transformed from golden hawk to man midair, did a somersault, and landed on his feet in the training field in front of Nea. He bowed with a flourish.

Nea acknowledged him with a nod, then excused herself from the training field and gathered Zen and Florinald together. A few minutes later the four Knights met up.

"I've been scouting," said Aurus. "I located the remaining two encampments and both are fairly near here, but in opposite directions."

"Which one are we hitting first?" asked Zen.

"That's open for debate. The one to the West is run by a forty-foot-long snake that has flying squirrel-girls for grunts. The eastern one has a demonic-looking, winged boss and its grunts are the same mauve-skinned lizard race with fangs and fin-ears that we saw at the portal site."

"Which one is closer?" asked Nea.

"The demonic boss," said Aurus.

"Then we should hit her first, yes?"

"No. If the grunts are the same as the portal guards that would probably make them part of the faction running the show currently. We'll hit the snake-thing first."

"Why?" asked Zen. "It would be logical to hit the closest first, and you said it was open for debate."

"Yes, to both statements, but there are other factors to consider: One, the squirrel-girls can probably respond faster if we attack the other faction. I know they don't help each other, but they could find us at our worst after a battle with the others. Two, if the lizards are of the dominant faction that makes demon girl the Final Boss of this worldlet, and you fight the final boss last."

"Are you equating this to a video game?" asked Zen.

"Why not? They tend to have logical patterns. As for your second statement, I said it was open for debate, but I'm still making the final decision. The one being closer isn't really a major factor, but the response time is. We're hitting the snake monster first."

"Fine," said Zen, "I don't suppose it makes much difference in the long run."

"Anything to add, Florinald?" asked Aurus.

"Not a blessed thing. I'll just go where you point me."

#

Zen parked their landspeeder at the base of a hill and climbed it with the others. It had a crown of low trees which gave them adequate cover.

"Like last time, this lot has captives, so we can't blast them indiscriminately," said Aurus. "There's eight hovercraft, eight holding cells, and fifteen metal personnel huts, along with electric street lamps. The snake lies coiled up in the middle, out in the open."

"I'll make sure to be wary of those lamps when it's dark," said Nea. "Won't let that take me by surprise again."

"With any luck we won't even be here in the dark," said Aurus. "It's only mid-afternoon."

"We have visitors," said Florinald, as he pointed behind them.

Five GEVs loaded with armed locals were roaring up behind them, the women hooting and hollering. With a look bordering on horror, Aurus flew down to meet them, hovering at the level of the GEVs.

"Folks, folks, cut the engines and the hollering. We're about to engage the enemy and were counting on the element of surprise."

The turbines stopped, the hovercrafts settled down, and the

yelling fell to a dull roar.

"That's better. Why are you here?"

A woman dressed in crude leathers, her face covered in black berry juice as a garish mask, held up a machine gun.

"Saw you leave in your floater, lord, and I knew you were going to assault the body snatchers. I decided we should follow and help."

"Well, that's admirable . . . Thessera, is it? But we have a plan. I don't want you all getting killed, especially without a purpose. You should go home now."

"Pardon me, lord, but this is our world, our homes, and our sisters. They don't get to take us without a fight. Besides, we have a god on our side, so how can we lose?"

"What god? A local?"

They all laughed and raised their guns high.

"Such humility. . .You, my lord."

Thessera laughed, and they all bowed, still in their seats.

"What makes you think I'm a god?" *Not that I haven't passed as such in my day.*

Thessera pointed at him.

"Your feet do not touch the ground, my lord."

Aurus looked down to find himself still floating at raised-up hovercraft level. He sank to the ground.

"I didn't mean to show off. Look, my fellow Knights and I will be attacking the body snatchers soon enough. You all just stay back and we'll take care of things."

He flew back to the top of the hill.

"The natives are getting restless. Can you believe it? They were going to attack the hollowback base on their own. I put a stop to that though."

They heard a roaring of GEVs behind them again.

"Looks like you aren't quite so persuasive as you thought," said Zen. "They're heading for the encampment."

"Oh, for crying out loud. They're all going to die," said Aurus. "I'd better stop them."

"Wait," said Nea, putting her hand on his arm. "I think our element of surprise is gone now, and maybe they'll be of some use in squirrel hunting."

Aurus grimaced.

"Fine. Having no good options, let's go with that. I'll go on ahead to soften up the hollowbacks, and act as a distraction again. The rest of you take the landspeeder and stay with the locals. Try to keep them alive, please?"

"Will do, boss," said Zen. "I've been itching to try out this captured blaster anyway."

"We're on the job," said Nea. "Give the hollowbacks hell while we ride herd on our new, annoying friends."

Aurus hit the sky as the other Knights ran to the landspeeder. He quickly caught up with the natives, as they were not running the GEVs at full throttle. He flew alongside the lead vehicle.

"Thessera," he yelled, "I'm going to try and blind the body snatchers with my radiance."

His body glowed briefly at low power to show her what he meant. When he stopped, Thessera's eyes were wide and filled with tears of wonder. Also from the glare.

"It'll be much brighter than that, so when I raise my arm, all of you close your eyes for a count of 'three.' Otherwise you'll be blinded as well. I'll tell the others."

Blank-faced, Thessera nodded as Aurus flew off to the other allied GEVs. When he was done, he flew toward the V'Laubi base, to meet the fleet of seven hostile GEVs now roaring in their direction.

The landspeeder of Knights caught up with the locals, so Aurus reminded them of the plan through his earpiece.

"I know you heard me talk to the locals, Zen, but tell the rest to make sure and cover your eyes as well. Don't need anybody stumbling about or driving blind."

He flew toward the approaching V'Laubi hovercraft. Drawing closer to them, he hovered in place for a moment.

"This is it guys, prepare for whiteout."

He glowed dimly, then raised his arm.

"Eyes shut."

He let loose a brief glow such as to make any sun jealous. Cutting the glow he glanced about to see the allied GEVs careening off course, but still intact, while the landspeeder was steady on. The squirrel-crewed GEVs had been in close formation and some had collided with each other.

Aurus was about to attack the enemy when a beam of blue-white surged by him from up ahead, burning a patch on the ground. The snake-thing in the camp had a glow in its mouth that was now fading.

"Great. Didn't know you could do that. Guys, did you see that?"

"Saw that," said Zen. "Didn't count on enemy artillery. Could be a problem."

"I'll take it out," said Aurus. "Since it's in the middle of camp, don't let Florinald blow it up, because the captives are still there. Take out the squirrel-girls and protect the locals."

Halberd in hand, Aurus flew toward the monster snake.

"I'm the distraction again, you giant hose monster. Comin' atcha."

He glowed again, not so bright as the first time, but enough to make him the most obvious target available. Not being immensely stupid, he flew in an erratic pattern.

Zen gunned the landspeeder, flanking the squirrel grunts and coming up behind them. Florinald fired precious arrows that became fireballs and lightning storms on impact, mostly making his precision archery unnecessary. Nea let fly a blaze of machine gun fire, while Zen tried to keep the landspeeder behind the line of enemy GEVs. He hoped to avoid any random gunfire from the allied locals that way.

Two of the allied GEVs had collided with each other, despite being widely separated at first. The men stayed with the wrecks, helpless, while the uninjured women jumped out screaming, guns blazing at the enemy.

Aurus closed with the snake, and decided it looked more like a chunky, armor plated worm. It was white, forty-foot-long and five in diameter, with jagged projections surrounding the mouth. A dozen blue, crystalline eyes surrounded that. It apparently had trouble focusing on him at close range, missing widely, so he flew to its back, or at least the side that was currently on top, and began hacking at it with his halberd. To no effect.

He focused his efforts on a discolored patch in the middle of its back.

"If you're V'Laubi, and you are, that's where the puppetmaster lives."

He assaulted the rough patch to little effect, and was rewarded by a blue-white beam knocking him to the ground as his energy shield went white. Tumbling about, he launched himself back into the air.

"You're more agile than I thought to be able to twist about like that, but I know one spot where you can't zap me."

He flew to the creature's front and grabbed hold of a jagged protrusion around its mouth, staying clear of the opening. He began smashing crystal eyes with the halberd and after the second, a high-pitched, electronic V'Laubi scream nearly shook him apart.

"Got you," said Aurus, grinning.

The snake writhed, smashed its head on the ground, then blasted at random. The beam damaged an inactive, large GEV and barely missed a shed full of captives.

Damn, you're going to destroy your captives trying to get me. Got to be another way.

While he dodged another blast, a glance at the battlefield told him things were going well enough for his side. A message from Zen said the same thing.

Only one other way, dammit.

"Things could be better here, Zen, but I've got this. Don't worry."

#

Three allied GEVs were in action against four of the enemy's. Gray-furred girls jumped high, using natural membranes attached to their sides, stretching from wrists to ankles for gliding. They were unclothed, save for colorful ribbons trailing from their wrists and necks. Big, fluffy tails completed the squirrel look, their hands bearing nine-inch claws as an added bonus.

Some squirrels carried machine guns, but couldn't fly while using them. Combat was a physical cacophony of melee, missile fire, and mayhem. The allied men charged into combat wielding axes while the women shot whom they could. Florinald took out large swaths of squirrels with ball lightning and ice storms while Nea used the mid-day shadows in the grain field to go where she would and take out choice ground targets. Zen drove the landspeeder to stay with the enemy, but had to stop in order to fire his new blaster. It was quite effective, and he took out an enemy GEV himself. He contacted Aurus.

"Things are good here, 'Great One.' Don't expect us any time soon to help with the giant white snake. Hope things are okay, love, Zen and the gang."

The snake swallowing Aurus grabbed Zen's attention, so he missed the reply.

Chapter Nineteen
Back From the Depths

The white snake fired a blue-white burst at the approaching landspeeder, but Nea jumped up in front on its engine cowling. The beam dispersed on her energy shield, sending it into the white.

"I'm going to hide us," she said. "Follow my directions."

Nea whipped her cloak about, raising a fog bank about them that traveled with her.

"Cut your speed, Zen. Hang right and keep going."

"I'd just fire into the middle of the fog, if I couldn't see in," said Florinald.

"Which is what I'm counting on. I don't have to be in the middle, and I'm not. The center is about fifty feet to our left."

"Excellent," said Zen. "Meanwhile the snake is focusing on us and not our allies."

"Speaking of which," said Florinald, "they need a little help."

He fired an arrow behind them, and it burst into a colorful lightning storm outside the fog.

"What was that for?" asked Zen. "I thought you didn't want to waste any arrows."

"Don't, and didn't, but our allies needed a little help, so I took out the last big mass of airborne squirrels. The locals should be fine now."

"Left turn, five degrees," said Nea. "How could you have known that, Florinald?"

He tapped his eyepiece.

"Told you, this baby has everything. I can see through the fog clearly with my left eye."

"Quite so. I forgot. Maybe you should be driving then?"

"Or you? I suck at it, but I can loan my scanner to Zen."

Zen fitted the scanner over his left eye.

"That's better. Wow. You've got quite the readouts here, and they're distracting."

"Ignore everything but your sight," said Florinald, "and drive us where we need to go."

Another beam of energy struck nearby, rocking the landspeeder.

"It's zeroing in on us somehow," said Zen, "unless that was random. I can steer on my own, Nea, so don't worry about directions."

Another beam struck, even closer.

"Hey, if I'm seeing these green bars right, that was weaker than the previous burst," said Zen.

"It's Aurus," said Nea, gripping her weapons more tightly. "I knew he wasn't dead."

Zen veered into a wide right as they climbed the hill upon which the enemy base and white snake sat. The creature fired another burst that went well wide of them.

"That one's even weaker," said Zen, "so I think you're right about Aurus."

A glowing form burst from the back of the snake, hurtling skyward until it exploded with radiance. The snake collapsed, its eyes and mouth dimming. From the mouths of the locals, the Knights heard a growing chant.

They bellowed, "Aurus, Aurus, Aurus," over and over for at least a minute.

Aurus, for it was indeed he, dropped into the landspeeder slowly, taking a seat in the back. His entire body was charred, with barely a scrap of clothes remaining.

Nea poured some water from a canteen into a cloth and rubbed his face gently. He responded with a smile, then grabbed the canteen and drained it. He coughed, than sat back and opened a box of ration bars.

"So what happened there?" asked Zen. "I saw the snake eat you and figured it was all over."

"It didn't eat me. I fed myself to it. In my attempts to blind it, random blasts could have destroyed the captives, so I went inside. Figured it'd go back to blasting the locals before I could kill it, but I knew you guys would be on the job."

"How did you kill it?" asked Nea. "Attacked delicate internal organs?"

"It barely has any internal organs. No, being armed, I was almost literally a heavy metal poison to the white snake, so the farther down I went, the more damage I did. The energy blast-generation area ended a third of the way down, and was basically the entire interior until then, so I couldn't destroy that, only damage it."

"Though it almost destroyed you," said Florinald.

"True, but my energy shield held out most of the way, until it didn't. My beams were useless, so I tried cutting the spine, but that was armored until I got to the spot where the V'Laubi was attached. I attacked for all I was worth, which wasn't as much as I'd have liked, considering how cramped it was inside."

"But the second main thing was that you did it," said Nea. "The first was that you lived."

"Now we can rest," said Aurus. "I'm in no shape for assaulting the last base right now. This one was really tough. In fact, I wonder if this damn snake might have been the actual final boss? We'll hit the other base later."

Zen was about to comment, but Florinald jumped in first.

"Unfortunately, we don't have that kind of time. The last faction is leaving their base, probably intent on taking their captives to the V'Laubi homeworld."

"Fuck 'em," said Aurus. "We destroyed the portal, so they're going nowhere. We'll get 'em tomorrow."

"I don't think we will. Since I could see their base from up here, I could see their leader in detail, and she's a doozy. I wish you'd described her better before."

"Don't drag it out. What is she?" asked Aurus, a touch of anger in his voice.

"A Quanilith demon. Those can traverse the planes on their own, and she's probably the one who opened that portal to this world in the first place. They can leave."

"Flaming bitches of every hell everywhere," yelled Aurus. "Let's get going. The landspeeder can go as fast as me at my best, and I'm not. Let me eat, drink, and nap. Then I'll be better at least by the time we catch up."

"None of us are in great shape," said Zen. "We'll need sleep too."

"That's okay," said Florinald, "I never sleep, so I can drive, at least well enough to follow them, if I don't have to make any crazy turns."

"You never sleep?" asked Nea.

"Never, though I can bring on sleep if need be, so hardly ever anyway."

"Eyes to the right," said Zen. "Aurus's fan club is here."

Two remaining functional GEVs were roaring up to the base, their crews screaming Aurus's name.

"Oh, bloody hell. I look like incinerated garbage. Hold them back and give me a minute."

Aurus ducked down while Nea leaped out to meet the locals. She was met by Thessera and her driver, Racknuh, who had both jumped out of their vehicle.

"Well met, Lady Nea," said Thessera, "we are here to give praise to Lord Aurus for defeating the Great White Snake."

"Well, he did that, but it isn't as if he fought alone, you know."

"Of course, my lady. I beg your forgiveness. Is he here?"

"Yes, but not in a state to be seen after that fight, and we have to get after the last of the bodysnatchers now."

"It's all right, Nea," said a pristine, glowing, clothed Aurus as he floated above the landspeeder. "I thank you and all your people, Thessera, but we really do have to chase down the last of the enemy now."

"Begging your pardon," said Florinald. "They've split their forces. The base is well-guarded by grunts. Only a token force with their Boss is transporting the captives."

"You heard him," said Aurus. "There are no prisoners at the last base but armed guards are still there. Leave it alone for now and free the captives that are here."

"Of course, Lord," said Thessera as she and all her people

bowed.

Aurus settled down into the landspeeder, glow fading, and the Knights departed.

"How did you regenerate so rapidly?" asked Nea.

"Didn't. I just pushed up layers of unburned skin from underneath and overlaid the damage. Can't hold it for long though, and it hurts."

"Impressive control," said Zen, "but all in the name of vanity?"

"No, just wanted to give the locals the sense we were in control of the situation, not barely dealing with it."

Once they had departed the battlefield Aurus's body gradually returned to its charred state. Nea watched in fascination as fresh skin retracted beneath the surface.

"Eat and drink your fill," she said. "Get some rest. Florinald has this."

"If I eat my fill there'll be none for the rest of you. The landspeeder isn't exactly overstocked with food. This box of ration bars will do."

He hugged the box to his chest.

#

"This is the front desk with your wakeup call," said a voice intruding into Aurus's dreams.

His eyes flickered open as Florinald spoke again.

"We'll be at the portal site in a few minutes. Since I know where they're headed I took a roundabout route to avoid being seen. I think we can ambush them."

"We're faster?"

"I could see them quite clearly as they left their base. Their GEVs are overloaded with captives, and slowed because of it. Grunts have a minimal presence, having left their base well-guarded, as I mentioned."

"You have a plan?"

"Not really my thing. I'll leave that up to the rest of you. I know Zen likes making plans."

"I do," said Zen, yawning. "Get us there and we can figure out something."

"Nice to have a chance to plan," said Nea. "Before that though, I must say Aurus is healing nicely. Very nicely, in fact. You might want to grow some clothes. I find it rather distracting."

Aurus glanced down at his fresh, pink, naked body, then concentrated. A gray bodysuit matching Nea's formed about him.

"Sorry. Didn't mean to make anyone uncomfortable."

"Didn't say I was uncomfortable, just distracted. Are you up for fighting?"

"Guess I'll have to be. It'll likely take all four of us to put down a Quanilith."

"Tell us what you know about them, Florinald," said Zen.

"First, I'll trade you the GEV controls for my scanner."

"Done, but answer me this first: everybody else has numbers that show up on it when I look at them, but not you. Why?"

"Well, I *am* ValDurian," said Florinald as he put the scanner back over his left eye. "We don't usually show up on any sort of surveillance. That's it, sole reason. Now, drive this thing like it was meant to be driven, Zen."

Zen did. He guided the landspeeder to come around the back side of the portal site. He even parked it in the original spot they had found it.

"And that's how it's done," said Zen. "We have plenty of places to hide in the rubble, so why don't we hear all about this creature while we set up the mortars."

"Don't bother with the weapon set-up," said Florinald. "The Quanalith is a high-level demon, and not vulnerable to common, mortal weapons like mortar rounds."

"Typical demon," said Nea, "vulnerable only to magic and magic weapons. Luckily, my rapier and main-gauche are magical."

"As is my halberd and heat-beams," said Aurus. "I was supposed to have that you know, the 'not being vulnerable to mortal weapons' thing. The Vals couldn't quite pull it off, for whatever reason, but it would have been nice."

"Very," said Zen, "and while Florinald has at least a few magic arrows left, I have nothing magical, making me useless in this fight."

"I can loan you a magic dagger," said Florinald.

"Some demons can be slain by pure iron or silver though," said Nea.

"Not the Quanalith," said Florinald. "It's a top-grade demon. It has awesome dragon-style wings, four arms, and fights with supercharged elemental swords. This one is only seven-foot tall, but bound to be a bear of a woman, similar to that Kelvaana you like so much, Aurus."

"I keep saying it's not that I like her, just that she was impressive. And what's with you and your description of the Quanalith? Are you her press agent?"

Florinald laughed.

"Sorry. It's that she looks really cool."

"I'll appreciate how cool she is while she's killing us. Time to work up an effective plan."

"I'm all for that," said Nea.

"A really cool plan," said Zen.

Chapter Twenty
Knock Down, Drag Out

"Enemy GEVs in sight," said Florinald to the other Knights, under the sparsely-starred night sky. "Ten all told. Demon boss in the front one, of course."

"How close for those not having telescopic sight?" asked Nea.

"About a mile out. They'll be visible to you in under two minutes."

"Right on schedule," said Zen. "Now we'll see if my plan works."

"*Your* plan?" asked Nea, her face worked into a disapproving frown.

"Okay, 'our' plan. We all had our parts."

"Here's my part," said Aurus, stepping from behind the apparently intact portal arch.

He bore the form of a mauve lizard woman, his throat a red ruin, as if it had been sliced open. He wore the bloody, scored and dented yellow plate armor he had scavenged from a corpse, and carried a machine gun.

"Very impressive," said Florinald. "That's a good imitation, and I know some top-notch shapeshifters."

"Thanks. I practice a lot on all sorts of odd forms and found it's about getting the small details right."

Florinald's hair went from red to black, then back again.

"All I can do is change my eyes, hair, and skin. I don't want to ruin the group dynamic, so I'll keep it red for now. Why does your throat look like it tangled with your halberd?"

"Because I don't know their language or what they sound like, or if they even make sounds at all. At least I know their blood is red. This way I can just mime it."

"Fair point. Do you think the 'portal' will pass inspection?" asked Florinald.

"It's nighttime, so 'yes' if they don't look too closely," said Zen. "The frames and fabric from our gliders, along with wood from our crates, and the remaining actual materials make for a fair Hollywood recreation."

"Just so long as they don't go behind it," said Nea. "It's obvious from back there. Aurus, you need to hang these tarps to complete the look."

Aurus grabbed a pile of tarps and flew up to hang them in the middle of the portal arch.

"Good enough?" he asked.

"Perfect. It's up to me for the finishing touch."

Aurus carried her up to the top of the tarp and glowed dimly. Her body blocked the light directly behind her, allowing the gradual creation of a shadow that filled in the entire portal.

Once on the ground, Nea completed her work, leaving a field of blackness filling the interior arch.

"There. No danger of that getting them home, and nobody will try to activate it now."

"Especially important, since we have no idea how that worked," said Zen. "Should allay their suspicions long enough for us to carry out the rest of the plan. It all depends on how convincing an actor you are, Aurus."

"Story of my life. The rest of you get scarce while I make like a wounded soldier."

The other Knights disappeared into the darkness while Aurus found the proper painful position to lie in wait. In a matter of minutes the lights of the enemy GEVs were seen coming through the forest. They roared closer while he watched, and were quickly in spitting distance.

The GEVs stopped dead. Fans still roared, keeping the vehicles off the ground as the Quanalith leapt from the lead one. She fluttered her ribbed wings and landed by Aurus as he 'snapped awake' at her presence.

Showtime.

"What happened here?" she screamed. "Who did this? How did you survive?"

He put hands to his throat and shook his head.

"You're bloody useless. Where did they go?"

He waved back the way they had come.

"Ha. They'll find I left a full complement of top soldiers at our base, not the wretched cast-offs like you, and with better weapons too, not the pathetic toys like yours." She pointed to the machine gun on the ground.

"Bring 'em on through," she yelled to the waiting hovercraft, while waving toward the portal. "I'll come back with more soldiers and we'll find out who did this."

She looked at Aurus.

"I suppose you can come through and get patched up. You're barely any use to me normally and not at all in that condition."

She turned to march through the gate, but cast her eyes up and hesitated.

"Something wrong here. I—"

Aurus flew at her hard from behind, taking them both through the shadow, which disappeared, leaving only hanging tarps.

The rest of the Knights struck from hiding, targeting the ten drivers of the GEVs. Nea traveled through shadows, plentiful thanks to the vehicle lights, cutting throats with her rapier. Florinald took out two at once with double dagger shots, while Zen used body throws to pull the lizards out and to the ground. Then he'd shoot them in the face with a pistol.

Panic set in amongst the drivers after Zen fired a few rounds. The remaining five lizards pulled out high-tech rifles and fired bursts of energy into the night, randomly. One burst hit Nea, whose energy shield went into the yellow.

Florinald took out two more drivers while Nea killed the one that hit her. Of the remaining two, one fired at Zen, hitting a nearby GEV instead. The panicked target rapid-fired back, killing the other grunt and some of the captives.

Zen pulled the last driver down and twisted its neck until it broke. Then he made the rounds of the fallen lizards to shoot the V'Laubi who were still in them, in case they still lived. None got free.

"Damn," yelled Nea. "Ladies, we're here to rescue you, and I'm sorry one of your captors started shooting. We'll save your friends if we can, but we have to go after the big demon who's trying to kill our friend right now."

There was crying and screaming until Nea bellowed.

"Stay calm. We'll free you all as soon as we can. Zen, check the grunts for keys and free the women if you can. Florinald and I will go after Aurus."

"We will?" asked Florinald. "How?"

#

Aurus tumbled through the shadowgate, then came to his feet, eyes blazing, firing energy beams into the Quanalith's back. They missed her purple blouse, which was open in the back for her wings. She whirled and backhanded him in one motion with her two right hands, sending him flying. He took advantage of the blow and extended the flight even farther with his own power, landing in a splayed pose amongst the discarded crates at their first campsite.

"What the hells?" she bellowed. "Guess I don't know my own strength. Why would you attack me, scum? Not to mention, how? That useless machine gun didn't do it."

She flexed the fingers on all four hands and a sword appeared in each, one blazing with fire, one frosted with ice, one crackling with lightning, and the last swathed in darkness.

Damn, she is cool, Florinald, but I just might end up dead if I don't play this right.

She walked toward Aurus, her long, silver hair billowing more than the wind would cause. Pupilless eyes of solid violet looked him over, probing for answers while all four swords swung about lightly, almost carefree. A smile split her face, a little too widely.

"You're extraplanar as well, and not in your own form. Let's see if we can get answers, assuming you aren't dead."

Aurus let loose his light in a nova-like burst, hoping to blind the demon. With an even wider grin she stood over him, then plunged all four swords downward into the armor he was suddenly no longer wearing.

Aurus shot backwards and upwards as his discarded armor exploded, swathing the demon in flames and smoke. He materialized his halberd and gained more altitude.

Not going to wait for the anime-esque smoke to disperse. Don't have the time.

He flew at her, halberd whistling through the air as it struck. The impact blew away the remaining smoke, showing all four swords having blocked the halberd. She smiled that wide grin again.

"This is going to be more fun than I ever expected to find on this worldlet, halberd-man. Come at me again."

Aurus flew up, did a midair turn, and faced her.

"I will, soon as I figure how this is going to play out."

"Why, do you have more cheap shots up your sleeves? The light-burst was pointless, since my eyes don't have irises to dilate. Have to admit the explosion hurt, but nothing stops Umaldra the Eviscerator."

"That's you?"

"Yes, that's me, you fool. Now are we fighting on the ground or in the air?"

"We can't just take it as it comes? You look about as maneuverable as a truck while flying, so why don't we plan on ground combat for now?"

"You're wrong about that, but it doesn't matter. I'll fight however you want."

Aurus landed and went for a wing strike, but missed when the wings vanished. She counter-attacked with a flurry of sword thrusts.

"None of that, halberd-man. If we're not flying I'll just put my wings away for now."

She whirled about, each sword striking at a different level. Aurus blocked them all by holding his halberd vertically. His halberd was then engulfed with fire, lightning, ice, and shadow in separate layers, so he sent it away.

"Very nice, but I hope you have other weapons, because that one's done for."

She stabbed from his left and right with all four blades, but he dropped into a split, avoiding them. At nearly the same instant, he brought back his halberd and struck up, narrowly missing her crotch, but slicing the blouse while leaving a cut from navel to top, stabbing up into her chin.

With a mighty screech, she dropped her swords and yanked the halberd away.

"Tha thin shou been done," she slurred, blood running down her neck as she hurled the halberd off the mesa, into the distance.

While she was distracted, Aurus scooped her swords up with a crate and dropped them into a fissure. As he turned to run, she tackled him from behind, bringing him to the ground.

"Doan needum. You die now."

She squeezed him with all four arms, each of which ignited with one sword power. Aurus simultaneously burned, froze, spasmed, and had his life force drained.

Perfect time for my energy shield to be dead.

He flew backwards, dragging her with him until he slid under a wooden frame arch.

The arch erupted into white radiance, causing Umaldra her own spasms and allowing Aurus to slide free. He stood to her left, supported entirely via his flight ability, and focused his eyes on her left temple. His heat rays burned into her head, bringing new wails of pain.

"Eaahh - I - will - eat - you – man."

"Not if I eat you first, woman."

He gritted his teeth and opened his eyes wider as the heat rays increased in strength. His desperation grew as his peripheral vision saw movement in her limbs.

With a great cry, she broke free of the arch and sprouted wings. Aurus leapt at her, but missed as she shot upwards.

"If this was your best, it's not good enough, tricky little halberdless man. Gotta admit it's the best I've faced in a long time though."

Aurus stared at her as he assessed his chances.

I'm too drained to attack, and I have no weapon. One chance, if I can survive that long…

He flew toward a stack of boulders piled three high, hoping she would follow.

Umaldra dove to the ground to pick up and throw a lone boulder at the stack, breaking it apart.

"Nice try. It's obvious you've got this place trapped, so do you think I'll just let you use them on me?"

"Y-you have so far. Why stop now?"

"Funny man. I'm actually going to miss you."

An arrow hit her, disintegrating the left wing and part of the connecting shoulder.

"But *I* don't miss," said Florinald as Umaldra fell into a patch of darkness.

She reappeared from the original mesa shadowgate in crystalline manacles with Nea astride her.

"It worked," said Aurus. "You guys were my one chance. My last ploy was to keep her worrying about traps and chasing me about until you showed up."

"All wrapped up," said Nea. "Pity about the wings and shoulder, lady. With the neutralizer cuffs on you won't be regenerating. We aren't trying to torture you, but you'd be too dangerous with powers."

"This is nothing, but you should just kill me now, because I won't tell you anything."

"That remains to be seen," said Florinald, "but killing you is out of the question."

"Why?" she said with a smirk.

"It's that you're a Quanalith, and if we kill you here your essence will reconstitute on the demonic plane eventually. Killing you would be your ticket out."

"Smarter than I thought. Can I bribe you all then?"

Aurus's eyes went wide with surprise.

"What? Look, we're just here to keep the V'Laubi from turning this worldlet into a 'new body' distribution center."

"And I was here to help that happen. Pity we can't be friends, halberdless-man."

"Yeah, pity, but I have to ensure the V'Laubi leave this world."

"Speaking of which," said Nea, "we should restrain hers so it can't detach."

Nea removed her cloak to bind Umaldra, then saw where Aurus had burned her in the back through the open blouse.

"She doesn't have a V'Laubi. She's not a hollowback."

Umaldra laughed.

"Hollowback. I like that. No, I'm not one of 'em, I just work for them."

"Yeah," exclaimed Aurus. "I saw that when I zapped her. Don't think that changes anything for us really. We still have to lock her up and take care of her remaining forces. Then we can worry about the rest of the plan when Master Julian gets here."

"Could you do one thing for me, pretty please?" asked Umaldra. "Could you tell me what the rest of your traps were? I'm dying to know."

"Sure. Don't want to torture you psychologically. The explosive armor I wore, and then the holding spell in the wooden arch were made by Florinald here, from his arrows. The third and last was mine, but it turned out to be useless."

He pulled a tarp from over a pile of wooden boxes, revealing a collection of mirrors.

"The idea was that they'd help me beef up my natural light-power to blind you, giving me the advantage. Not a great trap, maybe, especially since it turns out you're immune to it. In the end I was only leading you on a wild goose chase until my friends showed up."

"Oh, you are a fun one," said Umaldra. "I hope we spend a lot of time together in the coming days."

"Sure, but first I have to recover my damned halberd from wherever you threw it."

#

Aurus lay abed, eating and healing. Nea knocked on the door frame, then entered, her right arm still outside the door as she waited.

"Don't mean to disturb your meditation and healing," she said, "but I've got something for you."

She held out his halberd in her right hand.

"My halberd. Thank you," he said.

"You're entirely welcome, but it wasn't just me. In fact, it was barely me. I got the locals to look for it since they've got the numbers. Would have been here sooner, but they passed it around so everybody could touch it."

She handed it to him and he looked it over, then made it vanish.

"Thank you again. It's plumb hard to come by magical golden halberds these days."

Nea smiled.

"I suppose it is. And you're welcome. Are you sure you aren't a god? The locals have made the spot where it landed into a shrine."

"They're welcome to do so," he said, laughing, "but I get no benefit from it."

His face went somber.

"Not to concern you after we had such a victory, but I've been lying here, thinking."

"Yes, that is concerning," she said, while hiding a smile with her hands.

"I hate to get all serious," he said, "but I'm starting to think something is out to get us, apart from the hollowbacks. Just a feeling really, but there have been a few incidents now."

"Such as?"

"Marvin being taken down by the beastriders for one. We talked while I was flying him to the hospital, and he felt like they did something to him so he blacked out briefly. Couldn't define what. Speaking of blackouts, there was the incident when you forgot you could do shadowgates. You never forget anything."

"I'm hardly infallible, but yes, it was odd."

"'Like a cloud over your thoughts,' I think you said. Then there was the incident with street lamps coming on early, at just the right time to hurt you."

Nea's face grew pensive.

"Not only that," said Aurus, "when fighting Umaldra I was more panicked than I should have been. I've been in far worse situations before."

"Well, you had been wounded near unto death beforehand."

"True, but it just felt wrong. Am I looking for villains that aren't there? Evil mind controllers?"

"I can't say, but I can say we should be extra-cautious going forward. Should I say something to the others?" asked Nea

"Not yet. It's only been you, me, and Marvin so far. Let the conspiracy theories breathe for a bit first. Just be mindful," said Aurus.

"Will do, while you get some rest."

#

The Grand Elder sat at a large, wooden desk strewn with papers and obscure, misshapen objects of unknowable nature.

"I bring news most grave, O Grand Elder," said Javis with a quaver in her voice, bowing.

"Then get on with it, unless it gets better the longer you delay."

"It does not. The latest venture, this one into worldlet 236-342 —"

"Enough. The designation is not important. What happened?"

"The utter annihilation of all V'Laubi forces present," said Javis, tensing.

"Not just the Voaminid forces?" asked the Grand Elder, leaning forward with an intense expression.

"All, O Grand Elder."

"So long as the other losses had equal losses."

"You lost more, since you had more there—"

"We are always first and foremost. Do our losses hurt my standing?"

"I cannot say, as I am not an Arbiter. The gravest news is that they captured or killed Umaldra, the Quanalith demon."

The Grand Elder sprang to her feet, scattering papers and objects to the floor.

"This will not do. Umaldra was a valuable tool, and one not easily replaced. Were the foes Olgun, like on Miefurdra?"

"Mei—, uh no, I do not believe so. I also question whether those were truly Olgun."

"Makes no difference. I will contact the other factions and order reprisal. The will of the Divine be done."

"Praise the Divine," said Javis.

Chapter Twenty One
Oracles: Cridi

Raelani floated through a silver door into a gray world.

"Oh, Great Oracles, I'm here. You wanted to see me?"

A roiling cloud of red surrounded her, obscuring her, tumbling her about. She thrust both arms straight out to her sides, giving her a 'T' shape. She stopped tumbling, and the cloud resolved into thousands of playing cards with red backing. Her arms ran crimson from paper cuts as the cards combined into a woman's shape and spoke.

"This is your significator, the Queen of Swords."

A giant tarot card of a gold-crowned woman holding a sword appeared between the two.

"Accept your fate," said the lady in red.

The queen stepped from the card, swinging her sword at Raelani, who dodged.

"My fate is my fate, so acceptance is irrelevant, but my fate is not to die here."

She screeched, her voice shattering the queen's sword.

The queen placed the pieces at Raelani's feet and vanished. Raelani picked up the hilt, which still had a short length of blade, and drove it into the gray ground before the woman of cards.

"I name you Gid, cartomancer, and bind you to your place."

The cards became a woman of alabaster skin with flowing red gown, blank golden eyes, and long red hair who was bound to the ground with glittering chains. She bowed to Raelani. As Raelani bowed back, she was engulfed by an orange wave.

For a moment, the wave settled into a sea of orange, without a ripple or trace of Raelani. With a great frothing, she rose to the surface, drawing up a great spout of orange into her mouth.

Dripping wet, she pulled a porcelain teacup from her robe, then drew forth a saucer with the other hand. She put the cup on it upside down, sucking the orange wave into it, save for a humanoid pillar of orange liquid. She placed the cup-and-saucer down.

"I name you Jusa, tasseomancer, and bind you to your place."

The chains bound orange tea into a woman of alabaster skin with a flowing orange gown, golden eyes, and long orange hair who bowed to Raelani.

A lightning bolt from the gray struck Raelani. It was followed by metal-edged dice, razor-taloned birds, fish with nasty teeth, wooden letter tiles, and an 8-Ball. She hit the gray ground hard, but bounced to her feet and grabbed the broken sword point.

Extruding most of the point into a fine wire, she lassoed a humanoid spark. Her hair, now smoking and frizzed, bounced as she drove the remaining point of the wire into the gray earth.

"I name you Laba, electromancer, and bind you to your place."

Laba appeared in chains, with garb and hair in yellow, then bowed.

Raelani grabbed a handful of the still-raining dice, then tossed them before her.

"Critical hit," said Raelani. "I name you Cridi, astragalomancer, and bind you to your place."

Cridi appeared, a vision in green, chained to a desk, and bowed.

A face of clouds encircled by birds appeared high above Raelani's left. On her right, a pool of water with a woman's eyes bubbled forth a rushing river.

Three birds struck Raelani from behind, then veered off, leaving the back of her gown in tatters while three sharp-toothed fish bit at her toes from the water that now surrounded her up to the ankles. She hurled a handful of metal-edged 8-sided dice at the birds, downing them. While they lay before her, she made the dice into colorful mosaic metal collars on each bird.

"I name you Kelon, aeromancer, and bind you to your place."

Blue-haired Kelon appeared, and bowed while the fish still bit at Raelani and wooden tiles fell on her head.

Raelani touched the birds, which flew high until she gestured at the fish. They dove, each scooping up a fish in their large beaks, but could not swallow them because of the constricting collars.

"I name you Elyn, hydromancer, and bind you to your place."

Flowing indigo water became the chained woman, Elyn, who bowed to Raelani.

"Very good, my Lady, but now you face the greatest powers," said a new voice from a cloud of violet fog.

There was laughter from the bound women.

"Words conquer all," said the violet fog as it became a wordstorm.

Small wooden tiles drove Raelani to her knees while a giant pair of black-rimmed glasses watched dispassionately from the side, above a massive 8-Ball. Raelani disappeared beneath the tiles while the wordstorm laughed.

Raelani yelled, "Your words are weighty, but take care in their use."

She burst from the pile, scattering tiles everywhere, pelting even the glasses.

"You are the EX champion," she shouted, holding up 'E and X' tiles together.

"Pathetic. Your future is HAZY," said the wordstorm. The four tiles appeared before Raelani.

"I'll disabuse you of that notion in a JIFFY," said Raelani triumphantly, holding up the appropriate five tiles. "19 points."

The wordstorm ended, tiles crashing to the gray ground.

"I name you Trisyn, logomancer, and bind you to your place."

A woman in violet rose from a pile of tiles, to be chained, and she bowed while Raelani panted, trying to catch her breath.

A woman's deep voice came from the glasses, saying, "I must commend you for your progress thus far, but what does the future hold? Ask your question."

"Are you going to stop the nonsense and give me the information you wanted me to have?"

The 8-Ball, which came to Raelani's chest, rolled and stopped, revealing a glass window on what had been the bottom. Behind it, in a sea of blue darkness, floated the glowing message: **Reply hazy, try again.**

"Are you going to rein in the chaos and give me the information you wanted me to have *sometime within the next few minutes?*"

The 8-Ball rolled over, then stopped again with the window on top. This time it said: **It is decidedly so.**

"Then I name you Delu, crystallomancer, and bind you to your place."

The glasses shrank until they adorned the face of a woman in black, who bowed to Raelani. Delu's chains appeared, linking her to all the other women.

"Is it any wonder that we're using artificial intelligence more now?" said Raelani. "Watching over the AllWorlds is draining. I don't have the time or energy for this. The Omnimind is far less stressful."

Delu adjusted her glasses.

"We're all busy. Cridi has something for you."

Raelani floated around to the fourth woman, the one in green, who twirled her emerald hair about slender fingers while she waited.

"Lady."

"What needs to be dealt with?"

Cridi grabbed at a paper on her desk, which was strewn with dice of numerous shapes, sizes and colors.

"The dice tell me something is coming up regarding the worldlet of Gyi'stal."

She shoved the paper at Raelani, who took it gracefully.

"And who shall I delegate this matter to?

"Whatever decision you make shall be the correct one, of course, according to the dice," said Cridi.

The Oracles vanished, save Delu the Black.

"My Lady, a word?"

"You have a concern?"

"I fear that one of us Oracles may be a traitor working against the common good."

Raelani raised an eyebrow and said, "That is a matter for concern, or would be save for two things."

"Those are?"

"You're all oracles. It seems impossible that one or all of you would not already know this and have taken steps to stop such a traitor."

Delu pushed her glasses up again, her blank golden eyes unblinking.

"True. What is the other thing?"

"You're all multiple personalities of the same person. It is impossible that one aspect of you could keep something like that hidden from all of the other yous."

"Sadly, that does not prevent any of us from working against what you perceive as the good. It may be or have been necessary, as the tapestry of prophecy has been pulled taut for so long the fabric of reality is strained. We were never meant to have a perfect knowledge of the future for such a stretch of time."

"Has time been stretched out of shape?" asked Raelani.

"As the warp and weft fray, who is to say?"

"An Oracle?"

"We would dare not, but would dare to take whatever means are necessary to ensure that does not happen, or to mitigate it if it does."

"My faith in you remains strong," said Raelani. "You will guide us through this."

Both women bowed, then vanished.

Part Four: Convolutions

Chapter Twenty Two
Loose Ends

Master Julian sat across the conference table from the Knights, leaning back in his comfy office chair. Zen was just finishing up his summary of events.

"That's the end of the final garrison on this worldlet. It didn't go quite as expected, but it is a finish."

"Any surviving invaders?"

"None, as the locals involved themselves. Our original plan was to stupefy the garrison with dreamfruit, then merely capture them. To that end, the locals faked a raid with a couple of captured GEVs, then abandoned one when the garrison retaliated.

"What the grunts ended up with was a GEV requiring only minor repairs, and the back half full of dreamfruit. Having run through their original rations, the grunts quickly devoured the dreamfruit. Now, we figured it would knock them all into blissful comas, then we'd just capture them with ease."

"That turned out to not be the case?" asked Julian.

"Correct," said Zen. "With this particular species, or possibly because of the dual nature of V'Laubi and their host bodies, the grunts went insane, killing each other. Those few that ran off into the woods were slain by the locals."

"Hmmm. Perhaps not the desired outcome, but I'm not complaining. Saves our resources and solves the immediate problem. Now we must resolve the ongoing problem."

"What problem is that, Master Julian?" asked Nea.

"We have a bunch of barbarians zipping around in hovercrafts and carrying automatic weapons."

"That's a problem?" asked Aurus.

"Only because it violates our core tenets. Through whatever means, we've helped the natives acquire technology and weaponry far beyond their norm."

"You're worried about upsetting the local balance of terror," said Aurus.

"It's already upset. Now we have to do something about it."

"So, what's the plan, Julie?" asked Florinald. "Do we seize the guns by force? That could get quite unpleasant on both sides."

"No, let's not go there. You've already taken care of one local problem, the invaders, and we are working on the dreamfruit. Morninglight has analyzed the sample you gave him and determined it is not native to this world. Therefore, we can remove it and solve the second local problem, dreamfruit addiction. I think you can solve the out-of-place tech problem by trading it for fruit removal. They won't need the guns to fight dreamfruit dealers, so the locals probably won't kick too much."

Master Julian pulled out a sheet of paper and handed it to Florinald.

"It'll have to be done without Florinald, though. Raelani has other matters for him to attend to."

#

"Lady. You have something only my unparalleled skills can accomplish?" asked Florinald.

"That's the most I've ever heard you speak at once, and so boldly," said Raelani, "but yes, precisely. It's a little worldlet named Gyi'stal, and we are looking to make allies there."

"And, you first thought of me?"

"Why not? You are a ValDurian, and uniquely suited for the task at hand."

"In other words, everyone else is busy, and I'm available."

"I won't deny that's part of it, but this is important, and you can handle it."

"Fine, but I'm not operating at full strength, or any strength, really. I've exhausted my arrows."

"I know that, but you won't need them. Enak made this for you."

She tossed him a gold finger-ring with a rolled-up paper stuck through it. He donned the ring and stuffed the paper in a jacket pocket.

"You'll want to read that paper. It explains how the ring works."

"Wouldn't need this if he'd been making my magic arrows, as he would have already, I suspect, were he not busy making magical rings."

"Don't be that way. Enak will make you more arrows when he has a chance."

"I don't recall having been consulted on this. I like being an archer. I like being *the* archer. It's my one claim to fame."

"Congratulations. This is the first time I can recall that your true feelings were expressed about something that bothered you."

"And that's a good thing?"

"I think so. Time to stop hiding your light under a bushel basket. I knew hanging around with the knights would be good for you."

"They certainly let their feelings shine. You put me with them as a learning experience?"

"I put you with them because they needed help. Anything extra is a free bonus. Now, why don't you get on to Gyi'stal and do that job only you can do."

Chapter Twenty Three
Drinks and Dreams

Kalillit imagined for the fourteenth time that day how much better her life was going to be. She tossed back gwa-fruit beer dregs from the wooden mug and hollered for more. The bald, peg-legged barkeep thumped over to her, glaring all the while.

"You've had three mugs already. When am I going to see some money?" His bushy black eyebrows ran together as he scowled.

"Money?"

She lowered the hood of her brown jacket and pointed to her pure white hair.

"I'm Sunchosen. This leer is the beast you can do for me. I mean beer. This beer is the beast . . . least you can do for me."

She belched. The only other patron, a man wearing green and black, smiled from his corner table.

"Girl, you're no Sunchosen," said the barkeep. "Sunhair or not, your skin is pale as mine. Pay up and get out."

He smacked his hands together and she jumped in her seat.

"I'm not full-chosen yet. I haven't been to Sunspire. But I will, and I'll remember this." She scowled at him.

He spit on the floor.

"You'll pay in bits, or you'll pay in service. My sons would like a go at you, they would. You could even make some bits here by renting yourself out. 'Course, I'd get half your take to pay for your upkeep."

Kalillit looked at him in horror.

"By the Sun. How dare you?" she yelled while jumping to her feet. "I'm leaving. Be thankful you may still keep this place."

He grabbed at her, but she dodged and ran toward the door. Before she reached it a rough-looking man blocked her flight.

"Grab her, Dhun," said the barkeep.

Kalillit ducked, but Dhun grabbed her by the hood. He held her slight body around the waist, dwarfing her five and a half feet frame.

"Let me go, you assworm. I'll have the protections removed from this place."

The barkeep hobbled over, smacking his fist into his palm.

"Service it is then. We'll start right now."

Kalillit screamed, loud and shrill enough to make him flinch. He went to slap her face, but something stayed his hand.

That 'something' was the man in the green jacket and black trousers. He'd come up from behind and held the struggling barkeep's arm. A gold ring gleamed upon the right hand of the stranger, who said, "Excuse me, sir. What does the young lady owe you?"

The barkeep stopped struggling and turned to the man.

"Six bits. What's it to you?"

"Three bits, you robber-bastard," yelled Kalillit.

The stranger dropped a handful of corn-kernel sized and shaped copper nubs into the barkeep's hand.

"Ten bits. That'll settle both our accounts."

He poked Dhun in the bicep.

Dhun released the girl and rubbed his arm.

"I still want a go at her," he said, leering.

"Up to the lady, I'd say."

The stranger looked at her.

"What do you say to the gentleman's offer?"

Kalillit put on her most seductive expression and moved closer to Dhun. Her knee met his groin and he collapsed in a heap.

"That's what I figured," said the stranger. To the barkeep, he added, "Don't expect any further business from me with customer service like that."

Kalillit followed close on his heels as he walked out the door.

"Hey, you," she said, trying to match his rapid pace.

He turned and grinned.

"Heyou is my brother. I'm Florinald. What can I do for you?"

They stopped walking.

"You can explain why you butted in my business."

She glared up at eyes distanced by his six-foot-plus height.

"You're welcome."

"What? I didn't thank you."

"Sorry, I must not have been paying attention. Thanking's what people usually do when somebody helps them."

"I didn't need help. I coulda paid, but shouldn'ta had to."

She frowned and then stamped her foot at him.

"You deserved those drinks for free then?"

"Yes. I'm Sunchosen. I shoulda demanded more."

Florinald suppressed a grin.

"I heard you mention that before. What's a Sunchosen?"

Kalillit blinked in surprise.

"Were you spawned this Firstgood? Everybody knows that."

"Indulge me. I'm a stranger to your land."

"Oh. You must be from the Frozen Shores, where the Sun doesn't touch, past the Outlands. I thought you dressed funny."

"My mother will be sad to hear that. She bought me this outfit."

He flicked imaginary dust off the sleeves.

"Oh, I mean, the colors are odd for around here, and it looks too hot for the Midlands, that's all."

Florinald chuckled.

"No offense taken. Minor temperature variations don't bother me. I should be comfortable anywhere on Gyi'stal. Now, as to my question?"

"Oh, the Sunchosen. The Protectors, Chosen of the Sun. 'And lo, the Rakar fall before them. We, the Children of the Land, bow before the Chosen of the Sun.' And I'm Chosen now."

"A little light on details. How are you suddenly one of them?"

"Not suddenly. My hair's been changing for a year now. Only Sunchosen have pure white hair."

"I did notice everybody here has black hair, when they have hair, and pale skin. I fit right in. You're the first variant I've seen. But there's more to being a Sunchosen, yes?"

"Their skin color is Sun-blessed amber. Their eyes glow purple in the Goodlight and yellow in the Badlight. And power. They wield such power as the common can never know."

"Of course. How do you become one?"

"You don't. It's a birthright, but sometimes it shows up late, like with me."

"Fascinating. How do you become a full Chosen?"

"I need to get close to the Sun's purity at Sunspire, home to the Chosen. There I get my full power."

"Ah, then I too travel to the Sunspire, in search of the Sunchosen ruler."

"High Lord Indalakeir? I'll probably hafta meet him myself. I could maybe introduce you after."

"Then you wouldn't mind if we travel together?"

"I suppose not. Just know that I don't owe you anything."

"Only your name. I'd hate to call you by my brother's."

"Kalillit."

Chapter Twenty Four
Stuck in the Midlands with You

Florinald and Kalillit set an even pace toward Sunspire. Keeping their bearings proved easy, as the Sun never moved. Two candles had come and gone since they started, as she told him when they heard a great tolling bell.

"That's Lastgood. We only have a candle left to find shelter."

She walked faster.

Florinald matched her pace.

"What's Lastgood?"

"Just before the Sun changes from Goodlight to Badlight, of course."

"Is that when your sun turns purple?"

She nodded her head.

"Of course. What else would it be?"

"Raelani only knows. So many interesting new things here."

"There's a Sanctuary up ahead 'cause it's a regular road for Sunchosen offerings."

Florinald looked about the hilly, rocky path they trod.

"You and I have vastly different ideas on what constitutes a road. I'd be kind in calling this a footpath. What sort of Sanctuary?"

"The only kind, a building set up by the Sunchosen to protect travelers during Badlight. We should just make it. We'd better."

"Why all the fuss over purple light? I assumed it to be this world's version of night. I actually find it quite soothing on the eyes."

They assumed a jogging pace.

"Night? I don't understand," said Kalillit.

"As with roads. Where I come from, the sun remains the same color most of the time, but it travels across the sky. That's one of the ways we mark time without candles, generally in increments of hours. When it goes past the horizon, the world gets dark. That's nighttime."

Kalillit laughed.

"A scary story for children. Just imagine: Gyi'stal gettin' dark. That's when you throw blankets over their heads, I suppose?"

"No. Why is purple called the Badlight?"

"Because the Rakar roam then, of course. Goodlight creatures are bad enough. Badlight creatures are far worse. They murder at will, and weapons don't hurt them. Only the power of the Sunchosen keeps them out of homes and Sanctuaries."

"They fight these creatures every night, um, Badlight?"

"Never seen it myself. They place Suncanna on the buildings to keep out Rakar."

"Those twelve-pointed gold stars?"

"Staras? What is a 'staras'?"

"Stars, symbols of your Sun."

"Yes, the Suncanna. Their power keeps the Rakar away, except sometimes when Goodlight creatures steal them. Then we hafta wait for the Sunchosen to replace them."

"So, without these Sunchosen you'd all die?"

"Yes. The monsters of the Badlight are without end. Only Sunchosen can fight them."

Kalillit picked up her pace.

Florinald kept abreast easily.

"It's good to be Chosen."

"Very good, and I'm one of them now. Or I will be."

"Pretty sweet racket. They've got all the non-chosen helpless and dependent. Have you ever seen a Rakar?"

"No, but I've never seen air, yet I breathe it."

" Two different things. You can feel air; you know the lack of it means death. Have you ever seen a Badlight creature?"

"I have not, else I'd be dead. I've heard their howls and seen the remains of those unlucky enough to have met them. Why do you ask?"

"I've been on Gyi'stal for three days. Sorry, three Goodlights. I walked outside during Badlight, and it was pleasant enough. I did hear awful noises, true, but saw nothing I hadn't seen during the day, ah, Goodlight."

"You walked among the Rakar? You are a liar or a Sunchosen, and you are no Chosen."

She breathed more heavily as they ran.

"I am many things, but not Sunchosen. I admit my case is not typical. In all likelihood your Rakar could not sense me, unless they track by normal vision alone."

"You are a strange one, yet not a danger, I think."

She fell silent as they came in view of a one-story dome building of wood with no windows.

"Providence of the Sunchosen," exclaimed Kalillit. "Too soon to be a miracle, too late for good planning. The Badlight is swift upon us."

She sprinted for the dome, Florinald following. She entered while he walked around the building.

She stuck her head out and gasped for breath, then called out.

"Maybe you are a danger. To yourself. Get in here."

He walked in at a leisurely pace to find the Sanctuary in darkness. With flint and tinder, Kalillit ignited a kerosene lamp dangling from the ceiling, and then closed the door.

Florinald looked at the piles of rotted trash and broken furniture. Cabinet doors hung open, sagging. The smell of mold and feces hung heavy.

"Can't say much for the housekeeping here, now that I can see it."

"These are supposeta be kept up for travelers, but it's so close to town it probably don't get used much."

She shook out a couple of straw mats and used a ratty broom to sweep clean two patches of floor on opposite sides of the room.

"I just hope there's some food left."

There wasn't.

"You started on the journey of your life without any preparation? No food, no water, not even extra socks?" asked Florinald.

"I trimmed off the last ends of my dark hair this Firstgood. The others on the farm gave me money to buy supplies for the trip, but I thought the barkeep would treat me like my friends did. It could have gone better."

"Fret not, youngster," said Florinald. "I may be the least of my family, but food I can provide."

He stepped to his right, and there on a rough table behind him sat two foot-long, reddish-brown cylinders, a loaf of bread, and a bottle of water.

Kalillit grabbed the bread and ripped a big hunk loose with her teeth. After a few rounds of chewing and swallowing, she said, "What are those red things?"

"Smoked sausages. Do you eat meat?"

"Only if I can get it."

She sniffed one, smiled, and bit into it.

"Yes, I eat this," she mumbled through spicy sausage.

Florinald produced a knife, cut the sausage in half, and took the part she wasn't eating.

"You can slow down. I have more, and it won't disappear if you let go."

After she had finished stuffing herself, Florinald asked, "So do we spend the next twelve hours in here doing nothing?"

"Candles; ten of them, not twelve. I plan on sleeping for most of that if you stay on your side of the room."

"I have a high tolerance for boredom, but would you mind talking until you sleep?"

"We could tell stories, I suppose. Maybe explain what you meant about being the least of your family?"

"That's a tale all right. I'll tell you what I'm allowed. We're a secretive family, we ValDurians. Most of them have awesome powers, rivaling or exceeding your Sunchosen, I expect."

Kalillit smiled in disdain.

"A family of braggarts then?"

"Not most of us, but I'm adopted. My powers are more on this order."

He threw a dagger from his right hand into the wall, followed by one from his left. The first dagger vanished, and the second stuck in the hole made by the first. Then that vanished as well. When she looked, he held them both.

"That was amazing," she said. "Hardly the power of a Sunchosen though."

"As I said: adopted. I have cousins who can change the course of mighty rivers and bend steel with their bare hands."

"They steal?"

"No. Steel is a metal, stronger than the copper you use."

"Copper?"

"Those bits that act as money, that's copper."

"We say 'shuc'. Like this." She pulled a crude dagger from under her jacket. Made of rough, beaten, greenish copper, it had an eight-inch blade, wooden handle, and keen double edges.

"Yes, that's copper. Steel is stronger and holds an edge better."

He produced a dagger again. "This is steel, sort of, in some part."

He balanced it point-down on his finger, showing it before her eyes. She made a grab, but it was gone.

"I wanna see it closer."

"That was rude. Maybe you can see it if we improve your manners. In the meantime I could improve your dagger if you like."

"How?"

"Give it here, and I'll do a thorough sharpening and molecular readjustment."

"I don't know what molar tusks are, but I'm not giving you my only knife."

"I don't really know what molar tusks are either, but if you're worried about having a knife, here."

He tossed her his dagger.

Her eyes drank it in, and she tossed him her blade without hesitation. Hers had an upturned point, and looked rather like something a child might make without proper tools. Florinald placed a red lens over his left eye and produced a silver rod with a v-forked end. While she fondled his blade, he drew hers back and forth through the fork until he was satisfied.

"Here."

He tossed it to her, and she caught it without seeming to look.

Her eyes opened wide.

"What did you do?"

The blade, while retaining the same shape, was smooth and

gleamed like new. He had also added a gold knob on the end of the grip.

"I fixed the molar tusks and sharpened it. With magic. It's stronger, sharper, and will hold an edge longer. All the stress-cracks are gone, and the balance is perfect with that knob on it. It should go where you throw it."

He held his hand out.

"What? I'm not paying. Did I ask you to do that?" She crossed both daggers in front of her face.

"I don't want payment. I want my dagger."

"You gave this to me."

"So you wouldn't fret. If you don't return it, then you owe me for the knife-magic."

Her eyes narrowed as she stared into his.

"Fine. That's fair, I suppose."

She went to hand back his dagger.

"Wait."

He crooked a finger, and the knife appeared in his hand.

"Just to show I could have taken it, but I wanted you to acknowledge it as mine. When I threw them earlier, it wasn't some sort of performer's trick. They come when I call them."

He made a show of tucking it inside his jacket.

"I thought that's where you kept them. Where'd you keep the bread and sausage?"

"I may tell you. We travel to the same destination, and might as well talk along the way."

#

Florinald had extinguished the kerosene lamp, and lay on his mattress. His eye-lens made everything perfectly visible to him through slitted lids as he looked at the ceiling. Kalillit snored as a small section of the ceiling dropped open, held by the tentacles of a V'Laubi so as not to strike the floor. It fell to the floor silently and put the ceiling section back in place. After it had done so, Florinald transfixed it with a dagger, and the creature quivered for a brief time. In a short while, the tentacles shriveled up, so Florinald carried it outside into the purple.

He dug a small hole in the surrounding shrub line, then buried the already-collapsing mass. He took a small gold tube from his jacket pocket.

"Day four. Killed my twenty-first V'Laubi on Gyi'stal. I've learned how to kill them cleanly, avoiding their horrid screams. As I suspected, the places I've just learned are called Sanctuaries are prime locations for V'Laubi to claim victims. I doubt the original builders have any idea, so I won't spread that notion around. The rest of the worldlet is clean, provable in that no other V'Laubi show up on my quantum-signature tracer, apart from this area and a bit farther ahead.

"I suspect they are being cautious in not attracting the attention of the Sunchosen, but I'd be willing to bet they are dying to control them."

Chapter Twenty Five
Welcome to the Jungle

Kalillit woke to Goodlight on her face. She tucked her knife away and yawned. Florinald stood by the open door.

"How much Goodlight did we lose?" she asked.

"This is Firstgood, it just turned. I checked through this little sliding slot on the door before I opened it."

She rolled over and fell off her mat.

"What the Rak is this?"

"An air mattress. I put it under your mat while you slept. With magic. Did you sleep well?"

She yawned again. "Never better. I haven't ever slept so long before."

She looked about the Sanctuary.

"You've been busy."

The once dilapidated and messy building fairly gleamed. Cabinets and furniture had been repaired and both trash and smell were gone.

"I don't sleep. Even though I wasn't bored, it feels good to be useful. Grab your sausage; I want to show you something."

Behind the dome, Florinald pointed to a damaged spot that should have held a Suncanna. "I noticed it yesterday when I walked around here. I didn't mention it because you needed a good sleep."

"But we could have been killed. The back isn't protected."

"I'd have protected you. I never sleep."

"What, never?"

"No, never. Well, hardly ever. It's one of my ValDurian benefits. I asked for it. It makes for dull nights, but I can will myself to sleep occasionally. Sometimes I think I should have asked for superhuman strength instead."

"You can ask for stuff like that? Would they adopt me?"

"One never knows, but it isn't as much fun as you might think. We should get walking now, yes?"

"Yeah. After I attend to business." She made a quick trip to some bushes.

When she returned, she said, "Let's move feet."

In less than half a candle, they reached two white pillars, one on each side of the 'road.' Florinald looked through his red lens.

"These are very unusual. The stone is unknown, but I know their dimensions now."

"Is that important?"

"My forte is missile weapons. I like to know height and distance so I can calculate trajectories. These are thirty feet tall and three feet wide, by my system of reckoning. The scanner also picks up infra-red, ultra-violet, analyzes materials, reads power levels and makes maps as I travel."

"That all sounded stupid, and I'll bet it didn't tell you these mark the end of the Midlands. Past them are the Sunlands, the realm of the blessed Sunchosen."

"Are most of the Sunlands a jungle?"

He indicated the vast forest a mile in front of them.

"No, but it's the most direct route from here to Sunspire. I hear that offering-bearers always hafta trim it back. They make plenty of complaints saying the Sunchosen should do it, but nobody's actually dared to ask yet."

Halfway to the forest a green snake rose from the tall roadside grass, striking at Kalillit's foot. Florinald whipped a dagger, killing the snake.

She jumped.

"What was that for? Are you trying to give me a heart attack?"

"Trying to save your life, and you're welcome."

"Ekari in the grass aren't dangerous." She lifted her right foot, pointing to her boot. "They can't bite through these."

She picked up his dagger with the snake impaled on it. A beautiful green snake, with ribbed vanes folded along its left and right sides.

"They're not dangerous until you kill one of them."

In the distance, they heard an angry droning as hundreds of Ekari rose into the air.

"They only fly when they're angry. Unless we can hide, they'll drain our blood 'til we die."

She looked about frantically for cover.

"If they're up, we go down." Florinald grabbed Kalillit's shoulder and pulled her off the road into the tall grass. "Don't move. Their eyes are on the tops of their heads, so they probably won't be looking down. We can wait until they give up."

"I don't think so. Never heard of them stopping once angered."

"First time for everything. We can afford to wait them out."

A candle later Florinald changed his mind, or rather, Kalillit changed it for him.

"If we wait here long enough, it won't matter. The Badlight will get us."

"Damn. It's my fault, so I'll deal with them. I'll lead them back the way we came, then you run to the next Sanctuary."

Before Kalillit could say anything, he jumped up and ran back along the path. With a buzz of angry wings, the Ekari turned as a swarm, only three feet above ground level, and followed him as an undulating green carpet.

They caught up swiftly, covering him in a mass of snakes to the point he could no longer be seen. They brought nearly unbearable pain, like a hundred hot wires. His hands covered both eyes to protect them, and in doing so he felt his new ring touch his face.

"Son of a bitch. Rebelled against the ring so much I forgot."

He rolled over and over, crushing Ekari that oozed red and purple blood, the latter of which was surely his.

Don't have a choice if I want to protect her.

He concentrated on the ring and the instructions in his pocket until he felt them grow warm. Florinald stood and flexed his right hand. His eight-pointed gold-star-crowned ring glowed, and he produced eight yellow orbs, each an inch in diameter, clustered on his palm.

Florinald hurled the balls in an arc around him. They exploded into lightning balls, vaporizing the entire swarm within a hundred feet, save for the ones in the clear space where he stood. He dropped again and rolled until those remaining were crushed.

Kalillit, who had not run far, rushed to him.

"There, I've corrected my mistake," he said. "No child in my charge will suffer harm."

She coughed on the acrid smoke from the electrocuted snakes.

"How . . . did . . . what . . . child? I'm a full-grown woman. Do you think those tavern scum wanted sex with a child?"

"In my experience, it's entirely possible. My pardon; you seem quite young to me, but then I'm rather old in human terms. How old are you?"

"I'm over five Goodspans. That's more than five thousand Goodlights, since you're not from around here."

He hesitated.

"If I figured that right, you're only fourteen or fifteen standard years. Not adult where I come from."

"Adult enough. My mother had me around this age."

"That is as may be. My apologies, young lady. If there are any other harmless dangers, tell me about them ahead of time, yes? As to your not-yet voiced questions, I have equipment for emergencies. Sausage for hunger, bombs for mass enemies, and so forth.

"As for *my* question, why didn't you run as I told you?"

"I-I'm not a coward. Maybe I couldn't stop them, but I stayed in case you lived after they left. Maybe I could have dragged you to the Sanctuary?"

"Thanks. I appreciate it, but you were more likely to get yourself killed, and I couldn't live with that."

"But you'd have been dead before me."

"True. Guess it would have worked out then."

Kalillit grunted.

#

The trek along the jungle path passed without further incident throughout the day. Florinald had shown her his Ekari-inflicted wounds, which were pinpricks of purple. She snorted disdainfully at them, until he explained the snakes sucked blood right through the skin, rather than biting. He drank a clear potion that he said would help overcome his wooziness and blood loss.

As Badlight drew closer, Kalillit grew nervous.

"There should be a Sanctuary at the trip's halfway point. It might be overgrown, so look sharp."

They ate red, teardrop-shaped gwa-fruit off the trees as they walked, and Florinald saved some seeds.

"Cousin Morninglight will find these quite interesting. They remind me of both meat and bread, plus they can be made into beer. Sounds like a win all around."

He tucked away a whole fist-sized fruit under his jacket.

Kalillit pointed up ahead. "There it is; the Sanctuary."

She rushed forward.

"Azku shit."

He caught up and saw the source of her consternation. The wooden dome was shattered and overgrown, with no sign of a Suncanna.

"We're thoroughly baked," she said. "No way we make the next town before Badlight."

He pulled aside vines and pointed to skeletons.

"Even worse," he said, "there's still some fresh meat on those bones."

The vines grabbed him. Kalillit screamed. She ran to him, dagger drawn.

Florinald had been completely engulfed by vines. Kalillit sliced them away until the vines grabbed her dagger and right arm. She shrieked and pulled a small blade from her left boot, then cut herself free. She removed the vines around his face, the terror in her eyes replaced with determination, even as small vines lashed at her, drawing blood.

"M-my hand," he choked out. "Free my right hand. Don't worry about cutting me."

Blood leaked from his face and chest, staining the vines purple.

She sliced at his hand until he wiggled his bloody fingers.

"Move back and don't look," he yelled.

His ring glowed brighter and brighter. Kalillit cut herself loose from a few vines and ran.

A soundless explosion of light filled the broken Sanctuary. When it faded, she turned around to see Florinald standing, vineless and blood-soaked.

"You saved my life. Those vines leak acid from their razor-sharp leaves."

He pointed to his shredded, blood-stained clothes and the oozing purple gashes on his face. With his shirt removed, Kalillit gasped at the slashed skin hanging from his arms and chest, exposing muscle.

He drank another bottle of clear potion, and offered one to Kalillit. She drank it with a grimace, then they bandaged each other.

"I suppose it's what I get for feeling invincible," said Florinald. "I didn't think anything on this little world could hurt me much. If ValDurians have a particular weakness, I'd say it's ego."

"I'd have cried if you were plant food. There'd be nobody to bring me sausage."

"No worries there. I've got plenty left," said Florinald, then he frowned. "Another matter, young lady. You told me you had only one knife, yet I see that isn't true. Thank goodness."

"Your people aren't the only ones entitled to secrets," she said with a shrug.

Florinald produced a fist-sized brass ball and threw it at the broken Sanctuary. It exploded in a cloud of black gas, leaving dead and withered vegetation in a hundred-foot circle. He examined the area with his scanner, detecting a still-living V'Laubi hidden by the debris.

He tossed a red fireball into the spot, then stood back as the V'Laubi became ash.

A quick search of the wrecked Sanctuary grounds revealed a passenger coach. It was filled with large, sealed jars, which Kalillit identified as wine vessels.

"It's offerings to the Sunchosen, from all the nearby towns."

"What happens if the Sunchosen don't get their tribute?"

"Offerings. Don't know; never heard of it happening. It won't matter to us anyway; we'll be dead in a few candles."

"No, we won't. I told you before; I've walked through your Badlight."

Florinald went inside the coach, and exited scrubbed of blood, wearing a fresh change of clothes identical to his old. The harnesses were detached from the bovine skeletons, which Kalillit identified as those of Azku. He tossed the harnesses in with the wine, and produced a silver, palm-sized disk. It expanded into a green, glowing, three-foot-diameter floating platform. Finally, Florinald attached the harness pole to the platform through a convenient top loop that tightened around it.

"Hop into the driver's seat, Kalillit, and hang on."

She did, and he ran. The platform followed him, pulling the coach. Kalillit bounced and bumped in the cushioned seat, laughing with glee.

After a candle or so, she stopped laughing. "Why didn't you pull that floaty thing out before? You run a lot faster than I do. I coulda ridden on that. Why aren't you riding on it?"

"It only follows me, or travels in a circle around me, so I can't ride it and go anywhere. We didn't need it before and now we do. Any more questions?"

They had reached the edge of the jungle, so he slowed to a trot and breathed a little easier.

"Where do you get all this stuff from? You barely have pockets, and no backpack either."

Florinald slowed to a walk.

"You saved my life. I owe you that much at least."

"More, but talk first."

"I have more pockets. Pocket dimensions, that is. Tiny ones."

"What?"

"Magic, invisible pockets all over my body. In my ring, up and down my arms, legs, chest and back. Each holds some useful item or has room for storage. I have to open them with my hands, which is why I needed you to free mine. There are also regular pockets in my jacket."

"I guess that explains it. One of your pockets has sausages then?"

"Three pockets, actually. I like sausage."

Kalillit was about to agree when the Sun turned purple. Her eyes were wide with fright, and she gulped constantly.

In a dry voice, she said, "It's beautiful. We're gonna die."

"No, we aren't. Well, not right away at least. I expect you've got thousands of Goodlights left yet. As for me? Hard to tell. ValDurians usually live a long time, even the adopted ones."

She pulled her hood tight, closed her eyes, and shuddered.

"I'm serious," he said. "Even my poor powers are enough to get us to the next town."

"May it be as you say." Her voice trembled.

"It looks clear; we should be fine." He picked up his pace, walking with a jaunty step.

Florinald stopped short as a black fireball arced out of the sky, exploding in their path.

The flames never touched them but continued burning. From the midst of the fire reared up a greenish glob with a gaping maw and one giant eye.

"Congratulations," it said in a thick, liquid voice. "You will be the first human to be killed by a Rakar in quite a while. We've been picking Suncanna off the Sanctuaries to give us more chances, so it's about time. I'd have been here sooner, but we had to cast lots to see who got to have fun. Hell, I personally encouraged the reaver vines to grow at the last Sanctuary, so it's only fair it fell to me. Wait."

He blinked his massive eye in a slow, deliberate manner.

Florinald smirked and put the red lens over his left eye.

"So you're the unlucky winner," said Florinald. "And here I was thinking your kind were only stories to keep the gullible in line. Can you give me your name, so that I may put it in my journal?"

He held a book and pencil. Kalillit's legs gave out, and she fell on her ass, barely breathing.

"Where in Rak did you come from?" it said while pointing a globby tentacle at Florinald. "All we saw was the girl. Huh, well, I get the guy, and after time for her to run and scream, somebody else gets the girl. Otherwise, I'll catch it for killing two of you."

"We wouldn't want that now," said Florinald. "Since we're going to die, would you mind explaining how you can remove the Suncanna?"

The Rakar laughed in a burbling fashion.

"The Suncanna keep us twenty feet away from the Sanctuaries, so we developed a new technology…the twenty-one-foot pole. We pry them off, into a bag on another twenty-one-foot pole."

Kalillit gasped.

"I am truly impressed," said Florinald in a monotone. "No wonder the people fear you."

"It's so rare we find humans in the 'Badlight,'" said the Rakar. "I've got the whole act planned out. I'd better get in shape for the part. You may have a few moments to grovel and beg for your lives."

He began changing to a humanoid form.

Florinald looked at Kalillit and shook his head.

"We really aren't the groveling and begging types. We'll face whatever you dish out."

The Rakar was now fifteen feet tall, with huge bat-like wings, one big, red eye and an ebon-black standard human shape otherwise.

"Oh, brave types. I love it. This'll be more fun than I thought."

"You might want to put more effort into it than that. It's a pretty boring look. Maybe some cool armor with jagged points, and a demon-head shield? Oh, and a bad-ass sword would help."

"What?" roared the demon. "You're giving me fashion tips while I'm planning to kill you?"

"Look around." Florinald laughed. "The wagon is pulled by a floating disk, the girl is Sunchosen, and you didn't even know I was here. You're pretty slow in sizing things up, Squiggy."

"The name is Alfranazor," raged the demon.

Florinald wrote that down in his journal, put it away and pulled a dagger from his jacket pocket.

"I like you, Al. Tell you what, I'll let you fly away as a courtesy. Just let your buddies know to leave us alone."

He balanced the dagger on his right thumb.

"The girl is a halfer, nothing more. You've got a little magic, that's all. My fellows would never let me live it down if I let you go. Say, what are you fiddling with there?"

"Oh, just a little toy of mine. Take a good look."

He tossed the dagger right into the middle of the one, big eye. Alfranazor fell over backwards and pawed at his eye, doing still more damage.

Florinald recalled the dagger to his hand and put it to Alfranazor's throat.

"Leave. Now. Return to your fellows and say the Sunchosen denied and defied you."

He pressed his ring into Al's chest and the flesh sizzled, leaving an eight-pointed star burned into it.

Alfranazor dissolved into oily smoke and vanished.

Kalillit sat transfixed. "How . . . what . . . who . . .?"

"If I take your meaning; I distracted him by throwing my little dagger into his big eye. Thank Raelani the eye was so huge, else I might have missed. If I were blindfolded, facing backwards and upside down."

"But –?"

"My ring is the same stuff your Suncannas are made from. It's what keeps the Rakar away. Gold is sacred to the god Apurion, and in these little worlds it's deadly to demons. They can't even bear to be near a large mass, hence their need for poles. Now, throw your hood back and keep your eyes down. If his friends are watching, and they are, they'll see a Sunchosen. I don't think they'll bother us again this Badlight."

Black fireballs exploded around them, disgorging six Rakar.

"Why can't I always be right, like the rest of my family?" Florinald yelled.

He dove into four of the amorphous beings, twin daggers flashing. Two Rakar became skeletal humanoids with whips and went after Kalillit.

She dodged and slashed, but her dagger wouldn't bite into demonic flesh. Florinald cut, punched and dropped explosions, all the while drawing the main hoard from Kalillit.

"Hit them with the butt of your dagger. It's gold," he yelled.

Puzzled, she hit. The Rakar burst into flame and vanished, while the other near her just ran. Florinald, battered and bleeding, dragged himself from a pile of dead or dying demons.

Putting his foot on what looked like a neck, he asked, "What made you stupid enough to try again? Didn't you see what we did to Al?"

The creature choked and burbled.

"He told you our plan, about removing Suncanna. We couldn't let you tell the Sunchosen. They might actually do something."

The demon dissolved.

Chapter Twenty Six
Well We're Movin' on Up

A few candles later, Florinald and Kalillit walked, coachless, into Bylea, a robust town containing hundreds of wooden dome-houses. All were sealed for the Badlight. They made for a white stone tower in the middle of town at Kalillit's urging.

Florinald, in fresh clothes again, checked it out with his red lens. "Same stone as those pillars we saw before. About one hundred feet high, twenty feet in diameter, and Suncanna every ten feet up. This place is pretty well protected."

The door had a copper gong hanging from a pole to their left. Finding no hammer, Florinald pulled out a foot-long mace and two pairs of earplugs. After showing Kalillit the use of earplugs he beat the gong like rolling thunder.

Satisfied with the noise and dents, he replaced the mace and his earplugs. In short order the door-slot opened and a pair of drab green eyes stared at him. And continued staring.

Florinald asked, "Aren't you going to find out what we want, or invite us in, or tell us to get lost? Anything?"

The man behind the eyes said, "I'll wake the Master. This is unprecedented."

The slot closed.

"If he isn't awake already, he's the soundest sleeper I've never yet met," said Florinald. He turned to Kalillit. "Get ready to meet your first Sunchosen up close, if you were right about this place."

She gave him a blank look. "What?"

He started to yell but instead pointed to his ears. After a moment, she took out the earplugs and handed them back.

"Keep them. I've got others, and I don't need your ear goo," he said.

"What did you say?"

"About the ear goo?"

"No, before that."

"Get ready to meet a real Sunchosen, if you were right about one living here."

She put the earplugs in a jacket pocket and fluffed up her hair, trying to look as Sunchosen as possible.

After a short wait, they heard the beating of mighty wings. Looking up, they saw a brown, four-winged bull launching from the roof of the tower. It circled them at head-level, its rider a slender, amber-skinned humanoid with white hair and glowing yellow eyes. He wore a white tunic, white pants, and white sandals.

Kalillit trembled.

"And they shall ride upon the backs of divine beasts, with wings of storm and hooves of thunder."

The bull landed nearby, making a display of its mighty, white shoulder-wings and the smaller haunch-wings. The passenger jumped from the saddle and stood before them, imposing at six inches taller than Florinald.

"I am Meshalameir, Protector of Bylea. I suffer no Rakar in my presence. Leave or be destroyed."

Florinald sighed. "We are not Rakar. The girl is Sunchosen; I travel under her protection. Can a Rakar do this?"

He placed his hand on the Suncanna over the door. He held Kalillit up to do the same.

"Then how do you live in the Badlight? The girl has not come into her power."

"Luck," said Kalillit. "The Rakar saw my hair and didn't press the issue. We almost lost our offerings near town, though. I stepped away from the coach to attend to private matters, and then Rakar killed and ate our Azku. My attendant's luck held; he was inside the coach and they let him be."

"The offerings of wine are in the coach outside of town," said Florinald. "Once we lost our animals, we ran."

"Why did you not stop at the midpoint Sanctuary? That's what it exists for."

Kalillit spoke. "The Sanctuary no longer exists as anything but debris. The Suncanna are gone. We hoped we could make it here, and we nearly did. We didn't want the offerings to be late."

"They already are, but your effort is noted. You may enter my tower until Firstgood. We will talk after I sleep."

#

Meshalameir proved good as his word, and his word provided a long breakfast which they shared. After an account of their journey, which downplayed Florinald's role, the Sunchosen had a team take them and two draft Azku to retrieve the wine-wagon. Back at Bylea, Meshalameir had them quartered in a guest-home until the next Goodlight. At Firstgood they set out for Sunspire in the offerings-wagon, minus several jars for Bylea, but plus two new Azku. The Sunchosen made for the destroyed Sanctuary with a team of builders, supplies and Suncanna.

Sunspire lay before them fifteen miles away, clearly visible. Florinald measured its height at two miles, not counting the gradual rise of the land. It looked fragile, being scarcely a quarter mile across the base, and tapered to a point.

The path to Sunspire was still no true road, but level and hard-packed, making for an easy journey. Easy for speed, but not so much for comfort. The Goodlight shone much hotter than what they had experienced previously, leaving Kalillit drenched in sweat.

Florinald said, "You could take off the jacket at least. I don't think the boots are helping either."

"I'll suffer. I need the jacket to hide my dagger. I don't like being barefoot."

He produced a bundle of white fabric and a pair of lace-up sandals.

"Get in the coach and put these on. I won't see anything, so don't worry."

She snatched the bundle from him and swung into the coach through the window. After a few minutes, she rejoined him in the driver's seat.

She wore a loose, white, long-sleeved pullover top with loose white pants, lace-up sandals and a wide-brimmed white hat.

She held a copper dagger in each hand.

"I got no place to put these now."

Florinald handed her two white buckle-on sheaths, the big one for her left forearm and the smaller for her left calf. He showed her how to wear them.

"Now that we're on our own," said Florinald, "could you tell me about those winged bulls? Cousin Morninglight would love to see one."

"The Weirkien. Not much to say; they're rare, male Azku sacred to the Sunchosen."

"I'll bet the droppings are no fun to clean up. Their design is good, with a set of small rear wings to balance out the front ones. Many four-legged creatures with wings only have them near the front shoulders. Ofttimes those that can actually fly look silly with their butts hanging down."

"Huh?"

"Never mind. I'll tell you when you're older."

The trip continued monotonously for five candles. At that point, they saw tilled fields on both sides with workers garbed in red or yellow. They were harvesting what resembled deep blue sunflowers, piling them into wooden carts.

"What are those?" asked Florinald.

"No idea. I've never been this close to Sunspire before. Why, would your Cousin Morninglight want one?"

"Probably." Florinald chuckled.

At eight candles they saw workers clustered together, unmoving. Florinald stopped the coach.

"Anything I can help you folks with?"

An elderly male in yellow, with bald pate and long black beard spoke.

"No. Nothing can be done until a blessed Sunchosen returns."

"Explain, please," said Florinald.

"Young Lalangil went in too far for harvest. The hucha were not ripe, and reminded him of this, as we could tell by his screams."

"I know not your hucha. What did they do?"

"The young plants are sensitive and will hurl poisonous thorns at any who disturb them. In the older plants, the thorns fall out when replaced by the seeds we eat."

"I have medicines; perhaps they will help?" said Florinald.

"I have an anti-toxin," said the old man, "but he went in too far. Anyone who goes after him will suffer in the same way. A blessed Sunchosen is beyond such harm, but none have yet responded."

Florinald frowned.

"Point the way. I can bring him out without incident."

With an incredulous look, the old man pointed the way, and Florinald ran into the hucha. The workers fidgeted anxiously for several minutes, and the old man turned to Kalillit.

"Your friend is brave, but a fool. Only the Sunchosen have ever walked among the young hucha without harm."

Kalillit grinned and slapped him on the shoulders with both hands.

"Yep, he's a fool, but somehow I'm not worried for him."

He rubbed his right shoulder.

"May it be thus, but Lalangil has likely died already. The effort is in vain."

Florinald burst forth from the field with the afflicted boy across his shoulders. He gently placed the boy on the ground, and the old man rushed to give him the medicine.

The crowd watched breathlessly, and then erupted into gaiety when Lalangil stirred to life.

"Sorry it took so long," said Florinald. "He couldn't speak, and the thick undergrowth made him nearly impossible to find."

"Thank you, sir," said the old man. "How were you able to do such a thing?"

"Vitamins. Call it a blessing of the Sunchosen. Will he be all right?"

"I believe so. How may we thank you?"

"A big handful of those seeds will do, if you please."

Florinald pulled out a small satchel and the old man filled it with a healthy pile of seeds.

"How shall Lalangil call his rescuer?" the old fellow asked.

"Tell him Kenny Rabinowitz was here."

Florinald and Kalillit re-boarded the coach and went on their way.

"So, who's Kenerbelwits?" said Kalillit.

"Just a name I've used. If they say my real name, it could draw the attention of powers unpleasant."

"You told me your real name."

"Did I? Oh yes, I did. It isn't a problem while you're with me. Just don't say it when I'm gone."

"Why didn't the hucha kill you? You've had trouble with plants before."

"Didn't feel like dying this time. Plus, missile weapons, such as these thorns, are mine to use, not to be used against me."

"Sure, why not?"

They traveled on and reached the base of Sunspire at Lastgood. The path ended at a set of two white pillars identical to those at the beginning of the Sunlands, except that these burned with a ghostly white fire. An actual road paved with gray stone started past the pillars, but this was blocked by ten men in blue tunics and white trousers. To the right stood a small wooden booth occupied by a man in a blue tunic and blue trousers.

"State your business, please."

"We bear offerings of wine from the Eastern towns," said Kalillit. "In addition, I am a Sunchosen not yet come into my power, and I seek the peak."

She removed her hat.

The man nodded at the sight of her hair.

"You may proceed. Now you, sir; what is your business?"

"Me? I'm with her, as a traveling companion and aide."

"Young lady?"

"Sure. What he said."

"Very well, you may continue."

The guards allowed them through, and four escorted them plus the coach to a square wooden platform large enough to hold the coach and azku. The platform had chains at each corner attached to winches one hundred feet above. The guides halted them.

"The azku and the wagon stay here. We'll help you unload the cargo." Which they did, onto a long, low cart.

When all was unloaded, the two travelers and the precious wine were cranked to the next level. From there, two more guides escorted them along a stone ramp to another platform. This one had a counterweight mechanism which took them up another hundred feet to the next ramp, which took them to another platform, and so on. This went on for one hundred platforms, taking them up nearly two miles of the gray stone spire and seven candles into the Badlight.

Guides along the way assured them no Rakar would approach Sunspire under the purple light. This allayed Kalillit's nervousness but did nothing to decrease her boredom.

Just as she was about to ask, 'Are we there yet?' they arrived at the last stop with a thump.

Before them towered a gigantic white castle, carved in whole from the inner stone of Sunspire. It dazzled with an astonishing multitude of crystal domes and windows shining in purple splendor from the Badlight. There were no attendants waiting for them, but Kalillit saw a golden filigreed gate a few hundred feet ahead, across the glazed, white stone pathway.

She turned toward Florinald, and instantly jumped back, dagger in hand.

"Who are you?" she yelled at the copper man standing near her.

"It's still me, girl. All ValDurians have the ability to alter their form to some extent. All I can manage is the color and texture of my eyes, hair, and skin. This is my true skin, or near as I can remember, anyway."

"Yeah, with all that blah, blah, blah, it's you all right. Why the disguise before?"

"I don't like to make a scene while traveling, but now I need to stand out. I want a meeting with the High Lord, and this should get somebody's attention."

Sure enough, as they approached the gate, guards on the other side went running for the castle proper.

Florinald produced two metal folding chairs, and Kalillit plopped down with great relief after a day of standing. After a few minutes, the guards returned with three Sunchosen that glowed in yellow auras. All three were slender and well over six feet tall.

The center Chosen spoke.

"We suffer no Rakar on Sunspire. Begone." The other two solemnly nodded their heads.

"I've been through the drill already. Will this help?" asked Florinald.

He grabbed the golden gate with each hand, and Kalillit did the same.

"If not Rakar, then what are you?"

"ValDurian, Florinald specifically, and her . . ."

"Hi." She waved with her right hand.

"She's Kalillit Farwander, Sunchosen-without-portfolio. Both of us request an audience with your High Lord."

The Chosen looked at one another and appeared to be debating silently. Finally, the middle one spoke.

"Very well. This is unprecedented, and for just that reason I think you should see him. Come with us."

The Chosen opened the gate and motioned them on. Inside the gargantuan, glistening castle they were led to the baths.

Non-Sunchosen attendants helped them remove the 'lowerworld stink,' and fed them. At Firstgood they were taken to the throne room. The High Lord Indalakeir sat resplendent within, on a golden throne atop a twenty-one tier dais of glazed white stone. On both sides of him stood ten-foot-tall white pillars burning with ghostly white flame.

Dozens of willowy Sunchosen stood about, silently staring and nodding at one another. Kalillit was sure now that all Sunchosen were tall and slender, and she hoped her new height would kick in soon. Florinald bowed his head slightly and Kalillit did the same.

"Welcome to Sunspire," boomed the voice of Indalakeir. "Our eyes have seldom seen the like of you, O man. What reasons have brought you into the presence of our magnificence?"

"I am Florinald ValDurian, and my reasons are threefold, Your Highness: To establish an alliance between my family and the Sunchosen, to invite one or more of yourselves to travel back with me to Valeron, then lastly, to see this young woman become a full

Sunchosen."

Indalakeir's chin leaned on his right hand, and the left-hand fingers drummed on the throne's arm.

"It is not our way to have discourse with lower beings, any more than is required. None here would wish to leave, unless I so ordered it. I am not inclined to do so. As for the girl; she is no Sunchosen."

"What?" Kalillit squeaked. "I just don't have my full power yet."

Two Chosen stepped forward and forced her facedown to the floor. Florinald looked up to the High Lord.

"Your Highness? Is her offense so great?"

Indalakeir waved the Chosen away.

"Only in speaking out of turn. She may stand. Though we would welcome another to our ranks, she is not Sunchosen. If she were, her power would already have manifested, being this near the Sun. Still, she is not without her uses. Young, pure girls are sensitive to the presence of stonefire, and she will be put to work guarding against it."

"Stonefire, Your Highness?" asked Florinald.

"This," said Indalakeir, pointing at the flaming pillars to his sides. "Being this close to the Sun causes the exposed sacrestone to flame, unless a protective glaze covers it. Where the glaze has worn thin, stonefire bursts forth. Young girls are particularly sensitive to such possibilities."

Kalillit thought to protest but decided against it.

Florinald spoke.

"The Rakar have devised a means of removing Suncanna from your Sanctuaries. We have seen this on our journey here. My family can help you with that. In trade, you might give aid toward a great crisis approaching which will affect all worlds and worldlets."

"The Sunchosen neither need help from outsiders, nor do we offer such help."

"What would convince you my family is worthy of your attention?"

Indalakeir mused for a moment.

"If you could hold your own against our Champion, I might consider your position."

"In what sort of contest?"

In response, all the courtiers moved away, save for the two that had pushed Kalillit to the floor. She and Florinald were waved off to the side. At an unspoken signal, both courtiers glowed with purple auras, bowed to Indalakeir, then to each other. They straightened up and commenced blasting each other with purple rays from their eyes.

At first Kalillit was thrilled, but as the long minutes went by, boredom set in. The two combatants stood unmoving while their eyes blasted, and their auras flickered. At last, the aura of one failed and he was knocked on his backside. The audience applauded.

"That is the High Duel, where the strongest wins," said Indalakeir. "The battle ends when one is dead or unable to fight. Is this something you can do?"

A faint smile played on Indalakeir's lips.

"I'm willing to try, Your Highness, in the interest of relations between both our kinds."

Indalakeir smiled sweetly.

"Yes. Oh, one more thing, you may not use any sort of weapons or defenses from outside Gyi'stal. My Champion will use powers of this world only. In the interest of fairness, I ask that you do the same."

After a moment's hesitation Florinald said, "Yes, Your Highness. Certainly. When do I battle?"

"In three candles. You will be taken to chambers to prepare, unless you require rest, of course."

"That will be fine, Your Highness. May the girl come with me?"

"Of course. She may help you prepare."

Florinald and Kalillit were taken to a small room where Kalillit plopped down on the only bed.

"You don't sleep, right?"

"Correct. Not that I'd be able to now, anyway. I may be in over my head here."

"Seriously? I saw you take down a Rakar without half-trying, and destroy a good chunk of jungle."

"Yes, with equipment from other worlds. I don't even have weapons from this world. It isn't that Chosen are so strong. I scanned them during the 'fight.' I could handle them if I used my good throwing daggers. Even Indalakeir, and he's a sight stronger than the others. Dodging their beams isn't so hard either; they squint just before they fire, which is a bigger tell than I need. No, I just don't think I can hurt them without some throwing weapons."

Kalillit gave him her dagger. "This is from here. Use it, but I want it back after you win."

Florinald brightened. "Thank you. That helps. If I could just get more stuff to throw, I could do this."

"How about the sacrestone bed?"

"Little heavy for me, but I could break it up." He produced a large hammer and smashed a bed leg into small bits that immediately burst into stonefire.

"Scratch that idea," he said, as he produced two long metal forks and a bag of marshmallows. "But I have another."

He showed her how to toast marshmallows. After eating several, he pulled out metal tongs and sealed some pieces of the stone into a metal jar. "For Cousin Morninglight."

He paced about the room.

"I still need some projectile weapons. I'd use my copper bits, but those aren't from here."

"And I only have a few," said Kalillit, wiping marshmallow from her lips. "Wait, I got it. You're gonna' owe me for this."

Chapter Twenty Seven
If You Try Sometimes

Florinald faced his opponent in the middle of the arena. It was a thirty-foot diameter circle surrounded by a wall of sacrestone, with three tiers of seating surrounding that. Indalakeir came down from his box seat to the Champion, who knelt before him. After the High Lord placed his hands on him in blessing, the Champion stood; his six-and-a-half-foot height dwarfed by the seven-foot figure of Indalakeir.

The High Lord took his seat and waved for the fight to start. The Champion fired up his purple aura while Florinald watched his eyes, waiting. When the blast came, he dodged easily and it struck the surrounding wall. A gasp arose from the audience as the wall burst into stonefire.

"What is this?" thundered Indalakeir. "This is not how the High Duel is fought."

"Begging your pardon," said Florinald. "I have no resistance to your destructive power without using my other-worldly devices. As we all have feet, I assume there is no unfair advantage."

"The Duel is suspended until the wall is re-glazed."

Florinald sat with Kalillit in the meanwhile. She asked him, "Why do you need to dodge his beams? I thought that stuff couldn't hurt you."

"Missiles, not energy blasts. Still, between your knife and these, I think I've got this." He patted his bulging pockets.

The arena was soon ready, but this time the walls were lined with Sunchosen who had their auras up.

Indalakeir glowered from his box and addressed his Champion. "If you should miss again, your friends will absorb the blasts. Try not to let them be hit too many times. Commence."

The Champion tried his best, but Florinald always knew when a blast was coming. Many of the supporting cast were hit, but none of their shields went down. After several minutes of this Florinald reached into his pockets and threw a hail of sharpened hucha seeds at the Champion. None did any damage.

Changing his tactics, Florinald grabbed handfuls with supernatural dexterity, a row of seeds between every finger and thumb. He threw them in a tight stream, so that each seed in a row hit the same spot. After multiple handfuls, they penetrated, and the shield flickered. The Champion roared in pain and fired a blast in panic. It caught Florinald by surprise and hit him square in the chest, burning a hole in his jacket and shirt. He rolled as he fell, spilling hucha seeds from his pockets.

The Champion ran toward him, but Florinald swept the spilled seeds across the floor. The Champion slipped on them and fell backwards. His shield went out, and the crowd gasped.

"Have I won?" asked Florinald.

"He is not done yet, outworlder," said the High Lord.

As he blasted Florinald in the leg, the Champion sat up. His aura flickered to life as Florinald threw Kalillit's dagger, piercing the weakened aura and the Champion's neck. The Champion dropped again, and the aura died.

Florinald limped to the Champion and turned him facedown. "Your Highness, have I won now? He is not dead, but soon will be. You said only that one fighter must be unable to battle, not that there must be a death. If you declare my victory I can save him if you allow me to use my outworld tools."

Indalakeir drummed his fingers on the throne for a long moment.

"Fine. You are the victor. Save his worthless life if you can."

He and all his people left the arena. Kalillit ran to Florinald.

"You did it. I knew you would. Are you all right?"

"No, but I will be, and so will he." He salved and spray-bandaged the Sunchosen's neck and eyes, then gave Kalillit back her cleaned dagger.

"By the way, thank you for suggesting I sharpen hucha seeds as weapons. Took some fiddling, but in the end they worked just fine."

"You're welcome. Don't forget it."

He pulled out the bloody seeds with long tweezers and put them in a glass jar. After closing the little wounds, he put a few drops of liquid in the former Champion's mouth and stepped back.

The Sunchosen groaned and sat up. He pawed at his eyes. "I can't open my eyes." He coughed and hacked for a moment.

"No, you can't," said Florinald. "I used the bandage spray to seal your eyelids in case you had any funny ideas about revenge. Don't worry, I've got a solvent for that. You lost, but I didn't kill you. In fact, I patched you up."

"You should have killed me. My life is worthless since I failed the High Lord. He won't take this affront to the Sunchosen lightly."

"I figured him for the type. You could come with me. My family would be most interested in meeting you."

"Thank you, but he is my Lord. My fate rests in his hands, but you should leave if you can. He is the vengeful type."

"I will, and I have something that might help you."

Florinald pulled out a pile of silver rings and placed them on the former Champion's fingers.

"They're made of silver, and I've never seen that here. You might be able to buy favor with them."

He sprayed the Chosen's eyes.

"That'll dissolve right quick."

"Thank you. I am Salallen. May I know your name?"

"Florinald ValDurian, but it's best not spoken." He shook Salallen's hand. "This is a gesture of greeting and friendship between equals where I come from."

Salallen wiped his eyes clean and smiled. "I'll show you the way out. This place is a gargantuan maze."

"No need. I have my own way of leaving."

He gave Salallen a crystal ball.

"If your Lord wishes to contact us, that sphere will enable it. So that you know, what I said about the Rakar and the great crisis is true. I leave to see what can be done."

"Farewell then. Girl, you can come with me. I'll show you where the rest of the young slaves live."

"Slaves?" she asked.

"Well, yes. What did you expect?"

"More than this. Florinald, take me with you."

"I'm not sure if I can do that."

"Of course you can. I saved your life twice; first at the forest and here when I suggested the seeds as weapons. You owe me, and ValDurians pay their debts, yes?"

"Yes."

"Good. I want that name you gave me to be for real."

On the floor Florinald placed a box which blossomed into an eight-foot-high rainbow portal.

"Kalillit Farwander, the AllWorlds await."

#

The Grand Elder screamed at Attendant Javis.

"What do you mean, all of our bases belong to them? My reach and resources are infinite," the Grand Elder raged. "Have you and my other attendants gone insane?"

"We operate faithfully and efficiently as always, Magnificence," Javis said while bowing.

The Grand Elder hit her in the face with a blow that knocked her backwards to the floor. Then the Elder fell back into her chair.

"How can I trust such a report?"

"The same way you have trusted all my reports throughout the years," said Javis, rising to her feet. She avoided wiping at the red blood trickling from her mouth and it dripped onto her robes.

"It was easy because they were always favorable to me. Who would have the power to defy the V'Laubi?"

"More than you might think. You have always avoided confrontation with powerful enemies, but this time they have found you. My sources agree that the enemy is the Knights of Valeron, the main active force of the ValDurian family. They were probably also the ones claiming to be Olgun."

"Irrelevant. I shall marshal our forces and show these fools what it means to defy the Divine."

"Begging your pardon, but unless the Divine performs a miracle, you have no forces to marshal," said Javis.

Rage contorted the seething Grand Elder's face as she stared into Javis's eyes.

"Attendant Javis, contact the other factions and arrange a meeting. We have a matter of some importance to deal with."

Chapter Twenty Eight
Oracles: Jusa

Florinald straightened his green suit jacket for the nth time. Kalillit stood next to him, fidgeting with her knee-length white dress. She tried to tug it down farther.

"Relax and sit down," said Florinald. He waved his hand, pointing to a table in the Italian restaurant they occupied.

"Sit? I wouldn't dare. Why is it you get pants and a jacket?"

"Style, I guess? He brushed imaginary dust off the sleeves and trouser legs. "I just go where they point me, and wear what I'm told. We can stand at the bar if you like and order drinks plus garlic knots."

She stomped to the bar as hard as she could in stiletto heels. She slapped on the bar to get the bartender's attention.

"Gwa-beer and some of those garlic nuts."

"Nothing alcoholic for her," said Florinald. "Root beer and garlic knots for both of us."

"It's still beer. What's the difference?"

"Root beer is mostly caffeine and sugar. I think you'll like both."

Just then, a man approached them from the back rooms of the restaurant.

"Sir and madam, the proprietors will see you now."

He ushered them through a back room and closed the door behind him as he left.

A dimly lit, wooded clearing greeted them, showcasing a bubbling cauldron over a fire in the middle. Murmuring voices danced at the edges of their hearing while shadows flickered at the corners of their eyes. Kalillit shrank closer to Florinald and grabbed his hand.

The voices grew louder.

"A small one, isn't she?"

"Barely a nibble."

"Pretty though."

"Just what we need."

The ghosts of decrepit crones oozed out of the trees and surrounded the duo. The crones spun around them faster and faster, growing more and more solid. They grabbed at Kalillit and grew younger while her skin wrinkled.

Kalillit shrieked. Florinald hugged her.

"I told you before we came; they're just messing with you. None of this is real."

The ghostly crones stopped, no longer ghostly or crones. Eight alabaster women in colorful gowns linked hands in a circle around the pair.

"You shouldn't tell her that."

"Quite so."

"This is all real."

"Reality is relative."

"Not real in what way?"

"Shut up," screamed Kalillit as she stamped her foot. "Stop it. You're all crazy."

"She gets us, Flory," said the lady in yellow.

"You'll be the ones to get it if—"

Florinald put his hand over her mouth. She bit his hand. He pulled it away, uninjured.

"Look what they did to me. I'm old," said Kalillit.

She waved her wrinkled hand before his eyes.

"You aren't," he said.

Florinald rubbed at her hands, and the wrinkled skin vanished.

"It's all illusion," said Florinald.

"Why are we here? You said it was important, but these crazy people are making me crazy."

"These crazy people are the Purveyors of Portent, the Sibylline Sisters, the A-Team of Augury, the Octuplets of Oversight, The Eight

Who Are One, the Supreme Scrying Squad... I forget the rest."

"The Ogdoad –" they said in a collective stage-whisper.

"Yes, of course. The Ogdoad of Omniscience, the Eight Oracles of Valeron."

The women bowed with exaggerated flourishes.

"They help guide ValDurians and our Knights to deal with situations before they become huge problems. In some cases, to even prevent them before they start."

Kalillit scowled.

"What's an 'oddtoad'?"

"Ogdoad. It just means a group of eight."

"The Oracles are, from red to black: Gid, Jusa, Laba, Cridi, Kelon, Elyn, Trisyn, and Delu. Oracles, this is Kalillit, as you know."

"I won't say I'm pleased to meet them. And that's Kalillit Farwander."

Kalillit stomped her high heel into the dirt and nearly fell.

The lady in orange clapped her hands and a table with a tea service appeared in front of Kalillit. She jumped back three feet and did fall this time.

Kalillit flung the high heels into the woods in a fit of rage, then Florinald helped her up, and gathered the shoes.

"Relax," said Florinald. "They'll help you, but only while amusing themselves."

"Amusing themselves?" She grabbed the high heels. "I thought I was going to die while they sucked out my life, and you did nothing."

She held the shoes tightly by the toes.

"You let them terrorize me for their amusement."

She struck him savagely with the heels, again and again, and he did nothing to protect himself. Tears streamed down her cheeks.

"I liked you, and I thought you liked me, but you let them do that."

She dropped to her knees, the shoes falling from her hands. Florinald went down and hugged her tightly. She didn't pull away.

Florinald turned toward the Oracles with a fierce scowl.

"She's right. You're all assholes and I'm worse for letting it happen. We're leaving now. I don't care why you wanted to see us, but we won't be back."

The Oracles collectively gestured, then all but the one in orange disappeared, leaving Kalillit and Florinald sitting in chairs before a small, wooden table.

"As I predicted, of course. Yes, we Oracles are all assholes, but you aren't, Florinald. You're just too used to going with the flow, but I knew you had it in you. Can you two find it in your souls to forgive some crazy old ladies?"

The two looked at one another in confusion, then at the Oracle.

"I'm Jusa," said the lady in orange. "I'm going to do a tea leaf reading for you both, in hopes of gleaning more about the upcoming major crisis."

She poured tea from a pot into three cups.

"Drink."

Robotically, they both drank. After they finished, their cups were turned upside-down, then Jusa examined the residue of leaves remaining.

"Interesting," said Jusa. "Take a message to Lord Indra, Florinald, and then take some vacation time."

"A vacation in the face of an approaching crisis? I know to whom I speak, but is this wise?" he asked.

"It isn't here yet," said Jusa, "so I'd get all the rest I could in the meanwhile. If there were anything that could be done we'd have let you know.

"Young lady, if you could find it in your soul to forgive Florinald, I think you'd feel better. After that, some other ValDurians would like to meet you, and set you on the path to truly becoming Kalillit Farwander."

She handed a wax-sealed scroll to Florinald.

"Be off with you, and don't do anything we wouldn't do."

"That doesn't really exclude much," mumbled Florinald.

#

The golden flower-ship landed silently.

"We are here," shouted the Grand Elder over the intercom. "Depart the ship in your assigned groups, at your assigned intervals. I don't expect any more cooperation between factions than usual. Just keep to your designated targets and don't interfere with another group. When all are in play, I'll give aid to whichever units need it the most. Disembark now."

The hatch opened and the gangplank extended. V'Laubi units left the ship in groups of one hundred. First came the howling, tech-armored quadramorphs armed with netcasters, then clawed, tailed women wearing blue plastic body armor, carrying yellow-glowing swords, along with machine guns and bazookas. Behind them came four-eyed Clermann women behind steel shields, wielding gold paralo-ray guns. Rushing out flew squirrel-girls armed with pistols, followed by the Grand Elder's own Voaminid lizard women in yellow armor. Voaminid armaments varied, but included anything carried by the other groups.

"Go forth," said the Grand Elder. "I'll be with you momentarily."

She caressed her Battle Presence, which stood beside her command chair.

"I am restraining myself from plunging into you. I want to savor this."

She sank her hands into the armor and it began to flow up and around her.

"I-I, yes. This must be what our host bodies experience when we enter them. I almost envy them, but it is our divine right to control, not be controlled."

The armor sealed itself around her and she embraced herself.

"Enough. Time to assert our dominance."

She went to the lowest level, a hangar bay, where she entered a personal-sized flower ship. The doors opened and the ship flew out silently.

The five legions assaulted a five-walled city from each different side. While none of the combat was going well for the hollowbacks, her Voaminid legion was getting the worst of it. The Grand Elder landed behind her lines, and strode forth in slow splendor, enjoying the sparkle of sunlight on her armor.

"Attendant Javis, report."

"The city is built into a mountainside, with a five-sectioned wall surrounding it in a semicircle. Counting left to right, we have claimed the fourth wall as our target. I have called a halt to our advance, as it has some fearsome defenders. My hope is that the main three defenders will go to help the other walls."

"Main three? Three beings are making it difficult for you?"

"Yes, but if they expend their might on the other legions we should be free to enter here."

"We don't have time for waiting. Pull the low-born dregs back and I'll deal with this myself."

"But, your Magnificence—"

"Just do it. I'm going in regardless, but a withdrawal might save this pathetic lot some injuries."

The Grand Elder leapt forward a hundred feet in one bound, striking the fourth wall as she ended her leap. Chunks of masonry flew in an explosive fury, above and behind her, some pelting those Voaminids who had not retreated far enough.

A piercing sound preceded a rain of massive ice chunks which knocked the Grand Elder down.

"Uh, oh. No breaking the fourth wall," yelled a brown-bearded man in an orange kilt and red breastplate, standing in midair. He held black bagpipes which he put to his lips again. The shrill skirling brought down another storm of mini-icebergs on the already-buried Grand Elder.

"Get down there and check on her," he yelled.

A man and woman both leapt from the top of the wall, falling slowly to the ground. The red-headed woman looked up at the piper as she fell.

"Hey, Rayan, I thought real Scotsmen didn't wear anything under their kilts."

"Aye, but armor is always an exception. Now keep your focus on her, Gelda, and make sure she's done in."

"Looks done for to me, at least until the end of the next Ice Age," she said as they landed.

"What's the urgency?" asked the blond pony-tailed man. "The Oracles never give us a mission we can't handle."

"Aye, that's true so far, Eligar. Stay sharp and don't make liars of 'em."

Even as Rayan spoke, the ice pile shook, then exploded. The jagged, icy fragments might have been the death of the grounded pair, but Gelda defended herself with a whirling greataxe that had been on her back, mostly hidden by her mass of red hair, while Eligar outran the fragments with eye-blurring speed.

Rayan started another bagpipe solo, but the Grand Elder hurled an ice fragment that shredded the pipes and tore them from his hands.

"Clan MacCormac will neither forgive nor forget this offense," he shouted as he landed. Rayan rushed forward as he pulled a claymore, sheath and all from his back. He whipped the sword in a forward arc, hurtling the sheath as a missile weapon.

Gelda and Eligar joined in, surrounding the Grand Elder.

"I am enjoying your defiance," said the Grand Elder, "but it's your time to die now."

Chapter Twenty Nine
Here It Comes!

Aurus stood from a table and slapped on his fedora. He walked down the brightly-lit hallway, passing three doors until he came to an open one on his right. Knocking on the frame first, he entered.

"What's up?" asked Zen, who sat before a computer that took up most of a desk.

"Just waiting for the next big event. After all the near-constant battle, the waiting is getting to me."

"The peace is nice, but it's the proverbial calm before the storm, so I get it. You're looking good at least. Fully recovered?"

"Recovered my halberd, yes, and feeling tip-top. How are you and everybody else doing?"

"'Everybody else' is just Nea right now. Florinald is still on another mission."

The intercom buzzed. "Attention. This is Master Julian. All Knights and DemiKnights please meet me in the conference room."

#

A crowd filled the conference room. Julian stood on its oval table and made an announcement.

"Before we get into the meeting, it is my sad duty to announce that Knights Rayan MacCormac, Gelda Bronsten, and Eligar Windtalons have returned their badges to the Wyrd. They succeeded in their missions and now take their duties beyond this life. If any if you knew them, you have my shared sorrow."

Julian let the crowd speak amongst themselves until the talk quieted down.

"The rest of us still have duties, so let me introduce everybody to everybody.

"This lot are the Edgeriders." He indicated a group of eight that looked like a cross between construction workers and armored medieval knights.

"The Faybranded." These were seven dressed in various shades of green leather with three sporting stag antlers. Their sex was indeterminate.

"The Arcanen." Five obviously wizard types in robes of various colors. Two men and three women.

"Atom Heart and his Amazing Friends." Those three wore colorful superhero costumes. The biggest of them had a blue cloak, and a glowing disk attached to his chest.

The woman of the group, a redhead in white, said, "We did not agree on the group name. I'm Seerian and this is Battlescar." She indicated the other man near her. He had deep scars on his left cheek and throat, his outfit matching them in red.

"Aw, c'mon, Seeri. I thought it made us sound cool," said the cloaked man with the glowing disk.

"Sure, Lem, but it gives you top billing," she said.

"You can at least call me Atom Heart," said Lem.

Julian frowned, and rubbed between his eyes.

"Moving on, these are the Deadenders." He pointed to three men and three women, all gray-skinned and dressed in leather.

"Last, but hardly least, these three are Aurus, Nea, and Zen. No group name."

A new voice broke in behind them all. "Maybe no group name, but there are four of us."

Nea spun about to see a familiar brown-skinned man in the doorway, and nearly screeched with joy.

"Marvin, you're back."

"I am, and glad to be so. It is my understanding we're about ready for the Last Push against the V'Laubi."

"We are," said Julian. "That's where I was going after the introductions. There's a lot to talk about, so let me get to it. First, let me welcome you back, Marvin, and say I'm glad to see you.

"As Marvin said, we are nearly ready for the Last Push. You lot and other Knights have taken down all known V'Laubi outposts, leaving only their homeworld extant. Our final mission is to make sure the hollowbacks are rendered either harmless or nonexistent."

"Wouldn't that last be a job for the Untari?" asked a yellow and green-robed woman from the Arcanen.

"Yes, but there are two reasons why that won't be done. The first is that the ValDurians treat the ending of life, particularly that of an entire race, as an extremely grave matter, to be avoided under normal circumstances, as you know. The second is that the Untari are effectively useless on the central V'Laubi home worldlet."

"How so?" asked a Faybranded.

"The central part of the worldlet neutralizes the use of magic, explosives, or energy weapons. Ninety percent of the Untari's available weaponry would be ineffective."

There was a moment of intense chatter amongst the assembled Knights, until the largest member of the Edgeriders yelled out, "But most of us use either magic or energy weapons. How can we handle something the Untari can't?" An accompanying rumble came from the other Knights.

Julian raised his arms, then lowered them, palms down, until the talking ceased. "I'm getting to that. You all will be taking care of the V'Laubi portals. They are stationed on the outskirts of Lakachar, the V'Laubi homeworldlet. Far from the middle, the portals operate under normal bubble world conditions, else they would not operate at all."

"Then the Untari could assault the portals. Why the Knights?" asked Aurus.

"Frankly, with the Untari it would be over in an instant. We need a slower spectacle to garner their attention and divert resources from their city."

"We can cut them off from the AllWorlds, but not assault them directly?" asked Atom Heart.

"I didn't say that," said Julian, "but a direct assault would be most difficult. I hope it doesn't come to that. We'll know after Lady Raelani has finished speaking to the V'Laubi."

#

Nea walked alongside Marvin as he limped through the halls. "I'll be happy to help in getting your equipment organized," she said. "Julian won't need us for a while anyway, so it gives me something to do. Here we are now."

They stopped at a plain door, like a dozen others they had passed, and Nea paused before opening it.

"Just so you know, it's not in the same condition you left it."

She opened the door.

The lights came on and Marvin's face fell.

"What did you do to my stuff?"

"We had to use it a lot, so it's mostly depleted. I know we didn't clean and store it properly, so I'm sorry. If it helps, we were going crazy trying to keep up with the V'Laubi."

"Would it have killed anybody to use up one box of ammo before opening another? I just hope we have enough to do this last job against the hollowbacks. That stuff isn't easy to come by." He sighed. "I'll be thankful for your help."

"Help cheerfully given. It'll also give us a chance to continue the talk we were having, before you were injured."

"Were we talking about anything in particular?"

He started making a stack of boxes.

"Not really, I guess, so let's start anew. I was wondering how you healed so fast," she said while separating unopened boxes of handgun ammo from partial ones.

"I didn't. Same rate of healing as a normal, healthy person, I just had longer to do it in."

"Explain, please."

"My Bifrost shard was set to a time zone two weeks before any the rest of you were using. I went back there and started healing before I was actually injured, so I'm mostly recovered now. So is that the thing you really wanted to talk about?"

Nea nodded, then shook her head.

"No, there is one other. I was going to ask this the last time we talked. Do I seem like an okay person to you?"

"That's a curious question, if I may say so."

"I mean, am I the kind of person people like to have around? I haven't done a lot of interaction with people in a non-professional capacity."

He finished stacking some empty crates.

"I like having you around. Don't hang with average people myself much, so maybe I'm a poor person to question."

"What I mean, is, well, am I—"

"The kind of woman that men like to have around?"

"Yes, that. Don't want to put you on the spot, but since you brought it up. . ."

Marvin laughed. "So here I am, on the spot. Let me start by saying that I'm a lot older than I look, so this is a clinical observation, great-grandfather to great-granddaughter. You'd make some men nervous, but not any fellow Knights, I'd think."

"I was wondering, because Aurus seemed stunned by my appearance after the lessons with Madame Zygmeir at first, but seemed not to notice me at all later on."

"There was a lot going on, of course."

"Uh huh. Maybe it's because I dialed the makeup back, so I didn't look as much like a showpiece mannequin."

"Pardon?" said Marvin.

"I don't look as good as that first day. Didn't seem sensible to be using that much makeup on a mission."

"You don't really need any on a mission, or at all, by my way of thinking, but there's nothing wrong with putting your best face forward. You've been looking very attractive of late, if I may be so blunt."

"Thank you. Can't say Aurus has noticed though, except for that first look at Madame Zygmeir's place."

"Does that bother you?"

"No, of course not. Zen hasn't said anything either, but a woman doesn't mind a compliment every once and a while, so thank you again."

"You're welcome," said Marvin. "Not my business, I suppose, but are you and Aurus a couple, or are you working toward that?"

"What? No. Gods above, he's gorgeous, but thinking is not his strong suit."

"Yes, he looks like a movie star. As Aurus is a shapeshifter I assume it's a matter of choice."

"I don't know. He can't hold a new shape for an indefinite period, so it's probably his default human form," said Nea.

"That aside, he's been a Knight for quite some time, and has handled some impressive missions I've heard about. He can think when he wants to, but I'll admit he can come off as less than brilliant sometimes. From what I understand he used to act as a private detective, like from old-time movies."

"He's told me about that. Anyway, thanks for indulging me. I'll concentrate on business now."

#

Master Julian met with Aurus and the rest of his squad.

"While the other teams wait for the results of Lady Raelani's meeting with the V'Laubi, you'll be performing your own mission."

After he waited for acknowledgment, they gave him a collective shrug, and he continued.

"Glad to see you're all enthused. It's very simple: While the Lady speaks with their leaders, the other Knights will gather near the portals. The collective attention of the V'Laubi will be drawn to these things, allowing you to assault the city from underground."

"How?" asked Nea. "Do you have a map of their sewer system, or somesuch?"

"I do, in fact, courtesy of the Omnimind. Unfortunately, you'll have to dig your way to it from the edge of the worldlet, so they don't see you start. They may be smart enough to have continuous observation despite their worldlet having a foreign presence at its doorstep . . . or because of it."

#

"Javis, attend me," shouted the Grand Elder .

The lizard woman stepped from behind a tapestry.

"Yes, O Grand Elder?"

"I need my poison compressed-air gun needlebolts."

"Here, your Magnificence. May I ask the need?"

"We're having a meeting with those Valurdians, and my Battle Presence won't work here. I need assurance we are in control."

Javis handed her a packet of pencil-sized projectiles along with the gun.

"Good enough. I'm off," said the Grand Elder, "keep an eye on the proceedings."

"Very good, your Magnificence."

Chapter Thirty
Such Things are Beneath Me

Raelani rode in a carriage of alabaster and gold, drawn by a team of eight black horses shod and accoutered in silver. She poured herself a last glass of champagne, then handed the empty bottle to her silent companion. The brass-armored, close-helmed knight pulled out a box from under the seat, then took the bottle and placed it atop a dozen other empties. They kicked the box back under.

Eying her glass sadly, Raelani sipped at the champagne until they arrived at massive leaden gates set in a wall of gray stone. Finishing the drink, she placed the glass in a small cabinet on the coach wall, next to her bench seat. She stood, and adjusted her raiment, which consisted of a simple white gown and cloak, with a golden, gem-studded diadem upon her forehead. Picking up a hand mirror, she checked her look.

She rubbed the large, milky-white stone in the diadem's center and it showed rainbow colors briefly. Satisfied, she dropped the mirror and drew on long white gloves.

Reaching for the door handle, she stopped and spun about, her gown and cloak fanning out, but dropping limp when she stopped. No mysterious winds ruffled her garments. With a shrug, she opened the door to see a tall, gray-garbed, gray-masked footman awaiting her. He tipped his top hat to her and offered his hand, which she took to step down the short carriage ladder.

"Thank you, Coachman. I don't expect to be long, but if things go very wrong don't wait for me. There'd be nothing you could do to help, so get the horses and yourself out of here. The V'Laubi have allowed me one attendant, so Samus here will have to do."

She patted the brass knight on the shoulder, then they both walked to the leaden gates, which opened inward with ponderous slowness. They crossed the threshold, and the gates closed behind with considerably greater speed than they had opened. Raelani looked about, seeing a blocky city of gray stone with no visible populace or obvious doorways.

"Charming. Let's see how long they make us wait, Samus."

She pulled down one glove, and checked her wind-up wristwatch as she waited. At the half-hour mark several beings headed her way. She pulled up her glove.

"Not bad. Enough time to establish their dominance, but not too long for bad form. This appears promising. Makes me hope all the preparation was pointless."

Twenty-five beings surrounded her, five each of squirrel-girls, quadramorphs, four-eyed Clermanns, clawed/tailed women, and mauve-skinned Voaminid lizards. One of the lizard-women spoke.

"You will come with us to the Grand Chamber, where the Council of Providence will assess your words and intent. Your attendant may stay with you, as is proper, since it is not armed."

"Lead the way, my good women."

And they did, keeping Raelani and Samus in the horde's middle. After twenty minutes, by Raelani's mainspring watch, they arrived at a crystal-domed edifice, and were greeted by a seven-foot tall woman wearing plate armor and bearing a greatsword in each hand.

"Kelvaana, how nice to see you again," said Raelani. "You're doing well, I trust?"

"Yes, quite recovered from the thorough drubbing at the hands of your Aurus, thank you. I passed along your communications to the Council, verbatim and it was touch-and-go there for a time, before they agreed to meet with you."

"Sadly, many V'Laubi had to die before they agreed to this meeting," said Raelani. "I had hoped to avoid that path."

"As did I, but it took all that to sway their rather rigid minds. You must understand that the Council Elders are very old, having been hosted by numerous bodies. I do hope some sort of compromise can be reached between our peoples, as I don't believe a war is to either of our benefits."

"Agreed. Take me to your leaders."

#

Julian stood with Aurus, Nea, Zen, and Marvin on the shore of a fog-shrouded lake.

"As most of you know, the bubble worlds, of which Lakachar is one, rest on the Infinite Ocean, which is but a manifestation of the astral plane," said Julian. "This is only how our minds and eyes perceive it."

"Yes," said Marvin, "we know that."

"I didn't," said Nea, "but what's your point?"

"We can't use the Bifrost shards for a sneak attack, since the rainbows are too visible. To get around that, I've called in an old friend for an ocean voyage."

The fog disgorged an ominous spectacle. It looked like the ribcage of some gigantic beast, beaten with demonic hammers into the form of a ship, with the spine forming the keel. Where it might have once had sails, only black tatters trailed in the wind. No visible motive source moved it along, its only direction coming from a great, towering, skeletal figure in flowing black robes at the tiller.

"This is Zilbik, the Boatman," said Julian. "He'll take you along the Infinite Ocean to Lakachar. I must remain at our base to observe and control the operation."

The figure of nightmares waved at them.

Come on board, he said in grating mind-speech, *this will be only a short trip, but be wary, as the Infinite Ocean is no place for fools.*

They loaded numerous boxes of equipment aboard, where they discovered a transparent skin covered the ribs, keeping them separate from the Ocean. It made for bouncy walking, but seemed otherwise firm and solid. The Knights left Julian behind as they got underway.

The ocean manifested as starry night sky below them. Above them whirled heavens as from the imaginations of children, obeying no known laws of physics, filled with multiple planetoids careening about.

This is the Infinite Ocean, thought Zilbik out loud. *Do not dive overboard if you can help it. Your abilities may not work there, and I have no means to pull you back in. You could easily become lost in the AllWorlds. I know that for Knights of Valeron such may not be terrifying, but you could find yourselves in worlds where your Bifrost shards do not work.*

"All right then," said Aurus, "we place our lives in your hands and trust you to get us to our destination."

There were agreeing nods from the other Knights. Zilbik grabbed the tiller, and they could feel power emanating from him into it.

"And away we go."

#

"Are we there yet?" asked Aurus after what felt like hours. "Sorry, but I couldn't help myself."

Barring disaster we should be there momentarily.

The ship shook as they heard a thump on its side.

"I could see through the side membranes," said Nea. "Some sort of shark-beast hit us head-on."

Zilbik let loose a static-like sigh.

The Infinite Ocean is full of things like that. Many are just other travelers, but some are predators. Do any of you have extra-planar connections?

Nea and Aurus raised their hands.

Shit. I can smell it emanating from you now that I'm looking for it, especially the big guy. Let's hope it was just curious.

A wide-finned shark leapt at Aurus, who ducked, the beast sailing over the ship. Another followed, and this one Aurus split with his halberd.

There are more, and I might be able to outmaneuver them for a bit, but not the entire school, and not for the whole remaining trip. You'll have to fight.

"They're after me mostly, right?" asked Aurus.

I expect so, but it's not like you can leave. Wait, can you?

"Can we fly over the Ocean?"

If you can fly, I see no reason why not, but then they'll go after her, he thought, pointing to Nea.

"Not a problem, is it, Nea?"

"Not at all," she said as he picked her up.

Stay in sight of the ship. It's easy to get lost here.

Aurus launched himself and Nea into the phantasmagorical sky just as another flying shark leapt over the ship. This one hit the inside membrane and twisted around, teeth snapping. Marvin and Zen shot it to no apparent effect, and scrambled to avoid the teeth as it flailed. It quickly grew tired of playing with them and managed to heave itself overboard.

"Son of a bitch, I hate feeling helpless," said Zen. "I've got to acquire a magic weapon."

"What happened to that energy blaster you confiscated?"

"It's somewhere in our cargo boxes. Even if I had it out, I've yet to figure out how to charge it. The next shot could be its last."

"I know how you feel. While I have bullets for most every occasion, I don't know what hurts these shark-things. Hmmm, maybe sea-prism stone?"

You won't have to worry, said Zilbik, *the flying sharks are going after your friends. They might have to worry though.*

Aurus bobbed and weaved, dipping down, then up, leading the sharks away from the ship.

"This isn't too hard," said Aurus, "I can dodge them easily enough for now, but more are on our tail every minute. To add more trouble, I can't fly any higher. Infinite Ocean rules, I guess. I'm at maximum ceiling right now and well within their leaping range."

"I'll watch your back at least," said Nea, "and we're far enough ahead that any leap gives us plenty of warning."

"Thus far, but they're marginally faster than me and are catching up."

"You're faster as a hawk."

"You're suggesting I drop you?" said Aurus in an incredulous tone.

"Well, if it meant saving yourself —"

"Not ever. I'd rather be swallowed than sacrifice y – a teammate. I can fight them if need be. Only their numbers pose a threat."

"Behind."

Aurus banked right, narrowly dodging a flying strike.

"Damn, that was sooner than I expected. I can't fight while holding you, but I've an idea. Since my clothes are part of me I'll expand my belt. Slide down into it, facing away from me. I'll snug it up and hold you hands-free."

After a tense moment, Nea was in place, head between Aurus's shoulders, weapons out.

"Ready to repel boarders, Captain," she said.

Right on cue, three flying sharks came at them, missing as Aurus put on the air brakes. He bisected one as it passed overhead, then he put on the speed again.

"I'm only going to hit one by accident," said Nea. "Putting yourself in position puts me out of it, but don't change tactics. Do what works for you."

They flew on, Aurus zig-zagging and doing barrel rolls. The problem with those is that they slowed down his forward speed, so more sharks gained on them. As four more leapt at them, Aurus spun in place, decapitating three while Nea took out one.

"Got one," she yelled. "I just stuck my blades out and got him while you spun. Accidentally, as I said it would be."

"Awesome. Now close your eyes. I'm going to try and blind the next batch."

He let loose a small nova, which didn't stop those already in flight, but did send the next batch into a frenzy as they snapped at each other. The ones in flight were avoided with ease, relative to the previous batch.

"We're almost there," said Aurus, "I can see Lakachar ahead. Don't see the ship though."

"Aim for the shore," said Nea. "If these are like regular sharks they won't want to beach themselves."

"Unless they're also stupid like regular sharks, in which case they won't care."

He let out another nova flare and the sharks dropped back.

"There's the ship," yelled Aurus as they entered blue skies and sunlight. "I'm hitting the beach."

He aimed for white sand just as a voice pierced his head.

Pull up. Don't land.

Aurus's foot brushed the beach and it disappeared, becoming Ocean. Thankfully forewarned, he pulled up with nothing more than a wet foot. Dodging a lone shark, he flew to his maximum ceiling and spotted the ship nearby, with Lakachar not far ahead.

This time, having entered normal skies and sunlight again, Aurus hovered above the beach.

You're good. Take a break. What you encountered before was another predator, using illusion to snag a meal. Rare, but not rare enough.

Aurus landed, released Nea from the confines of his belt, and they waited for the boat.

#

Using telescopes, Julian and members of the other Knight squads observed from afar as Raelani entered the crystal-domed building.

"Seerian, you can read lips?" asked Julian.

"I can, and we're positioned perfectly to the side so that I may see the lips of the Lady and the Elders."

"What is the point of this?" asked Atom Heart. "I know if talks break down we'll attack their portals, but why put the Lady in such danger? We would not be able to save her without our powers."

"It's not her way to order a final assault without giving them a chance to negotiate. As for her being in danger, she did bring an aide. Don't dismiss her ability to take care of herself, for that matter."

"Of course," said Atom Heart. "No disrespect intended, but I worry."

"As do I," said Julian. "As do I."

#

Raelani examined her surroundings. Under a dome of crystal, she stood in a semicircular assembly hall with five stone pillars before her at the flat end. Now-closed steel doors marked her entry point, and her twenty-five escorts stood to the left and right, following the walls. Samus stood by the doors, with a mauve lizard-woman on either side, crossing pikes before the brass knight. Four of the five pillars were the same height, at around fifteen feet high, with the middle one five feet taller. Upon each lower pillar sat a yellow-robed Elder of fay appearance, with green skin and pointed ears. The middle pillar seated a gold-robed Elder.

Raelani stepped forward until the center Elder spoke.

"I am the Grand Elder. Come no closer, outworlder. We do not know if you are contaminated with deadly spores or some other means of ending our lives."

"Though we could unleash deadly pollen, such would alter the ecology of your world, so is forbidden by us. I carry nothing that could end your lives. Even if I could, such things are beneath me."

"You wanted to meet with us, and we wanted to avoid further bloodshed. Speak your piece."

"Avoiding bloodshed is what I do best, but your tendency to kidnap women from other worlds is making that difficult. Stopping all that would be a good place to begin talks," said Raelani.

"That is our only means of survival. You are asking us to die as a race."

"A simple moratorium on kidnapping would end your race?"

"The V'Laubi were divinely created to be the minds and souls of lesser races. To that end we sacrificed the ability to exist separately for long periods of time. Now that our original host-race is dying off, we have no recourse but to find others."

The Elder waved her hands up and down her body.

"This is the original host race, sacred to the V'Laubi. There are very few left, and fewer all the time. As hosts die, we require new ones. You ask that we allow ourselves to die, in order to conform to meaningless moral standards of yours."

"Meaningless?" asked Raelani. "To you, perhaps. Those women being abducted and forced into becoming your vehicles are condemned to a living hell not of their own making."

"Blasphemy. The hosts coexist in glorious harmony with their new souls. To suggest otherwise is unthinkable."

"I'm not 'suggesting' anything. Some of the hosts we released from bondage described precisely the horror they were going through.

To your point, some of the hosts were fine with the occupation, but data suggests they are in the minority."

The Elders turned to one another and mumbled. Finally, the center Elder spoke.

"Lies. You make it sound as though the body-sharing were not mutually beneficial. You think we are such foul creatures?"

"I'm saying that in the zeal to save your race you might be taking incompatible hosts. We could devise tests to determine compatibility, but would only consider using them on willing volunteers. There might be other things we can do to help. We've been informed the V'Laubi were cloning bodies with parthenogenesis, but that there are problems with the process. We could help perfect that," said Raelani.

"We have determined that is a dead-end. Only fresh, natural hosts will suffice."

"And there we have an impasse."

"You will tell us how to live our lives, what is proper and acceptable by your rules and standards? You have killed so many of my people. Who are you to determine what is right?"

"I am Raelani ValDurian. Our family has taken it upon ourselves to keep peace throughout the AllWorlds insomuch as preventing invasions from world to world. What you do to and among your own people is your concern only."

"Then your authority is self-determined? There is no vast governing body giving you directives?"

"We simply do what seems right, based on our core moral principles and our Wyrd, which is the Fate determined for all ValDurians."

"Then you are as much the invaders as we."

"If you choose to see it that way. Unlike yourselves though, we gain no inherent benefit from interference. No power, no wealth, and in many cases, not even gratitude, as we usually work in secret," said Raelani, with a trace of wistfulness in her voice.

"We would subject ourselves to your authority, giving you the power of life and death over the V'Laubi, a race created by the Divine? Nothing gives you that right."

"Only the right to protect those that cannot protect themselves, the rights from a fellowship of sapient beings looking out for their neighbors, an investment in the common good."

"Then you have no right. The V'Laubi will continue on as we always have."

"You might want to bear in mind that our forces have eliminated your outworld bases, and that we would cut you off from the AllWorlds to prevent the formation of others. This is only if we cannot come to some sort of accord, of course."

"Your pitiful family cannot dictate to us on Lakachar. Here you have no power. Here, we dictate terms. You will be held so that your family will leave us be."

"If that is your final decision then I must take my leave of you. I had hoped for something better, but it is not to be."

"Bind her," said the Grand Elder.

She pulled the poison needle-gun from beneath her robes.

The twenty-five women encircled her as she vigorously rubbed the white stone on her diadem. A rainbow flare burst from it through the crystal dome as winds tore at her cloak and gown. Multiple beings hesitated as she flew up, landing at the entrance where Samus stood.

"Samus, open," she said.

The brass armor's chest opened to a hollow interior, which Raelani entered, curling into a fetal position. It closed over her just as poison needles ricocheted off the armor. The Grand Elder fired several more, then reloaded and pumped the pistol with a lever on its top.

"Samus, engage travel mode," came Raelani's muffled voice.

The brass suit morphed into a five-foot high fat disk standing on edge, then it spun in place, a wheel in an aura of green flame. Having recovered somewhat from their hesitance, the women launched spears, but those which hit the disk bounced off harmlessly.

The disk traveled straight up the wall, pausing at the base of the dome, where it spun furiously for a moment until the flame changed to red. At that point it melted through the glass and traveled down the outside of the hall, leaving a scorched path behind it until it hit pavement. Changing back to green flames, the disk spun through the city until it came to the leaden gates, where it traveled up and out of the city.

The horses and carriage awaited her. She disembarked from

Samus as the Coachman opened the door and waved her aboard. She took his hand as she paused to step inside.

"I told you to leave if things went wrong, Coachman."

"Yes, but did you expect me to leave you behind?" he asked as she sat.

"Not really, Indi."

She reached over to remove his mask, then kissed him.

"Here's where things get interesting again," he said, "Oh, and here's your bodyguard."

He lifted Samus and placed it in the coach, where it took a seat.

"How did the microverse work?" he asked.

"Half-microverse, and as expected. It gave me a personal bubble of 'normal' rules, where my powers and those of Samus worked. Not sure how long it would have lasted though."

"Excellent. Speaking of Samus, how are they doing?"

"Just fine, Lord Indra," said five little indigo people that popped out of Samus's head, arms and legs.

"Buckle in," said Indra, "I'm kicking the horses into overdrive."

#

"That's the signal," said Julian, as rainbow rays shot from the crystal dome. "Talks have broken down. Everybody to the attack, that means you too, team MANZ."

Zen's voice came in over Julian's earbud.

"What the hell is team mans?"

"You guys. M-A-N-Z, Marvin, Aurus, Nea and Zen."

"Hard pass on that. Call us team Aurus if you have to. We're on it, Zen out."

Chapter Thirty One
Into the Breach

"Got the call from Julian," said Zen. "Talking didn't work, so the plan goes as discussed."

"Which is why you had us load all the equipment into the prefab cabana beforehand, yes?" asked Aurus.

"Of course. None of us thought there'd be much chance of an accord."

With various mumbles of assent, they took seats in the cabana, which rested near the base of the thousand-foot high cliffside at the sandy beach where they had landed.

"We'll skip most of the trip with the teleport," said Zen, "then we follow the map and break into their underground levels. Then we rescue any prisoners and cause whatever damage we can to their infrastructure."

"Wait, teleport?" asked Aurus. "I must have missed that. Thought I was going to fly in through one of the fissures in the rock wall carrying one of Nea's shadowgates. We're going to teleport for miles to an area the spellcaster has never been before? Not only is that dangerous, I wasn't aware any of us could do that."

"Pardon me for misspeaking," said Zen. "Nea will be using a shadowgate, but I've got a better way than you carrying it while in hawk form. This way we'll be on our mission while the other Knights are assaulting the portals. Only if you approve, of course."

"Okay," said Aurus, "lay it on me."

#

A rainbow bridge touched down at a V'Laubi portal. Julian communicated with Seerian by radio.

"Wait for them," he said. "Whatever faction that controls this portal will be sending reinforcements, but if you destroy it too soon they'll likely return to the city before engaging. I hate to say it, but we need to bring as many of them out as possible."

"When should we attack?" asked Seerian.

"Yours to determine. Use best judgment. Julian out."

Seerian viewed the area through binoculars, and saw a small horde of clawed, tailed women. These wore blue plastic body armor, and carried yellow-glowing swords, along with machine guns.

"This is a good batch," said Seerian, "and I don't see any others on the way. I remember that the different factions don't help one another, so this is probably the lot of them. Let's go."

Atom Heart, Seerian, and Battlescar rode the rainbow down.

"Nothing to it but to do it," yelled Atom Heart as he charged, cape flapping in his wake.

Seerian and Battlescar rolled their eyes, then broke left and right to flank the enemy. She belched forth gouts of flame while he punched at great speed with bladed knuckles. Atom Heart took the brunt of machine gun fire which left no lasting impression on him. He struck hard and often, flinging bodies left and right as he approached the portal.

Breathing heavily, flames gone, Seerian stopped and looked around. Her eyes went blank white as she called out.

"Lem, dodge left, then jump up. Scar, dive in, take out the one with the bazooka. They'll be pulling out swords now."

She skipped backwards, avoiding gunfire, then dropped into a split, seeming to avoid swordplay accidentally. She grinned, conjuring a firebolt from each hand, taking out the nearby swordswomen while doing a backflip onto another. That one's neck she broke while pushing off with a handstand on its shoulders.

"Scar, behind," she yelled, prompting Battlescar to spin about, eviscerating two soldiers about to stab him.

A dozen soldiers opened fire on Seerian, but she dodged easily. Almost. Two rounds caught her, and she fell.

"Sheila," yelled Atom Heart as he raced toward her, scattering soldiers before him like toys. He smashed through those that had shot her, leaving none standing. Gently, he picked her up, blood from her leg and abdomen staining his yellow shirt.

Her eyes were normal as they stared into his.

"Duck, you dummy," she groaned, as a bazooka shell caught him in the back.

He dropped her in the explosion, then fell on her.

The one who had fired tried to load another round, but Battlescar removed her head. He looked about, but that was the last enemy standing.

"Lem, get off me," squeeked Seerian, "I can't breathe."

Battlescar pulled Atom Heart off her, then laid him facedown and looked at Seerian with concern.

"I'm okay. Well, okayish," she said. "These bullet wounds are minor, compared to him taking an armor-piercing, anti-tank round in the back."

She peeled off his ruined cape and used it to wipe his back, revealing a gaping and burned wound.

"I think he'll be okay, if the hydrostatic shock wasn't too much. It's broad, but not too deep, and the blast cauterized the wound, so he isn't bleeding much." She smiled. "He'll be more upset that his cape was destroyed, I think."

Battlescar nodded toward the portal.

"Yes, we're supposed to destroy it, but Lem was going to let loose an 'atomic blast' from his dynaheart. It depowers him, and would likely kill him right now, so I don't know how we'll destroy the portal."

"No, no, I can do it," rasped Atom Heart, struggling to rise, but only succeeding in flipping himself to his back.

"No," yelled Seerian. "Destroying the gate isn't worth your life. It can wait. Don't be a hero."

"But, isn't that what I'm supposed to be? What we all are? We have a mission."

Battlescar picked up the enemy bazooka, then pulled a shell

from the dead wielder's backpack.

"See, Lemmie, there's a better way. Any other way is better than you dying."

Battlescar fired, seriously damaging the portal, but it remained standing. As he attempted to load another round, one of the fallen savages rose and stabbed him in the back. Battlescar fell.

With a cry of rage, Atom Heart rose, and loosed a white beam from his chest-disk, incinerating the creature. He fell to his knees, but pulled himself to Battlescar.

"He's alive, but we're not done here yet."

He snatched up the bazooka. Loading and firing the last four rounds, he brought the gate down in a pile of crashing rubble.

"It's done," said Seerian. "Mission accomplished, Atom Heart, my hero."

"You're my hero and my heart. And call me Lemmie."

#

"Team one, successful," said Julian. "Team two, summon Bifrost and attack when ready."

Another rainbow touched down at a portal, and six gray-skinned beings in leather waited at its apex on jacked-up motorcycles that looked suspiciously like modified Harley-Davidsons.

One man in a spiked helmet watched through binoculars for a few minutes, then shouted,

"Deadenders, go."

The motorcycles roared down the rainbow, handlebar machine guns blazing. Before them stood multiple ranks of four-eyed Clermann women behind steel shields, wielding gold paralo-ray guns. Bullets bounced harmlessly from shields, while paralyzing rays were equally ineffective against the Deadenders.

"Attack formation Alpha," yelled the character in the spiked helmet as they closed with the first line of Clermanns. Two bikes sped left, two took the right, and the remaining two gunned for the middle.

The Clermanns braced themselves and drew swords while the middle bikers held a device with two hand grips between them. They rode wide when almost upon the Clermanns, drawing forth a glowing blue line between the grips and gunning their bikes. When the line hit it sliced through whatever was in its way: shields, swords, heads, or bodies. The bikers dropped the line and pulled their blades, thin with glimmering blue edges.

The other four bikers hit the outlying Clermanns with their own blue blades, decapitating four. By this time the other enemy ranks had moved forward, engaging all the Deadenders with machine gun fire that was only marginally more effective than the paralo-rays.

The bikers wobbled as they were hit, but otherwise ignored the gunfire until a camelcat rider jumped up on her steed.

She screamed out, "Their machines, shoot their machines."

The gunfire upon the bikes brought them down and they skidded to a halt, taking Clermann soldiers with them. The Deadenders leapt from the wreckage, and fought the soldiers afoot.

Despite their superior blades, the Knights fought a losing battle against the vastly greater numbers of Clermann soldiers. The camelcat rider herself took the head of the spike-helmed man with her battleaxe. As the head bounced to the ground, bloodless, the rider shouted in triumph while she jumped onto his chest from atop her beast. Barely a dozen soldiers remained apart from herself.

"We have beaten the invaders. Many of our sisters yet live despite the loss of their hosts. Well done."

The headless corpse stabbed her through the crotch, and rose, carrying the blade up through her heart, then through her surprised face. As her corpse fell, other partial Deadenders struck with paralo-rays grabbed from fallen Clermanns, or with captured machine guns. It was a scene from nightmare as legless Knights dragged themselves about, firing guns or grabbing at the terrified soldiers.

Those soldiers that didn't run in terror along with the camelcat struck back, ruining the Deadenders further, but eventually lost.

"Zalk, the runners may bring reinforcements," said a woman missing both arms and her lower body.

The body of the spike-helmed man poured a black liquid on his neck-stump, then lowered his head into place and fiddled with it momentarily. He held up a finger toward the woman while he coughed experimentally.

"Ah, there. Vocal cords are back together. Why didn't you stop them then?"

"Funny. You're the only one of us who can control their body when your head's not with it."

"We're lucky they did run; I think they could have overwhelmed us otherwise. Anyway, pull yourself together, Imelda, we still have work to do."

"You're a laugh-riot today. Little help, Zalk?"

Grinning, Zalk started to attach an arm to her torso.

"That arm's not mine, jerk."

Exaggerating a pout, he attached her proper right arm with the black liquid.

"Thanks, Zalk. I can take it from here. Maybe see if the others need help?"

Imelda pulled herself about with her one arm, first attaching her lower body, then finally her left arm. Meanwhile, the rest of the Deadenders were in varying stages of reconstruction.

Zalk stood in the middle of the group.

"If everybody's got it together, we still have a portal to destroy."

"Hey, I can't find my foot," said a large, muscular, blond woman.

"Got it, Crunch," said a man with an eyepatch. "Can you imagine how much pain we'd be in right now if we were still alive?"

"Pretty sure we'd be dead again at this point, Wrecker," said Imelda. "Know I would be."

"As I mentioned, there's a portal to destroy," said Zalk. "We'd use the Dividing Line, but we'll need two choppers going for that. Work on your own bikes first, see if they're salvageable. Make it fast, just in case the hollowbacks send reinforcements."

For the next several minutes they tinkered with the bikes, until Imelda spoke.

"My bike is running, but the engines on most of them are full of bullets, just like we are."

"You got that right," said Wrecker, "I'll be coughing up slugs for a week."

"Not an issue," said two in one voice. One was male, one female, with faces each tattooed with half of a red phoenix. If they were to put their heads together correctly, the halves would make a complete bird. "We can cobble together enough good parts to get another engine going. Give us a bit."

"You got it. The rest of you, while Marlon and Maria work, get four good tires mounted on the bikes we'll use," said Zalk. "No point waiting until the engine is done."

Half an hour later, two bikes were good to go. Zalk and Imelda took the double-grip device between them and roared off for the portal.

"Up your speed," said Zalk, "we're not going fast enough."

"Up yours, Zalk. I know how the Line works. I made it."

After a burst of speed, keeping the bikes in perfect tandem, they spread out with the Dividing Line extending between them. They hit one leg of the circular portal together, low, nearly ground level, the thin, blue line cutting through cleanly. As it cut, they lifted their arms higher, making the cut much higher in the back. They whipped around and headed the way they had come, bikes moving together again until the Line units touched.

In perfect sync, they spun around and headed back toward the other leg. Once again they cut through flawlessly, making an angle cut. They gunned it back to their friends, and waited.

And waited.

"Where's the Earth-shattering kaboom?" asked Wrecker.

"Don't know. I think the cut was so perfect the pieces are joined like Johansson blocks, despite the angle cuts. Stupid gravity's slacking off. You got explosives?"

"When do I not have explosives, Zalk?

Wrecker pulled a box from his bike and placed it at the base of the left portal leg. He lifted his eye-patch and pulled out a small tube which he pointed at the box, then pressed a button on the tube. He walked back to Zalk.

"Good placement, Boss?" asked Wrecker.

"Perfect. Remind it of how gravity works."

Wrecker pressed the button again and the box exploded.

The portal wobbled with one leg damaged. Unable to stand up straight, it slid on the angle cuts and slowly collapsed from its own weight, becoming a twisted heap.

"Good job, gang," said Zalk. "Back to base."

Zalk summoned the rainbow, and they pushed their bikes up and off Lakachar.

#

Aurus and friends stepped from the blanket Nea had enchanted. It was being held up by Zen's drone, and hung in the middle of a small cavern that was lit by the drone's lights.

"Nice work, everybody," said Aurus. "It navigated perfectly with the Omnimind's map you installed, Zen, and Marvin's explosives that it carried neatly eliminated those damned blockages. Oh, and of course, we wouldn't be here at all without Nea's shadowgate."

"Yay, us," said Zen.

Aurus paused to look around, and saw a cleft leading out.

"Now that we've experienced a moment of victory, we still have to release all the prisoners from the underground levels. Lakachar's world-rules will kick in beyond this tunnel, so everybody prepare for the worst."

"I've got a cart full of crowbars," said Zen, "and all sorts of hand-tools."

"Lockpicks are on me," said Nea, "along with acids and poisons, all of which will presumably work here."

"The cart has crossbows for everyone," said Marvin, "with plenty of bolts to go round."

"The cart has melee weapons as well," said Aurus. "Magic and science are equally damned here, so all we've got going for us is brute strength, skill, and hard, pointy objects."

He materialized his halberd.

"Won't be able to do that beyond here, probably, but I've brought back-up."

He pulled open his shirt, and the skin peeled away from a milky-white stone on his breastbone. When tapped, it had a rainbow iridescence that quickly faded.

"That's our ace-in-the-hole, a micro-universe, half of the one Lady Raelani has."

"Meaning what?" asked Nea.

"When activated, it creates a pocket dimension of its own rules. It gives us a place where magic and electricity work, like in most worlds."

"How big a pocket?" asked Zen.

"Not big. We'll be a very close family. Also, though I'll regain my full power, it won't leave the pocket. My energy beams would dissipate upon leaving, but it won't stop inertia."

"So my bullets would keep going once fired," said Marvin.

"Yes. We have that going for us at least. It'll probably be of short duration as well, since it'd be fighting against a vastly larger dimension."

#

Julian directed the Faybranded into action while a wizened, old, green elf in a city tower looked on through a telescope.

"Take a look, Kelvaana. The next portal outpost is being invaded."

Kelvaana stepped up to the eyepiece, looked through and nodded.

"Yes, it is as you say, O Mighty Elder. Are you making a point here?"

"The point is that our portal is next in the sequence. You need to observe them to see what tactics they use, that we may be ready to counter them."

"In deference, that is likely pointless, as each group of invaders has been completely different."

"Different, yes, but they may use similar tactics. We need to learn as much as we can, so that our portal remains. We will become the dominant faction and rule Lakachar."

"Begging your pardon," said Kelvaana, pulling back from the eyepiece, "this group is using plants of the earth, springing forth and strangling our people. In my experience, that will be unique to this group."

"Keep looking. You never know what secrets may be revealed."

"So far, I can see that our paralyzing rays don't work on them. That's something at least."

"What?"

The Elder grabbed the telescope, throwing it out of alignment, then fumbled with it.

"Blast. Give me a minute here."

"Would you like me to re-align it?" asked Kelvaana.

"No, I can do it. Your giant hands would just mess it up more."

"At your will. In the meanwhile, maybe we can figure out why the ValDurians are doing this."

"To conquer us, obviously," said the Elder. "They're cutting us off from gaining new bodies, condemning us to death."

"What I meant was, why this method?"

"Explain."

"Why are they attacking our outposts one at a time? They clearly have more than one attack force. Why not hit us all at once and be done with it? For that matter, if they concentrated all their forces on one base at a time, the defenders would be easily overwhelmed."

"Perhaps, like us, their factions do not cooperate readily?"

"I have spoken with them while their prisoner, and there are no factions, to my knowledge. They are logical beings, so there must be a sensible reason for this behavior."

"Whatever the reason, it gives us an advantage in being able to prepare ourselves. We know they won't attack again until the current raid is done, and I've had time to reinforce our outpost with troops from the city."

"That's it," said Kelvaana, "they want to give us time. Pardon me, O Mighty Elder."

"Whatever. I've got to fix this viewing device."

#

Giant plants burst from the ground, vines grabbing squirrel-girls from the air. Some of those on the ground fired paralo-rays at the Faybranded while others fired machine guns. None had any noticeable effect.

"We have them countered, Moonbrow," said a blond, hoodless Branded. "What must we do now?"

A slender, antlered person with a crescent moon brand on their forehead spoke.

"Allow me time for thought."

They gestured, brand glowing brightly, and the air turned dark blue. Moonbrow engaged mindspeech.

"I have stopped time for the nonce. Neither we nor they will be able to move until I have resolved this matter. They are the enemy and have kidnapped women or killed men from a number of worlds. This cannot go unpunished, but have we the right to kill them?"

"They are mutant squirrels, an abomination of nature, and we slaughtered the last such we encountered. Why not now?" said the blond person.

"That was in my dark phase. I now look upon the situation with new eyes, Starheart."

"Look faster, Moonbrow. They're sending reinforcements, and those are outside your timestop. If we don't deal with this group soon, they'll overwhelm us when it ends," said one of the antlered Branded.

"It is as you say, Firehand. I apologize for my new moon phase, as I'm always a bit scatterbrained for a while. I pass the leadership to Windeye for the current mission."

An antlered person with a tornado brand under their left eye spoke.

"Accepted. There is no resolution save death for the enemy. All other discussion can wait until a better time. Everybody, unleash your power upon our foes, keeping to those nearest you. Moonbrow, let time march on."

The blue dissipated and time lurched forward. The vines holding squirrel-girls ripped them asunder and pulled the remains underground.

"Oakarm, that being done, concentrate your power on protecting us from their weapons."

They nodded, and each Faybranded felt a surge of power in the thin, flexible, wooden armor on their bodies.

Firehand sent forth roiling flames, leaving little of the enemy but the stench of burned fur. Starheart bathed their foes in glorious light, sending squirrel souls to the heavens. Windeye unleashed a small tornado that spelled doom for those flying foes near them.

"Stormthew, withdraw from combat and prepare a welcome for those approaching. Wavewalker, do the same, and unleash your attack just before Stormthew," said Windeye.

They both nodded and stepped back, eyes closed and concentrating. In the meantime, the rest of the Faybranded finished off those squirrel-girls they'd already engaged.

Stormthew and Wavewalker opened their eyes and pointed at the approaching enemy. Water rose from the ground and rushed toward them, gathering into a wave which pounded the running squirrel-girls before Windeye's tornado drove much of it into the sky. Flying enemies were soaked and knocked to the ground, the water collecting into an ankle-deep lake around those still standing. Stormthew yelled to the skies, which grudgingly went dark until they disgorged lightning upon the squirrels both grounded and still flying. When the sky lightened, all the squirrels were down.

"Worked as I'd hoped," said Windeye. "They were electrocuted like drunken fools with a hair dryer in the bathtub."

"Sort of stretching that analogy, aren't you," said Moonbrow.

"Maybe, but felt I needed to say something of import."

"Don't worry. We can rewrite it in the transcript. Let's move out."

#

"How many prisoners was that now?" asked Marvin, holding up a paper tablet and pencil.

"Five hundred twenty," said Zen, "Sorry, five-twenty-one. Why is it taking Nea so long to send them back? How long has she been gone?"

"I don't know," said Aurus, "my watch doesn't tell time here. Feels like too long though."

He held up his watch to the torch they had jammed in the wall, showing the second hand stopped.

"Why did you let her go back alone?" asked Marvin. "If attacked, she's helpless."

"First of all, she asked to go it without our help," said Aurus, scowling darkly. "Second, she's got the latest batch of prisoners with her, and many are armed now. Third, if you think Nea is helpless without magic then you don't know her at all. She's one of the most skillful swordswomen I've ever known. Fourth, I'm more worried about you two if I'm not here, since guns won't work."

"Fair point," said Zen, "but you don't have magic either, just a halberd, and it's not even magic at the moment."

"I can't fly, eye-zap, or regenerate, yes, but I can do this."

He hefted the equipment cart over his head, then put it down gently.

"How can you do that?" asked Marvin, "that has to be at least five hundred pounds with the equipment still in it."

"My strength isn't entirely magical. A lot of it comes from the supernatural quality of my muscles, maybe half or a third, so I'm still way stronger than most normies."

"I'm willing to wait here with a torch while you two go on ahead," said Marvin, "just so she can find us. My body is still aching from the wounds and I'd slow you down."

"Should you even be on this mission?" asked Zen. "You've lost more than a step. If we have to flee you're in trouble."

"True, but I'm a long-range fighter, so I'm just as effective as usual in that regard, even with a crossbow. My original point remains."

"Leave the torch, bring the cart," said Aurus. "We'll light another torch to carry with us, because we've got to get moving. The assaults on the portals won't last forever, and we're lucky it drained most of the guards from down here. We've only had to fight twice and those were laughers, even without powers."

"I'm good with laughers," said Marvin.

"As am I, said Aurus, "But my luck has never lasted this long before, so let's get moving."

#

"They're coming," shouted the wizened green elf as she danced up and down. "Wait until these Vaalrudians meet our fully-powered, four-legged forces."

Five mages in robes of differing color floated down the rainbow toward the outpost.

"We will capture these five, then their power will be ours, and we will rule the V'Laubi. Follow the plan, Kelvaana, lure them in and take them. Wait . . . where is Kelvaana?"

She moved the telescope back and forth frantically, looking for Kelvaana on the field.

"How dare you? Are you running scared? No matter, our forces can win without you, I'm sure."

#

The Arcanen floated over the battlefield. This portal was at the tail-end opening of a canyon, with a great, solid metal gate behind it. The gate was open now, but if closed would cut the portal off from the city.

"What'll it be?" asked the woman in blue robes. "Subtle magic or simple overpowering? Everything I do is blue, so they're through. Not sure it makes any difference either way."

"Blue, Cecilia?" The woman in red snorted. "I'm no less powerful, so if I do red, they're dead."

"Oh, Faya, so sure of yourself. You want to settle this right here, right now?"

Bong sounded a bell held by the woman in yellow and green.

"Enough, you two monocolored morons. You can settle it later, if we live."

"Use our best discretion, Karamandia?" asked the man in pink and purple.

"Always, Bremuj. Pick your territories and try not to interfere with each other, especially you, Faya and Cecelia."

"I've picked out the hot targets," said the man in heliotrope and white, as he handed out papers to the others.

"Thank you, Jemelex." She studied her paper, which had moving text and pictures, then smiled.

"Arcanen, annihilate!" *Bong.*

Each Arcanen unleashed magic upon their targets, and continued for several minutes with unrelenting fury. Until it relented. As the multicolored smoke cleared away, the Arcanen cursed in one voice.

"Damned of all the hells," said Karamandia, "Not a one of them has fallen. How can that be?"

"Anti-magic shells?" said Bremuj. "Starting analysis."

The V'Laubi returned fire with a multitude of paralo-rays, which dissipated on an invisible energy barrier surrounding the Arcanen.

"Touché, my hollowback girls," said Karamandia. "Keep up the analysis, Bremuj. Meanwhile, does anybody have a suggestion?"

"Duck," said Faya, "incoming V'Laubi netshells, I think."

The shells missed completely, hitting the ground and exploding into clouds of gray-green smoke.

"Might be poison gas," said Karamandia. "Fly back and up."

As the Arcanen retreated, more shells flew their way, releasing smoke, much of which engulfed the V'Laubi quadramorphs and their entire outpost, filling the canyon.

"I was going to say we should blow the smoke away," said Karamandia, "but it could be doing our job for us if it's poisonous. They're supposed to be pretty stupid, I think, so stand down for a minute or so and let's see."

The quadramorphs did not fire upon the Arcanen, but there was a great deal of noise coming from their outpost.

"What are those colored, blinking lights behind them, coming from the city?" asked Jemelex.

"Some sort of code, I wager," said Faya, "how else could they communicate, lacking radio transmissions?"

Karamandia slapped herself on the forehead.

"Arcanen, blast the smoke away. They're pulling something here," shouted Karamandia.

The smoke blew away from a magical onslaught, to reveal quadramorphs in full retreat, driving twenty hovercraft toward the city. Two more GEVs remained at the base as the four-legs worked on disassembling what remained of their portal, which wasn't much. Mostly it was only the oval frame which remained, ninety percent of the inner tech modules having been removed.

"I can't believe this," said Karamandia. "Now they get smart? Everybody, after the main fleet and maybe we can stop them before they get to the null zone. We can get this bunch afterwards."

The Arcanen flew after the twenty hovercraft, but were considerably slower.

"They're going to hit the zone any second now," said Cecelia, "but that'll stop them cold, so we can catch up."

"Yeah, but we won't be able to hurt them then," said Faya, "they'll still be in the null zone."

"We can't hurt them now," said Jemelex. "Our long-range attacks dissipate."

"Some part of the vehicles will still be stuck on this side," said Bremuj, "we'll blast what we can, maybe latch on and pull them to this side to finish the job."

A bell sounded.

"Analysis complete," said Bremuj. "I can't believe it."

"Believe what?" asked Karamandia.

"This canyon channels wind from the null zone. We couldn't hurt them because the very air neutralized our attacks. That great gate must be for closing off the wind so their portal will work."

"Yeah?" snarled Faya, "then how do their vehicles work?"

"Get to the sides, out of the canyon, everybody," said Karamandia. "Faya, send your magic through the ground and melt it ahead of them. Cecelia, make an ice storm above them. It should work now. The ice is non-magical once formed."

The GEVs were battered by ice, which pushed them into the molten ground, bringing the fugitives to a halt.

"We've got them now," said Karamandia. "The anti-magic wind was above them, leaving their vehicles powered, and we couldn't send magic through it. Now it's all over."

"What the flaming hells? Look at the last portal way over there," said Jemelex, pointing.

A giant humanoid figure was carrying the last portal away toward the city, intact.

#

"I knew we were pushing my luck," said Aurus, staring at Kelvaana, who blocked his way, swords crossed.

"I rather expected it would be you here," she said. "So very nice to see you again."

"You expected . . . they figured out what we were up to?"

"I figured it out. Just a bonus it was you."

"While I respect your fighting ability and determination, I didn't think you were this smart, no offense."

"None taken. We are of two minds, of course. The V'Laubi mind is the calculating thinker in the calm moments, while the human takes over in the stress of battle. A perfect partnership."

"That's debatable," said Zen. "I've seen too much opposing evidence to believe that."

"I'm not here for a debate. I came to stop you from stealing my people's future."

"Good luck with that," said Aurus. "Your leaders have already done it."

"I still can't let you go any farther in. You don't have your powers now, so I can take you, plus, I've got a back-up squad around the corner. I just wanted a chance to talk."

Multiple sets of eyes peeked around the corner while snarling howls filled the background.

"Talk then," said Marvin. "I'm all for a peaceful resolution, or as close as we can get to it."

"I understand that our kidnapping of host bodies is unpalatable to your people, but we have no choice if we wish to survive."

"Explain how," said Aurus, changing his grip on the halberd.

"There can be no normal birth and growth on this world. Males become sterile after a time, and fetuses die stillborn anyway. We are told it's from some background radiation."

"So move then," said Aurus, "there are plenty of empty worlds."

"But none with Lakachar's natural defense zone where both magic and science fail. Our people have become paranoid about such things."

"I'm sure the ValDurians could find a solution to your predicament, given time," said Zen.

"And I agree, but then we are allowing outside forces to control our lives, something that does not sit well with our rulers."

A new voice broke in.

"In other words, it interferes with them controlling your lives," said Nea.

"Nea, glad to have you back," said Aurus.

"So glad you couldn't wait to replace me with another woman, I see." She made a sniffling noise and wiped her eyes.

"What, no, wait, that's, huh?" said Aurus.

"Relax, I'm messing with you. The problem we face, Kelvaana, is that your people can't be allowed to run free, taking whom they like, whenever they like. If some sort of solution can't be found, you'll have to be exterminated as a race, and we don't want that either."

"Exterminate us? We are inviolate and unconquerable on Lakachar. The ValDurians have no power here."

"You know that isn't true. Not only are we in the process of cutting you off from the AllWorlds, you were in the council audience hall when Lady Raelani activated her power. Do you think the ValDurians wouldn't use that if they needed to?"

"I assumed it was very difficult to do, and of limited duration, else she would have done it earlier."

"She wanted your Elders to be at ease, and to not feel as though they were groveling before a superior power. I can't in truth say how difficult it was for her, or how long the power would last."

"None of that changes my situation. It is my duty to defend my home, which you have invaded. I think there are enough four-legs to take you all out in your current condition."

She held the greatswords crossed over her chest.

"Let's hold off on all-out battle," said Aurus. "So you know, I too can activate my powers for a brief period, but have been saving it for an emergency. Rather than annihilate you and your entire force, I challenge you to a battle, one-on-one, you and me, right here. I swear not to activate my powers. If you win, we leave, those who live anyway. If I win, you let us take the unpossessed captives away."

"I don't think –"

"Of course not," said Nea. "Let me help you with that. After a bloody battle, which we'll win, since we can access our powers, the captives will still be released, and your forces will all be dead.

Kelvaana started to speak, but Nea shushed her.

"It ends well for you, assuming you live. After we free your prisoners, we'll be heading to the section controlled by your ruling faction. Rest assured we'll get through their doors like we have everybody else's. Then we destroy all their underground forces, and free their prisoners. What this means is that your faction will be the only one able to field at least a reasonable depth of soldiers."

"Then we could become the ruling faction. My Elder might even forgive me for abandoning the field right now."

"Perhaps you might even become the new Elder," said Zen. "It sounds as though your people could use someone more clear-thinking."

"Something for the future," said Kelvaana, "right now my host wants a go at you, and I'm finding it difficult to restrain her.

"All forces stand down. I'm fighting the pretty boy now, winner take all. Your head is mine. It'll look great on my wall."

Kelvaana lunged forward, swords swinging high and low. Aurus ducked back, avoiding both strikes, then hit her in the head with the butt-end of his halberd. She staggered back, but he pressed his attack, leaving her reeling.

"This is nothing, puny man. Without your magic strength you are no match for me."

She lunged again, one sword cutting his hat, but the other slicing his leg. The move left her off balance, and he dropped his halberd to take her down with a shoulder throw, which was especially easy because of her great size. She landed on her chest in a great crash of armor, her swords flying from her hands. Aurus put her in a full-nelson hold, keeping her facedown, straining to control her.

"You cannot win, man. Your noodle arms hold no magic and cannot hold me."

"Only some of my strength is magic. Ugh. This is me and I am enough. Yield. I am more than enough."

The struggle went on for several minutes with both fighters weakening, but no sign of either giving up.

"Please, Kelvaana, don't make me kill you. For the good of your people and your faction, yield."

Kelvaana went limp.

"For the sake of my people, I yield."

"Tell your people to surrender and back off."

She did and they did.

Nea and Zen came forward to grab Kelvaana's swords, and held them to her neck when Aurus released her.

"You needn't worry," said Kelvaana, "I keep my word, or our words, I should probably say. Where do we go from here?"

"Pull out every guard from your detention facility," said Aurus.

"Say they're going up to fight if you have to. We're going to free all your prisoners, then go for those of your ruling faction."

"This still leaves us very weak."

"But not dead. We'll do everything possible to save your people," said Nea.

"Then I should tell you we know the rulers have a 'secret' high-tech area in the normal zone, with a tunnel from their facilities."

"Thanks, but we know that," said Zen, "so it'll be dealt with in its proper time."

Kelvaana took her swords and sheathed them on her back.

"Retreat, the lot of you," she said to her quadramorphs. "We're going up to the surface. Spread the word to the others."

Chapter Thirty Two
What's the Big Hurry?

"Has the giant brought in the portal, Javis?" asked the beautiful, green, Grand Elder of her mauve, lizard attendant.

"She has, O Grand Elder," said Javis.

"Excellent. Have it disassembled and pulled behind us to the Secret Area. No point in leaving it."

"May I ask why we retreat?"

"It's obvious. When the Valian demonstrated the ability to use her powers here, I knew we weren't safe. We'll find another world, free from their interference, and start over."

"ValDurian, O Grand Elder."

"What?"

"They call themselves 'ValDurians,' O Grand Elder."

"I don't care, and never correct me again. See to the portal, then take it to the Secret Area. And make sure you bring my Battle Presence."

"Yes, O Great One."

The Grand Elder stormed out of her tower, down a spiral staircase to the underground levels. She climbed aboard a horse-drawn carriage and proceeded to the cell level. Once there she talked to more lizard attendants.

"How goes the withdrawal?" asked the Grand Elder, pulling on her cloak against the cold.

"With great efficiency," said one lizard. "Most of the prisoners have been moved to the new location, along with weapons and supplies. The new base already has a generator in operation, so it's defensible. We were only waiting for you to arrive so we can wrap up the operation."

"And I am here. Proceed with the evacuation, but only shut down the portal once the giant and main portal have gone through it."

"As you command. What about us?"

"What about you?"

"We can only deactivate the portal from this side. Are we expected to remain behind?"

"Not all of you, just enough to carry out the shutdown."

"And what will we be doing after that?" asked the lizard woman.

"Defend the secondary portal with your life, or lives, if more than one of you remain." She swirled her cloak about herself and walked into the escape tunnel, leaving the lizard attendant alone.

"Of course, O Great One, anything you say, O Great One. Run for your worthless life, you useless piece of shit."

She walked around the empty cells, calling out, but getting no answers. At that point, the giant arrived, crawling through the tunnel that wasn't big enough for her to stand. Behind her she dragged sections of the main portal that had been disassembled and strung together with cables. In the darkened tunnel, it looked rather like a lumpy train engine pulling its cars in tow. Attendant Javis walked alongside the giant, who now carried the Battle Presence.

"That way," said the second attendant, pointing to the escape tunnel. "You're taking it to the secondary portal. I'll just bring up the rear, and watch for any stragglers, since I have nothing else to do right now."

The giant continued down the tunnel on hands and knees, with the first attendant behind her. Just as she passed a white line painted on the floor, the attendant's radio buzzed.

"Attendant Javis here," she said.

"What's taking so long, Javis?" asked the radio. "I've called a dozen times."

"Apologies, O Grand Elder. I had to wait for the giant. I've just left the null zone, and I'm right behind her. I don't think she can go any faster on her hands and knees."

"Speed her up. I don't want to wait any longer than necessary."

"Yes, O Great One. Of course, O Great One." *Eat shit, O Great One.*

The giant proceeded exactly as she had previously, but Javis walked as fast as she could until she caught up to the Grand Elder's party.

"Oh, there you are," said the Elder. "Where's the giant?"

"Not far back, O Great One. She picked up her pace at my urging, so you should be able to hear her about now."

The Grand Elder's pointy ears flicked, then she focused on sound from the tunnel.

"She also has your Battle Presence," said Javis. "It was faster having her carry it."

"Excellent," said the Grand Elder. "We can get going now."

With a great noise, the tunnel ahead of and above them collapsed, opened now to a sky that was barely seen through a cloud of dirt. A golden beam from above illuminated the cloud.

"I was so close," yelled the Grand Elder, pulling herself from the rubble.

"Stand down and surrender," shouted an amplified voice from above, "by order of the Edgeriders, Knights of Valeron."

More V'Laubi dug themselves free. As the dirt cloud cleared further, the Grand Elder could see, above them, a large, octagonal metal disk with a central glowing orb on its underside. A golden beam from the orb shut off.

#

Aurus and company walked through the recently vacated prison of the ruling faction. His fedora was little more than a brim, the top having been cut off by Kelvaana. He walked with a limp, and used a crowbar as a cane, since his left leg was tightly bandaged.

"Took us too long to break in here," he said. "Maybe I should have activated my powers? Would have healed me up, at least."

"You said that was for emergencies," said Nea. "We know where their exit is, so we can just go after them."

"The bonus is that we'll eventually be at full power along the way," said Marvin.

A noise came from their left, followed by a dozen mauve lizard-women.

"Unfortunately," said Zen, "this lot is already at full power, it seems."

Each bore a crossbow with a magazine of bolts on top.

"Dive for cover," yelled Aurus, as he was struck by a brace of bolts. The other Knights found cover, but Nea risked crossbow fire to drag Aurus behind a wall of stacked barrels with her.

"Not fair," shouted Marvin. "They have repeating crossbows, while I have only the boring, ordinary kind."

He took out two soldiers as clean kills, while Zen missed, then the other lizards scrambled for their own cover.

"Not good," said Nea to herself and Aurus. "Only one wound is life-threatening, but that's enough. I don't have time to drag you out of the null zone, so get the micro-universe going."

"No, I can –"

"Don't argue, Do it."

Aurus pulled open his shirt and went to rub the node, but it wasn't there.

"It's deep under the skin. Must have pulled it in reflexively, but I can't open it up now without my shapeshifting," he said.

"Then how –"

"You've got daggers. Use one right here." He pointed to his chest while grimacing in pain. "Cut me, Mick."

"What?"

"I'll explain later, but open me up now, so I can touch the node."

Meanwhile, Zen and Marvin had taken down two more lizards, but their position behind stacked ceramic washtubs was in danger of being surrounded.

"At times like this I really appreciate the Garand," said Marvin.

"This has happened before?" asked Zen, as he eyed their situation warily.

"Not specifically, but there have been situations I was without it."

"Hopefully, you'll live to have more of those," said Zen.

"Luckily, this is no longer one of those," said Nea, suddenly beside them, holding Marvin's rifle. "Got it out of the cart on the way over. Now, get ready for the most important group hug of your life."

Aurus appeared, and they all huddled together. Marvin grabbed his gun, and the eight remaining lizards were dead in about the time it took him to spot them. The magazine ejected with a 'ping,' and Marvin slapped in another. He kissed the rifle.

"Good timing, Big Guy," said Zen, "but you don't look so good."

Aurus bled from multiple crossbow bolt wounds, and the bolts were still in them, but broken off near the heads.

"I've got my powers for the moment, and even the invisibility watch is working. I had to leave the heads in the wounds so I wouldn't bleed out all at once. I am getting better, though."

He pulled the remains of his fedora from a pocket and set it upon his head atop the brim, where they merged back together.

"That alone makes me feel better. I must leave the node on to keep healing, so you may as well all get in the cart and I'll push it along while I fly behind."

"Sounds good," said Marvin, "but I'm not leaving without a few of these."

He grabbed some repeating crossbows and their bolts, then tossed them in the cart.

"And we're off," said Aurus.

The second attendant watched from behind steel drums as the Knights left the area.

"Well, I've done all I can do here. Maybe I'll just show myself out to the surface and surrender unconditionally."

#

"Where's that giant?" asked the Grand Elder. "She's got to take that flying disk out."

"The name is Thunder Hills," said a great, rumbling voice from the rubble behind the V'Laubi. "What is it I'm doing now?"

"Do you see that dish in the sky? Destroy it. Then I'll need you to dig out the tunnel ahead of us," said the Grand Elder.

"One thing at a time, Elder," said the giant as she stood. At sixty feet tall, her head and shoulders poked through the newly open ceiling.

"Whoa, big girl," said one of the Edgeriders, peeking over the side of the disk. "There doesn't have to be a fight. Your side has already lost, but you don't have to go down with them."

"Not my choice," she growled. "I'm bound in service to the backeaters."

She bent her legs and jumped from the tunnel in an obviously magic-assisted leap. Standing on the surface, she raised her fists to the sky.

"If you Knights value your lives, leave now."

"Can't do that, so bring the fury, big girl."

"I'm a woman, and the name is Thunder Hills."

She opened her fists, and spread out her fingers. Lightning flashed from them to the sky, which darkened in an instant. All eight Edgeriders stood at the rim of the disk and fired energy beams at her.

The beams hit to no effect, then the giant brought her hands down, bringing lightning from the sky with them. Nature's unnatural fury blasted the disk, then all was quiet while smoke arose from it.

"Edgeriders, Disassemble," cried out one of the Knights.

The disk broke into eight wedges, each carrying an Edgerider. They stood on the flat fronts of the wedges, points trailing. The Riders scattered in the sky, then came back in random positions, blasting at the giant, again not harming her.

"Edges to the sky," shouted the man in the yellow hard hat.

The edge-wedges met well above the giant for a quick conference. All the Knights wore chrome high-tech armor.

"She's not just immune to our rays, she's absorbing them," said the man in armor and yellow hard hat.

"You know how this must end then, Walt," said a woman in armor with yellow trim.

"I do, Arlene. Everybody, listen up: Attack Plan Theta is in operation. Donni and Earl; left arm, Arlene and I; right arm, Mickey and Sylvia; left leg, Henry and June; right leg. Let's show her why we're called Edgeriders. Attack."

They broke up and came at the giant from all sides, this time with their edge points in front. Thunder Hills swiped at them when they came within range, narrowly missing. Donni and Earl drove their edges into her left forearm and bicep, making the arm useless. Mickey and Sylvia took down the left leg, spilling her to the ground.

The giant swiped again, this time knocking Henry flying. It was her last swing, as Walt and Arlene took down her right arm. Walt jumped from his edge, and ran to Henry as June nailed the right leg. Walt checked a readout on Henry's suit.

"Unconscious but okay. I'll drive your edge now."

Walt ran to Henry's edge and jumped on. He blazed to the giant's right leg and jammed the edge in place.

"Thunder Hills, you are our prisoner. I suggest you stop struggling before you permanently injure yourself."

The giant glared at him, but said nothing. She did stop struggling.

"Arlene, keep an eye on things here. I'll bring the mobile base around to check out Henry and then wrap things up."

Below ground, the Grand Elder screamed.

"Get up there, the lot of you," she said to her remaining troops. "Take out those Knights and free the giant. We're going to need her."

"That's flat-out impossible," said Attendant Javis. "The opening is too high for us to reach. Even if we could, this lot is no match for those Edgeriders."

"Don't you dare tell me something is impossible, you low-born maggot. Get it done," shrieked the not-so-Grand Elder.

"Yeah, do it yourself, you useless shit. I'm out of here, and the rest of you might as well come, before those Edgeriders remember we're down here."

The lizard-women all nodded, then followed Javis back into the tunnel.

"Hate to break up a good rebellion," said Aurus, standing in the tunnel with the other Knights, "but none of you are going anywhere. Name is Aurus, Knight of Valeron."

He brandished his halberd.

The V'Laubi troops automatically pulled out paralo-ray tubes but couldn't fire them.

"You needn't have bothered. I'm Zen, DemiKnight of Valeron, and I've already reversed the polarity of the neutron flow. None of your tech will function until I say so."

The Grand Elder pulled a repeating crossbow from a soldier's back. She was, however, unable to fire it as Nea had emerged from a patch of shadow, and now embraced her tightly.

"I'm Nea, DemiKnight of Valeron, and you're in my hands now."

The Grand Elder struggled until Nea applied pressure to her neck.

"I'm Marvin, DemiKnight, and I will shoot the next of you that tries to fight. Got that?"

He held the Garand over his head for effect.

Javis shrugged and dropped her ray-tube.

"If I may speak for everybody, we surrender, and will cooperate in any way possible to end this peacefully," she said.

Surrender? thought the Grand Elder as she regained consciousness. *After all my travails, all my anguish, it will not end like this.*

She struggled to rise, and as she did, revealed a glint of gold beneath her.

And it will not.

The Grand Elder's Battle Presence flowed up and closed about her body.

"All of you Knights and traitors will die now," she screamed.

"Oh, bloody hell," exclaimed Aurus. "Now what?"

"I'll take care of you all later. The giant is more important right now," she said.

The Grand Elder jumped through the ceiling hole, into the field above.

"Take care of the surrendered," said Aurus to Zen and Marvin. "Nea and I will stop Her Majesty before she lets the giant loose."

Zen and Marvin nodded while Aurus carried Nea into the world above.

The flying edges were moving the giant onto a platform carried by a floating dome. Aurus dropped Nea and rammed into the Grand Elder from behind, knocking her about fifty feet away.

"Get the giant out of here, all of you," Aurus shouted. "She must not rejoin the fight."

"Don't you need help with her, sir?" asked Walt.

"If she gets the giant lose it won't matter. It'll take all your edges to hold her. Go."

Walt saluted and waved the other Edgeriders on.

"We'll be back as soon as she's secured," said Walt.

"Go," said Aurus as the Grand Elder regained her feet.

They left.

"Valurdian fool. One Knight is no match for me, especially if that first attack was your best."

"It wasn't. I was just in a hurry, and the name is ValDurian, but I only work for them."

She closed in a blink and punched him in the gut, sending him sailing nearly a hundred feet until he stopped in midair.

"You're fast and strong," Aurus gasped out, "but I bet you can't fly."

He rose hundreds of feet into the air, but she jumped right to him. Barely dodging her at the last split second, he barrel-rolled away as she fell.

"You jump good," he said, "but you can't turn in midair."

The Grand Elder fell into a dark hole on the ground, and the soil closed over her head as Nea appeared behind .

"I've got her," she said, "but I wanted to keep her head above ground so you could cut it off."

Aurus hurtled down and stabbed at the ground, but the Grand Elder caused a small earthquake as she broke free, laughing.

"That wasn't nearly time enough to suffocate me, weak fool." She threw a boulder at Nea, who avoided it by dropping into another black hole. Aurus struck at the Grand Elder with his halberd, barely scratching the armor.

The Grand Elder laughed, then kicked Aurus away. As he regained control over his flight the Grand Elder dropped into a black hole again. This time the ground closed over her up to the neck.

"Got her, Aurus. Lop it off before she gets free."
With blazing speed, Aurus rushed in, but only made a cloud of sparks where the halberd struck her neck.

"Keep at her. We can do this," said Nea. "I had time to set plenty of black holes while you talked with the Edgeriders."

"Pity you won't get the chance to use them," said the Grand

Elder.

She broke free of the ground and grabbed Aurus's right arm. She twisted it, bringing a scream from Aurus and making him drop the halberd.

"My, my. You Knights are much more delicate than I expected."

Using both hands, she ripped Aurus's arm off at the elbow.

"You bitch," screamed Nea as she ran at the Grand Elder.

She dove into a black hole at the Grand Elder's feet, widening it beneath them. The Grand Elder dropped again and the hole closed over her. Nea ran to an unmoving, slowly bleeding Aurus while carrying his arm.

"Are you alive? I've got her trapped for a moment."

His eyes snapped open.

"Been better. I was playing possum because I had an idea. Don't want her to hear."

He whispered to Nea, then used his watch to vanish.

With a massive ground shake, the Grand Elder broke free from the earth and found Nea alone.

"All by yourself now? This is going to be such fun—"

The Grand Elder's words choked off as she suddenly flew high, her closed helmet covered in blood. She struggled, swinging around and whirling her arms about her for several minutes. Gradually she grew limp and fell to the ground, Aurus appearing above her, then landed nearby, grinning before he collapsed.

Nea ran to him, still carrying his arm.

"Here's your arm. Can you make it regrow in place?"

"Don't know for sure, but I hope so."

He stuck the forearm on his stump and made the shredded skin close over it.

"How did you do that to her?" Nea asked.

Shaking off a wave of pain, Aurus sat up.

"Got the idea when she said you didn't have time to suffocate her. You gave me the chance to bleed all over her, and since it was my blood I could make it go where I wanted. Packed it all over her helmet and figured it would close up any air holes even if I couldn't see them. Had my belt around her middle so she dangled low and couldn't hit me accidentally, then just rode it out until she stopped moving."

"Is she dead?"

"Hope so, because I can't go another round with the Grand Elder."

"Have no fear on that matter," said the Arbiter, who had appeared behind the Grand Elder, tapping the Presence with her pointer. "The Battle Presence works only for the Grand Elder, and as an Arbiter of the V'Laubi, I certify she is no longer that."

The Battle Presence flowed away from the former Grand Elder and stood stock still, bloodless, and empty, waiting for its next inhabitant.

The Elder gasped, her eyes opened, and she stared up at the Arbiter.

"How dare you?"

"If you had won this fight, it would have been a different matter, but you have lost. This latest debacle has lowered your score to a point we Arbiters have declared the Elder of the L'Orenn to be Grand Elder," said the Arbiter.

"Those losers?" asked the Elder. "They were always at the bottom."

"Which is why they are now on top. They lost the least of anybody. Their caution has finally paid off."

The Arbiter waved her pointer and the ground opened, dropping the Elder with the other V'Laubi waiting below ground.

The Elder came to her feet with difficulty while Aurus and Nea floated down.

No, no, no. This is not how it ends. I am always in control. The Elder clutched her stomach with both arms and squeezed to rally herself. And felt a lump as she did. *I am still in control.*

She pulled out her needle pistol and fired, first at the Arbiter, then the assembled Knights. Aurus pulled Nea to his chest, turning around to protect her, while some of the assembled V'Laubi were hit. Marvin lay on the ground, but Zen was nowhere to be seen.

From a prone position, Marvin emptied eight rounds into the Elder's gut, blowing her torso apart, then slowly came to his feet while changing clips.

"Warned you," said Marvin. "Anybody else with a death wish?"

"No," yelled Javis, "but those needles are poisoned and you

might die."

The V'Laubi who had been hit writhed in pain, then fell. Aurus stumbled, then looked at Nea with an expression of helplessness.

"Is there going to be anything left of you after today?" she asked.

He stumbled again and made his shirt disappear. His back was peppered with poison needles and the skin around them was turning black.

"Oh, my lord," said Nea as she began to pluck them out.

"Doan warry," said Aurus, "the Eggraiders got a doctor ship. They can fix me."

He fell to his knees.

"No time," said Javis. "The Grand Elder's body should have an antidote on it because she was always afraid of poisoning herself."

She went through the corpse's pockets and pulled out a bottle of blue liquid, then handed it to Nea.

"Just a capful to each victim should do. Can you help my people also?"

Nea gave a capful to Aurus, then moved on to the V'laubi, then the Arbiter. She and the hollowbacks all responded well, but Aurus was still down.

"Give him more until he responds," said Javis. "I never saw anybody take so much poison and live."

"That's Aurus for you," said Nea, as she poured about half the bottle down his throat.

"I'm almost back to regular pain now," rasped Aurus. "You know it's been bad when you start to enjoy ordinary pain."

"Where's Zen," asked Nea, looking about.

"There somewhere," said Marvin, pointing at the largest pile of rubble. "Whatever you guys were going through, we felt it down here too. The ceiling started caving in again, and took out some of the hollowbacks. Almost took me too, because I couldn't move fast enough, what with my injuries."

He paused to draw a ragged breath.

"Zen could have run, could have saved himself, but he slammed me out of the way. We barely knew each other, but he chose my life over his."

#

Three days later, Aurus met with Master Julian.

"That went worse than expected, with the tragedy of losing Zen," said Master Julian. "We got lucky with the former Grand Elder though. How'd you pull off that raid on the final base?"

"Pretty simple," said Aurus. "Changed myself into a lovely lizard lady again, then Javis helped. We traveled to their last base and entered without challenge. Which is a good thing, considering the state of my arm and general health. We used Zen's codes to turn off their power, and Marvin brought in a mini-howitzer for shock value. Nea breezed through the installation, freeing prisoners, while Javis and I explained the situation to the remaining V'Laubi.

"They are very reasonable beings when they realize everything is stacked against them. Surrender was total from that base, though I don't know what to expect now that they have a new Grand Elder. Now what?"

"The remaining factions on Lakachar have also surrendered. Now it's up to the ValDurians to deal with the aftermath. Your only concern right now is that both the Oracles and the Omnimind have decided the Knights need a vacation before dealing with the next big thing."

"I don't think I've ever had a vacation," said Aurus, "at least, not an enforced one."

"Even you need a rest, especially after what you went through, so grit your teeth and enjoy it, Knight. That's an order.

"When you return, there'll be a formal goodbye for Zen."

This Might be Important

Raelani squirmed uncomfortably in a cushioned wicker lounge chair while winds whipped her hair and gown about unmercifully. She drained the last sip of wine from a glass, then hurled it to the marble patio where it joined the remains of other glasses, along with wine puddles. Flinging herself back into the chair, she reached over the side and grabbed a corked wine bottle. She stared hard at the bottle until the cork popped itself. Without sitting up, she took a slug of wine, spilling some on herself.

"A lovely sight, to be sure," said Indra, who had appeared to her right, along with a wicker chair beneath him.

"Stuff it," she said, taking a smaller sip this time.

Indra gave a wan smile.

"So why are you here playing the drunk?" he said.

"Who's playing?"

"Alcohol does not affect you, so I assume you're play-acting for reasons unknown."

"Does so affect me, if I want it to."

"Only in that you could convince yourself you're getting drunk."

"Hey, I also like the taste, so why not drink a lot?" asked Raelani.

"I've known you for a little while now, and you aren't acting like yourself."

"A little while? We've had five kids together."

"That was you?" he said, smiling.

"Yeah, me. There'd better not be anybody else."

"Sorry, I was only trying to make light of the situation."

"I get that you were joking, but you don't do it well. What I don't get is why things are going so badly for our Knights."

"In what way?"

"We lost four Knights. In that way. And in addition to suspicious things happening that none of them can explain."

Indra heaved a sigh and sat back straighter in his chair.

"I know you think of the Knights as if they were your grandchildren, but they do things that have to be done, and sometimes they die. If I—"

"I know that, and I can deal, except that ..."

Indra waited, his face set to impassive.

"There might be a problem with the Oracles," she said.

"Explain."

"Delu came right out and suggested there might be a traitor among the Oracles. I dismissed it, of course, but what if she were right? What if one or more of them have lost their collective mind? Or minds. If their prophecies have been tainted, how would we know? We've let them give us direction for a very long time. What if we can't depend on them any longer?"

Indra gripped his chair arms tightly and sighed again.

"The Oracles are doing their jobs properly, as always. Sometimes their job is not very pleasant, but you must remember they can do nothing without us enabling them."

"What do you mean, Indi?"

He stood, tearing the chair arms away as he did. They turned to splinters in his grasp.

"I caused it. Everything. The near-misses, the deaths, save for Zen. It was me. They said it was imperative, that the AllWorlds depended on it."

Raelani jumped to her feet, winds blowing away her lounger and the glass fragments.

"How could you?" she wailed. "More than that, they talked to you directly? They never do that. Why not me?"

"They would not. You could never do what was necessary, because you cannot cause harm to a living being."

"But why cause any harm? We're supposed to be the good guys."

"No, we aren't. We work for the greater good, but that doesn't necessarily mean we're good. We've done what was necessary, and kept things running so smoothly for so long that reality is beginning to rebel, even to unravel. If it isn't dealt with then we'll have caused greater harm than we ever prevented. Oracles were never meant to give perfect knowledge of the future, which is why, mythologically speaking, they were always vague."

Raelani nodded.

"In the old days, half the time, heroes actually ended up causing the problem they were trying to avoid, because they had only a little knowledge," she said.

"Exactly. And that's how it was supposed to work. Things have gone too well for us for too long and we're going to pay the price unless drastic steps are taken. I've only just started to mitigate the damage."

"But you've killed Knights. You almost killed Marvindius."

"Marvin Dees."

"I don't care what he calls himself now. How can you do this?"

"Because I can detach myself from the personal present and look toward the needed outcome. Does that make me evil? Maybe. For that matter, I haven't killed anybody of late, but did set up situations in such a way that the outcomes will help keep reality from shredding. I regret some of our people died, but better them than everything as we know it. I even offered to sacrifice myself, but was told that wouldn't help."

Raelani cried. A constant waterfall of big teardrops would have wet her gown, save that her winds blew them away.

"I don't know what to think. This isn't what we do."

"True. It's what *I* must do until the crisis is averted."

Chapter Thirty Three
Island Getaway

Aurus and Nea appeared on a silver platform hanging over the whirling vastness of Chaospace. The platform, along with hundreds of others, connected to the floating space island below via crystal escalator ribbons placed along its rim. It looked rather like a giant millipede on its back with legs in the air.

Aurus, blond and tanned, sported white shorts, flip-flops, and a red Hawaiian shirt. Nea, pale and black-haired, wore a wide-brimmed black hat, sunglasses, green jumpsuit, and black sandals. They both studied an image that had flickered into view before them.

"Greetings," said the shimmering vision of a bearded gnome, resplendent in rainbow robes with silver highlights. "Welcome to the Hotel Cosmapheir. Please take the moving steps to the front desk where I will assist you. For your protection, please note that spells do not function on the hotel grounds. If this does not suit you, then you may depart now, with no charges. Have a pleasant day."

"Doesn't really apply to me. I don't do spells," said Aurus. "While we're here though, call me by my middle name, Harry."

He jumped on the escalator and Nea joined him.

"It does apply to me," she said, "not that I cast many spells anyway. Why call you Harry? We aren't undercover."

"Aurus is a far more distinctive name than Harry. I'd rather not get the attention of any mystical beings that have heard of me."

"Makes sense. Maybe you should have changed your face then?

Little too late at this point, though."

Aurus grunted in agreement. "I thought the Cosmapheir had been destroyed in the Outerwars a hundred years ago."

"It had. Apparently they rebuilt it. The current quality of service remains to be determined, I suppose."

"Sure, I guess."

Aurus craned his neck, taking in the view as the escalator moved them down.

"How'd you find out about it?"

"Carl Helsir told me. Since he's well-connected, I asked him if he knew of any high-end vacation spots. He thought I might be interested in this one."

"Oh, Loki? Yeah, he was okay, I guess, if a little shady. Being as it's a resort for wizards, why'd he think you'd care?"

"Why wouldn't I care? I'm a wizard, Harry."

"You know what I mean. You aren't some lazy, poufy wizard that uses magic for everything. You're a hard-working DemiKnight of Valeron."

"Damn right, and this hard-working DemiKnight could use a great vacation, especially after that latest mission. You know that better than anybody. How's the arm?"

"Still attached at least, and mostly pain-free. Thanks for asking. So why am I here also?"

"Your orders also were to take a vacation. Besides, most wizards bring a bodyguard since spells can't be cast."

They reached the end of the escalator.

The lobby, as it were, looked exactly like an open-air park with numerous kiosks. A white, sandy beach ran adjacent, with an ocean beyond, and the tang of salt in the air. The deep blue sky, complete with pleasantly warm yellow sun, looked like that of a typical world rather than the awful glory of Chaospace.

While approaching the nearest kiosk, they recognized a few faces in the crowds.

"I've studied some of our fellow check-ins," said Nea. "The minotaur and goblin are Vork and Velak, respectively. They're free-lance troublecausers that are definitely not friends with the full-stars. I think they work for the Twilight brothers now."

"You mean Bellos, Plagos, Mortos, and Murray?"

"The very same," she said, with a sour look.

Nea gave the park a visual once-over.

"Quite an amazing crowd. The dwarf with the stormcloud golem floating on a tether is an Undercairn. I don't know which one," she said.

"Well, there goes our vacation. That lot is high on our do-not-play-nice-with list."

As they had just reached the kiosk, the attending gnome said, "I couldn't help but overhear. Don't worry, sir. There's a strict no-violence policy at the Cosmapheir, along with the spell negation. Fighting will get you ejected, as will bringing in weapons. Technically, that golem could count as a weapon, so it got shut down."

Aurus shrugged his shoulders.

"Fighting wouldn't bother me. How do we sign in and where do we go?"

The gnome, whom they'd seen in the greeting image, three-foot-tall in a two-foot hat, smiled.

"That's what I'm here for." He pulled out a bowling ball-sized crystal orb. "You deposit your SMUs into this. Twenty per guest per day for the room and basic package."

"What are Smoos?" asked Aurus.

"Ess-em-yous, Standard Magical Units," said Nea, "the basic breakdown of magical power for spell usage. The amount needed is what determines a high or low order spell."

"Whatever happened to cold, hard cash?" asked Aurus.

"Acceptable for most places," said the gnome, still smiling, "but magic is universal. It can be stored, and if used properly, can create or destroy, extend life or end it. It also powers the hotel and the spell dampening field."

"What are the basic amenities?" asked Nea.

"Well, the room itself, of course. We no longer maintain the existence of rooms that aren't in use, in order to maximize profits."

"Another universal thing," mumbled Aurus.

The attendant continued. "Then the most basic of magical experiences, travel to imaginary worlds with no interaction. Finally, a magical extravaganza; this would be a spectacular stage show experienced by other guests as well, not something private."

"How much for the works?" asked Nea.

The gnome's smile grew faint.

"If you have to ask, then you probably can't provide that much power." Upon seeing Aurus's glower he quickly added, "One hundred SMUs per day, per person. Will that be in crystals, or straight from the source?"

"He's right, Harry." Nea sighed. "I don't have that kind of power."

"Power, schmower. I got your smoos right here, junior." He grabbed the orb and concentrated. It glowed so brightly the gnome hid his eyes, and Nea stood behind Aurus in his shadow. He handed the solar orb to the gnome.

"There. How many smoos is that?"

The gnome put the orb under the counter and waved a wand over it. "That, that's more than enough for seven days, sir, for the both of you, with full service."

"Keep the change," said Aurus. "That should increase your profit margin. How do we get to our room?"

The gnome held out a golden stylus and crystal tablet for them to sign.

"Zaeph," he bellowed. "Kiosk fifty-seven."

A young, beardless gnome in a red bellhop's outfit with matching pointed hat popped in.

"Zaeph, take these VIPs to Suite One."

Zaeph waved a silver wand and he, Aurus, and Nea appeared in a luxurious hotel suite. 'Luxurious' in the way that the Golden Gate is a nice little bridge. Every standard of opulence Nea could think of was extant. While she attempted to take it all in, young Zaeph handed her two crystal cards with gold etchings.

"These are your key cards. They let you enter the room at will."

He pointed to a minivan-sized cornucopia made of gold.

"The megacopia will provide anything you might need in the way of food, clothing or in-room entertainment. Remember that all material created will dissipate outside the hotel grounds. You must eat only non-magical food the day before you leave. Physical mementos may be obtained at the numerous gift shops.

"The Green Door will take you to any magical adventure in its memory, or make new ones following the instructions on the plaque.

"The mirror will explain how to seal the room against uninvited guests. If you have any further questions, the mirror will contact a staff member. If you have any complaints, please address the mirror.

"The suite has three bedrooms. One for each of you, if you wish separate quarters, and a third for guests.

"I hope that my service is acceptable. I normally work Magical Systems, but Customer Service is understaffed at the moment, so I'm filling in. If anything I've done is below expectations, please accept my humblest apologies."

"Not at all," said Nea. "It's superb, in fact."

Zaeph bowed before her and held up a palm-sized crystal. Nea gazed at it in confusion. Aurus grinned at her.

"Tip, he wants a tip, girl. It's customary in Earth hotels, and here too I'll bet. Zaeph, you want smoos?"

Zaeph smiled, but bowed his head lower and held the crystal higher. Nea looked to Aurus, but he waved at her with a hand flourish. Nea took the crystal and concentrated while it flared briefly. Zaeph bowed even lower, then vanished with a wave of his wand. Nea heard a thump behind her.

She saw a desiccated, gray and shriveled form in Aurus's Hawaiian shirt sprawled on the floor, facedown.

"Aurus."

The still, skeletal figure whispered dryly, "Smoos."

Nea placed her hands on his back, under his shirt, and concentrated. After a few moments color returned to his skin, which plumped a bit, hiding his skeletal structure. Still, Aurus remained a pale shadow of his usual robust self. Nea turned him on his back and put a pillow under his head.

"What the hell, Harry?"

"I gave a little more than I could afford. Deficit spending they call it. I'd never pumped out pure magic before."

"I don't understand."

"Neither do I. The full-stars gave me a body that's a magical engine, but it goes to my flight, sun-powers, strength, and shapeshifting mostly. I can't do spells. Literally not built for wizardry."

"But you were fine until the gnome left."

"Nope, just used my shapeshifting to look normal until we were alone. I don't want the garden gnomes to see me like this. It's okay. I'm used to appearing as something I'm not. I may not have earned this body, but I care for it with pride."

"So, you going to live or what?"

"Hope so. I should recover okay, but I don't know how long it'll take. Never been like this before, not even after all those harrowing battles of late."

"How can I help? I don't have enough power to give more than I already did. I can help you walk to your room. I could even carry you if need be. Can I get you something else? Food maybe?"

"Yes, that."

"What do you want?"

"Everything on the menu. Doubled."

Chapter Thirty Four
Cheap at Twice the Price

The following made-to-order morning found Aurus in better spirits. He polished off his tenth plate of scrambled eggs and bacon, followed by his third roast wild boar. Nea's tea and scones somehow seemed pathetic by comparison.

Aurus let loose a massive belch, sat back in his chair, and watched his distended belly shrink down to his usual rock-hard abs. Nea looked on in pure envy.

"It must be nice to eat whatever you want and not gain any weight."

"It is, but that's not usually how it works for me. I do eat more than the average superhuman as a rule, but now my body is converting the magically-created food back into magic. I guess I'm feeding off the power I provided."

"So, you're good then?"

Aurus's fingers flexed and a golden halberd appeared in his hand, to be immediately dismissed.

"Well, I'd say I'm at about thirty percent, so lots better than most people. More than good enough to start enjoying this enforced vacation. I suppose it could be worse, though.

"It isn't a place recommended by the Oracles or the Omnimind. If it were, I'd expect some hidden agenda. As it is, I brought the trouble on myself because I was trying to show off."

He finished up the remains of his breakfast.

"Let's make a good time of it, okay?" he said. "Anyway, do you have any clue as to what we could be doing?"

"I went through the list while you were stuffing yourself. We could be superpowered defenders of humanity fighting an alien invasion."

"Too much like our day job."

"Covert operatives on a mission to save the King or President?"

"Again, our regular stuff," said Aurus.

"Normal teenagers and a talking dog solving mysteries and fighting ghosts?"

"Zoinks. I've seen that cartoon show, so no."

"Pilots in giant robots fighting other piloted giant robots?"

"Only if they're really awesome, or we get to design our own," said Aurus.

"I'll put that on the 'maybe' pile. Little fairy-types in a giant world, having fun making fools of the bigger creatures?"

"Well now, that does sound like fun. Let's do it."

After getting the proper costumes from the megacopia, a crude brown vest and red pants for Aurus, then a green Tinkerbelle dress for Nea, they went through the Green Door.

They found themselves on a forest floor where red-spotted mushrooms towered over them like trees, and trees were like pillars of the heavens. They now both had gauzy fairy wings.

"Wow," said Aurus, "I guess you get what you pay for. This is amazing. Is it like the Star Trek holodeck?"

"I don't know what that is. It's part solid illusion, part mind tricks, part I don't know what. I only know this girl wants to have fun."

She grinned as she vibrated her new wings and took off into the trees.

Aurus flew after her. The race was on, but even though Nea had a head start Aurus soon caught up.

"How is it you're so fast?" she asked as he did loops around her.

"Always have been. Did you forget I can fly under my own power? For me, these wings are just show."

His eyes glazed over and he dropped.

"Aurus," she screamed.

Nea flew down and caught him before he fell very far, landing on a gargantuan tree branch.

"Wake up," she said while slapping his face.

Aurus's eyelids fluttered and opened.

"I may only be at twenty percent, come to think of it. My power is recovering more slowly than usual, I think. Then again, I've never taxed it so much, all at once."

The tree shook, and the treetops dissolved, leaving the spectacle of Chaospace staring down at them.

"Is this part of the scenario?" he asked.

"I don't think so. Emergency exit." Nea pressed fingers to her crystal card and the Green Door appeared. She carried Aurus through to their room.

The room seemed normal, but the mirror yelled at them.

"Emergency. Please exit through the manual door immediately."

They opened the white double doors and stepped onto an elevated crystal walkway with gold handrails on both sides. Up and down the walkway their neighbors had done the same.

On the outside, the four-story hotel seemed much like any other mundane brick hotel, but windowless, with the crystal walkway encircling the building, connecting all floors. Their building was only one such of a line stretching into the distance. Nea set Aurus down, and he used the handrails to keep to his feet.

The sky was still blue, and the day warm, with no earthquakes to ruin the mood. With no disaster to grab their immediate attention, the two looked over the crowd. Many of the other guests were in fanciful costumes.

"The lady in the over-the-top crystal gown is Iradiel, the Mother of Glass. She's friends with our bosses," said Aurus.

Nea smiled and said, "It looks like she was having a great fantasy."

"Maybe, but I believe that's how she normally dresses."

Leaving Aurus for a bit, Nea walked around, looking over the neighbors, most of whom seemed none the worse for wear. Then she saw their nearest fourth-floor neighbor slumped against his door, with a brown-haired girl putting her hand on his chest.

Nea called out, "Sir, may I be of help?" She reached them before he could respond.

The man regained his footing with an ebony cane.

"No, no, I'm quite all right, young lady, but thank you for your concern. Didn't sleep well, I suppose. First night in a new place, and then this alarm nonsense, that's all."

He pushed himself to his full height with the ivory-headed cane, but remained several inches shorter than Nea. He straightened his black, Victorian-style suit, smoothed back his white hair, and placed a dangling monocle to his left eye.

He gazed approvingly at Nea, and let the monocle drop on its gold chain.

"Where are my manners? I am Augustine Silverwind, Gentleman Investigator." He bowed slightly from the waist. "This is my granddaughter, Neramira."

The girl, looking to be in her early teens, pulled at the sides of her white gown and curtsied.

"Charmed, wot?" said Neramira.

"Investigator?" asked Aurus, who had made his way over, behind Nea. "Like a detective?" he said, too loudly.

"Why, yes, young man," said Augustine. "That's it exactly."

Nea scowled at Aurus.

"We must apologize for the rudeness. This is my partner, Harry Keaty, and I am Nea Nystoros. We too are investigators."

"Indeed?" said Augustine. "A small multiverse, is it not? I have been bringing my hard-working niece here into the business, but felt we needed a vacation. I had hoped the new hotel would meet the standards of the old, but it seems I am to be disappointed."

"Don't fret yet," said Nea. "This is the shakedown cruise as it were. Everything new is bound to have minor issues at first."

At that point, a great, pure tone sounded three times, followed by a booming voice. "Guests of the Hotel Cosmapheir. We apologize for the inconvenience. The Green Door reality generator system is experiencing a temporary problem and is non-functional until tomorrow." A collective groan went up from the various guests. "Those who have paid for the service will be gifted an extra day's stay, and meanwhile all other services are working properly. Thank you for your patience."

"Then that, I suppose, is that," said Augustine. "We hope to see you around and about, as the only other entertainment is the nightly stage show for the inexpensive rooms."

Having said their goodbyes, Aurus and Nea returned to their room to change back to the clothes they arrived in.

"I meant to ask them at the time, but you interrupted me, 'Harry.' Maybe you know? I found it curious that Neramira said 'charmed,' but then asked 'what.' Strange, don't you think?"

"Not 'what,' but 'wot.' Double-you-oh-tee. It's a Britishism, basically the same as 'you know.' I'd assumed from their accents they were British, so that tracks."

"Oh, interesting. Kind of cute, too."

A leisurely walk along the beach in lieu of entertainment brought them to the check-in kiosks.

Arriving guests flowed in as usual. It wasn't long before a loud commotion at one kiosk got the couple's attention.

"I can't take an extra day," roared the minotaur, Vork. The goblin, Velak, stood behind him, shaking his head. "Either get your system up and running now or give us a refund. Double for the inconvenience."

"Sir, be reasonable," said the gnome behind the counter. "I don't have the authority to do any such thing."

"Then get someone with the authority," thundered Vork. Velak nodded his head.

The terrified gnome replied, "B-but all the H-high M-management is w-working on repairs. I-I can't contact them."

Velak tapped Vork on the leg. Vork stepped back and Velak moved forward. "My dear sir, you are upsetting my associate. This is generally considered unwise. Furthermore, we are under contractual obligations to Bellos Twilight, a being high on the list of those who should most particularly not be upset. If you do not resolve this matter to our satisfaction then I shall be forced to bring it to his attention."

The gnome looked ready to have a heart attack before Aurus spoke up.

"So, the bullies aren't scary enough on their own? You have to threaten in your boss's name?"

Vork bellowed loud enough for Nea to cover her ears.

"We're plenty scary, pipsqueak. Mind your own business now or tend to your wounds later."

"You two even work for the weakest brother." Aurus laughed. "Everybody knows Legality is the strongest of the Four Horsemen."

Vork threw his head back and roared, then snorted and charged. Aurus did a quick side-step and Vork tumbled into the sand. He scrambled to his hooves faster than expected, hitting Aurus in the gut with a left hook. Aurus crumpled to his knees, and Vork raised both fists to crush his skull.

Two chrome-armored figures appeared on either side of Vork, bathing him in beams of blue light from their eye-slits. He went rigid and each figure grabbed one of his arms. They disappeared, taking Vork with them.

Nea stood watching, a neutral expression on her face. Velak smiled at her with an evil, sharp-toothed grin.

"I know who you two are," he said. "I always study the enemy. Vork will be quite happy to learn who he took down." He turned to the gnome. "As for you, this is not over, though I will return to my room for the nonce."

The gnome turned his eyes from a video screen in front of him.

"Your companion has been neutralized and returned to his point of origin. Violence is not tolerated here, save in the simulations. Have a nice day."

Velak walked off while Nea helped Aurus to his feet.

The gnome asked, "Are you well, sir?"

"Never better. I'm glad I was able to turn their attention away from you. Lucky those armored guys showed up."

"The paxitons show up at the onset of violence, but I thank you for taking their initial assault off me."

"You're welcome . . . Nea, I'm feeling a bit tired. Perhaps we should return to our room?" They left the beach.

"Aurus, you took that punch on purpose, didn't you?"

"Well, I knew violence wasn't allowed, and I figured they had some way of enforcing that. If I had hit back they might have ejected me as well. But no, he hit me fair and square. My reflexes are still off."

"So, what do you want to do now?"

"Hang out, relax, eat, see if the megacopia can make a punching bag that looks like Vork, eat, and then maybe eat. Or we could stop by Augustine's place and chat with him and his granddaughter/niece."

Nea laughed, loud and long.

"I had wondered if you picked up on that."

"Of course I did, wot? That old pervert."

She laughed again.

"It's not what you think, Aurus. She isn't a real teenaged girl. I could sense she's some sort of summoned creature, an elemental spirit maybe."

"Doesn't mean he isn't a pervert."

Chapter Thirty Five
You Can Checkout Anytime You'd Like

The following morning Aurus awoke with a grin.

"I'm much better today, Nea. Let's try that Green Door again after we have breakfast."

"I've been up for hours and already ate. You know I don't sleep much."

"Nor do I as a rule, but these are trying times in which we live. A few dozen magical breakfast burritos and I should be good to go." As he spoke there came a frantic knocking at the door. A glance at the mirror showed them it was Neramira. "Now what?"

Nea unsealed the door.

"Come in, please. Is something wrong?"

Neramira drew quick breaths. "Maybe. I returned after an early morning run but realized I had forgotten my key card and couldn't open the door, wot? Uncle August won't respond to my knocking, so he might be sick. It was faster running to here than the reception area, so can you call the staff for me?"

"Of course."

Within moments Zaeph opened Augustine's room remotely and promised to bring in a medical team. Aurus and company entered, finding the white-haired gent immobile on his bed.

Neramira rushed to Augustine's side and unlaced his nightshirt down to the navel, revealing several crystals attached to his abdomen. She put her head to his chest, and then put her hands over his heart.

Her hands glowed slightly and Augustine stirred.

"It's not enough," she said. Her dress exploded into two white wings growing from her shoulder blades, revealing a body covered by, or composed of, swirling mist. She lifted him from the bed and enfolded him and herself into a cocoon of wings with only their heads exposed. Just at that point, two gnomes in white robes emblazoned with red crosses appeared.

"He needs mana to live," she shouted.

One gnome waved a silver rod and vanished along with Augustine and Neramira.

The other gnome questioned Aurus and Nea. "Anything you can tell me about this?"

"Not much," said Aurus. "He was having some trouble yesterday during the alarm. I thought maybe it was his heart, but if it is I'm guessing he strained himself paying too many smoos for this room." The room, though well-appointed, was a third the size of Aurus and Nea's.

"That's it?" The gnome looked disappointed.

"Sorry," said Nea. "We just met them yesterday. We didn't discuss the family medical history."

The gnome said, "Right then. I'll be off." He made to wave his little silver stick when Nea stopped him.

"Can you tell us how to find the infirmary? We'd like to check in on them."

"Just ask your mirror. It'll put a map up on your key cards."

"Speaking of which, we'll bring them these," said Aurus. He picked up two key cards from the nightstand. "It might make things easier for them later."

#

Aurus and Nea sat on a couch while Augustine rested abed, Neramira sitting on a chair at his side. Neramira touched the old man with her wings and said, "I'm sorry I have no tears to give for him, but as you no doubt see, I am not human." Puffs of white vapor rose from the corners of her eyes. "I am a free-willed sylph, conjured by him long ago, though I play at being his niece, or granddaughter."

"And you stay with him by choice?" asked Nea.

"He is a wonderful old man, and I love him as much as a sylph can love anyone. My life's goal is to make his final days easier, yet he thought I needed a vacation. He went to an awful bit of trouble to bring us here, and it may kill him." More vapor arose from her eyes.

"What happened to him?" asked Aurus.

"He paid too many SMUs for the room. It must have hurt him deep down because he hasn't been able to recover. He is not a young man, after all."

"I apologize for being nosy, but what are those crystals on his stomach?" asked Nea.

Neramira folded her wings back into the form of a gown and sighed. "The source of his life. Each is a mana battery."

"I don't understand," said Aurus.

"If I may," said Nea. "Mages tend to live longer than the average human simply because they have a greater store of mana through dedication and training."

"Well, I'll be damned."

The sylph sniffled, clouds leaking up from her eyes.

"Neramira?" said Nea.

"Please, just 'Neri' would be nice."

"Neri then. He feeds off the crystals?"

"Sort of. They maintain his life rather than provide power for spells. His personal power does that, but it hasn't recovered as it should."

"Has this been an issue before?" asked Aurus.

"No, but he ages, as humans do. The mana extends his life but not his youth. There must come a time when his body no longer functions. I know this, but can do nothing to stop it."

Neri's face disappeared in a cloud of vapor tears.

Nea tried to hold her, but could not, as Neri broke up into vapor.

"Neri? I'll help if I can," said Nea as Neri re-formed.

"It's okay. I really shouldn't have human emotions anyway. If he dies I'll lose him and my emotions. I can't bear the thought now, though I suppose I won't care afterwards."

"Because he's the one who summoned you?" asked Nea.

"Yes. Everything I am is tied to him. I'd rather kill myself than lose all that and have to remember what I had."

Augustine reached out his hand and grabbed hers. "That won't happen. Not today, at least."

Neri embraced him, vapor streaming up from her eyes.

"Gus. You're awake. Next time you go, take me with you."

Augustine stroked her long, brown hair.

"Enough of such talk. I'm here for some time to come. There are other things to talk of right now. Be a dear and elevate my bed, would you?"

While Neri fiddled with the bed, Augustine went on.

"I have come to a conclusion, besides discovering hospitals are universally uncomfortable. My loss of personal mana is not natural. It has naught to do with exhaustion or my advanced age."

"How can you be sure?" asked Nea.

"I have a wand with which I check myself habitually, much as how one would check their own blood pressure or blood sugar in some of the more advanced worlds. Last night my power was recovering normally, and I worried over no more than getting a good night's sleep. Then I found myself awake here, amidst the glory of rectal thermometers and bedpans."

"Meaning what?" asked Aurus.

"Meaning that someone or something is draining my power. Only my own, not from the crystals. This could be a natural occurrence of Chaospace that has remained undiscovered thus far, or a matter nefarious. Either is concerning, but particularly the latter."

Neri hugged him tightly.

"We need to leave then," she said.

#

After making sure Augustine and Neri were safely back in their room, Aurus and Nea took a walk.

"I vote for nefarious," said Aurus.

"As do I," said Nea. "It seems less believable that an unknown danger of Chaospace suddenly picks on some poor old wizard than if he were targeted on purpose. Maybe an old enemy of his followed him here?"

"Not just him. It could explain why my power's taking its sweet time building up."

"Then not a personal enemy? Maybe an opportunist? For those who can read it, Augustine would seem to have a tremendous amount of personal power, and you actually do. Usually."

"I'm thinking Velak. He's pissed off that his friend got the bum's rush. Maybe he wants to recoup the smoos he spent, or to make trouble for the hotel."

"Perhaps, but we'll have to speak with the management about this. It'd be hard to investigate without their cooperation."

They approached the closest kiosk, which turned out to be the one they had signed in at. "May I help you?" asked the gnome in attendance.

"You may," said Nea. Their badges appeared in outstretched hands; Aurus's had a quarter-sized hole in the middle, while Nea's had an inset black onyx cabochon. "We need to speak with your top management."

The gnome gulped visibly. "Of course, though as guests you could use the mirror for any questions. May I know what issues concern you?"

"You may not," said Aurus. "Your higher-ups will let you know should they feel the need. Beat feet now, buster."

#

The Main Office was very impressive, even by the standards of Aurus and Nea's hotel room. Miles of crystal corridors merged in a vaulted conference room of silver and sapphire, lit by hidden sources.

Aurus and Nea stood before a silver throne encrusted with diamonds and sapphires, a throne clearly made for a very large man. Aurus had transformed to his semblance of a bronze-skinned man with a gold-feathered hawk-like head, wearing only a chainmail kilt about his hips. Nea wore a gray bodysuit with a matching, hooded cloak that shaded her eyes.

While they waited patiently, a gnome sped toward them from one of the corridors, riding a floating disk decked out with side rails for each hand. He parked midair and stepped onto the throne, his disk obediently settling to the floor behind. The gnome topped out at six feet, half of which was his stove-pipe hat, tasteful in violet with silver spangles. A simple robe of ornate gold brocade showed off his ankle-length, jet-black beard and completed his attempt at imitating a parade float.

"Gentlemen." He coughed. "Pardon me: gentlepeople. I am Artifus Vohn Mackleweiser, Grandiloquence Supreme of the Mackleweiser Consortium, and Absolute Authority of the Hotel Cosmapheir. I apologize for the wait, but teleportation is impossible within the Central Complex, as you have no doubt seen. Now then, what have we done to incur, um, to deserve the honor of this visit?"

"I am Daernea the Undark, DemiKnight of Valeron, and this is Aurus Keaty, a full Knight. There is a customer safety issue that must be addressed immediately."

"All conceivable safety issues have been met and protective measures enabled which exceed guidelines. We even had to invent some issues that could not have existed without our help. I'm sure the matter has already been dealt with."

"You're saying the ValDurians are wrong?" said Aurus, his voice crackling with power.

Artifus winced and patted his brow with a lace kerchief.

"Of course not. I would never argue with the Ones of Power, or the Knights of Valeron who speak in their name. Are you here in that name?"

"We are here as guests," said Nea. She launched into an explanation of the matter, concluding with, "Since this is a very delicate and possibly dangerous matter, Aurus felt we needed your cooperation to make a proper investigation."

Artifus, who had ah-hummed and harrumphed throughout Nea's monologue, tapped a finger to his bulbous nose.

"Hmmm, quite so. Such a situation, if known, could ruin our reputation and destroy this relaunch. Plus, think of the liabilities should any customer perish."

"Not to mention the moral obligation to step in and prevent tragedy at all cost," crackled Aurus.

Artifus flinched and closed both eyes.

"Oh, yes, of course. That as well."

"We require only your cooperation," said Nea, "along with certain supplies."

"And I need to discuss this with Gus, again," Aurus said.

Chapter Thirty Six
Party at Aurus's Place

At midnight, the door to Aurus and Nea's suite slowly opened. The lights were low, and plush, white carpet showed indentations of footsteps moving toward the bedrooms, stopping at Aurus's room. His door opened, revealing Aurus's still form on the bed. Lightning struck the unmoving form, streaming from the now-visible form of Velak in a bejeweled harness.

"Die, you ValDurian lap-dog. Nobody messes with Vork and Velak."

The lightning continued, and the still form remained just that.

"Why aren't you dying? This thing isn't sucking up any power at all. What the hell?"

Two paxitons appeared with a 'thump,' engulfing Velak with their blue rays. His crystals flared into blinding brilliance, darkened, and he collapsed, unmoving.

Zaeph appeared, along with Aurus, Nea, and two red cross gnomes. The healers checked Velak's body while Zaeph and Aurus talked.

"What is this, sir?" Zaeph pointed to the form of Aurus on the bed.

"An original reproduction of myself, thanks to the megacopia. I just baited the trap with a little help from your boss."

Aurus lifted up mannequin-Aurus's shirt, revealing its body to be studded with mana crystals.

"I was sure he couldn't tell the difference between personal power and stored power," said Aurus. "Thanks to a pal, we knew he couldn't snitch the stored power, so your boss provided these.

"Knew it was him." Aurus pointed to Velak. "Another case closed. This guy's due for punishment, just as soon as we figure out who has jurisdiction."

"How did you know it was him, sir?" asked Zaeph, eyes wide.

Aurus puffed up his chest. "Gut feelings. When you've been doing this as long as I have you just know."

One of the red cross gnomes exclaimed, "He's dead. I think his crystal harness electrocuted him. What happens to the body? Do we notify next of kin?"

"I'll take care of it," said Zaeph. "You guys can leave now."

They did so, with a quick 'pop' of air as they vanished.

Zaeph spoke to the paxitons.

"Pick him up and we can take him to Artifus."

"Wait a moment," said Nea. "I need to ask him some questions first."

Zaeph gaped.

"But, but he's dead. How can you ask him anything? Spells don't work here. You shouldn't even try."

"No spells. My shadow over his captures the soul before it completely leaves the body. It would be so much more painful if he still lived, but I can work in an eternity of torment in a very few minutes."

Nea stood over Velak, engulfing him with her shadow, when he suddenly jumped up.

"Wait, wait. I'll talk. Anything you want to know."

Nea blinked in exaggerated surprise.

"So, you live? I am surprised. Not. I know you've faked your death before, and it didn't seem a stretch that you had a way to fake your death now, spells or not. I need to know who gave you that bejeweled harness."

"What benefits do I derive from this outlay of information?"

"Keeping your for-real life, but that's only from Aurus and me. I don't know what the Mackleweisers want."

Zaeph coughed.

"Hrm, probably reparations for damage done. I'll take you to the Grandiloquence Supreme right now. Let's —"

Aurus grabbed Zaeph's arm.

"We still need him to talk."

"I haven't caused any damage here as of this moment," said Velak. "I only acquired the harness within the past few hours."

"Don't grease me," said Aurus, "there've been at least two hits within the past two days."

Velak held his hand over his heart.

"I swear by my goblin mother's heart that I speak the truth. This is my sacred vow."

Nea smiled thinly.

"Truly a sacred oath, but I know you weren't born a goblin. That and a hill of beans leaves us only gas. Feigning death is hard, but the truth is harder. We too study our enemies."

Velak gave a nasty grin.

"As I know you won't kill a prisoner. Still, someone in a hooded black robe hired me today and gave the harness as payment. He tried to pass as one of the taller races, but I could tell he was a gnome with stilts. He said tonight would be my only chance to strike at you."

"I don't recall pissing off any gnomes recently," mumbled Aurus.

"You piss off so many people it's hard to keep track," said Nea. "Still, it sounds as though the Mackleweisers have a traitor on their hands. Only a staff member could open these locked rooms. It could take ages to find him or her."

"Got him," called a voice from the air.

Four more paxitons appeared, surrounding Zaeph. Behind them stood Augustine, Neri, and Artifus. The blue eye-beams of all six paxitons bathed Zaeph on all sides, paralyzing him.

"That was quick," said Aurus. "I really thought it'd take longer, but I guessed right."

"Well-targeted, sir," said Augustine. "My little mana-examination wand showed what had to be a vast number of powered crystals on his person while I was afforded the concealment of invisibility."

He handed Aurus back his wristwatch. "Quite an amazing device, hiding us from sight while marking perfect, soundless time."

"Harrumph," coughed Artifus. "Indeed, youngster, can you explain yourself? You carry a fortune in SMUs on your body, property of the hotel, no doubt."

Zaeph laughed, a high, squeaky screech.

"They're mine, created on my own time, and powered on my own time."

"Perhaps so," said Artifus. "But they'll be removed from you until we can sort this out."

"No, I don't think so," said Zaeph. "Paxitons, subdue them."

The six magical mechs turned their blue beams on the assemblage, save for Zaeph. Stretching out his hand to Velak, he gestured, then the crystal-laced harness detached itself and came to him.

"You're one tough goblin. This was supposed to kill you when caught, to throw suspicion off me." He donned the harness.

"How dare you, youngling?" yelled Artifus. "Paxitons. Override his orders. I, the Absolute Authority, command you."

The paxitons didn't even twitch.

"I helped create the system, you old bean-counter," said Zaeph. "I made sure I could control it. Still, time to get out while I'm ahead."

He waved his little wand and nothing happened.

This time Artifus gave a laugh, a healthy, hearty one.

"I shut off the teleporter system after the last mechs arrived, just in case you tried to escape. You can't control a system that isn't on."

Zaeph screamed unintelligibly, then coughed and spit.

"You old shit, I'm better than you, better than any of the others. I'm a genius and you made me a bellhop."

"We all started at the bottom," said Artifus. "You'd have had your chance in good time."

"Screw that, my time is now. Forget escaping. I'm going to drain all your life energies and tell them the goblin did it. Then I'm going to take over the hotel so I'll have a continuous flow of fresh power."

Up the shaded backside of the paxiton paralyzing Aurus crept a shadow that became Nea, who covered its visor with her cloak, cutting off the beam. Aurus pulled the construct's head off.

"Get the little jerk, Aurus," yelled Nea. "We'll be fine."

His golden halberd appeared in Aurus's hands as he flew toward Zaeph. He cut the heads off the two paxitons holding Augustine and Neri without slowing, while Zaeph ran out the bedroom door into the living room.

Aurus intercepted Zaeph before he left the suite, flying between him and the outer door.

"You can either surrender now and take your medicine," said Aurus, "or I can exercise my option to apprehend you with enthusiasm. Your call."

He slapped the halberd into his left palm as he dropped down. Zaeph rolled to the floor, diving under Aurus before he landed. He was out the door in an instant with Aurus close behind.

Aurus used the flat of his halberd, knocking Zaeph back ten feet on the walkway.

"Give it up, buddy. You haven't really hurt anybody yet, so this doesn't have to end in blood."

Zaeph scrambled to his feet.

"You have no authority over me, and I don't have to run."

The harness he wore expanded into a three-foot sphere of gems and wire, interposing itself between him and Aurus.

"My dranna is more than a match for you," yelled Zaeph.

The dranna glowed like a miniature sun, emitting a blast that knocked Aurus off the crystal walkway and sending his energy shield into the white. Zaeph glowed as well, and flew toward the arrival platforms, followed by the dranna.

Aurus halted his fall in midair and flew after Zaeph. Catching up in a moment, he hacked at the dranna with his halberd, causing one small section to go dark.

"This isn't ending well for you, Zaeph. Your magic sucker won't stop me, and you certainly can't."

Multiple blue beams hit Aurus from behind, stopping him dead in the air.

"Maybe I can't stop you, but the paxitons can. You've violated the weapons ban," yelled Zaeph. From the beach below, seven paxitons unleashed their azure fire on Aurus.

Zaeph shuttled his way up toward freedom on the escalator. "And don't call me by that childish nickname. I am Zoraepheum."

#

Hours later, the Mackleweisers had put things to right, save that Zaeph, or Zoraepheum, had escaped.

Aurus rested in bed, recovering from paxiton paralysis overdose and low mana, surrounded by burritos, burgers, Artifus, Augustine, Neri, and Nea.

"I don't understand," said Artifus. "How could such a promising young gnome go so wrong?"

"He thought you treated him like a chump," said Aurus, "that you ignored his genius and made him a lousy bellhop."

"Genius, peh," spat Artifus. "I've known smarter, though he has managed to create a lot of self-charging mana crystals. That's very difficult, but he made errors while creating them. We found where he had removed fully charged crystals and botched the bridging to bypass them. That's why we had the malfunction with the Green Door system."

Artifus removed his hat and wiped his bald pate.

"He was treated the same way we all were. Damned whiny kids these days. I cleaned toilets in the original Cosmapheir. Customer Service is King, and we are all servants to it, even me."

"What happens to him now?" asked Nea, tossing her cloak over a chair.

"Nothing until we find him," said Artifus. "We've spread the news through the regular channels. We only mentioned that he stole from us, not what he did to the guests, or that it endangered the hotel. We'd appreciate that you also keep it to yourselves. In return, the Hotel offers each of you a lifetime VIP pass."

"Most gracious," said Augustine, "though I'm not sure that my niece and I did very much."

"Ah, but you did," said Aurus. "You made me realize there was someone behind our drained mana. It had to be someone who knew their magical security systems, and which guests were loaded with SMUs. I really did think it was Velak at first, but the trouble with him didn't start until after both us had mana issues. Speaking of, where is the jerk?"

"We sent him on his way with a warning to never return," said Artifus. "We thought it the best solution, considering he works for Bellos Twilight. We don't need that one mad at us. Velak didn't truly know what the whole story was, so I don't think he can harm our reputation. Especially if people know it comes from a lying weasel such as himself. The only positive thing gained from all this was the exposure of the weakness in our anti-magic system."

"True," said Nea. "It only prevents the gathering of magic in order to cast a spell, not the activation of spells already stored in an item, or on one's self. That's how Velak feigned his death. It also doesn't prevent the use of inherent abilities that draw on magical energies, as when I used my shadow power. I don't know if you could cover that without shutting down everything here."

"Still, something to look into," said Artifus.

"I think it's time we leave, and let Aurus get some rest," said Neri. "He's taken enough of a beating, I think."

"Thanks," said Aurus, "but we Knights of Valeron deal with that sort of thing on an almost daily basis."

"Oh, I see. I'm sorry you have to do that. See us when you're feeling up to it," said Neri.

Aurus, alone with Nea, said, "I think our energy shields need some sort of upgrade. They wouldn't stop the paxiton beams, just like with the V'Laubi paralo-rays."

"I think they're only meant to stop damaging attacks."

"Yeah, I guess, but you take seven beams at once and tell me they aren't damaging attacks."

"Something to bring up at our next meeting?"

"Yes. By the way, you can't really torture souls with your shadow, can you?"

"No, that was only to get Velak to react. I assumed he faked his death, somehow, based on what I know of him."

"Thought so. Anyway, this place is getting me down. We might as well be working for all the rest I'm getting. What say we blow this pop stand after I eat my fill of real food?"

"We could, but then you'd miss the giant robot battle tomorrow."

From the nightstand she held up a sheet of poster paper with a robot design on it.

"I thought you might like this. Designed it myself."

"Oh wow, yes. That's what I'm talking about. Now we can finally start to enjoy this vacation."

Chapter Thirty Seven
In Passing

Aurus, Nea, Marvin, and Julian stood in a cemetery, facing a freshly-placed marble headstone that read:

ZEN SMITH

LT

US ARMY

HE PROTECTED HIS FRIENDS

HIS COUNTRY AND THE WORLD

"He's unknown no longer," said Julian. "The ValDurians made sure his record, modified for this Earth, reflected his deeds and heroic death. In the end he was recognized as a hero after all. That's all they could do. He had no living relatives of any kind. The only family he had was the Knights of Valeron."

"I didn't think we were going to mesh well at first," said Aurus, "but he was a team player. I think we even became friends by the end. I regret his passing."

Nea wiped a tear away.

"I can't help but think if we'd beaten the Grand Elder faster he'd still be alive," she said with a sob.

"No point in dwelling on that," said Marvin. "If I could have moved faster he wouldn't have felt the need to sacrifice himself, and I'll have to live with that."

"You were barely recovered from near-fatal injuries," said Nea. "You probably shouldn't have been on any mission to begin with."

"Knights do what Knights do," said Julian. "I approved his placement, so I have at least as much guilt as any of you."

"Dwelling on guilt does us no good," said Aurus. "I will dwell on how much he meant to us in the short time we knew him. Also that I always thought Zen was a nickname. Never thought it was his given one. Always meant to ask though. Not the way I wanted to find out."

"Zen Smith," said Julian, "You accomplished your mission and I return your badge to the Wyrd."

Chapter Thirty Eight
The Weight of the AllWorlds

Indra stood on the precipice. Below and infinitely beyond him swirled the sea of Chaospace. He had lost track of how long he'd been staring at it, but was time even relevant in this place?

"Seven hours and 18 minutes," said Raelani, who may have just appeared. "That's how long you've been here."

"Does it matter? They say those who contemplate the abyss too long will hurl themselves into it."

"And will you?" she asked, grabbing his hand.

"I don't know. Was going to, but the longer I stand here the stupider that idea sounds. It wouldn't kill me, but I'd lose myself in it. I'd feel no responsibility, or anything at all, in all likelihood. The trouble is that everything would be dumped on you, and I can't bear that."

She pulled herself closer to him, burying her head in his massive chest.

"The Oracles finally spoke to me," she said, "and I now have a more clear idea of what it is you're supposed to do."

"Could you explain it to me then?"

She looked up at him.

"Since we have drawn the fabric of reality so taut, the little acts of chaos you caused have loosened things up. The prices paid in blood count the most, unfortunately. There is less danger of collapse now."

"Less, but not none. There is still The Big Thing coming up, and if I can pull that off we should avoid the complete breakdown of the AllWorlds."

"You mean 'if *we* can pull that off.' You aren't alone in this."

"I should be. There's no need for you to be involved."

"Were it not for me none of this would be necessary. We could have fought evil where we found it, not gone looking for trouble. There would have been no tightening of the multiversal violin strings to the point they'll fold the instrument onto itself. More importantly, you're my husband and my heart. Where you go, I go, for better or for worse."

"There is much worse to come."

"And I will be with you, to do what I can."

They embraced.

Simultaneously they said, "Together, we can do anything. Let the AllWorlds tremble in anticipation."

END